*Also by Shelby Foote*

# September September

# September September

## SHELBY FOOTE

*Random House New York*

Library of Congress Cataloging in Publication Data

Foote, Shelby.
September September.

I.  Title.
PZ3.F73918Se   [PS3511.0348]   813'.5'4   77-12523
ISBN 0-394-40721-0

Manufactured in the United States of America

9  8  7  6  5  4  3  2

First Edition

SEPTEMBER

| 1 | 2 | 3 | 4 | 5 | 6 | 7 |
|---|---|---|---|---|---|---|
| 8 | 9 | 10 | 11 | 12 | 13 | 14 |
| 15 | 16 | 17 | 18 | 19 | 20 | 21 |
| 22 | 23 | 24 | 25 | 26 | 27 | 28 |
| 29 | 30 | 1 | 2 | 3 | 4 | 5 |

*Vice may be defined as a
miscalculation of chances.*

—JEREMY BENTHAM

# Contents

# September September

# 1

# *Three Came Riding*

It was a bad time in many ways, some of them comprehensible, others not. We had a great big kewpie doll in the White House, commander-in-chief of all the cold-war warriors on our side, and the Russians were up to something they would fling skyward from the dusty steppes of Kazakhstan just one month later. On this hot clear Wednesday in early September, twenty years ago, the morning paper bulged with yesterday's news from Little Rock, where Orval Faubus had drawn the line at last. Triple-decked, four columns wide, in type so black it fairly seemed to shout, the headline was racked above run-on stories that broke beyond a full-page ad proclaiming E-Day for the Edsel in dealer showrooms all across the land. "A real crock," Podjo said from the back seat, the *Commercial Appeal* spread along his thighs like an out-of-season lap robe. He was talking about Faubus, not the Edsel, though later he would see how well the phrase applied in that direction too.

Three of them in the weathered Ford drove north up Highway 61 out of the Delta, first with the midday sun at their backs and then to their left rear, beyond the river hidden westward behind the levee sometimes visible in the distance. From Bristol to the Tennessee line, all hundred and thirty-odd miles of road and half-drowned farmland, gridded with silver pencilings of water in the furrows on its flanks, were flat as the palm of your hand until the car struck the rising ground of the Chickasaw Bluff, where the cotton and corn and beans left off and Memphis had its being. Podjo Harris was forty crowding forty-one, a hale-seeming man with a broad mustache, dark hair and eyes, a chin that resembled a naked heel, and a powerful-looking nose. The couple in front, a man of twenty-seven and a woman in her mid-thirties, were Rufus Hutton and Reeny Perdew. Slim and blond, he sported a duck-tail haircut, trained in a wave across the top, an indefinite mouth, and eyes of as pale a blue as Confederate violets. He drove with a certain indolent skill, taking the curves with such ease that you might have thought the end of the steering shaft reposed in a cup of oil.

"Yair," he said, in confirmation of Podjo's reference to the governor of the state across the way; "a real crock. But remember, he's on our side," and went abruptly into one of those keyless transitions habitual to his nature. "What a year; Jesus. I read about it yesterday in the *Scimitar*. Four point three-one inches of rain in August alone. That brings the total to better than fifty-two inches so far this year. The wettest eight months in this century, it said, and a whole lot more to come this fall, not including the planters' tears. But what the hell. It isnt like we came up here to farm."

He grinned, looking over at Reeny and all the way round to grin at Podjo too, then took another sudden conversational veer as the car began its climb up the rising stretch of highway. "This looks like country I never wanted to see again, even in my dreams. Korea, and the goddam slants in their padded clothes coming at us up the hillside out of the darkness, ringing cowbells, blaring bugles, yelling 'Amellican you die!' Man, did we cut them down." He turned again toward the back seat. "How bout yours?"

"I dont know," Podjo said presently, still reading the *Commercial*. "Mine was a different kind of war; I was mostly too scared to get my face out of the mud. All I remember about Europe is the rain, like on a tin roof. There's a helmet rim along the top of every scene I saw."

"We never had much use for helmets except to boil things in. You know how Marines are."

"No. How are they?"

Rufus started to answer, then saw it was a joke. He laughed. "Semper Fi, pal," he said, and turned his attention back to the road.

Off to the left, as they reached the crest of that first hill, they saw a dilapidated roadhouse, half of its sloped roof burned away and the rest gone to ruins.

"Hey!" Reeny cried. She had been musing for the past ten miles or so, withdrawn into herself. Now she emerged as if into daylight. Her face brightened. "Look at yonder. We used to come up here to dance and see the sights."

In back, behind the charred and vine-invaded ruin, there were a dozen one-room cabins, gutted too; tourist courts, they were called in their day; linoleum-floored cubicles, oven-hot in summer, icebox-cold in winter — so cold your breath congealed — each with its tin-lined shower stall and sighing toilet, a rickety washstand, one straightback chair, and a double bed with rough-dried muslin sheets, a cotton blanket, and a pink or blue chenille bedspread so reduced by repeated washings that its fringes barely reached the bottom edge of the thin mattress.

"Gone with the wind," Rufus said, watching over his shoulder as the ruin slid by and flicked away. "My God, my youth. I used to get a hard-on every time I rode past one of those places, remembering all the hot-eyed little girls I shared them with. But not that one; Jesus. Not with all that scorch and all those creepers snaking in through the doors and windows. Man, that's *sad*."

Reeny seemed to agree. At any rate she lapsed again into musing, whether the cause was old mortality or not.

Podjo watched her over the rim of his paper. Tall, with most of her height in her legs, she had high, firm-looking breasts, which he guessed by now had begun to go a little, and wore a sweater and skirt, loafers, and no socks. Her hair, so light a brown it passed for blonde, was cut in a modified page-boy, held more or less in place by an elastic headband that showed above her bangs and was hidden elsewhere by long straight tresses which turned inward at the ends to avoid contact with her shoulders. A wide, rather thin-lipped mouth and sloe eyes, so dark a blue that they seemed black in all but the strongest light, were her best features, but their aspect was considerably diminished by the narrow, vaguely divergent nose, perhaps a quarter-inch too long and with nostrils crimped to the near rim of pain. His first impression of her, just under two weeks ago, had been that she was a whore; some sort of call girl, available on short notice, he decided, rather than a regular in a house. But that was partly because she was with Rufus, whose tastes he guessed ran mainly in that line, and it had passed, so far at least as the present was concerned, though not as a probable factor in her background. Something came off her; you believed, or anyhow imagined, you could smell it at close quarters such as this. Bed, he thought, and resented the distraction, now as at the outset, two weeks back.

Her sadness, if that was what it was, had begun six miles this side of Bristol, just short of the Jordan County line, when they came in sight of a lofty flat-topped Indian mound beside the highway. "I always meant to climb that," she remarked, "but I never did." Rufus slowed and made as if to stop. "You want to climb it now?" She shook her head. "No," she said. "I waited too long." It was then that she went into her first spell of intermittent brooding, and Podjo had assigned it to the common condition of women who tie in with younger men. Rufus was a good half-dozen years her junior, if not more.

Now they purled along, the car's engine sounding happy to be on the flat again, free of the unaccustomed strain and with even an occasional dip to a culvert where a creek or bayou drained riverward in the olden days before the highway was laid down. Up ahead they saw the state line coming toward them, and short of it, on the left, a roadside store with a broad gallery and hand-lettered signs nailed at random along its eaves: *Pistols. Rifles. Ammunition. Fireworks. Last Chance.*

Just beyond it, on the opposite shoulder, the back of a large billboard marked the line itself. Turning sharply in his seat as they went past, Rufus looked rearward and read the words printed boldly in white against a background of green: MISSISSIPPI. WELCOME TO THE MAGNOLIA STATE. "Good old Missy Pissy," he said, "where men are men and women like them that way."

Reeny laughed, and presently, as the car soared over the high arch of Nonconnah Bridge, giving a sudden lifted-curtain view of downtown Memphis, five miles off — the scattered hotels, Chisca, Gayoso, Peabody, Claridge, all of different shades of brick, and the Sterick Building, tall and slender, gleaming white as any tombstone in the sunlight — clicked on the radio in time to hear the announcer burble in a breathy nonstop voice: "Hi, folks, all you folks out there this fine bright afternoon. We're moving on with Clint Whitehead next, a new version of that old favorite, 'I'm Waiting in the Lobby of Your Heart.' Hope you like it, all you Whitehead fans and others roundabout. Here she goes!" While the guitar twanged and jangled and the singer complained of unrequited troubles through his nose, Reeny hummed along, caught up in the excitement of thickening traffic, four-lane now, and the lift of spirit that always came with entering the city.

Podjo had laid the *Commercial* aside and leaned forward, hands on the back of the seat ahead. "Pull over there," he said, pointing, and when Rufus drew up alongside the newspaper vending machine at the curb, got out and put a nickel in the slot. He looked up and down the sidewalk, in a quick theft-reflex, then bent forward and took two papers from the box, one of which he dropped on the front seat as he got back in and unfolded the other, scanning the headlines — sans-serif, blacker and thicker in the *Press-Scimitar* than in the one he laid aside — before he settled down to the text beneath them. He was a great reader of the papers, a habit he had picked up in the penitentiary.

"I see the church is with us," he said, displaying a streamer that ran across the top of the second page: 15 LITTLE ROCK PASTORS BACK FAUBUS ACTION.

Reeny nodded as she read it, her own copy untouched on the seat beside her. "My daddy was a preacher. Is," she said in quick correction. "I bet he's siding with him, too."

"What church is that?" Rufus asked, surprised.

"His own. Foot-washing Baptist, Total Immersion, True Vine Pentecostal; lots of things. They change its name from time to time."

"Jack-leg, hey?"

"I reckon," she said reluctantly.

Podjo was into the text by then, having studied with care a double-column front-page photograph. *Vacation Time*, the caption read. *President Eisenhower escorts Mrs. Eisenhower from the car at National Airport in Washington as they prepare to leave for a vacation at Newport, R. I. On hand to say good-bye to their grandparents are Barbara Anne, Susan (practically hidden behind her sister), and David.* "Get this," he said, and read aloud parts of the adjacent story. " 'President Eisenhower flew to New England today for a seaside vacation of golf and fishing as the Navy's guest at Newport, R.I.' Mumble, mumble. 'They will occupy a tree-shaded twelve-room white stucco house which the new commander of the base, Rear Admiral Henry Cromellin' — poor outranked bastard — 'is yielding to the commander-in-chief. There has been no official word on how long the Eisenhowers will vacation at Newport, but — '

"Hold it," he said, wetting his thumb to riffle several pages (including a repetition of this morning's full-page ad in the *Commercial*: MORE THAN A NEW MAKE OF CAR, THE EDSEL IS A QUARTER BILLION DOLLAR MEASURE OF A COMPANY'S FAITH IN THE AMERICAN ECONOMY) until he reached the breakover. "Here. 'they may stay until close to the scheduled mid-October visit to Washington of Britain's Queen Elizabeth.' Mum, mum. 'Eisenhower is accompanied by a small staff and two White House physicians.' Yair; that's the ticket. Just let him stay right there, golfing and fishing. It's where he can do us the most good."

At the intersection of Third and Crump — Highway 61 had become Third Street, some blocks back — Rufus waited for the amber light and then turned left, on beyond the foot of Main, under a railroad viaduct, past a large brick church with steep concrete steps, to Riverside Drive, where he turned right — north again, with the river once more on their left, still unseen but certified now by a view of the superstructure of three bridges etched in spidery geometric black against the cloudless blue late-summer sky — for three more blocks till he turned left again on Carolina, just short of a Chinese grocery store on the northwest corner.

"Almost there," he said, and jerked his thumb at a sign above the entrance to a converted residence two doors behind the corner grocery: MEMPHIS NIPPLE Co. "My favorite hang-out," he told Podjo over his shoulder.

Reeny had laughed hard at this on Sunday, but now she leaned forward, the heels of both hands braced against the dashboard, and peered intently through the windshield to where Carolina dead-ended into Arkansas Street, a residential stretch only two blocks long, one north, one south of the junction they were approaching, isolated and remote, yet only one block off busy Riverside. They would see it now, Podjo for the first time, Rufus and Reeny for the third.

Turning left at the junction, short of a double-stooped raw brick duplex on the west side of the street, Rufus eased past a white frame house, older and larger than the rest, with a pair of dormers like two eyes in its roof, and pulled up at the curb in front of another, also frame but newer and much narrower, just beyond. He reached out, turned off the ignition, and dropped both hands in his lap in imitation of an exhausted oarsman. "End of journey," he announced. "All out for home sweet home."

Podjo stepped backward from the car, bringing his suitcase with him, while Rufus went around and took two others from the trunk. Reeny by then had gone up the walk and three front steps to the low stoop and removed a key from the pocket of her skirt. Using both hands she turned knob and key simultaneously and bumped the door ajar with her hip, then stood back to keep the screen from slamming in the faces of the two men coming up with the bags, and followed them in, stepping as if at a stride into midsummer. "Woo," she said. "Let's get some windows open fore we roast." Outside, the temperature was just over ninety degrees, but inside, with the front and back doors locked and all the windows firmly shut, it was close to an even hundred, the air stuffy and rather musty too, with a smell of feathers and dusty plush.

Moving quickly through the three rooms, opening windows as they went — living room, bedroom, kitchen, the last beyond a narrow hall that flanked the bath — they reached the back door, which Rufus unlocked and snatched ajar to lead the way onto the screen porch at the rear.

"How about that?" he said. He gestured with a proprietary sweep of his arm, and Podjo saw the three mile-long bridges, amazingly close, striding westward across the river and the Arkansas flats beyond. They went out with a rush, lightsome and parallel, keeping step as they walked the water on stilts of stone. "Aint that something?" Rufus insisted.

"Something," Podjo agreed, gazing out past the lip of the ninety-foot bluff some thirty yards from where he stood on the screen porch.

When they went back into the house they found that the rooms had already begun to freshen from the light breeze lifted off the river by the updraft of the bluff. Rufus led the way. In the hall beyond the kitchen Reeny stopped and turned to face Podjo, one arm extended overhead in a pose he found puzzling until he saw a light brass chain suspended from the ceiling near the bedroom door, the ring at its end dangling near her hand. "Watch this," she said with a note of pride not unlike the one Rufus had struck when he made his panoramic gesture toward the bridges, rather as if he owned them or at any rate had discovered them on an expedition into an unknown land. They had, after all, come up here and found this, and they seemed to expect high praise for their success. Reeny took hold of the ring and tugged on it, bringing what seemed to be most of the hall ceiling yawning down at a sharp angle to within a couple of feet of the floor. Rufus reached from behind her and unfolded a short flight of steps leading up to a longer flight to which the first was hinged, so that the two, now joined end-to-end, led steeply up to what Podjo at last perceived was the attic.

"Look up there," Reeny told him, still with that tone of anticipatory pride, "and youll see what we liked best about this place, first time we saw it."

He did as she said, stepping gingerly up the ladderlike contraption, and when his head was clear of the rectangular opening, two feet by five in width and length, saw by the faint gleam of light from louvers set in the gables at each end, west and east, a large area inclosed by raw lumber, tentlike in effect because of the light-brown quality of the air and because of the rafters slanting sharply down from the ridgepole to the eaves. About half the floor space was boarded over, the rest exposed joists, and off to one side a gas-burning hot water heater sat in a shallow square zinc tub. Except for this the place was empty, though an unshaded lightbulb dangled from its cord in the center of the expanse, naked as a hard, inedible piece of fruit suspended from the tip of a vine that was otherwise barren.

Reeny was talking down below, he realized, her head about on a level with his knees. "We thought we'd round up one of those folding canvas cots. You know? Maybe two."

"Yes, and a fan," Rufus broke in, raising his voice to be heard in the attic overhead. "What do you call them? Oscillating. It could get awful hot up there for the little nigger and whoever's guarding him from time to time."

"Right," Podjo said, descending. "First, though, let's get it taped. See what we have to do, then figure how."

Clear of the steps, he refolded the bottom section, lifted the whole until the counterbalancing springs took hold, and used the chain to ease it back in position, flush with the ceiling. He stood in the hallway, looking first through the frame of the back door, where the bridges soared in geometric silhouette, then in the opposite direction, through the living-room window toward the dusty street out front. Both views were blurred by screens. "It looks like a good set-up," he told Rufus and Reeny. "You did fine."

Shortly after five oclock that afternoon, as usual in all but the worst weather, Eben Kinship left his office on Beale just west of Third, cater-cornered from Handy Park, and walked the accustomed four blocks to his home on Vance, midway between Abel and Hernando. Strictly speaking, neither the office nor the house was his; he just called them that, much as you might say 'my desk' or 'my doctor,' 'my wife' or even 'my God'; they belonged in fact to his father-in-law, for whom he worked and from whom he rented, like so many others — cooks and maids, chauffeurs and yardmen for the most part — in this and other Negro sections of the city, whether adjacent, near its dusky heart, or peripheral, in the fast-growing white outskirts they were learning to call suburbs. A portly man, beginning to go somewhat to fat at thirty-eight, he enjoyed this way of ending the day, particularly when the weather was as fine as it was now. Though he took pains to mask his pleasure behind a dignity composed in roughly equal parts of careful posture, sober clothes, and a burgeoning corporation, his satisfaction was evident from his demeanor, which included a smile of self-congratulation for thus combining, in this one act of walking home, the double virtue of losing weight and working up a healthy appetite. He was commonly thought of as handsome, and he was, with his chiseled nose, well-defined mouth, and amber eyes, proportioned about a clean-shaven face whose skin was of an even tone a little darker than light brown. Women marveled at his fidelity to his wife, and it was true that he was faithful to her, both for her sake and his own, thereby linking principle and desire. They also said he knew which side his bread was buttered on, and that was true as well.

When he came in sight of the green bungalow on the south side of the street — a good deal smaller than the largest houses in the neighborhood, but somewhat larger than the smallest — he saw his daughter rise from her waiting place on the top step of the stoop. She was six and her name was Lucinda, though no one ever called her that; they called her Sister Baby. This had been her first day at school, and she was dressed accordingly in one-strap patent leather pumps and short blue socks, a wide-skirted red-check gingham dress, and twelve tight pigtails distributed about her scalp and tied at their ends with bits of yarn. Quite pretty, she closely resembled her father in the shape and color of her face and eyes.

"Hi," she said as he turned in at the gate.

"How was school?"

"It let out early. For us I mean. Teddy's grade had to stay later."

"Ah." He leaned down and kissed her. "Where's he now?"

"Watching TV. Little Rascals was on and now it's Mickey Mouse. Next comes Popeye. I'm waiting for that."

"Dont you like Mickey?"

"I like him all right," she said, "but just not much. I like Farina. And Popeye; I like Popeye."

"When I was a boy, back down home, Little Rascals was called Our Gang. I used to go and see them every Saturday that I had fifteen cents to buy a ticket. We sat up high, way over everyone in town."

"I know. You told me."

"I did?" he said. "I guess I did. I guess I tell you most everything, one time or another."

They had come into the house by then, and on the television

Donald Duck was involved in some kind of vigorous dispute with his three nephews, who were all alike and all like him, except smaller. "Hello, Teddy!" Eben shouted above the quacking. By way of reply the boy raised one arm in an undistracted salute, never looking away from the ruckus on the screen. While Sister Baby joined her brother on the couch, Eben went back to the kitchen where his wife Martha was fixing supper. Two pots bubbled on the stove and she stood at the counter breading veal chops. "Home," he said.

Martha was thirty-five, three years younger than her husband and much darker, with a wider, heavier mouth and nose, a frame that tended to thinness, especially in the arms and legs, a rounded jaw, and prominent, goitrous eyes. Though the combination was considerably more attractive than the parts that made it up, she did have what was uncharitably called a bullfrog look, and what was worse she was painfully conscious of the charge, sometimes with unfortunate results. For example, she bought clothes designed in theory to hide or disguise certain defects, only to find those defects emphasized in fact; or she employed a cosmetic grease that did indeed straighten the kinks in her hair, as advertised, but produced withal the effect of a fluted lampshade, worn at a rakish angle, or a badly fitted horsehair wig, hurriedly clapped on her head and lacquered to a hard high gloss, unbendable as stovepipe. In any case, even allowing for the exaggeration of a mocking or jaundiced eye, husband and wife made an oddly assorted pair as they stood there in the kitchen, waiting first for the Disney and then the Popeye cartoons to end so that Eben could return to the living room for his usual fifteen minutes with Douglas Edwards and the News.

Just as he clicked off the set at straight-up six oclock, Martha called from beyond the dining-room curtain that supper was on the table. He took his place at one end, she at the other, and the children sat between them, on opposite sides, Sister Baby with a volume of *Stoddard's Lectures* for a chock to help lift her shoulders clear of the table edge, which otherwise would have been about on a level with her chin. In addition to the veal, there were mustard greens, corn on the cob, a double stack of sliced bread, two sticks of butter, and coffee and milk, followed by store-bought lemon pie with a second cup of coffee for Eben and, on second thought, a second piece of pie.

Teddy wanted another piece, too, and was given it, only smaller. He was eight, two years older than his sister, and bore as striking a resemblance to their mother as she did to their father, so that each was a miniature switched-sex reproduction of a parent.

Eben rose, and while he returned to the living room to stretch out in his Morris chair and read the evening paper — a nightly ritual — the children helped clear the table and dry the dishes Martha washed. It was crowding six-thirty by now, getting on toward sundown.

By the time Martha came out to join him, settling on the couch with the *Ladies' Home Journal*, Eben was deep in his lounge chair and the *Scimitar*. From beyond the curtain, where brother and sister were stationed for their lessons under the glare of the lamp suspended above the dining-room table, Sister Baby appealed for release on grounds that, unlike Teddy, she had no homework to do. "Then sit there and get acquainted with your books," her father told her, not looking up from his paper. "And mind you dont bother your brother. Or your mama and me," he added. This too was to be a ritual, coincident with his own, and he wanted it inaugurated properly on this first school night, homework or no homework. Martha paused in her reading, ready to intervene if necessary, but Sister Baby abandoned her complaint.

After a while there was one more interruption; Teddy wanted to know the answer to six times seven. "Look it up," Eben told him, "or figure it out for yourself. And dont bother your sister. She's studying."

"I'm not studying," Sister Baby called promptly through the curtain. "I'm just looking at my books."

"All right," Eben told them. "Just settle down now, both of you."

"I didnt say anything," Teddy said.

"All right now. Settle back down," Eben told them.

They did, and things were quiet except for the rustle of his paper and the occasional whisper of a page as Martha turned it, reading the continuation of a regular feature on beauty hints. "Your Skin: What You Can Do About It," the one this month was called, and from time to time she paused, as if to ponder the finer points of what she read, and gazed thoughtfully in the direction of the pictures on the walls.

One, by the curtained entrance to the dining room, was a gilt-frame chromo of a girl-faced Christ in profile, eyes uplifted, with light brown hair worn shoulder length and the trace of a smile on the lips inside the beard. On the opposite wall, between couch and television, the pictures were all family photographs, including one of Eben and Martha on their wedding day, nearly ten years ago, Eben smiling, fifteen or twenty pounds lighter, almost lean, and Martha looking solemn and possessive in square-necked white satin and a different hair-do, shorter and more becoming in effect, alongside a recent studio portrait of the children posed together on a bench. In their paired case it was Teddy who looked solemn and Sister Baby who was smiling, thereby emphasizing their crossed-gender resemblance to their parents in the adjoining wedding picture.

Dominant on this wall, however, and set knowingly or unknowingly on a balance with the one across the room, was a large oval portrait in a burled walnut frame of a man so altogether solid-looking, despite his more than sixty years, that even looking at him from dead ahead, as you did here, you could tell he had thick folds of fat across the back of his neck but absolutely nowhere else. The small round eyes peering intently out of the otherwise uninterrupted dark expanse of face contained a sentience beyond interpretation on short notice. He wore a hat, a heavy watch chain linking the bottom pockets on his vest, a snub bow tie, and square in the notch of the V of his starched shirt-front, which had the glazed, milky look of mother-of-pearl, one tiny polished gleam of gold so central to his aspect that he might have been built around it. His close resemblance, first to Martha, then to Teddy — or rather theirs to him, on an increasingly smaller scale — left no doubt that he was her father, and lest some viewer mistake the identification, obvious though it was, his name was written across the bottom of the oval, just above the curve of walnut, in a script almost too flowing to be real: *Theo G. Wiggins.*

Beside him, but hung a little lower, was a small round picture of his wife. Aristocratic of mien, with skin a good bit lighter and paler than high yellow, she had intelligent eyes and a high-bridged nose, aquiline in contrast to his broad flat one with its two fuliginous nostrils, black on black, that put you in mind of a double-barrel shotgun trained on a point exactly midway between your eyes. In the juxtaposition of their two photographs, as different in style as they were in subject, she might have been some distant forebear in an old-time ambrotype; a quadroon or octoroon great-grandmother, say, whose white blood had been abolished in his and his father's and grandfather's veins by some progressive, highly virulent form of male genetic domination.

These were the pictures on the walls of the Kinship living room, though whether Martha actually looked at them when she glanced up from her beauty hints would have been hard to say.

Eben had moved steadily through both sections of the paper, reading most of the time with a look of stern or querulous scorn not unlike the one he wore an hour ago while watching Douglas Edwards and his film-clips of the news. Both narrow hightop shoes propped toes-up on the pull-out of his chair, and observed unblinkingly from above by the two round eyes of the patriarch on the wall, he seemed not to approve of much that was going on in the world, at home or abroad. This look intensified during his perusal of a background story on

Little Rock, beginning wtih Faubus's defiance of a federal court order, two nights ago, by calling out two hundred and fifty National Guardsmen, armed with rifles and carbines, who next morning — yesterday — turned back nine Negro students who tried to enroll, along with two thousand whites, in Central High School.

Six of the nine had shown up again this morning, with similar results. TENSION HIGH: / SIX NEGROES / SHOOED OFF, the *Scimitar* headline read, alongside the two-column cut of the Eisenhowers, headed for Newport, over the caption announcing that this was vacation time.

"Those damn people," Eben said.

"What people?" Martha asked, surprised. She thought he perhaps meant Ike and Mamie, whose photograph showed uppermost on the paper he had folded angrily and dropped into his lap.

"Those poor damn people over there," he said with a jerk of his head toward Arkansas, and launched at once into the tirade he had been building up to for the past half-hour or more. "It will be the same for them that it's been for others elsewhere. The ones who moved in to stir things up will get what theyre after, or else they wont, and then theyll move on to something else and leave the locals to take what follows. And what follows? I'll tell you. Lost jobs, foreclosed mortgages, white resentment; all that. Like that city-bus business last year in Montgomery, that preacher's son, King — a preacher himself, I understand; some kind of preacher anyhow. Lord God. Who cares which end of a bus he rides on, just so it gets him there? The thing to do, and everybody knows it, is hump hard inside the system, so youll own your own car and wont even have to think about busses, let alone ride one."

"You sound just like Daddy would sound if he'd talk about it," Martha said when Eben paused as if for approval.

"Why not? He's right, aint he?"

This time he had in fact asked a question, but she knew better than to venture a reply. He had used the word 'aint,' which he had spent the past twelve years avoiding, though not always with success, and she knew from this that he was upset. She was right, as it developed, for he was barely launched on all he had to say.

"It's like that old time, after the Civil War; Reconstruction, they called it. Ha. They had the whole Yankee army and all the U.S. government on their side, and they got every single thing they asked for. Yes, and a lot they didnt. And what came of it? I'll tell you. Trouble came of it; Jim Crow, alienation, repression like nothing our people ever knew. Back before that time, a man who really made it had a freedom, a respect these outsiders dont even know how to aim at. Now what are we fixing to have, just when we're close to getting back on our feet again? We're fixing to have the anger and enmity of every white man in the region; not only the Kluxers draped in bedsheets, the yahoos who do the whipping and the lynching, but also the ones that hold the purse strings and pass out favors. Theyre fixing to fix it so we wont be able to do business even with men like Mr Crump, men right here who know us and respect us enough to give us a chance to get what's coming to us under our own steam. You watch and see if what I'm saying is coming dont come about. It will, as sure as shooting, whether they get their way or not, win or lose, and then move on. Winning or losing, whichever they call it, dont matter a-tall when you start out with the drawback of being a loser even if you win."

He subsided and sat looking at the Eisenhowers in his lap, including the grandchildren, as if for counsel in his distress.

"I think so, too," Martha said when she was satisfied he had no more to say just then.

She returned to her magazine, glancing sidelong from time to time at her husband. Evidently the Eisenhowers had failed him, for he brooded now upon the blank screen of the television, gipsy-like, in contemplation of the clouded crystal ball which it resembled.

They sat that way, together yet apart, until just before eight oclock — time for the Wednesday Night Fight: Gene Fullmer vs Chico Vejar — when she called to the children to put their books away and come get ready for bed. By the time she got them undressed and washed, into their nightclothes and back out into the living room to say goodnight, Vejar had been down for a seven count in the third and Fullmer had bulled and dundered him around the ring for two more rounds in so dull a fashion that Eben was glad to switch over to Whirly-birds, ostensibly as a special treat for the children on this first school night, but partly too as a release from his own boredom. He switched back during a late commercial to find that Fullmer had won the decision, as expected, and when Whirlybirds was over he leaned forward and clicked the set off.

"Let's go now," Martha told the children.

"I want Daddy to care me to bed," Sister Baby said as usual. She wore a pair of her brother's hand-me-down pajamas and felt slippers. Her pigtails bristled in orderly procession round her head.

"Well, I might do that," Eben said. He turned and looked at Teddy at the far end of the couch. "How about you?"

"I dont need anybody to care me to bed," Teddy said; "I'm getting on toward grown. But I wouldnt mind if you want to."

Eben laughed as he rose from his chair. He hoisted his daughter onto his hip and took his son by the hand. "We're off," he said.

Martha followed back to their bedroom, a smaller one beyond the bathroom adjoining hers and Eben's, to hear their prayers, tuck them in, and turn the light out. When she returned to the living room Eben had the television on again and was watching Ozzie and Harriet; something about the shock of a new hair-do for Harriet, and Ozzie telling his troubles to a friendly soda jerk. Then a movie came on, *The Romance of Rosie Ridge*, but Eben soon wore out on it.

"Let's turn on in," he said, and clicked it off before ten oclock, without even trying another channel for Father Knows Best or Vic Damone or waiting for the late-night news.

They undressed in the bedroom, Martha using the opened closet door for a screen. She took off her shoes and stockings, then her dress. Still in her slip, she eased the straps off her shoulders and arms, along with those of her brassiere, put on her long-sleeve nightgown, over her head, and tugged it down till the hem fell past her ankles; which done she removed slip and brassiere from beneath the gown and stepped carefully out of her bloomers, all without showing so much as an inch of flesh that had not been visible two minutes ago, when she was fully dressed. In fact, there was a good deal less of it visible now, for the gown was higher-necked than the dress had been, and for good measure she then put on a pair of white athletic socks and a lace-trimmed nightcap, the former to keep her feet from getting cold in the night and the latter to keep her hair grease from staining the pillow.

When she emerged from behind the door, wrapped close as any mummy, Eben was in his nightshirt; he had just returned from the bathroom and was climbing into bed. She went to check on the children, already asleep, and then, returning, went around to her side of the bed.

"All right?" Eben asked, one hand on the bedside lamp switch.

"All right," she said, pulling the covers up snugly under her chin, and he turned out the light.

He lay there, hearing the faint complaint of the springs when she turned on her side, away from him, and as his eyes grew more accustomed to the darkness he could see her, or almost see her, a low ridge under the covers, inert and so far across the mattress that she might have been clinging to the welt. While he was undressing, and she was still behind her screen, he had felt the stirrings of desire; he had even gone to the bathroom and, hiking the tail of his nightshirt round his waist, washed up hurriedly in preparation for what he had in mind. But when she emerged from behind the door, capped and gowned and shod in her wooly socks, he put it out of his thoughts, or anyhow began trying. It came back stronger, that stirring of the flesh, while she was checking on the children. Then she returned. All right? All right. He clicked off the lamp; she turned on her side and he lay flat on his back, looking up toward the ceiling, invisible beyond the dim sheen of moonlight coming through the bedside window.

She had already fallen asleep, or she seemed to have, a low ridge on the far side of the mattress, and he held his breath to get rid of what remained of the erection, a trick he had learned overseas in the army. It worked, as it generally did except when the condition was extreme, which tonight's was not. He lay there contemplating the slack expanse of his body, as inert now as the one across the way. "I got to take some of this weight off," he said, and only knew he had spoken aloud when he heard Martha stir. She quieted, her breathing once more a series of drawn-out sighs, each of them broken off at the end, and he looked over at her, still as still, her nightcap a pale blob in the moonlight, then again down the length of his own body, slack as slack and crowding forty.

Jesus Christ, he thought, risible but querulous too, in self-mockery and in earnest, both at once: What became of all the fucking white folks think that niggers do?

And having reverted to that language, those accents and that syntax, he thought back to his boyhood and youth in Vicksburg and Bristol, remembering his mother and father, the smell of frying meat wafted up from the cafe to their living quarters, and his sister Julia wearing a red dress. The last he heard, she was in Chicago with her third husband, a clothing merchant close to twice her age. He reckoned by now she'd be giving him as hard a time as she had the others, the ones she married as well as those she shucked beforehand. She was two years Eben's junior, and the last time he saw her he told her that was no kind of life to live — only to have her grin at him with her painted mouth and say, with a purposely broadened accent, "I sho dont want to be living yo kind, no matter who gets hurt; including me."

He frowned at the memory, but not for long. Before he

finished thinking of her he had fallen asleep, and in that sleep he seemed to see old Theo G. still glaring down at him from his walnut oval on the wall.

Rufus and Reeny had come up here ten days ago, a Monday, and had spent that week — they returned to Bristol on Labor Day, driving both ways after dark — in search of something they could rent on a short-term basis, say for a month. Furnished or unfurnished hadnt mattered. What mattered was privacy; privacy of a particular kind that would fit the purpose now at hand. However, despite an unremittent combing of the classified sections in both papers and several trips to various parts of the city for a look at what sounded best in print but in every case turned out to be unsuitable in fact, they had come close to not finding it at all. Then at a club on Saturday night — a beer joint with an oldstyle juke box, bubbles moving bullet-like in slow motion through tubes of colored water — they met a young man Rufus's age, a bachelor salesman type, and got to talking.

At the outset he had been after Reeny, sizing them up to make his pitch, and by the time he heard their story he was more or less committed. Besides, it not only solved their problem, it also solved his own. He was in the cotton business, he told them, a Front Street firm that was sending him out to Arizona to a staple-classing school, and he had this place to sublet through September.

"Rufus was on his best college-boy behavior," Reeny told Podjo when they got back to Bristol with the news, "and this fellow got to talking about his digs being up for sublet, furnished, and we told him about our little boy and the eye operation, the whole bag about getting it done before we went

back to Ole Miss to graduate from law school and having
nowhere private to stay while we waited for the kid's eyes to
heal enough to make the trip to Oxford. He bought it all the
way, hook, line, sinker, and we were ready to take the place,
sight unseen, just from the way it sounded. So we went home
with him to look it over, and sure enough it was just what
we'd been after all along; especially the attic, which we didnt
even know we'd been looking for till we found it. We gave
him the hundred dollars, cash down, next day when we came
back to get the key. That was Sunday, yesterday; he was flying
out that night. No papers to sign, nothing. That's how far he
bought the package — plus I guess the fact that he was feeling
sheepish anyhow from having made a play for someone whose
little boy was going blind, whose husband was scrabbling to
get through law school, and didnt have so much as a pillow
to lay her head on through that time. Brown his name was.
Rufus told him ours was Keller, something like that; Mr and
Mrs John T. Keller, I think he said, and John Junior, five
years old and going blind if the doctors didnt save him. Aint
Rufus something when he gets going on a pitch?"

"He's something, all right," Podjo said.

"Yes, but wait; I left out the funniest part. This fellow Brown
hadnt meant to rent the place until he got to thinking about it
sitting there empty, at the mercy of burglars. That was what
made him extra glad he met up with us, he said; so the place
wouldnt be sitting there empty, at the mercy. Burglars!" she
cried, and Rufus joined her in the laugh that followed. They
both laughed so hard that even Podjo had to smile, a thing he
seldom did.

So now they were there, the three of them, settling in. For
sleeping, Rufus and Reeny took the middle room, the bachelor
bedroom with its chifforobe and double bed, and Podjo the
couch up front, a kidney-shaped piece with a tufted back,
covered in velure and stuffed with down, which he would
discover, night after night, accounted for and reproduced in
his nostrils that original fusty smell of feathers and dusty plush

which hung about till they opened the doors and windows to air the house out. The other two had more space and far more comfort, but he had the television — a minuscule compensation, he decided after watching the Fullmer-Vejar encounter that first night, not to mention the lack of privacy (Reeny was an insomniac) and the resultant loss of sleep because of late-night cowboy films whose sound tracks tended to be crowded with shouts and shots and whinnies. Still, the worst to bear by far was the couch itself; not only that musty smell, acquired in someone's unventilated basement over a period of years, nor the cow-pie brownish yellow color that once had passed for gold, but also its awkward size and shape. Too low to stow his suitcase under, and not quite long enough to let him straighten his knees while trying to get to sleep, it had arms of a height that gave an illusion of supportive comfort for his head when he first lay down, then a crick in his neck when he awoke next morning. In time he learned to hate that button-studded couch as much as he had ever hated an inanimate thing in his whole life.

Otherwise, even aside from the sense of ease and solitude afforded by the ninety-foot bluff, the river and its outward-soaring bridges, the updraft breeze, the screening elms and mulberries and magnolias, his companions could scarcely have done better in their search for a base of operations. Separate and remote, yet no more than a five-minute car ride from the heart of the downtown business district — Beale and Vance were even closer — this had been an all-Negro section, one street two short blocks long and another as brief that dead-ended into it for access, until three years ago a writer moved into one side of the raw brick duplex, down the way, and other whites followed hard on his heels, including a woman painter, a newly-wed architect, a television junior executive, a pair of interior decorators, a hard-working plumber, and several others, married and unmarried, to transform it into something resembling an artist colony, at least in the sense of being conglomerate and apart. Not that there was any feeling of shared endeavor; quite the opposite, in fact. As the cotton man said on the night he brought Rufus and Reeny home from the beer joint, people here tended to mind their own business, black or white, and that for them was the principal attraction. That was what they had been seeking from the outset; that and the attic they hadnt even thought of till they saw it.

"Right," Podjo said with ready approval when Rufus repeated his own. "You did fine."

They were unpacking at the time — Rufus and Reeny were, that is; Podjo would live out of his suitcase, already parked alongside the living-room couch — and each had among his effects, along with spare clothes, shaving gear and the like, one important tool of the trade they had undertaken. Podjo's was two sets of extra license plates, worn but current, from adjoining states, Arkansas and Missouri, to avoid attracting attention as outlanders. "There's all kinds of nuts," he had explained while installing the North Mississippi plates now on the car, "including ones that write down numbers just because theyre numbers and theyre there. I tell you, lots of well-designed jobs have wound up bummers because some straight-world bimbo took a notion to jot down something that didnt even concern him. You cant tell when there's one of them snooping round or staring out of a window just because that's what he spends his spare time doing. Real nuts. They can throw you before you know it."

He could be didactic on occasion, and this was one of them. Rufus listened respectfully, finding in this admonishment still further proof that he had been right to bring Podjo in on the operation. Reeny however paid little attention to the exchange, even though the Ford was hers and the discarded plates were in her name. Her contribution, unpacked now without comment, was a pint-sized dark brown bottle labeled *Noctec*, bought in a Bristol drugstore with a prescription from a friend who had it in turn from a friend who was a doctor, though not much of one any longer. She had secured it after conferring with her companions and asking around.

Rufus's contribution, on the other hand, came as a surprise. It was a pistol, an Army .45, which he lifted with a flourish from among the folded shirts and balled-up socks in his scuffed Gladstone.

"Just what the hell is that?" Podjo said angrily; as if he didnt know.

"It's in case we find ourselves in a tight with some rube cop or something," Rufus told him. "Or we run short of cash when we're coming down to the wire. What the hell? All we have to do is pull a small-time heist or two; one of those all-night burger places, say. Nothing to it. They dont want trouble. It's not even their money. They just fork it over when you show them this."

He hefted the automatic for their admiration, heavy and black in his hand as a lump of coal, and altogether deadly.

"Mother of God," Podjo said. He glared at the weapon, his letter-box mouth clamped in a frown beneath his dark mustache. "Put that goddam thing away and forget it. Better yet, get shed of it off the bluff there." The longer he looked at the pistol the angrier he got. "Goddammit, Rufe, I dont think you heard a word I said these past two weeks. Dont you know, havent I told you time and again, once this job comes down to violence the whole goddam thing's gone up in smoke, and us most likely with it? Jesus. Put it away; forget it. Heave it off the bluff."

"It's just insurance; sort of an ace in the hole," Rufus replied defensively.

An apprentice rebuked by an irate master, he laid the weapon away in a drawer of the chifforobe the cotton man had left empty for him and Reeny, and they went on unpacking. I got to watch this fellow; I got to watch him, Podjo thought.

The fact was, he had been thinking more or less along those lines — I got to watch him — ever since they renewed acquaintance, just last month in a Bristol pool hall. Acquaintance was all it had been till then, even at Parchman, though they both were from Jordan County and were assigned to the same camp. At any rate, the pool hall was where he first heard Rufus tell about the Greenlease job, four years ago in Kansas City, Missouri.

Carl Austin Hall and Bonnie Brown Heady snatched the young son of a local Cadillac dealer, Bobby Greenlease. They killed and buried him under a flower bed, early on, then collected the ransom — $600,000 in readily-spendable tens and twenties — and went on a spree to celebrate their coup, scooping the money in handfuls out of two suitcases loaded to overflowing with the stuff. That was when they were apprehended. Promptly tried, they were promptly convicted and promptly executed in mid-December, within three months of the crime in late September. What interested Rufus most, in this first telling, was the way they went — their final scene in the gas chamber, strapped side by side in chairs less than two feet apart. That had been their last request; that they go together. "Are you all right, honey?" Bonnie Brown Heady called to her partner when they heard the cyanide pellets, a little smaller than pullet eggs, drop plopping into the acid in the bowls beneath their chairs. "Yes, mamma," Carl Austin Hall replied, and the fumes came up.

"Aint that great? Just great?" Rufus insisted, his pale blue eyes shining with admiration.

"It dont sound too great to me," Podjo said after thinking it over.

Rufus grinned to mask his disappointment at Podjo's failure to appreciate this ultimate togetherness in that airtight chamber at the Jefferson City penitentiary, and they went on with the game. Whatever else he was, he wasnt much of a pool shot, certainly not enough of one to make a living at it, which he claimed to have in mind. However, as they went on playing he continued to talk about the Greenlease job, not about the closing scene, which he found so attractive, but rather about the caper itself, the way Carl and Bonnie had planned and carried it out, despite the personal shortcomings that undid them in the end.

"Even those clucks could bring it off," he remarked between shots as the game approached its end. "There wasnt a hitch between the snatch and the payoff, and there wouldnt have been one then if they hadnt gone ape when it was over — spending all that money, right off like that, and boozing it up to celebrate how well the thing had gone. It got me thinking."

He chalked his cue and shot, and missed. Then Podjo sank the twelve and the fifteen balls and the game was over.

"Nice shooting," Rufus told him. "Wait; I'll get us a beer." He went up front and returned with the two beers. "Come on. We'll drink them back here." He led the way to an empty domino table in the far rear corner. "It got me thinking, as I said, and here's what I came up with."

His first clew, he went on to explain, had been that the Greenleases were Jews. Wouldnt that perhaps make the police less energetic in their handling of the case? The answer was no, it wouldnt; not any more. Things had moved a long way from the days when Billy the Kid boasted that he had killed twenty-one men in his lifetime, and one Jew. Yes. But then the thought came to him, struck him: How about Negroes?

"I asked myself that, and knew I was onto something: How about niggers?" He patted the green felt table top. "Wouldnt that slow the cops down? And, what was better, wouldnt it slow the niggers down even more? The parents I mean. Wouldnt they be even readier than the Greenleases were to pay off quick and get their boy back, knowing the cops were white — Ku Kluxers, for all they knew, a good part of them at least — and wouldnt care too much, if at all, what happened to the kid, just so they solved the case and grabbed the ones who had him, that is until he got caught in the crossfire of the shoot-out? You bet they would, the niggers I mean, especially with things popping all round the South over that Supreme Court ruling on the schools, all that bus hooraw in Montgomery, and things fixing to come to a head across the river in Arkansas with Faubus up for reëlection and the polls showing him down so far it looks like he'll never get up. It's enough to make anyone jumpy, let alone them. My guess is they wouldnt even let the cops *in* on it, local or FBI. You follow me?"

"I follow you," Podjo said, and it was true. He followed him with something approaching awe, not only that Rufus had thought up what he was telling now, but also that he had gone into it so thoroughly; so professionally, so to speak. Nor was that the sole cause for wonder. Rufus had explored the matter practically, as well as theoretically, including a trip to Memphis to examine the possibilities on the actual chosen ground. He told about that too.

It couldnt be Bristol; Bristol wasnt big enough to hide in, he went on; nor was Birmingham either, quite. Only Memphis, Atlanta, or New Orleans would serve in that regard. This narrowed the choice to Memphis, partly because he already knew the geographical layout, but mainly because of the law's attitude there toward Negroes and the Negroes' attitude toward the law; Mr Crump, dead three years now, had laid the groundwork in advance, and laid it well. So it would be Memphis, and Rufus went up to look it over. He knew where; now he wanted to know who, and he was not long in solving that one, too, by a similar process of elimination.

He wanted someone rich, with a child young enough to be taken without the troubles an adult would give. Alas, he soon found there was no one in that category; all the rich Negroes were too old to have young children. That gave him pause, but having paused he moved on to grandchildren, and here a new problem arose. So many of the rich ones who had grandchildren had so many of them that he feared the law of diminishing utility would obtain; they might not value one child greatly if there were a dozen or so brothers and sisters and cousins in reserve. It was then, combing the papers and asking around, that he happened upon Theo G. Wiggins, whom he really ought to have thought of in the first place. Wiggins had only one child, a married daughter, and she in turn had only two, a boy and a girl, aged eight and six. The boy was thus the perfect candidate. And that was how the choice came down to Teddy Kinship, firstborn child of Eben and Martha and only grandson of old Theo G., who had money.

Podjo had not known what close attention he'd been paying until he looked down at the beer in his hand and realized he had yet to take a sip. Why me? he was asking himself when Rufus paused. Then he knew. It was because the other mistrusted himself as much as Podjo did: as if he knew that if he tried it unassisted — unled — he would be likely to fail in much the same way he had just failed at pool and had failed at so much else in his life, Ole Miss, the Marine Corps, and more recently crime, which had landed him in Parchman.

Sure enough, Rufus had paused to phrase a question in his mind, and now he asked it. "You want in?"

"I might," Podjo said, knowing he did, and took his first pull at the cold brown bottle in his hand.

That in itself was a kind of acceptance, including the drink that sealed it, and from then on Rufus proceeded on the assumption that they were partners. So in fact did Podjo, who began at once making improvements in the plan. Mainly these were modifications, simplifications required by Rufus's unbridled flights of fancy. One put up the notion, the other the know-how, and Reeny — she was presently in on it, too, and had been all along, Podjo discovered with some initial shock — the car. Between them, with the help of a good run of cards for Podjo a few nights later — that was his trade: gambler — they got up the $500 stake they figured was required.

They were waiting for the time to be right; waiting, that is, for a maximum of disturbance across the way in Arkansas, and in Memphis as well, to provide a background of fear and discord, a heightening of tension and apprehension. Podjo knew it was coming but he didnt know when. That depended largely on Faubus, and also in part on Eisenhower, on the quality and timing of his response. They were biding their time, watching the newspapers for clews, many of which were highly misleading. Then, the last week in August, Rufus and Reeny rode up to Memphis to locate a base. They returned early Labor Day morning, and that night Faubus made his move, going on television at ten oclock to announce that he had called out the Guard an hour before. The time was ripe, or getting ripe. They left Bristol soon after midday, Wednesday, and were in Memphis by late afternoon, unpacking for a stay that might last as long as a month but would certainly last no longer, since that was the length of the sublet lease for the house they had found on the bluff.

Next morning — although Podjo, after that first night spent on the yellow velvet couch, woke with a crick in his neck that gave him the bent-posture look of a hanged man who had been cut down just in time — they began at once to attend to such practical incidentals as stocking the larder in accordance with their individual tastes, which ran variously to Wonder Bread and peanut butter, Corn Flakes, beer and cigarettes, half a dozen fifths of Old Crow, assorted candy bars, Pet Milk, and powdered coffee. They came back to the bluff for lunch, scrapped together from the above, then set out for an army surplus store, where they bought two folding canvas cots, and a South Main hock shop where they chanced to see an electric fan in the window, an oldstyle three-speed model with an oscillator switch; Podjo was so pleased with this, which called up memories of boyhood, that he forgot the crick in his neck until he remembered and found it gone.

That night, taking a bottle of the bourbon along, they blew themselves to a meal at a restaurant called Grisanti's, across Main Street from Central Station. All three ate the roast beef dinner, which cost seventy-two cents with four vegetables. They had thought of going afterward to a movie, *Around the World in 80 Days* at the Crosstown, but decided instead, full as they were, to go home and flake out.

"I dont know about you two," Reeny said when Dragnet was over, "but I'm turning in."

Rufus joined her, and Podjo, after watching the local ten oclock news, bedded down on the couch, still full and reasonably happy: especially about the fan, which was just like the one — if indeed it was not the same old Emerson — he remembered buzzing and humming all night long, through July and August, in his mother and father's room when he was a boy down on Lake Jordan. He woke next morning, however, to find the crick was back.

It was Friday; they had planned a reconnaissance, the three of them, along Beale and Vance and the school route over to Linden. But when leaving-time came, Reeny changed her mind. "I think I'll stay home and wash my hair. You-all go on. I'll be here when you get back."

"What the hell," Rufus said. "Your hair?"

"Yes my hair. Why not? Goodness. . . . Well, if you just must know — it's my birthday."

"Which one is it?" Podjo asked without thinking.

"Never mind," Reeny said, bridling. Then she relented. "Ah, what the hell. I'm thirty-five." Her tone was reckless, but the recklessness was forced. "September sixth, nineteen twenty-two, around midday. Virgo, that's me, the virgin." She paused before adding, almost angrily, "My mother died that night."

"Look; I'm sorry," Podjo told her. He meant he was sorry for having asked her age, but she took him to mean the loss of her mother.

"Not nearly as sorry as I was. Am," she said.

"Well, o.k. then," Rufus said. "Come on, Podj. We'll study it up like we planned." He looked at Reeny, whose hair in fact was hanging rather lank by now, and patted the wave atop his own blonde head. "Happy birthday, Reen. We'll catch us a movie or something tonight, and maybe get you some ice cream and cake if youre good. Come on, Podj."

When they returned, around midmorning, Reeny was sitting in a chair in the back yard, her damp hair spread fanwise on her shoulders to dry in the sun, legs propped on another chair she had brought out to use as a footstool. They stood on the screen porch, looking out at her about midway between them and the lip of the bluff, with Arkansas for a backdrop.

Rufus glanced at Podjo, whose attitude, with his head cocked sideways to favor the crick in his neck, made him appear to be studying her intently.

"Man, I'll tell you," Rufus said, "there's more to that than meets the eye; lots more. That's the best rim job this side of Paris. I'm not kidding."

"You ever been to Paris?"

"N-no" — he hesitated, and Podjo could see that in the course of that drawn-out consonant he was making up his mind whether to lie or not — "but Ive been lots of other places in that direction, and I can tell you this one takes the cake." He did not mean Europe; he meant the direction of his proclivity, and Podjo, still looking at Reeny with his head cocked sideways in doglike speculation, understood this. "Ive seen you watching her," Rufus went on, "you being up here on your own, I mean, with nothing to cuddle up to. I'll give her the word, if you want, on condition you dont try to steal her. I'm broad-minded, but not so broad-minded I'd step all the way out of the picture. You want? It's really something; I'm not kidding. She'll make you think a whole covey of quail came whirring up out of your crotch. You want?"

"No thanks," Podjo told him after seeming to ponder the offer. He turned his head cautiously in Rufus's direction. "I always managed to get mine on my own. But thanks anyhow," he said drily.

"O.K. It was just a notion. All in the family, so to speak. Let me know if you change your mind."

"Yair," Podjo said, thinking: Or let *her* know. Then he added, "We better keep our attention on what we came up here for. Except in your spare time, I mean."

"Hi!" Reeny called from her chair in the yard. She had just opened her eyes to find them looking at her through the screen.

"Hi, baby," Rufus said. He raised one hand and waved at her, as if across a considerable distance, though she was less than forty feet away. "We were just telling each other how pretty you look, out there like that on the half shell."

They went out that night for eggs and country ham at Earl's Hot Biscuits, over on Crump, then to see *Around the World*, which they had passed up the night before, and came home late to go straight to bed, worn out by the long movie. It was not until the following night — Saturday — that Podjo was given at least an aural demonstration of what Rufus had told him yesterday in the course of his offer of Reeny's services.

He stayed behind when they left to go what they called juking, a cruise of the city's outlying joints and dance halls. The implication was that they were going to make a night of it, a belated birthday celebration, but to his surprise they returned early, around nine-thirty, just as the Miss America Pageant got started on Channel 3 from Atlantic City. He was sitting there having his third beer, settling down to watch the contest, when they came in and passed through the living room in such haste that they barely took the time to say hello. What's this? he wondered when Rufus closed the bedroom door behind them, nodding goodnight through the rapidly diminishing crack as it swung shut. Then he knew. I reckon they took them a notion, he thought, and he put them more or less out of his mind; that is until he heard, through the thin wall behind the couch, what he thought at first was singing; a duet.

One voice was shrill, mostly an *ee* sound, high, prolonged, operatic. The other was somehow obstructed, submerged, like someone moaning under water or maybe oil, a gargled growling. Both continued, mounting in intensity, melded in a common need, an urgency only just short, if short at all, of unbearable. Then it stopped, not suddenly but on a dying fall, a double suspiration, followed not by applause, as might have been expected for so virtuoso a performance, but by silence, also prolonged and profound. "Oo, good. *So* good," he heard Reeny murmur, and soon afterward Rufus said fervently, in a tone of prayerful gratitude: "Sweet Jesus." It was what he had been saying, or singing, all along — *Jeee*sus — only it sounded now as if a long-distance swimmer might have said it, just reaching the beach. Silence returned, then after a while the gently rasping sound of snoring, though whether from one or both of them Podjo could not tell, it was so faint. He went back to the pageant on the screen.

The snoring was Rufus, he presently learned. By now the proceedings had moved into the swim-suit competition, the girls parading across the stage in a curious minuet, as if each had her own pelvis for a partner in the dance and the pelvis was doing the leading. "That one's a looker," he heard someone say, and he looked around to find Reeny standing in the bed-room doorway, Rufus's snores sounding louder behind her with the door ajar.

She had on a peach-colored wrapper of imitation silk, held loosely together in front with one hand at her waist, and she was barefoot; bare-everything, he decided, but the wrapper. You wanna be next? he thought her look said. The contestant she indicated was Miss Colorado, twenty years old, five feet eight and a quarter inches tall, and she was indeed a looker. "I bet youd like some of that," Reeny persisted, boosting her choice.

Podjo grunted by way of reply, but the truth was he would very much have liked some of that, especially after all he had overheard in the next room. They watched the parading on the screen, the repetitive minuet, and before long Reeny, still standing in the doorway, remarked offhand: "They put Vaseline on their teeth."

"Their *what?*" It seemed outrageous.

"Their teeth — to make them shine like that in the lights when they smile that smile, and to keep their lips from sticking to them."

"Jesus," Podjo said in a tone quite unlike Rufus's a while back.

"A girl I knew was in one. Not up there; over in Alabama. She didnt win but she told me that's what they do — put Vaseline on their teeth to make them shine. A real bunch of clucks, she said, all just crazy about their shapes and saving them up for rich husbands. Their hope chest is their tits; theyre what they bring to the marriage. They dont allow them to be touched."

Podjo shifted uncomfortably on the yellow velvet, more than ever convinced that she had come out to ask that question: You wanna be next? Or maybe not. He decided not to think about it any more, unless of course she asked.

"Why dont you turn on in?" he said.

"I'm not sleepy. Who could sleep with Rufus cutting up all that racket in there? Besides, I want to see how this comes out."

It came out just as she had predicted at first glance. After the contestants put their clothes back on, the semifinalists were selected, then the finalists. These four survivors were questioned by the master of ceremonies, a vigorous man with a grimaced smile and patent-leather hair, barely able to contain the ebullience it was his job to supply, and the judges handed up their verdict. First the alternates were presented, then the winner: Marylin Van Derbur, Miss Colorado. "*There* she goes — Miss A*mer*ica," Bert Parks exulted, and she stepped out onto the runway, caped and crowned, smiling around her teeth, eyes luminous with tears of joy, as if they too had been Vaselined to make them glisten.

"Didnt I tell you? Didnt I tell you?" Reeny cried.

# 2

## *Voices*

So we settled in, and I had time, after all the scurrying round those first few days — Wednesday, when we got there, through Saturday night, when Miss America paraded; now it was Sunday — to look back over what the deal had come to, by way of groundwork, since Rufus first laid it out for me in the pool hall. He didnt mention any third party till the night of the following day. Then he did. "I'll be bringing my girl along," he said.

I didnt like it. God knows they have their uses, but I always had the feeling that they tend to fly apart, all too often over things that have nothing to do with the work at hand. Just so. Then I met her, Reeny Perdew, and at least she was a woman, not a girl, and likely to be useful on such a job, if only as a cook and nursemaid. So I thought, and I no sooner thought it than I found I was no more than half right, at best.

One thing I was wrong about, first off, was the cooking. You had to see what she could do with an egg and a hot skillet to believe it. I saw it once, back in Bristol, and I believe it, though only by the hardest. Once was not only enough; once was too much. It looked as if someone had bounced the eggs off the ceiling, shells and all. Country fried, she called them, but I'm a country boy myself, or was, and believe me that was never the style we woke up to in *my* day. One result, so far as home cooking went, was that I lived mainly on Chesterfields and Jax,

Rufus on candy bars, and Reeny herself on Corn Flakes and coffee, both with Pet.

I spent most of Sunday morning with the paper. FAUBUS SAYS GUARD WILL KEEP/ NEGROES OUT OF HIGH SCHOOL/ DESPITE RULING BY U.S. JUDGE, the headline read. He was holding firm; it was shaping up just fine. We had all the time we needed, yet not too much if things broke the way I had them figured. It was shaping up just fine.

Midafternoon we went over on Crump and ate again at Earl's — country ham, hot biscuits, and eggs fried the way they should be, over easy, with the edges crisp as lace — then came back and took three chairs out on the lip of the bluff to watch the sun go down behind the bridges, flaring red behind the grill- work of the girders and coating the flats across the way in Arkansas with blood. The evening sky darkened so slow you couldnt see it change until each change was past. I went in, got the Old Crow and a glass of ice, and came back out. Bullbats were flying in the dusk by then, making that farting sound they make, and the lights on the bridges began to glow, ruby, emerald, topaz, like sparks in the wake of a trio of rockets whooshing out across the river, hidden down below. Behind us, masked by the house till it rose higher, the moon came up full, murky orange from the fumes of the city till it sailed clear of the roof line, bruised-looking, then bright as hammered gold, balanced on the point of the near gable, bigger than the house itself and absolutely round. In the background, Reeny was talking, talking, the way she sometimes did; something about coming out of a cake.

"I'm drawn to the notion," she was saying. "You know, like at a party, a stag affair. Theyre all sitting round the table and the cake comes in on rollers. It gets there, and pow! a girl comes out, hands up by her head, fingers wiggling, and sort of kicks up her heels, bare titties and maybe a little strip of G-string, bobbed hair and high-heel shoes. You do your dance, a sort of Charleston, then go sit in the guest of honor's lap and muss his hair up. . . . I couldnt do that. I never knew anyone

who could, not really the way I mean, unless they were dumb
enough, free-spirited enough, and I was never either. I think
it's a worthwhile ambition, something to aim at — to be someone who could come powing out of a cake like that and enjoy
it, really enjoy it; not to be shy or ashamed of doing a crazy,
foolish thing, maybe even for a living, or of being a fool while
everybody watched and laughed, right up to the time you lost
your figure and maybe after. That would make it even funnier,
more foolish; after you lost your figure, I mean. I wish I could.
You know?"

I didnt follow it any too well, mostly because I wasnt listening except to hear it as a sort of twitter coming birdlike through
my thoughts while I sipped the whiskey and looked back over
how we got from there to here, from the Bristol pool hall to
light housekeeping on the Memphis bluff. Mainly it was a
process of scaling down. Rufus, for example, had fixed on that
Greenlease figure of $600,000, which I knew was away out of
line, no matter how rich this Wiggins was or wasnt. What we
wanted was a figure he would turn loose of without calling in
the law. I explained that about one tenth of that amount was
the most we could count on without bringing on a hooraw.

"Hell fire," he said, jerked up short. "A third of that doesnt
come to but twenty thousand."

"What third? Half," I said. "And it comes to thirty." He'd
been counting on a three-way split, including Reeny's third,
which combined with his own would give him two. It was
quite a come-down, a drop from $400,000 to $30,000. His face
took on the look of a man who's just been clobbered in the
market or threw snake eyes on a roll for all his winnings. "What
you do with your half's up to you," I told him, "including sharing it with her. She's with you, not me."

He came round; how not? and we moved on to other matters.
A similar one, and I stressed it, was the tone we'd take in dealing with the Kinships and old Wiggins. Just as we had to settle
on the right amount for the payoff, one theyd accept without
kicking up a fuss, so we had to decide beforehand how to strike

a proper balance, in our contacts over the phone and in ransom notes, that would frighten and reassure them, both at once; one that would scare them into doing what we said do, when we said it, yet not scare them so much theyd lose their heads and start yelling for the cops. The answer, we agreed in talking it over back in Bristol, was to combine an impression of cold professionals, old hands at capers such as this, with an impression of wild-eyed fanatics, new at the game and hot for blood; especially nigger blood, which would be why they got into this thing in the first place. Our job, we decided, was to make ourselves sound as if the Ku Klux Klan had joined with the Mafia to bring off the snatch, the gangsters holding the klansmen back from violence only so long as the conditions they laid down were being met.

That was where Faubus came in. He would provide the backdrop, the atmosphere of tension when the time came. And Eisenhower; he too would do his part up there at Newport, golfing, fishing, hanging back. We counted on them both, and every passing day the papers seemed to show we'd counted right in both directions. They made a good team, Ike and Orval.

Other, lesser matters had to be worked out, too; not less important, just less large. Names, for example. We had to have names to use while the boy was around, so he wouldnt be able to tell who we were when he got back home. Accordingly, Rufus, Reeny, Podjo became Brother, Sister, Joe, on the theory theyd be easy to remember — for us I mean, not the boy; that didnt matter, so long as they were false. Rufus didnt like his until I told him Brother is a name used by carnival women to mean a husband or a steady. "I got a brother," they say, meaning they are tied up or committed. He liked it better then, and made a joke about it; "Ive always been an only child, till now." I think he also liked the notion of added closeness, even incest.

Reeny laughed. She enjoyed seeing things work out, and would clap her hands when you came up with an answer to a problem, much as she might do after watching a magician pull an egg or a silk handkerchief out of someone's mouth or ear.

Fact was, she had worked out one such problem on her own, and by no means an easy one at that.

We wanted something that would make the boy docile, first on the ride from the school to the bluff and then on the walk from the car to the house; something that would calm him in short order, so he wouldnt yell or kick up a fuss, yet not so strong it would knock him so far out he'd have to be lugged along like a sack of potatoes. I thought it would be one of the barbiturates, Phenobarbital or something, but Reeny came up with the answer. NOCTEC (chloral hydrate) it was called, an orange-flavored syrup. *An effective sedative and hypnotic agent*, the inside folder read. *Somnifacient doses promptly produce drowsiness and sedation, followed by quiet, sound sleep,* and went on to tell how two teaspoons would put him under, or next to under, and three others given daily would keep him gentle. *Especially for the ill, the young, and the elderly. Allays anxiety and induces sleep without depressing respiration.* In short, it was just what the doctor ordered. And in fact that was where Reeny got it; from a doctor, or anyhow from a woman friend who got it from a broken-down old pill-roller who had given her the prescription before, for use on her kids on car trips, and she passed it on to Reeny on request.

A similar problem, having to do with getting the kid back to the bluff and into the house, was the color thing. Mostly it worked *for* us, but here it worked against. What would three grown white people be doing riding one little eight-year-old black boy around and then hustling him into the place they lived? Arkansas Street was what you might call integrated, in the sense that both races stayed there, but not in the same house; not by a long shot. Once he was inside, thanks to the windowless attic and the Noctec, there was no problem; the cover story about the eye operation was reason enough for keeping him hidden, out of the light, in case anyone came calling or snooping. But how were we going to get him there, first through the public streets, then from the car to the house, safely stowed away and sedated, without attracting attention?

This time it was Rufus came up with the answer. He mused

his way into a brainstorm. "There was an actor, coal black —
Canada Lee!" he cried, proud of the sudden recollection.
"Evilest-looking man I ever saw, bar none. I remember when
you looked him straight in the face you were staring right up
both nostrils. He played a white man once in some Elizabethan
drama; *Duchess of Malfi*, something like that. Did it in clown
white, I remember. We'll get that; clown white. Put it on him
in the car, and the kid will be white as the rest of us. Maybe
whiter."

Rufus often came up with things like that, farfetched but
pat, most likely because of all the reading he'd done and that
college education he was always letting you know he had.
Inventive, I guess youd call it. But there was another side to
it, too; one I discovered early on.

He said off-hand, one day we were alone, "My grandfather
was a banker here in Bristol."

"What bank was that?" I wasnt trying to pin him down or
anything; I was really interested.

"Planters Trust."

I tried to think back to times I went in there with my old
man to get an extension on a loan to keep from losing his truck.
Those were hard times, the Thirties. I remembered Lawrence
Tilden, who owned the place; a smooth-haired fellow named
Sanderson — he was a teller, always in his cage — and Harley
Drew, who sat at a desk out front until he went away; I even
remembered a porter whose name was Rufus, too. Then all of
a sudden it came to me, and before I could stop myself I asked
him, "Was his name Cilley?"

Rufus nodded, trying to pass it off by moving on to something else, and I thought of old Mr Cilley. He was a bookkeeper there for years, ever since Tilden's father's time; wore
detachable collars and cuffs, to show he'd come up in the
world I guess, and had a crusty way of never speaking, back
there in the back with his books and his green eyeshade and
sleeve garters. Some banker. I remembered then he had a stroke
and they took him home paralyzed. He lived that way for a

year or so, and then he died; a really terrible old man with
two round-heel daughters and a jerk-water politician son-in-law
who was always running for sheriff and never winning, except
when run-off time came round and he could peddle his few
votes. Old Mr Cilley.

Well, I guess it made sense if Rufus wanted to make him out
to be a full-fledged banker, even if it was only for brag, not
even a real con. Everyone has needs, and I guess we could all
use a banker in the family. But other things began to develop;
claims he made that didnt jibe. I thought I'd better ask around,
and then it all came out. Ole Miss, for example. He went there,
all right, but left in the middle of his second year, kicked out
for cheating and petty theft. The same with the Marine Corps;
he was about as much a Marine as his grandpa was a banker.
He went through boot at Parris Island, then out to Pendleton,
en route for Korea, and wound up in the brig for pilfering
lockers. Back home with a bad-conduct discharge, he tried his
hand at burglary till the police walked in on him and his
partner in a warehouse. The partner made a run for it, but the
police are still laughing at the way Rufus stood there, too
scared to move, wetting his pants while they put the cuffs on.
Parchman was a short trip; his politician uncle collected on a
favor owed him down at Jackson and got him out in three-four
months.

Just so. And now there was this, up in Memphis, and me
with him, and all the time all these lies about where he'd been,
what-all he'd done; Ole Miss, football, Korea, big-time crime;
all that. None of it was easy to put up with, coming at you
steady as it did. There's worse things than a liar, by far, but
Rufus had gone beyond lying to become the things he told.
He wasnt just a liar. He was a lie.

All the same, you had to give him credit. It was this very
lying, this inventiveness — imagination I guess youd call it —
that brought us up here in the first place. I wouldnt want to
take that from him. The plan was his; he dreamed it up; all I
did was scale it down to workable proportions. And it would

work. How not? His shortcomings werent the kind that would interfere, I kept telling myself, at least so long as I was there to ride herd on him. So I'd say; so I'd tell myself, each day that passed. Then we drove up and he came out with that goddam Army .45, and I knew I had more to fret about than I'd lulled myself into thinking because of the ache I had for those thirty thousand dollars. I got to watch this fellow, I got to watch him, I told myself.

We sat there on the lip of the bluff, sunset through moonrise Sunday night, and while Reeny went on about powing out of a cake I sipped my bourbon and thought back over what things had come to, up to now. After a while the mosquitoes drove us indoors and I bedded down on my velvet rack, put to sleep by a cowboy movie Rufus and Reeny watched till sign-off.

Youd think they had enough of Hollywood off the tube, but no. "How about a flick?" she said next night.

"Let's catch the Malco," Rufus said. "It's closest."

"What's playing?"

"Mm. *3:10 to Yuma.*"

"Who's in it?"

"What difference does that make?"

"O.K. Let's go."

So they went. I stayed behind. That was Monday; we were into the second week in September. They came home late — straight through, and closed the bedroom door behind them. This time she took the soprano part and Rufus did the moaning. I had a hard time getting to sleep, partly because I'd been asleep a good two hours already.

Reeny had taken to reading the papers, from boredom I suppose. I dont think she read much of what I read, but she had a way of finding things I missed; mostly in the entertainment section.

"I see Elvis is back," she said on Thursday.

"Who?"

"Elvis."

"Elvis who?"

"*Elvis,* for God sake. Elvis *Presley.* He's back from tour."

"Oh."

I guess I sounded unimpressed, or anyhow not impressed enough. It irked her and she said so. "Good Lord, Podjo. For someone who's smart, you can be awful dumb sometime."

"Well," I said, "I reckon we've all got our blind spots. Mine just happens to be Elvis."

"You ought to keep up better with what's going on in the world. Besides, he's from Missippi; Tupelo. You ought to take more pride."

I guess I ought. In fact I will, I told myself.

That same day there was a story, FAUBUS TO GIVE SCHOOL STAND/ IN DRAMATIC TALK WITH IKE, about a meeting that coming weekend up in Newport. Faubus had asked for it; I wasnt worried, knowing he was only jockeying for position when showdown time came round. Nashville had popped off by then, whites parading in protest round the schools, but Governor Clement let us down; agitators, he called them, and ran them off the streets.

We bided our time, Rufus and I, sometimes driving the route from the house on Vance to Leath School on Linden, during and after hours, with and without Reeny. Once we followed them going, the boy and his kid sister, and once coming home, a little over four blocks each way, both times past their granddaddy's house, a block up Vance from their own. Theyd wait for each other, whichever got out first, by the flagpole in the schoolyard at the corner of Turley and Linden. We had it taped, down pat. I didnt see how it could miss; except of course I knew it could, for reasons that had nothing to do with planning, good or bad. A squad car spots us, right after the pickup, and for no reason at all — a broken tail light, or the cop didnt like the way Rufus combed his hair or I sat sideways on the seat, or he wanted a better closeup look at Reeny; in other words, for nothing — pulls us over. "What you got there?" he asks, and sees the little nigger sitting there goggle-eyed with Noctec, half painted up with clown white. "What you got there?"

It could happen. There's where luck comes in, and I never

had much of it, especially in the clutch; a serious drawback for a man who calls himself a gambler. If it was raining diamonds, Moon Mullins used to say, he'd be up a flagpole with a tennis racket. That's me.

Truth is, we're not very smart, those of us who go in for crime. We have to make up in risk for what we lack in skill and insight. Not that the work of burglars, con men, counterfeiters, whatever, doesnt call for a certain amount of know-how. It does. But it also requires a lot of pure hard work and sweat; including the sweat that comes from fear, and that's the rankest kind, the hardest of all to ooze. And not that it doesnt pay. It pays, but not enough to balance out. We need a union. The pay is small for the time put in; including jail time, another hardest kind. What we have as a replacement for smartness — and no smart man would join up anyhow, except a certain variety of twisted feeb who's not out after money in the first place — is a willingness to cross the line and stand beyond the law, paying whatever the court says pay if we're collared and convicted. Just so. But as for me, I was out for the money; just the amount we settled on, thirty thousand. I wanted those green felt tables out in Vegas, the down-funneled blue-white light, clicking dice and clacking chips and slithering cards, all those wide-hat cats in string ties and hand-tooled boots, and the bets going round. Thirty thousand; I planned to break it down into three ten-thousands, a triple shot at the big time, three nights running. One of the three was bound to hit, I told myself, knowing it wasnt necessarily so. But how would I know, for sure, if I never tried? And this was my chance, courtesy of old Theo G., who'd never miss the outlay.

As for me, what would it cost me if it failed? Another five or six years of my life, I figured, at the most. And what the hell, it wasnt all that much of a life in the first place. My father was a logger, heavy-handed. He was from Joplin, Missouri, where I was born, and my mother was from Tonti Town, in northwest Arkansas, just across the way. She was Italian (or Sicilian, which is more-so) and wanted me to be a priest, perhaps as a way of paying back for having married Protestant. That wasnt the only wish she didnt get; not by a long shot. All religion did for me was make me scared to death of God. After all, I had plenty of evidence, from the Bible and in sermons, of what-all He'd been known to do to sinners no worse than I was. And Jesus too — he could be downright savage if you touched him where he was tender. What I kept wanting, kept looking for, was a lazy, mild-mannered, *simple* kind of saint and guardian who'd be inclined to indulge me in my lapses and not even take the trouble to pass my transgressions along to higher authority, God or Jesus or one of those ten-foot angels who carry keys or a sword they would use to lock you up or chop your head off.

The army cured me of most of that. Two years under that goddam Patton, who'd swap a regiment for a ribbon in a minute, made me one of the many athiests in Third Army foxholes. All I really got from it otherwise, including the Silver Star they gave me for my part in a fire-fight no different from a dozen others we'd been through up to then, was a beginner's love of the poker I learned to play on R&R. I came home to go for it in earnest, then ran into a serious interruption. Women.

This one was a good few years older than me, about the same span Reeny had on Rufus; society type, a Buick dealer's wife. I took her home from a club one night and her husband stayed there drinking. So we thought, till he walked in and found me banging her bass-ackwards over the foot of a nearly waist-high big brass bed they had. That was what made him so mad I think, the position. He went on through to the kitchen at a run, giving off a kind of screaming moan — I barely had time to hitch up my trousers — and came back with a foot-long butcher knife that wound up inside him in the wrestling match that followed.

D.O.A. The unwritten law works two ways, forward and reverse, especially when one of the men is a high-placed businessman and the other is what the newspaper has begun to call "known gambler." Manslaughter; I got eight years and served five, 1949 to 1954, then came back home to take up where I left off, more or less marking time for another three years till Rufus turned up with the proposition that brought us up to Memphis.

He was something else, that Rufus. Not just the lying, the pretending; they were only the means for trying to chase what he was after and knew he'd never get. What he wanted was manhood — wholeness — on his own terms; that is, by sacrificing nothing to achieve it. And he not only knew he'd never have it, he also knew he'd never stop trying to get it, *his* way, till he died. That would be his release, his only possible release. He knew that, and even sought it — Catch me! Catch me! he kept shouting, whether in lies or petty crime — but always flinched when it was offered, up to now, including a one-way trip to Korea. Sooner or later he would get what he was running toward, and that was what made him scary, especially now that the crime was far from petty. If there was any way to screw it up he'd find it; he'd head for Parchman — or in this case Fort Pillow; I kept forgetting — like a pigeon winging homeward to its roost.

And Reeny, whose notion of living was to come powing out of cakes; she too. She was an altogether different breed of cat, but they certainly made a pair. Two-three nights a week I'd hear them through that thin partition, singing those duets, and I'd remember her, Miss America night in the doorway in that damn peach-colored wrapper, when I was torn two ways, front and rear — and stayed torn, then and since, front and rear. A man's got to watch himself; know where he's headed, where he might get hurt. Just so. But the notion of her was starting to creep up on me. And more than the notion, she herself. It was all right wanting her for *my* sake; I could handle that. What worried me was I might start wanting her for *her* sake. I began to see that, and it scared me.

The week wore on, the second we were there. Then on Saturday, at its end, Ike and the governor had their meeting up at Newport. FAUBUS AND EISENHOWER AGREE/ TO WORK FOR FAST SETTLEMENT/ OF LITTLE ROCK SCHOOL CRISIS, the headline said next morning. A subhead read, *Troops Expected to be Withdrawn; New Moves May Come by Friday,* and the story: "While separate statements issued after their two hour and nine minute closed meeting were vague in details, it was obvious from their smiling faces and parting handshake that a full understanding had been reached."

Sure enough, a three-column cut alongside the text showed them shaking hands, Ike with his chin down, Faubus with his lifted, and both were smiling. Herb Brownell was in the background, smiling too. Vague, I thought; that's the word, all right, and passed the paper to Rufus and Reeny. "My money's on the governor," I told them.

Events were moving faster all the time now; all the time. Any day, we'd get the signal that said go.

Sunday morning we went to church as usual — Beale Street Baptist — then back to Tio's for Sunday dinner, and that was as usual, too. The children named him that: first Teddy, when he was barely one, mispronouncing Theo, then Sister Baby when she came along. Martha picked up on it next, and finally I did, first only in referring to him within the family, then afterwards to his face: at home I mean. Always before, I'd called him Mr Wiggins, that is until Martha and I were married, and then it became Mr Theo, which I still called him at the office, like most people. Names are strange, the way they are arrived at. I didnt know till years later, and only then by accident, that Tio was Spanish for uncle.

He was of course at the head of the table, Mamma Cindy at the end. Sister Baby and I were on one side, Martha and Teddy on the other, and lame Dolly in her apron and headrag limped from kitchen to table and back again, fetching and clearing, without the time for sitting down even if there had been a place laid for her, which there wasnt. She lived, or anyhow slept, in a spare room downstairs — up before daylight, Monday through Sunday, lighting a fire in the range for breakfast, and never done till she washed up after supper and turned the beds down. Lincoln they say freed the slaves almost a hundred years ago, but Dolly never got the word: unless, that is, emancipation didnt apply within the family. She was Tio's niece, an older sister's daughter, close to his own age and born with a crooked leg. He brought her here from Moscow at the time he married, gave her a home for life and five dollars all her own every Saturday, out of the goodness of his heart. After dinner we went into the parlor and could hear her back in the kitchen, washing up. Tio was in his chair with the antimacassars, solid as any rock, and Mamma Cindy sat in her own spindly one beside the unlighted fireplace, pale-skinned, with her high-bridged nose and dignity, hands folded in her lap: edgy though, I knew, from wanting a dip of snuff she couldnt have till she was alone. The children were restless, mostly Teddy, but we stayed on until the regular leaving time, past two. Then we left, glad to be walking the one block down Vance after all that heavy food.

Martha took Sister Baby and Teddy back for their nap, and before I could get settled down to my own, there on the couch in the living room, she came back up and started in on me, more or less the way I knew she would.

"I told you before, I'll tell you again," she told me. "Those children are too old to be sleeping in the same room, let alone the same bed."

You could tell she'd rehearsed it, probably all the way home if not through dinner, being in that roomier house of Tio's. She'd been through it too often, just as I had with my answer that Julia and I, with the same two-year age span, had shared the same bed till I was past eleven. "Memphis isnt Mississippi and you know it," she said, "and neither are the times. We said goodbye to the Depression long since: you just wont turn it loose. Going around flipping light switches and all that — "

It came up every Sunday, if not betweentimes. She'd be off and running, like now, the bit in her teeth, telling herself it wasnt for us or her, it was for the children. That made her bold. What she wanted was a bigger house, and she even knew the one, a block up Vance at 318, almost opposite her daddy's at 311: brick veneer, with three bedrooms. He owned that one too, the same as this, and she was forever after me to press him on the subject, along with another. A raise.

"You know how he is," she'd say. "He'll never give anybody anything of his own accord. They have to ask for it, and even then he's got to see they mean it: mean and *need* it, by his lights as well as theirs. Surely you know that of him, by now."

And I'd come back at her. "Yes I know it, and I dont like it," I would tell her. "We've got enough to call our own for the time being. I'll see to all that when the right time comes."

"The right time!" she'd say, and push her mouth out, pouting.

She thought I meant when Tio died, but that wasnt it. In the first place I'd long since come to know he was going to outlive us all, hands down, if that was what he wanted. What I meant was I didnt want to talk about it: didnt want to ask favors of him — over those, that is, she'd already talked me into asking and sometimes getting. The house we lived in rented for fifty dollars, just under a third of the $166.66 I made a month, while the other was likely to run some ten or fifteen dollars higher. He had owned them both for years, about as long as he'd owned the one he lived in, along with others hereabouts and elsewhere, and I was proud that in the ten years we'd been married, Martha and I, I'd never once missed paying the rent and paying it slap on schedule. I'd pay him before I'd even pay the doctor for delivering the two babies: go out and borrow it, if need be, even from one of the loan sharks on Beale.

He knew that, and I was bound and determined to have him

know it, as one of my few ways of being able to tell myself that I was unbeholden, independent, at least to that extent. That was why I sent the rent check on the last day of the month, by mail and without fail, so it would be there in the office on the first, even though the envelope, stamped and addressed in my own hand, was only one among the many Miss Lucy would sort and open, right there in plain view of my desk. I wanted it regular, like the others, only prompter: more punctilious, they call it. I wouldnt even hand it in by hand, even though it wouldnt be him that opened it but Miss Lucy. He'd still know, the way he knew everything, and I would know he knew, and what's more he would know I knew he knew.

Finally Martha let up, having said her say. I already had my coat and tie and shoes off, so I undid my belt and waistband and lay back, pulling the front page of the paper over my head for a tent. As it came down I saw my old commander — Supreme, they called him in those days — shaking hands with Faubus up in Rhode Island, smiling at him and Faubus smiling back, along with the Attorney General, who seemed to be taking turns smiling at them both. He was President now, in civilian clothes, but he didnt look much different except for being a good deal less pink-faced in newsprint, just as he was on television almost every night, and a little wispier round the fringes of his hair. He was the last thing I saw before I drifted off, digesting all that heavy Sunday dinner. I dreamed a child-hood dream about a crook-tail bulldog I once had, named Buster, till he died of a stomach ailment from something my sister Julia fed him on the sly.

When I woke up the children were engaged in some kind of squabble and Martha was scrapping together a cold supper in the kitchen. We ate it, watched some TV, and turned in early. She let me have some, the way she generally would on Sunday nights. I kidded her a little, afterwards, suspecting she liked it better than she let on, and she even laughed at some fool joke I made when she got back from washing up: something about clothes, all those clothes — a surprise package under all those layers. I went to sleep happy, and woke up more-so. I was eating my eggs and bacon in the kitchen when Teddy and Sister Baby came in for breakfast, dressed for school. This was the third week, and I gave them the same talking-to I'd given them at the start and on the first Monday, a week back, about going together to and from school, all four blocks, and being careful crossing streets.

"Whoever gets out first waits by the flagpole, understand? And neither leaves without the other. Especially you," I told Teddy, "or I'll tan your hide. And you too," I told Sister Baby. "You hear me? Tan your hide."

Both of them grinned at me over their cereal bowls, knowing I wouldnt, if for no other reason than that I never had.

I turned the key in the office door at straight-up eight oclock, ten minutes ahead of gray-haired Lucy Provine, and was already settled down to my books when Tio came in at eight-forty. You could have set your watch by all three of us, any weekday morning there at 185 Beale, and it had been that way — in that order, I mean — ever since Teddy was born and named for him, back in late August of 1949. The day was already getting hot when I got there, I remember, and found him waiting on the sidewalk. "Here," he said, and gave me a duplicate key, something no one had ever had before, not even Miss Lucy who'd been with him from the start. "I opened up for the first thirty years," he told me. "Now you do it the next thirty. Then we'll turn it over to little Theo, if he's able."

It was his way of saying he was glad to have a grandson, not knowing yet the boy would be nicknamed Teddy. That came hard but we stood firm, Martha and I, even under the threat that he might take the key back, along with the title he gave me that same week, Associate Vice President, and the twenty-five-dollar pay raise to $150. A year and a half later, April Fool's Day, Baby Sister came along, named Lucinda for her grandmother, and his cup about ran over: mainly I think because she was light-skinned, taking after my side of the family. I think that was why he chose me in the first place. For Martha I mean. And I know for a fact that was why he chose his wife Lucinda, called Mamma Cindy by the children even before they named him Tio.

Over the years, I studied him up close: first as a boss, the way you always study your boss, and then as my wife's father, the way you do that too. Yet I couldnt say I ever really understood him, any more than anyone else could, though many tried. In business it's like poker: you dont want them to know what you are thinking, and he was very good at that. I could never even say for sure when he was making a joke, no matter how much it sounded like one at the time. One day early on, for instance, I listened in while a man was trying to float a loan. Tio wouldnt go for it at all, and finally the man sat back — he'd been sitting up on the edge of his chair till then, hoping against hope that Tio would hand him just a little of all that money he knew he had — and came out with what he thought was his ace in the hole. "You know what they say, Mr Theo. You cant take it with you."

"I'm not going anywhere," Tio told him. He didnt smile. His face was perfectly straight. I think he meant it, just that simple: "I'm not going anywhere."

Another time — this was a caller, not on business, though this too was in the office in those first days, early on — I heard someone ask him, "Dont it bother you, Mr Theo, that youve got the same first name and middle initial as Senator Bilbo?"

"Well, no," he said after thinking it over. "I dont see how I can rightly complain. He had them first, by about fifteen years, though I'm fairly certain my daddy and mamma didnt know so the time." He thought some more. "Still," he went on, sorting it out in his mind, "you cant tell. We might be some kind of distant kin for all I know, the Senator and me. Who knows what went on, back in slavery days? In both directions."

The man laughed but Tio didnt. He sat there, looking chunky in his chair, built solid around that little gleam of gold on his shirt bosom. You couldnt tell.

While he never voted so far as I know, he contributed freely to most campaigns, including both Republican factions, Lily Whites and Black-and-Tans, though not as much as he did to the Democrats, who were mostly the winners: especially Mr Crump, whose first political race was underway when Tio arrived in 1909 to find W. C. Handy's band playing on street corners, drumming up crowds for what called itself the reform ticket, with Mr Crump at its head in the run for mayor.

> *Mr Crump dont 'low no barrel-housing here,*
> *Mr Crump dont 'low no barrel-housing here.*
> *I dont care what Mr Crump dont 'low,*
> *I'm go' barrel-house anyhow —*
> *Mr Crump can go and catch hisself some air.*

He didnt have much use for that, either then or later, neither the music nor the man who made it. In his eyes, even at seventeen, new to the city and city ways, Handy was some kind of clown, performing at people's beck and call, for very little cash and no credit whatsoever. More to his liking was Booker T. Washington, who came to Memphis on a speaking tour in November of that same year. Tio went, watching from back on the fringes of the crowd, and there began a lifelong admiration. "Let down your buckets where you are," he liked to quote, if only to himself, and: "No race can prosper till it learns that there is as much dignity in tilling a field as in writing a poem."

Not that he intended to get involved with fields or poetry. No: he put tilling behind him, where he came from, and the other he just never got into at all, even to read it. Howsomever, he did let down his bucket. He did indeed.

He was born and grew up — or almost up — near Moscow, on the Wolf River forty miles east of Memphis. His father was a cropper, once a slave, and had done a hitch in the Union army, so they say. He was the youngest of six children, born in 1892. The other five were girls and he supported them after he prospered, the three that survived their parents, until those three died too, still around Moscow and Grand Junction. It was a point of honor with him, and not too costly, one being widowed, the other two unmarried. But that was later. When he came to town at seventeen, walking because he didnt have the rail fare, he went to work in a livery stable, grooming horses, scrubbing down buggies, things like that, along with tips for doing them extra well, which he did. He'd had about six months' schooling, all told. For the most part he was bootstrap raised, self-taught by lamplight after hours, alone in a half a rented room over the stable while the others were out carousing. *Arithmetic and Its Application* was one text I heard him mention having got by heart, and pretty soon he had a small-scale loan business going among the people he worked beside: five cents a week on a dollar until you paid it back — which few chose to do because it seemed like such a bargain to have the use of a whole dollar for only a nickel, all week long, and no pressure brought to bear. He was fat when he first got here, so I heard. Then he got thin. Then he filled out, broadened to nearly the size he is today, with next to no fat anywhere on him. It was as if he abolished what he had been, rubbed himself out with an eraser, then started all over again to be what he became. Once he decided he was where he wanted to be, and when, he did indeed let his bucket down: in Memphis, that is, in the teen years of the century, the early and middle twenties of his life.

It was a high-rolling time and Beale was in its heyday, paved end-to-end with pimps and whores and gamblers, easy riders and their marks, parading daylong-nightlong past the pawnshops, hot tamale and pigfoot vendors, clothing stores, saloons and pool halls such as the Hole in the Wall and Pee Wee's Place, where Viglio Maffi and later Lorenzo Pacina tended bar and did the bouncing, Joe Raffanti's Midway, the Monarch Club and the Panama, where Jake Redmond and Irish Jim Mulcahy ruled the roost, Will Stewart's Marble Hall, Hammit Ashford's, and lots more, all before my time and long since gone. Tio never so much as glanced over their swinging doors when he went past them on the sidewalk, going about in those early days selling burial policies in the district. The sporting life meant nothing to him, if for no other reason than that the ones who lived it were too much of a risk for him to deal with on a bet they wouldnt die before they finished ponying up their costs. Maybe he knew already they couldnt last, even aside from the high mortality rate. And a good thing, too. Good riddance, right-thinking people would say of Handy and those like him when the time came round for Mr Crump to close them down and run them off, because of the way they detracted from the solid achievement of such men as the two Bob Churches, Tio, Matthew Thornton, and others like them, not to mention getting Memphis known as the murder capital of the entire U.S.A.

As for Tio there at the outset, moving up, he was plowing his earnings into real estate: shacks at first that rented for five dollars a month if you could collect it before the tenants skipped, then abandoned tumble-down houses that could be knocked back together by a jackleg carpenter-painter, a make-do genius kind of fellow he found who'd work for little more than the bread he ate, a sack of whiskey, and a place to lay his head down between sprees. All this time he kept rolling and expanding, raking in the dollars and plowing them back. Before he was thirty — 1920: he was twenty-eight and already had the office on Beale: *Theo G. Wiggins Development Corp.* printed in gold-leaf letters on the door, bent in two bows above and below the number 185 — he reached the first stage of what he was climbing toward, beyond the now, and went back to Moscow after Lucinda, this time on the train, in a broadcloth suit, box-toed shoes, a high boiled collar and bow tie, and a brown derby. She was two years his senior, just turned thirty, living with her old daddy, and hadnt even known she was waiting for Tio until he reappeared and claimed her, along with his lame niece Dolly to keep house for him and her.

Lucinda couldnt read or write, but he didnt intend for her to have to, any more than she would need to learn the housework. All he wanted was for her to look the wife part, which she did, and bear him children. She did that too: one child, anyhow. That was Martha, my wife Martha, born on his and Washington's birthday — George's, that is, not Booker T's — in 1922. But she was all. Either Mamma Cindy changed lives early, as they say, or else something went bad wrong under the midwife's ministration. In any case, the doctor told him this was all there was going to be in the way of children, and he wasnt long in adjusting to it, the way he always managed to do with things he couldnt alter.

As for me, I came along right at twenty-five years later, and only found out afterwards — too late for turning back, even if I had wanted to, which I didnt — that I too was part of the plan, as much as Mamma Cindy or Martha herself or in fact almost anyone Tio came in contact with in earnest. It wasnt that he intended anyone's undoing, exactly, though it sometimes came to that if undoing you turned out to be the best solution once the deal was under way. That's business, and business was what he mainly concerned himself with, in and out of office hours. Yes. What he did was, he dealt with facts as he found them, meaning problems that loomed in his path, and he expected others to do the same, including his wife and daughter, Miss Lucy, lame Dolly, various hard-breathing bargainers he encountered during his climb, and finally me, who passed the test — his test and, incidentally, hers — and so became his son-in-law, a near member of the family. Let the buyer beware, as they say.

My parents named me Ebenezer, out of the Bible, when I was born in Vicksburg on a cold mid-January day in 1919, right after the World War we later learned to call the First. Stone of Help, it means. My mother I think was going through some kind of religious thing at the time, though it didnt last much past her pregnancy. She and my daddy ran a cafe there and later in Bristol, where we moved after my sister Julia's birth, some two years following my own. Ebenezer, Stone of Help, had become Eben by then. I grew up there, a bright little light-skinned fellow, in a smell of cooking from

the kitchen down below and wails from a crank-up phono-
graph always playing the blues: mostly Bessie Smith, I realize
now, along with Robert Johnson from upriver — *32–20* I seem
to remember, and *Last Fair Deal Going Down* — till he died,
and so did Bessie: he by poison from some woman, she in a car
wreck up at Lyon. I worked at Goodblood's department store,
a porter, sweeping out and making deliveries when called on.
They liked me and I liked them: at least I thought so at the
time. I finished high school and went off to the army in the
draft before Pearl Harbor.

Engineers they called us, but we werent engineers. What we
mainly were was truckers, loaders and unloaders, all of us
colored except of course the officers. We went overseas to
Northern Ireland before the invasion and did our training near
a town called Magherafelt, not far from Belfast. White outfits
were stationed around it, too, and there was friction over the
girls — fights in pubs, things like that — until the district commander ordered the whites and coloreds to go by turns, getting
their passes on alternate weekends. "Nigger night in Magherafelt" soon grew famous for miles around, and the girls all told
us they preferred us to the whites: because we respected them,
they said. But I dont know. Most likely they were telling the
whites the same thing, to our backs, or it could just have been
that we were freer-handed with our Hershey bars. I mostly
stayed clear of them anyhow, knowing I'd be going home
some day.

We went over to France as soon as they made the Normandy
breakout, running something they called the Red Ball Express
to keep Patton's tanks in gas. I didnt see much, but one frosty
day Eisenhower himself doubled our column in a command
car, red-faced from the cold and looking worried. It was the
Bulge, they told us afterward, and we had done as much as
anyone to save it. So they said. Up in the spring, Hitler folded
under pressure from the Russians and they began getting ready
to send us to Japan. Then all of a sudden it was really over:
VJ Day, and I came home and got out fast on points.

I headed for Tougaloo, under the GI Bill, before I even

shucked my uniform. Business Administration. I had decided, since I was going to have to work more or less for the rest of my life anyhow, I might as well try to amount to something, or anyhow work with my head instead of my back.

It turned out so. I came on to Bristol with my certificate, waving it like a flag, but there was nothing there for me, or next to nothing. Goodblood's already had a bookkeeper: all they could offer me was the porter job again. My mother and daddy had moved to New Orleans during the war and Julia by then was off on her second marriage. Within a month I left for Memphis, which for us was always the City anyhow, and looked around for books to keep. I found them: first a dry cleaner, then a dime store, two filling stations, a cafe — part-time work, all for Negroes except one Jew: he had the dime store. I lived in a rooming house on Pontotoc, five dollars a week including breakfast, and planned to enter night school as soon as I was able, beginning my move toward becoming a C.P.A. That was my goal.

Around that time I first saw Tio — meaning he saw me. He sent for me, called me in. I hadnt even known he was watching, asking round. By then the year was into September, the hot September of 1947, and I was the same age he'd been when he married.

"I can use you if youre willing," he told me, sitting there across the desk. I said I was. "We'll see," he said, and told Miss Lucy, whose eyes had begun to trouble her, "Show him round."

What was going on was stranger than I knew. Close to thirty years he had been there in that office, and never once had anyone but Lucy Provine had so much as a glimpse of the inner workings behind his name on that glass door. Yet here *I* came. And why? I thought at first it was because he saw me as a repetition of himself — anyhow a potential repetition, once he got me shaped to suit him — fresh up from Mississippi, the way he'd been fresh in from Moscow close to forty years ago. But I was wrong. That wasnt it, and he had known it wasnt, from the day he lined me up. Business for him was deals and dealing, not the book work, while for me it was just the other way around. I liked the quiet, inside work, not the sweaty outside scrambling, outdoing the other fellow before he outdid you, and Tio not only knew it, he also knew I'd never change. I had the greed, all right: I just didnt have the necessary share. He could say of me what Joe Louis said of Floyd Patterson around that time: "He aint vichy enough" — meaning vicious. And I wasnt and he knew it.

Then what is it? What is it he wants? I wondered, and before long I found out from Miss Lucy. She couldnt believe it, either, when she passed the word along, the invitation. All those years, the only time she was ever inside that house on Vance was once when he was laid up with the flu and had to sign some papers. This was in October. I'd been at the office just under a month, and he was up the street on business: on purpose, I realized later, for he was shy in unexpected ways.

"He wants you to come to Sunday dinner," she said, doubting the words even as she spoke them. "Sunday dinner, this coming Sunday. He said to say so, and make sure you understood."

Miss Lucy made sure, the best she could, but the fact was I didnt understand at all: that is, until I got there and found him and Mamma Cindy sitting in the parlor — Mr and Mrs Wiggins to me, then — along with Martha in her church clothes. She was why, and I knew it as soon as I saw her standing there waiting for us to be introduced. Here I'd been thinking he viewed me as a possible repetition, when all the time he already had one — his own daughter. That was what she was, all right, a smaller-scale female repetition of himself, about the same height but thank God a good deal less broad, frog-faced, all the way black, with bulgy eyes, shotgun nostrils, and a wide mouth lipsticked thin inside its borders.

I knew, right then, and fell into the first of several panics I experienced in the course of the next three months. First I saw my room, over on Pontotoc — narrow cot and straightback chair, reading light and heavy textbook, like a monk's cell with its Bible — and all the cozy lonesome nights I planned to spend working up to the day I'd be entitled to write *Eben Kinship, C.P.A.* at the bottom of tax forms and reports. I saw it in my mind, and saw it fade: saw the cot replaced by a double bed, wide as a wrestling mat: saw chair and lamp abolished, the walls move outward to make a full-size bedroom, and children coming steady every year, all standing there in a row with their mouths agape, like baby birds cheeping to be fed. *Eben Kinship, C.P.A.* became *Eben Kinship, Husband* or, more precisely, *Eben Kinship, Son-in-Law.*

That was what brought on the first panic, that sudden vision in the parlor there on Vance, and it continued through the courtship, all three months, even after I got so I wanted her more than I wanted what I knew I'd be losing. The last one before the marriage itself, in early February of the following year — two weeks shy of her twenty-sixth birthday — was on the way to the church, our wedding day. I had to keep a steady grip on myself to keep from jumping out of the car, right there on Beale.

By then I knew a good deal more than I had known when I first panicked, and what I learned — asking round — had a double-barreled effect, pulling me toward her and driving me away. For one thing, there had been others, two at least that I know of.

One was Lydel Partridge, from a good family here on Vance, just up the street, in the undertaking business. He was married before we were, Martha and I, and already had four children, including a set of twins, by the time Sister Baby came along. It turned out Martha didnt want him — mainly because of the second one, who came in by the side door, so to speak, though the fact was he never came in by any door at all, knowing only too well the reception he'd get from Tio if he tried. His name was Snooker, from the pool game: Snooker Martin, low-born and too black, a long tall drink of water, as the saying goes, with crinkled hair and zooty clothes, already making a name for himself among the lower element, pool sharks, gamblers, fancy women, and the like. He was after her, bound to have her, until Tio cut him off.

I saw him once, years later on a visit from Detroit, lounging against a lamppost outside a billiard parlor, and he had a look of mockery on his all but chinless face. He was pointed out to me beforehand and I only glanced at him sidelong as I passed. I wondered if he got it during one of those secret meetings before Tio found out what he was up to and cut him off. I decided he did: not only got it, but had her begging for more, the way she never did from me. I decided she was comparing us and I didnt come off well in the result. I decided that was why she wasnt too fond of what I gave her, those nights she'd let me, including the times that got us our two children, when I felt something pass from my spirit into hers.

For some reason — surely nothing to do with what was fixing to come down — I thought about him a lot in the course of that third week in September, the tenth anniversary of my going to work on Beale for Tio and therefore close to the same anniversary of my marriage to his daughter Martha. Even aside from the raucous life style, Snooker Martin was too low-born and too black to pass Tio's muster, the way Lydel Partridge had done when she came home from that thousand-dollar girl school in Saint Louis, the way I too would do — not only mustered but recruited — a couple of years later, after Snooker Martin broke her in. I passed muster, first at the office, then on Vance, and despite those several courtship panics, including the last one on the way to Beale Street Baptist, almost before I had time to know what hit me here I was, hog-tied and committed, suffering ten years later from visions of Snooker raunching her roughshod on the back seat of some car or up some alley, riding her down, roweling deep up in her innards with that long black thing he no doubt had, yet always leaving her room to beg for more, the way she never would from me. These fits were as sharp and painful as the panics, ten years back, and a lot more specific in the pictures they called up.

Things went like that all through the third week of the

month, the moon in its last quarter at the start, then dwindling down to nothing but a paring. On Friday, the Mid-South Fair began its eight-day run, out at the fairgrounds, and the children were after me all week long to take them so they could see the shows and exhibits, the Lone Ranger, and ride the rides. I promised, if they were good, I'd take them after school on Thursday, the day set aside for the colored: not knowing, then, I wouldnt be able.

That was Friday. Next day was Saturday. Then would come Sunday and dinner at Tio's and Mamma Cindy's, rounding out another week. They went like that, dragging, till trouble came.

This time Podjo rode up front with me, the way it would be when the real thing went down, and Reeny rode in back to be with the boy. She even brought along the Noctec and the clown white, for this was a dress rehearsal, a pre-enactment. It was Friday, the last school day of the week, and we wanted everything to be the same as it would be when we played for keeps — maybe Monday, Podjo said, depending on developments over the weekend. All that was lacking was my pistol, which was on purpose; I was persuaded he was right about that, and left it home. "Well, here we go," I said as we pulled away from in front of the house, crowding two oclock Friday, September 20, in the Year of Our Lord 1957. So much for Our Lord. As for me, I was midway through my twenty-seventh, a good half-dozen years younger than he was when the Romans nailed him up, cheered on by his fellow Jews.

We eased our way a block up Carolina, past the nipple company and the Chinaman's, where I turned left into the northbound Riverside traffic, slack at this hour, and went with it, just under a mile alongside the chocolate-colored Mississippi humping and dimpling its way south toward Bristol and Vicksburg, Natchez and New Orleans, until a right turn under the viaduct took us onto Beale, first across Front and Main, then Mulberry and Second, and pulled up short of Third, looking ahead and across to Handy Park, which was nothing more than a scatter of empty benches, a double phone booth, and some worn paths flanked by patches of starved grass that looked as if they had been seared with a blowtorch to discourage the growth encouraged by the past nine months of record rain.

Nigger heaven was going badly to seed; not just the park but the street itself, unless (more likely) it had never amounted to any whole hell of a lot in the first place, and was never anything more, even in its heyday, than what we were looking at now, a four- or five-block dusty gully of signs and store fronts, dominated by three-ball fixtures over the entrances to pawnshops, the dead neon that shouted and beckoned at night to fieldhands come to the city in search of dice games, cruising whores, and various eat-shops dealing mostly in fried catfish and smoked pork. Interspersed among them were narrow-fronted establishments, places of business, such as the one we stopped to look at.

To our right, just across the sidewalk from the curb we had pulled up to, was the glass door with its bull's-eye medallion, gold-leaf letters edged in black and bent in a circle around the numeral in its center.

We had no real need or even purpose in being there except as a way of touching base at the outset, so to speak. "That's where the money lives," Podjo said, looking across his elbow at the name and number, ten feet beyond the open window of the car. "O.K. Let's get rolling."

I eased away from the curb, past Third to Hernando, then right, past Linden and Pontotoc, to stop again just short of Vance. To our right, across the street, we could see the Kinship house, frame green, and to our left the Wiggins house, pale brick, two-story. Both had shallow porches, and all of a sudden something came to me.

"Kinship," I said. "There used to be a couple ran a cafe on Bantam Street in Bristol when I first started going down there, still in knee pants. I remember they had a good-looking brown-skin daughter a friend of mine laid once — by way of changing his luck, he thought, till he found himself going back and back for more. Kinship. Maybe there's some connection, those and these, but I doubt it. There must be plenty of Kinships in these parts; white ones too."

"Let's get rolling," Podjo said.

He was right, for my watch by now was pushing close to letting-out time. The route was simple. We had done it twice already and once with Reeny along, all three times when we could watch the two children walk the four blocks together while we followed in the car. I turned left on Vance and drove on past the Wiggins house to Fourth; left on Fourth, past Pontotoc, to Linden; then right on Linden — all but vacant along one side, with Church Park on the other — to Turley, where the school was.

Leath School it was called, a big oblong red-brick building stretching nearly the whole block up to Wellington, close to seventy years old, with white-painted concrete lintels over the windows on all three floors, a flat roof, and two main entrances, one on Linden, one on Turley, equidistant from a flagpole set in the near corner of the shallow yard, behind a low wall that ran along both sidewalks where the two streets came together. It had thirty-odd classrooms and an enrollment of about five hundred, grades one through six. I knew all this, and more, because I looked it up in the library one day when I had nothing else to do. Originally it was called Linden Street School, until they renamed it for some philanthropist, and in those days, right up until the war, it was an all-white institution. Abe Fortas, a big-time Washington lawyer, went there as a boy, along with a number of others the local historian seemed proud of, people I never heard of till I saw their names in the back-file paper. Then, about the time of the war, the Board of Education changed it to all-colored and it began to go down, down, until now it looked every one of its nearly seventy red-brick years.

Parked there on Linden short of Turley, with a good view of both doors, we didnt have long to wait. After perhaps five minutes — two-thirty, on the dot — the bell went and a host of little Negroes of all colors, shapes, and sizes began to pour out of the two entrances. Ours was among them, not too hard to spot on this fourth expedition, and came straight to the corner flagpole, as before. He didnt have long to wait this time either. The little sister with the pigtails joined him there and they set out together, also as before, west on Linden past where we sat waiting in the car. He was kicking a rock along the sidewalk, intent on that, but the little girl glanced sidelong at us as they went by, lugging her booksack. We hadnt risked this close a look at him before, but Podjo thought it worth the gamble, just this once, for the sake of positive identification in case of a mix-up when the time came.

"Teddy. He's kind of cute," Reeny said when they passed out of earshot. The fact was, she said that about lots of males, whatever their age or color or situation. It used to make me angry until I stopped and realized how flattering it was, that out of all the ones she praised, of whatever age or color or situation, it was me she chose to be with, round the clock.

We took our time making the U turn, then came back, cruising slow on Linden, trailing and keeping our two in sight among all the others along the houseless stretch to Fourth, where they took a left and so did we, short of old Saint Patrick's just across the way.

Fourth was residential, both blocks down to Vance, and

that was the problem: whether to take him there, where people might be watching from their houses, within easy reach of phones for calling the police, or back on Linden along that vacant stretch, which was a lot more crowded with other home-bound children and was also likely to have more traffic on it at that hour, cars with drivers who might follow us or otherwise interfere with the operation. It had to be one or the other, Fourth or Linden, because once they reached Vance, with all its bustle, the odds against a quiet snatch would grow too long. We werent worried about being spotted. The plates would be untraceable anyhow, and in fact, if they were re-ported to either the Kinships or old Wiggins, the Arkansas tags we would be using then would only add to the fright, considering what had been going on over there for the past three weeks. What we didnt want was interference by anyone at that critical stage, either the cops or anyone else; especially a carload of angry six-foot bucks, with me without my pistol. We talked it over, Podjo and I — Reeny just sat back listening, if in fact that was what she was doing — and Podjo as usual came up with the decision, which was to play it by ear when the time came.

"We'll judge by what's going on. How it looks," he said. "Watch out now. Dont lose them and dont crowd them."

I didnt lose and I didnt crowd them; I hung back, just right, and pulled to a stop at the curb after making the turn on Vance. Across the way, a bit farther down, their grandmother, old Wiggins' wife, was waiting on her porch, the way she always did on schoolday afternoons, with a hug for each and some-thing else for both; in this case, cookies. They took them, two apiece, and called out past her, "Thank you, Dolly," to a little old shriveled-looking woman who came to the door just then in an apron and headrag. She resembled a witch, with a dust mop for a staff.

They went on, across Hernando, to their own house in the next block, eating the cookies as they walked. We drove by as they went running up the steps, met by their mother in the doorway.

"O.K." Podjo said. "Let's head for home."

That did it. We were as ready then as we ever were likely to be, and most of the credit — once the thing had been conceived — went to Podjo, who knew how to be careful about little important matters that might never have occurred to me or Reeny if we had tried it on our own. The dangers that lurk in iotas, someone said.

Not that I hadnt expected it of him, from the first time I saw him up at Parchman. You dont handle cards the way he did, down to the final low-lying deuce, without attention to details. He had that; cool and steady, raking in chips or shoving them out, with no change of manner or expression (the mustache helped; I think it was part of his game plan) and an underlying reserve of daring that might break the surface any minute, no matter what cards he was holding or not-holding. I knew right then, practically at first glance, though I barely spoke to him in the few weeks I was there before my uncle got me out, he was the man I'd want to have along, for both the planning and the execution, if ever something real went down. In the pool hall back in Bristol, when I first broached the Wiggins-Kinship operation after researching it in Memphis, I watched him turn and turn that cold brown bottle in his hands, not taking a sip till I finished laying it out, and let me know, with no real need for saying it, that he was with me. I knew then we couldnt fail.

As for Reeny, she came earlier; last spring. It was at a night-club called Bull Eye's outside Bristol, a converted Quonset with a rounded roof, like being under half an outsized barrel sawed through lengthwise. She was with some kind of businessman, gray-haired, well past forty, and I was with one of those hungry-eyed little nineteen-year-old chookies — hair ironed flat, pullover sweater a couple of sizes too small, white socks; nothing. Then I saw Reeny come in with this fellow and I said to myself, right off, *That's for me.* We sat at adjoining tables and I let her know by looks: Youre for me. And so she was. Come leaving-time for the businessman, he rose to go but she told him she wasnt ready. They fussed a couple of minutes.

Then he left and we moved over to her table, my date and I, and got to talking. I had my uncle's car and after a while we left too, the three of us. Up close, she looked older than I'd thought, but not much; just right in fact, for me.

I let the chooky out at home, spitting mad, and we went on out to the Shady Rest — old-style cabins with rough-dried sheets and outdoor plumbing. That was the beginning, and there was never anyone else for me since. Nor for her I think, though of course you can never really tell for sure, where women are concerned. Or men either, come to think of it.

We met often; daily, nightly. I was working the dog shift at U. S. Gypsum, pushing wallboard through a micrometer, hot and heavy work, and when I'd come off shift, all sweaty, she'd be waiting in her Ford and we'd go back to this room she had, which by then I was paying the rent on. I almost couldnt believe it. After all that looking, all that scrabbling, here I was and here she was; Jesus. It wasnt just the coming, though God knows it was the best I ever knew — "Babe, youre an artist," I would tell her — nor the pleasure she took, too — "So are you, hon," she'd reply. It was also that she liked me, really liked me, for myself. Lots didnt, for whatever reasons, and I could see she thought as I did about that; that it was their loss, I mean.

I felt that, and it made for good times together, out of bed as well as in, pitching or catching. I saw my life get straightened out and show that it would *stay* straightened out, right down to the wire, if only I could find some way for us to live accordingly — meaning money, and the more of it the better, so our outside life could match what I was feeling inside all this time. That was when I came up with the Wiggins-Kinship thing, and once I thought of it, working out the angles, I knew how Shakespeare must have felt when he wrote *Flourish. Exeunt* at the bottom of the last sheet of *Macbeth.* I was an artist, sure enough.

That was in late July, early August. I quit Gypsum and we went up to Memphis for a look-round and came back and lined up Podjo, and all this time I had this feeling for her, deep inside me. I guess you could call it love if there was such a thing.

I came up the hard way; I mean *hard* way. Grandfather Cilley was widowered early, working long hours down at the bank, with two young and, as it turned out, loose-minded daughters to raise, Edna and Eva. Both married early, which was a help at least for a time. Eva was my mother. My father was a cabinetmaker or furniture repairman, some kind of Scandinavian — "maybe a Dane," she said once — passing through. Conrad was his first name; so he said. He had stiff upstanding hair, pale as cornsilk, and a peculiar way of speaking through his teeth. That's all I knew, even by hearsay. He moved on by the time I was four, leaving nothing behind, not even a snapshot. I used to think I might run into him most anywhere; except how would I know him if he changed his name? or went back to this real one, for that matter, if, as I suspected, he only called himself Hutton during his Bristol interlude? I stopped thinking about him, is what I finally did, and felt better from that day forward. All he left me was his name, if it was his name, and even that turned out to be a burden. Hutton-Hutton, they started calling me at school, making that sound they used to imitate racing a car engine: hutton-hutton, hutton-hutton!

My mother clerked in a store — still does in fact, but she was younger then. We lived in a series of two-room apartments around town. She'd come in late and take me out of the double bed to spend most of the rest of the night on the couch in the living room. I'd hear them back there, hunching, hunching. Fun, she called it, always out after fun. Some fun. Christ; you could tell by the pitch of her moans she was only pretending. Then Grandfather Cilley came down with a stroke at the bank one day and they brought him home to Aunt Edna's to live, paralyzed, and she and Uncle Pat asked us to move in and help nurse him — meaning me, as it turned out. This was during the war, the big one; I was twelve. My job was mainly to feed him, wipe his mouth and backside, handle the bedpan and put the head of his little old useless pecker into the spout of the urinal when he signaled he had to piss, not always in time. Those were my schoolday afternoons and nights when Eva was out after fun and I was getting homework done between trips to his bedside and back. It didnt help my grades, I can tell you, and sometimes it was downright scary.

Late one afternoon we were alone in the house and he signaled for me to come over, making a sort of strangled whinny in his throat. Sometimes he could speak a little and this was one of them. I brought the bedpan over with me because of the urgency in his voice, but that wasnt it. What he wanted was to tell me something, something heavy on his mind.

"Lean down," he said; I just barely understood him. I leaned down, and his eyes, the irises pale and blurred without his glasses, seemed to spin round their pupils with the effort he was making. "Dont trust'um," he said. "I trusted um. Dont trust'um."

Thirty-odd years he put in at that bank, thousands upon thousands of other people's money passing down the nib of his pen as it moved across and across the ledger pages, tinted green from the light filtered through his eyeshade, and he'd never touched an unauthorized penny all that time. Now here was how he wound up, paralyzed back to infancy, flat on his back in the house of a daughter who didnt want him, supposedly being cared for by another who seldom came near him. No wonder he turned bitter near the end.

He wasnt talking about them, though. He was talking about the bank, those that owned it, those that ran it, those that used it and him with it — a fixture, with his eyeshade and sleeve garters, like one of the machines now junked and chunked aside.

"Honest always, I was," he said, mopping and mowing to get the words past his twisted mouth, irises spinning like little pale blue wheels round the pivot of pupils shrunk to pinpoints from the strain and earnestness. "Never touched so much as a dime, one thin dime," he said. "Mistake. Mis — take. You take um,

Rufus, hear me? Take um. It's the only way youll get justice. Steal'um blind."

He seemed to feel better for having said it. His eyes stopped that crazy spinning and he just lay there looking up at nothing, hands outside the covers, speckled over with liver spots on their backs.

A few months later, when he died, I found he'd left me close to two thousand dollars in life insurance, stipulated to go for my college tuition and expenses. What's more, he had it locked up tight and binding, with an executor — Mr Tilden at the bank — so Eva and Aunt Edna and Uncle Pat couldnt get at it, any way they tried. I know; for they tried and couldnt, not even Uncle Pat who knew all the angles. I went to Ole Miss in the fall of the year Truman was re-elected, if that was what you called it when he hadnt been elected in the first place.

I dont claim the old man's advice had much to do with what followed — though it seemed to. Likely, it wasnt even the genes carried down, his or my vanished father's; I just did what I did on my own account, never mind what he came out with on his deathbed. Ole Miss was perhaps the best two years, or nearly two, I ever knew. I majored in coeds, mostly hill girls unfamiliar with Delta ways. By the time it came down to dismissal (pilfering was the charge, a funny use of an old word, and as for the cheating, it was a question of cheat or fail, right down the line, and I chose cheating — a sensible choice, except for getting caught) the two thousand had about run out anyhow; Grandfather Cilley misfigured badly on that, back in the Thirties when I was in grade school. I came home and looked for work befitting a college man. Then came the draft, with Panmunjom in progress, if you could call it that, and Pork Chop Hill and the Punch Bowl already over. I might as well go whole hog, I told myself, and joined the Marine Corps.

Parris Island, Pendleton; I did my time in the stockade awaiting trial. They didnt call it pilfering, this time. They called it theft, conduct detrimental, and sent me home. Dishonorable, the discharge read, but at least I didnt get my head or an arm or leg blown off in that last Red offensive, a month before it was over in July of '53. Then came Parchman, which was no worse than the Marine Corps in some ways. I didnt even have to get my*self* out; Uncle Pat did that, swapping a favor he'd saved up, though he begrudged it and made it clear this was the last. That didnt bother me. All that bothered me was the story making the rounds about how I wet my pants when the cops walked in. They told it on me, laughing, and it was true. I didnt consider it characteristic though. It was just that they came down on me so fast, there in the warehouse, that I didnt have time to get set in my mind and my bladder failed me.

I came home again to Bristol, floundered around for a while, then went to work for U. S. Gypsum on my own. No Eva — that whore — no Aunt Edna, no Pat Shanahan to call uncle. Good riddance, I said, and I guess they said it too.

Being on your own is fine in some ways, terrible in others. I didnt know that, though, till I met up with Reeny, and even then it took me a while to see what I'd been missing. First off, I was after her all hours, day and night. Beaver, beaver. It wasnt till it leveled off that I could stop and think. Then I began to see a pattern to those past few years, Ole Miss and the Marine Corps and the rest — a pattern of failure rushed to completion as soon as I saw failure looming. I saw now where I'd been headed; "Die young and make a handsome corpse," as the fellow said in the Bogart movie. And the lies; my God, the lies. Some served a purpose, to shore myself up, but others I told for their own sake, the joy of invention. I should have been a writer, except I could never really get down to it as a trade like any other; bank-robbing, say, or carpentry, if I'd only had the patience.

Now at least, post-Reeny so to speak, the problems were all practical, and here too my inventiveness stood me in good stead for both our sakes; not only the big Kinship-Wiggins project, but also incidentals, such as offering her to Podjo almost as soon as we got to Memphis, even boosting her up to tempt him. I thought I saw him getting edgy, and the fact is

he's the kind of man some women feel a pull toward, not ex-
cluding Reeny, and after all we were likely to be there a full
month, all three in the same house round the clock. If he had
taken me up on it, right then and there, o.k. It would have been
with my encouragement and permission, no more an infidelity
than if it had been something that happened before we met at
Bull Eye's. My real theory, though, was that he not only
wouldnt accept her on those terms, he also wouldnt go after
her, then or later, on the sly. And I was right. "No thanks," he
said, just as I expected, "I always managed to get mine on my
own."

I thought about that on the way back from the pre-enactment, after we followed the boy and his sister home from
Leath School to their house on Vance. "Let me know if you
change your mind," I told him, and he accepted it on those
terms of trust and honor; "Yair," he'd said, nailing it down. It
began to rain while we were coming up Riverside, back toward
Carolina and the bluff. We had planned to go to the Mid-South
Fair — it was opening night and Reeny wanted to see the Lone
Ranger, among other attractions — but the rain by then was
coming down in buckets, still building up its all-time record
for the year. She was well up into her period anyhow, which
tended to make her cranky; that, and having to help scrap up
supper there at home. So I decided to work some more on the
ransom notes.

They were my job and I wanted to do them right. The first
was easy, the one we'd give the little sister to take home when
we snatched her brother there on Linden or on Fourth: *We got
your boy. If you say anything to any one, expecially the cops
local or other wise, you will have seen your last of him. We
mean this. So stand fast, you will hear from us in the next day
or so. Wait till then.* I did it in pencil, on cheap ruled paper,
to keep up the notion of nigger-hating rednecks, and wrote it
in a clear, rounded hand, about like that of someone in the
sixth or seventh grade, which I figured would add to the scari-
ness when they puzzled over it, wondering what to do to get

their boy back. Arrested development was the suggestion I aimed for, and it seemed to me I struck just the right tone, both in what it said and how it said it, as well as in looks, the rounded hand on that cheap paper.

That one I had done already; it was easy, as I said. The others — other two — were a different matter, different jobs of work. They only extended what the first began, but they called for a lot more clarity, involving specific directions as they did. Money, for example; the $60,000. We broke it down, Podjo and I, into two batches of two thousand bills apiece, $20,000 in tens, $40,000 in twenties, and I calculated their weight at just under fifteen pounds, combined. What's more, they would fit comfortably in a shoebox, with room for padding at the ends. That not only surprised me — I thought at first they would fill a good-sized suitcase, even a barracks bag — it was also something of a disappointment, despite the handiness, to find that so much wealth could weigh so little and occupy so limited a space. It was as if I had discovered that money didnt amount to as much in this world as I had thought; except of course I knew better, no matter how little it weighed or how little space it took up when you stowed it away for future spending. In any case I had all that to work in, together with much more in regard to the route and the drop, the standing-by for phone calls and such, always with that double threat of the amateur and professional, both deadly; Klansmen and the Mafia, Podjo said. There was where the writing came in, the over-all tone and choice of terms and such. Composing both notes I would throw in a few misspelled words and grammatic errors for authenticity to make the Kinships and old Wiggins think we were near-illiterate but altogether deadly, as I said. I planned, that is, to write them with all the care youd take in writing a sonnet if you wrote sonnets.

Finally I turned in for the night, about worn out. Writing is hard work, I'm here to tell you.

That was Friday. On Saturday things took a jump, beginning with the headline in the morning paper, six columns wide:

Faubus Orders Guard Withdrawn/ In Face of Government Injunction;/ Promises Thorough Appeal of Order.

It didnt sound good to me but it did to Podjo. *Claims that Violence Was Close at Hand Belittled by Judge Davies,* the subhead read, and Podjo grinned. "The judge can belittle all he wants," he said, "but violence is sure as hell close at hand now. Or it will be Monday morning, when Central High School takes back in."

"You mean we go?" I asked him.

Reeny stopped reading the other section of the paper to hear what he had to say to that.

"Let's wait and see what Orval has to tell us. He'll give us the word, most likely, before he jumps."

So Podjo said. His notion, now that the Guard had been withdrawn, was that the yahoos would take over, if only by way of proving that Faubus had been right all along. He was their boy and they would back him up. Anyway we could hope so.

As for me, I was saddened by something else on the page, a small story near the bottom. Jan Sibelius had died of a brain hemorrhage the night before, at ninety-one, at his home outside Helsinki. I thought of all the hours I spent over in the Music Department when I should have been in class — mostly math — listening to that crashing, spooky music he wrote, with the icy wastes of Finland in it and the loneliness of all men everywhere. That was in my freshman year; I gave it up for other pursuits, the year that followed, and now it came back to me, whole stretches of sounding brass, croaking woodwinds, singing violins. I thought of him off and on, all day, until we went to Grisanti's for the roast beef, making up for last night's skimpy supper, then back home to the bluff — in the rain again — in time for Gunsmoke on the tube at nine oclock.

We had quite a discussion about that; or I did. Reeny got to wondering whether Mr Dillon had ever been upstairs with Kitty at the Long Branch, and I felt called upon to set her straight. Probably not, I said. It seems he had this thing going off-camera with Chester. Chester you see was a cripple, and that's what Dillon was into — cripples of all kinds. That's why he crippled up so many men, himself, with that great long hog-leg pistol he carried all the time. Kinky. But I'll tell you, I said, a six-foot six-inch fairy is a fearsome thing to contemplate coming at you, let alone one wearing that damned hog leg on his hip. "Go right ahead, Mr Dillon," I'd say. "Go right ahead and have your way with me."

Reeny got to laughing and even Podjo smiled, though he hadnt paid much attention. He was waiting for the ten oclock news to find out what Faubus had to say. The news came on, on schedule, but not Faubus. He was off to Sea Island, Georgia, the announcer said, for some kind of governors' conference, apparently biding his time. We turned in early, leaving Podjo to his bed-of-roses couch, and I went to sleep with Sibelius bonging and gonging in my head, a ghost by now in the far beyond.

Sunday was no better, at least at the start. It was still raining, and would rain all day — a possible flaw in our plan, whatever schedule we finally settled on, if their mother came to the school and picked them up. Fair-goers all but drowned, the paper said, and the Memphis State football game, the first of the year, was played in such a sea of mud you couldnt tell one side from the other, they were so slathered over with the stuff. Faubus was still biding his time, apparently, off the coast of Georgia. We were left wondering. Arrests Promised by Mayor/ If Troublemakers Gather/ At Little Rock To-morrow was the headline, and we had trouble trying to figure whether that was a warning or a blanket invitation. One item, buried inside, seemed to show that some of the people up-country were also getting in on the act — except that, as usual, they did it in reverse. *Huckleberry Finn* was banned by the New York Board of Education from the approved list of text-books for elementary and junior high schools because it con-tained what the board called "some passages derogatory to Negroes." I could see the Wanted circulars now, put up in post-office lobbies all across the land: *Mark Twain, Racist.*

Tomorrow would be the autumnal equinox, the weather section said, and there would be a brand-new moon.

Then it came; the five-thirty news. Faubus was there at Sea Island, a break in the Southern Governors' Conference he was attending, and the reporters were jumping round him, egging him on. He gave them what they wanted, all right, and us as well. Without the Guard on hand to stand in the way, he told them — along with the folks back home — he was "apprehensive of violence" if those black scamps tried again to get in Central High when the bell rang next morning. That was all there was to it, and it was enough. I looked at Reeny, she looked at me, and we both looked at Podjo.

"O.K. That does it," he said. "We go tomorrow."

# 3

# A Piece of Cake

Of dark red brick, three stories tall and nearly a full block long, the schoolhouse seemed to tick like an outsized time bomb during those final dragging moments before the bell went. Then it did, strident and peremptory, signaling dismissal, and for still a few more seconds — five: ten: almost fifteen — the pregnant, somehow ominous span extended beyond itself, much as dynamite will seem to do when the fuse burns down inside it and the stick has still not quite yet blown. Even so, the suspension did not end with the bang or crash it seemed to apprehend, but rather with a muffled, reverberant thunder of feet down stairs and along hallways, faint at first, as if distant, then suddenly nearer, grown to a clopping not unlike the sound a herd of unshod ponies might have made while crossing hardpan at a trot, and there emerged in twin gushes from the two doors, one on Linden, one on Turley, two clotted streams of children of all sizes, shapes, and shades of black and brown and yellow, multifariously clad, pushing and shoving, carrying books in a variety of ways, satcheled, strapped, or unrestrained, lugged by hand or hugged against narrow chests. Their cries resembled the cries of birds, familiar and exotic, wrens and sparrows, cockatoos and parakeets, with the occasional wilder cry of some small animal mixed in the general din, which diminished as they dispersed about the schoolyard and along the streets that defined its limits, north and east and west.

One among the lesser figures that emerged from the doorway on the left had by now detached itself from the parent stream and crossed the yard diagonally to take station beside the flagpole set in concrete within the angle of the low wall at the corner where the two streets intersected. It was Sister Baby. Dressed today in a checkered skirt and shirtwaist, Mary Janes and short ribbed socks, she leaned against the metal pole and waited, Griselda-like, in a pose of weary patience, yarn-tied pigtails bristling round her head. Her book satchel dangled from one hand, while overhead the flag hung limp in the windless air and the sun was shining brightly, for the weather had faired after two long days of rain. The worn grass, the old red-brick building, streets and sidewalks, gutters, trees, all looked freshly washed in the fine clear weather, especially welcome after the spoiled weekend. She did not mind waiting at first, but presently, with only a few laggards still in sight in all directions, she grew restless and began to fidget, changing hands with the satchel and shifting her feet from time to time in an attempt to relieve the tedium. Fully fifteen minutes she waited, the longest ever, before two boys came out of the doorway on the right and parted without a gesture of farewell, going their separate ways, one down Turley, the other toward the flagpole.

This was Teddy, and he explained the estrangement between him and his companion. "Got kept in," he told his sister. "For talking in class — me and Juny Partridge. Humph. It wasnt me, it was Juny did the talking; I just listened. I told her so, old Miss Pitkin, but she kept us both in anyhow. Durn that Juny. Come on; less go." He paused though. "Dont tell Mamma, or Daddy when he gets home. They might not care us to the fair. If she asks, we just say we stopped off at Mamma Cindy's for a spell."

So they set out down Linden, she with her satchel, he without; he scorned such devices, having outgrown them, and walked with his books held casually under one arm, as became an old third-grader. While they paused before crossing Turley, Sister Baby asked, "Did Juny Partridge say you talked too?"

"Not this time. That was earlier," he told her. "We didnt get kept in for that one. Just fussed at."

"Oh," she said, as if singing a one-note song, happy to be convinced of her brother's innocence in the matter.

After crossing Turley they proceeded about fifty yards west on Linden, and there was a white lady in their path, half on the sidewalk, half on the grass that grew between it and the curb where a car was parked with two men on the front seat, white like her. "Hello, Teddy," she said, to their surprise, when they came abreast.

He stopped and turned, as did Sister Baby alongside him, hugging the satchel to her chest. "Yessum," he said. Beyond the lady he could see the two men watching from the car. One was blond, blonder than she was, and the other wore a broad dark mustache like a bar across his face, midway between the naked chin and cold hard eyes.

"Your daddy, back on Beale, told me to get you for him," the lady said. "He — he wants to talk to you. Maybe give you a present, I think. Anyhow he wants you to come with us."

She spoke rapidly, stammering a bit, as if repeating something not quite memorized. Her purpose was clear enough when she finished speaking, however, for she reached out and laid one hand on the boy's shoulder, fingers already curled to grip if need be, and addressed herself to Sister Baby beyond him, also as if by rote. "Here," she told her, tucking a piece of paper held in the other hand into the pocket of the girl's shirtwaist, just above the satchel clutched to her chest. "Make sure your mamma gets this. Now hurry home. And remember, it's important. Give it to her soon as you get there, without fail."

"Yessum," Sister Baby said.

Her eyes had stretched wide with surprise when the lady first stopped them, then narrowed with fear when she put out her hand and touched her. Now they registered more startled emotions as she saw her reach back, still keeping a grip on Teddy's shoulder, and open the door of the car behind her. "Let's go," she told him, louder than before, and when he bridled, straining rearward, she shifted her grip and caught him under the armpits with both hands, lifting him bodily so that his feet dangled clear of the ground, and swung him sideways, sacklike, into the back seat.

"Books, my books — I got to get my books!" he cried, for he had dropped them when she hoisted him sidelong into the car.

"Dont worry. We'll get you some more," she said as she climbed in beside him, slamming the door behind her. She seemed flustered. The window was down and she leaned partly out to call to Sister Baby, still standing on the sidewalk hugging her satchel, "Go home. Go on home now, like I said. And remember; give that paper to your mamma soon as you get there. You hear me?"

Eased away from the curb, the car was in motion before she finished talking. Sister Baby had one last look at Teddy, seated beyond the lady on the far side of the seat, and then he was gone, his head too low to show in the rear window of the car. It gathered speed as it swung south on Wellington, gliding swiftly out of sight around the red mass of the school. She stood looking for a time at where it had been, then bent and took up her brother's three books from the grass where he had dropped them — a speller, a reader, an arithmetic text, all with different-colored covers. She put them under one arm, more or less as Teddy had done, holding her satchel with the other hand, and set off again down Linden, just as the white lady had told her to do, bound for home.

In the car, as he steered it skittering south on Wellington, Rufus's elation soared beyond all bounds. "Got him, by God, got him!" he exulted.

"Easy now," Podjo said, first to Rufus, there beside him, then to Reeny, busy in the back.

"It's all right. It's all right," she told Teddy, who was badly frightened. "We'll have you with your daddy in no time. Just you wait and see."

She seemed to have her previous flustration under control. Rufus, though, could not contain his exuberance. He turned frequently to look in the back seat, as if to reassure himself that the boy was really there, then forward again to peer through the windshield at the traffic up ahead, threading his way with so firm a grip on the steering wheel that his knuckles were white from the strain. "Got him, by God, got him!" he kept exclaiming. "A piece of cake!"

"Easy. Take it easy," Podjo told him, calm by contrast.

For all his level-headed caution, Podjo felt great relief from the tension that had been building up within all three of them in the course of the past twenty days. Moreover, this sense of relief had been progressive ever since they woke that morning to find that the rain had stopped in the night and fair weather was at hand, forestalling a postponement of the job for which they had planned and worked so hard, even before they left Bristol for Memphis just under three weeks ago. Not only was there a measure of gladness that the day had at last come round; there was also, now, delight and self-congratulation at how well the thing had turned out so far, especially the actual event, the snatch back there on Linden within a hundred yards of the school.

"Luck. What luck," Rufus had said at the outset, looking out at the weather when he got up that morning, the hot bright sunlight beaming down on the bluff and giving the river a coat of gold as it glided south beneath the three bridges striding west to Arkansas.

It was only from that direction, the state across the way, that a touch of disappointment had intruded. When Podjo clicked on the Today Show for the early morning news, there was no mention of Little Rock.

"Maybe they didnt get the word," Rufus suggested.

"They got the word, all right," Podjo said. "Most likely theyre a little leery of the cops without the governor there to lead them. Or theyre like roosters at a cockfight; they have to strut a bit and crow and peck at straws a while, before they use their spurs. Theyll come round soon enough to suit us. Tomorrow will do as well as today, so far as our uses go."

His tone was reassuring, but there was for Rufus and Reeny — if not for Podjo himself, behind his facile modification of yesterday's prediction — a touch of foreboding in the notion that he seemed to have been wrong, at least this once about Faubus and his people, and might be wrong again in other matters; highly critical ones, for all they knew. Presently, though, he was proved right after all. The first bulletin came within fifteen minutes, and within the hour there were pictures of the action.

Groups it seemed had gathered in the Arkansas capital overnight, country people mostly, come in from farms and crossroad hamlets roundabout, but with a leavening of locals, urban types, younger for the most part and somehow athletic in dress and build; "Jocks," Podjo said approvingly when he saw them later that morning on TV. Early on the scene, they milled about the borders of the schoolyard, rather aimlessly at first, then bulged against the sawhorse barricades the police had set up in preparation for trouble. Occasionally one or another of them would cut loose with a rebel yell of pure exuberance, but nothing really strenuous happened until, shortly after the bell rang for classes and all of the white students were inside, they spotted a quartet of Negro reporters approaching. "Here come the niggers!" someone hollered, and a platoon of about twenty of the more vigorous among them — shock troops, so to speak — set upon and began to pummel these interlopers.

Satisfactory as this was, by way of diversion, it defeated the crowd's larger purpose by distracting attention from the arrival of two cars bearing the nine Negro students, or would-be students, who had been turned back, three weeks ago, by the Guardsmen then on duty and since removed. They were unloaded and hustled into the building before the crowd knew they were there. A howl went up, and by way of easing the frustration brought on by word that the nine were lodged inside, more or less beyond reach, the shock platoon went into action against three more reporters — white ones this time, with northern accents — and pummeled them in turn. By then the first bulletin had reached Memphis, and presently there were pictures. While the police stood by, looking apologetic for their presence in the first place, the crowd, swelled to about a thousand by reinforcements, began to dismantle the barricades in preparation for storming the school.

Shortly after eleven oclock, Podjo, Rufus, and Reeny rode over to Crump for a last-minute check on the Ford, a tank of gas, a quart of oil, and a hot breakfast at Earl's, the first they had had since their arrival, two days short of three weeks back. When they returned to the bluff, around noon, they learned from the television that the nine Negroes had been removed from the school to forestall a storming, and the crowd's mood had changed from rage to jubilation.

Podjo nodded approval of this as well, then went back out to the car and changed its license plates from Mississippi to Arkansas, screened from the neighbors by a pair of thick-leaved mulberry trees that grew beside the driveway on the south side of the house. Reeny meantime was getting her gear together, Noctec and clown white, the note to be given the little sister, a teaspoon from the kitchen, and a patchwork quilt they decided to take along. Rufus stationed himself on Podjo's couch and continued to monitor the television coverage of what now resembled a carnival, in and around the Little Rock schoolyard. Here in Memphis too, just over a hundred miles to the east, the weather was fair and seemed likely to remain so, with a high for the day — the autumnal equinox, the weatherman reminded them — predicted to be in the upper seventies. At last, with their watches crowding two oclock, the three set out.

One stop they made, at Carolina and Riverside, while Podjo went into the Chinaman's for an ice-cold bottle of cream soda, its cap sprung for easy removal when the time came, then proceeded slowly up Riverside Drive to Beale, one block south on Second to Linden, then four blocks east to where Rufus parked with care in the same place as before, some fifty yards short of the Turley intersection. Both schoolhouse doors were in plain view from there, and the three settled down to wait for those final minutes to tick away, dragging slower and slower as their watches, like the clocks on the walls inside, nudged toward the half hour and the dismissal bell that would clang when the big hand pointed straight down, vertical and decisive.

When at last it rang, it did so with such sudden, strident urgency that it seemed to be trying to make up for the drag of the past few minutes, and after the muffled thunder of a thousand feet, reverberant down stairwells and along the hollow halls, two happy streams of children poured from the doorways, pushing and shoving, chirping at each other like so many uncaged birds. Almost at once, all three watchers spotted the little sister and saw her cross to the corner flagpole, where she took up her vigil while her schoolmates went their ways, dwindling quickly to no more than a handful in the several distances. Her impatience, seen in the way she began swinging her satchel, shifting her stance, and tossing her pigtails as she leaned against or swung clear of the pole, was mild compared to Rufus's, who soon began to drum on the steering wheel, first with his fingers, then with the sides of his fists, in exasperation at the delay.

Presently though, as time wore on, it occurred to him that the explanation might involve something other than delay. "Maybe he got sick or something, and went home early."

"Maybe he did," Reeny agreed from the back seat.

"No," Podjo said. "The girl wouldnt be waiting. Let's sit it out. It might even be better this way. Just sit tight."

He was right, as it developed, though by the time the boy appeared the cream soda Podjo held sweating in his hand had lost its chill and was beginning to fizz a little around its loosened cap. Again with almost instant recognition, the three in the car saw Teddy come out of the Turley Street entrance with another boy, part curtly with him just clear of the doorway, then join his sister at the flagpole, where they spoke briefly before they traversed the angle of the schoolyard and paused on the far side of the intersection. They crossed, and as they drew closer Reeny got out of the car and took up a position in their path, one foot on the sidewalk, the other on the grass, holding in one hand the note Rufus had written for her to give the girl. When she spoke, the children stopped abreast of her, eyes widened. "Yessum," the boy said, and Podjo noted with approval that no one was in sight in either direction along that houseless stretch on Linden. Reeny appeared flustered and uncertain, however, speaking first to the boy, then to the girl as she stuffed the paper into her upper pocket, then to the boy again. "Let's go," she said, one hand on his shoulder, ready to clutch, and reached behind her to open the rear door she had closed when she got out.

So far, as Podjo watched through the window at the curb, not quite within arm's reach of the participants, the scene had a painful deliberation about it, almost as if it occurred in slow motion. Observing Reeny's confusion, he was about to get out and help her, when suddenly, as if hidden gears had meshed, the action took a leap and became headlong. Reeny caught the boy under the arms and with a single deft motion, such as a well-trained athlete or even acrobat might have performed, swung him up and sideways to deposit him abruptly on the back seat, startled but intact.

"Books, my books!" he cried.

"Dont worry," Reeny told him, entering too.

She slammed the door behind her and spoke through the open window to the girl on the sidewalk, words and tone matching those she might have used to admonish a tag-along dog. "Go home. Go on home now," she said, almost shouting, as the car eased away from the curb. In the rear-vision mirror, Rufus saw the little girl still standing on the sidewalk, her vanished brother's books on the grass nearby, until he made the turn and she slid sideways off the mirror, left to right and out of sight.

Headed south on Wellington for Calhoun and, eventually, Carolina and the bluff, he picked up speed to celebrate the ease with which they had gotten past, or almost past, this critical stage of the job. "A piece of cake!" and "Got him, by God, got him!" he exclaimed over and over as he threaded his way through the light midafternoon traffic.

"Slow down, dammit," Podjo told him. "You want half the cops in Memphis on our tail?"

Rufus slowed, and though he still drove with a white-knuckled grip on the steering wheel, the reduction in bounce and swerve as the car moved along was helpful to Reeny at this juncture. She had taken the teaspoon from the pocket of her skirt and was unscrewing the cap from the brown pint bottle she had brought along. "It's all right," she kept assuring Teddy, who was not only badly frightened but also had his face bunched up to cry.

"I want my mamma," he announced to anyone who would listen.

"Yes I know," Reeny said earnestly, "I know you do. Soon now. And your daddy; your daddy, too. Any minute now. Youll see."

"And my books," he said, as if by sudden inspiration.

"Yes — I know," Reeny agreed.

She had the cap off the Noctec by then, and poured a teaspoon level-full, mindful of the shocks and jiggles. "Here. Take this," she told him, and moved the medicine directly toward and into his mouth, which came obediently ajar, then closed around it. When she upended the spoon and withdrew it clean from between his lips, he grimaced and began to shudder. Reeny did not wonder at the reaction; she had tried the stuff herself, a couple of drops on one fingertip, and instead of finding the sticky pinkish syrup orange-flavored, as the brochure advised, found its taste to be that of grated orange peel, only just short of bitter if short at all. Podjo, grimacing unaware in sympathy, extended the uncapped cream soda over the back of the front seat, and Reeny, also wry-mouthed without knowing it, took the bottle and extended it in turn to Teddy, who gulped thirstily at its lukewarm foamy contents, still shuddering as he did so.

Reeny lowered the soda when he had drunk a little less than half, handed it up to Podjo, and after waiting for Rufus to complete the right turn into Calhoun began to pour the teaspoon level-full, as before. Teddy watched her, knowing what was coming.

"Thank you maam, I dont want no more," he said, lips clamped tight against his teeth.

"Here," she told him, extending the brimfull spoon again. "Take it anyhow. It's good for you. Then we'll go find your daddy."

Again, with no apparent choice in the matter, he took it as directed, grimaced and shuddered as before, and gulped at the soda, passed by Podjo to Reeny, who held it at a high angle until all that remained in the bottle was a little foam. He clutched it with both hands as he drank, and when it was empty she let him have it on his own. "There now," she said, screwing the cap back on the Noctec. "That wasnt so bad, was it?"

"Yessum," he said, when at last he caught his breath.

Podjo nodded approval. "Good work," he told Reeny. "Now for the rest."

Across Fourth Street by then, a block off Wellington, they were abreast of the Rock Island freight depot on their left. Except for a few other industrial concerns, smaller in scale, this stretch of Calhoun was residential and all-Negro, populated at this time of day by women, children just home from school or dawdling along sidewalks on the way there, and the elderly of both sexes, out on their porches to enjoy the mild, sparkling weather. Rufus drove west at a moderate pace, obedient to Podjo's admonition about speed and its consequences, but he still turned to look rearward over his shoulder from time to time, as if to reassure himself that the boy was actually there behind him, in the flesh.

He was indeed, though clearly not by choice. Sunk low in the seat, still clutching the empty bottle, he darted his eyes this way and that at his captors, so that he resembled — or in any case put Rufus in mind of — a pigmy hostage recently seized by a tribe of giant, warlike strangers and by no means certain, so far, whether he is about to be fed or eaten. He held tightly to the soft-drink bottle, though by now even the flecks of foam had subsided, and looked apprehensively at the flat round can Reeny took up from the seat beside her when Podjo said, "Now for the rest."

It was the clown white. Teddy looked alternately at her face and at the can in her hand, wondering, and his apprehension mounted when she removed the lid and he saw, inside, a smooth-surfaced pure-white substance he thought was lard. He assumed this too was something he would be required to swallow, and he began to shudder at the prospect; especially when she said, as she did next, "Here, Teddy. This is good for you, too." He clamped his lips shut, even tighter than before, but was relieved, albeit considerably puzzled, to hear her add: "Hold still now, while I put it on."

On *him* she meant, he realized when she scooped up a sizeable dab of it with her fingertips, then laid the can aside to free her other hand, and took him by the chin in order to steady his head while she began application of the cool white greasy substance to his face. She had not tried the clown white, as she had done the Noctec, and was therefore unsure of its properties and effect. Although she rather thought it harmless, used as it was said to be by clowns throughout the world, she did not like to take a chance and therefore avoided, as best she could, the rims of his mouth and eyes, lest they be stung or irritated.

She worked carefully, one feature at a time, left and right, giving particular attention to the convolutions of his ears, his nostrils, and the area under his jaw — which she noticed, when she released his chin, was trembling with something other than fear; perhaps a yawn. It was the eyes, however, now that she came to observe them, that impressed her as most strange. By this time Rufus had crossed Hernando, within two blocks of the Kinship house on Vance; they were passing Olivet Baptist Church, a dark-brick structure squatting castle-like on their right, with two bold towers flanking the central entrance, one square, the other round. Reeny paid it no mind, any more than she did its less pretentious rival, Ellis Grove Baptist, just short of Abel, a hundred yards farther on, absorbed as she was by the change she saw in Teddy's eyes. They had begun to look glassy — from the chloral hydrate, she realized, which had begun to take effect. Half-whitened, he stared languidly at her from the depths of his still-black sockets; or if not at her, then anyhow in her general direction. Unfocussed as his eyes had begun to be, it was hard to tell.

"Hypnotic," Podjo remarked from the front seat, looking over Reeny's shoulder at the boy. "The stuff is beginning to work."

"I dropped my books," Teddy said, more dreamy than distressed.

This Monday — despite the Little Rock explosion, just over a hundred miles across the way — was more or less like any other until around three-thirty when the phone rang for perhaps the fifteenth time since Eben opened the office at straight-up eight oclock. "Wiggins Development," Lucy Provine said, gray-haired, her thick-lensed pince-nez catching highlights from the sunlit glass of the door onto the street. Mostly the calls had been for Tio, who was out; but not this one. "For you," she told Eben, busy at his desk. "It's Martha. She sounds excited."

Excited was scarcely word enough. "Martha?" he said, and she began at once a rushed jumble of words and phrases too confused for him to sort and reassemble into sense.

"Eben? Eben? It's Teddy, Eben; Teddy! Something's happen. Something — somebody — got him, Sister Baby says. White. Come on home! Mamma Cindy — "

"Got him? How? What got him? Got him how?"

"And a note. Sister Baby, Mamma Cindy . . ."

"Martha? Martha!" He thought he'd lost her.

"Eben," she moaned, speaking now as if from a distance or perhaps about midway down a well. "It's Teddy. Teddy — "

"Wait there," he told her. "I'll be right home."

He didnt bother to get his hat, but he called over his shoulder to Miss Lucy on the way out, "Home. Be back."

"If you — " she said, and the door swung shut behind him.

After the cool dimness of the office, sunlight struck him like a slap across the eyes. Half blinded, he looked up and down the street, waiting for his pupils to dilate, and when they did, as luck would have it, the first thing he saw was a cab right there on Beale, empty and creeping eastward for a turn on Third, not twenty feet away. He had his hand up, mouth set to whistle, but then, as his vision sharpened, he saw that the luck, if you could call it that, was bad. The cab was a Yellow: for white only. He lowered his arm and looked again, up and down the street, and seeing no other, east or west, set out on foot, past Handy Park to Hernando, half running, half walking. I'm all out of shape, he told himself, partly to keep from thinking about what he might find when he reached home, just over three blocks south on Vance. I'll never make it running, he thought, already beginning to puff and about to wheeze.

When he rounded the corner, however, his luck came back. There at the curb, barely a dozen feet away and also headed south, was a cab. Moreover the luck held, for this was a Littlejohn: colored only.

The driver dozed at the wheel, engine off, while the radio chattered on about Little Rock. "279 Vance," Eben told him, opening the rear door.

"Check," the driver said, before he was even awake, and reached for the ignition. Heavy-set, with a broad Asiatic face badly pitted by smallpox, he looked in the rear-vision mirror, from which a pair of baby shoes were suspended by their strings, and studied Eben, who had gotten in, slammed the door, and sat forward on the seat. "Something wrong?" the driver asked, turning the key.

"279 Vance, and hurry," Eben told him.

"Check," the driver said again, and clicked the radio off.

They made the three blocks in good time; Linden, Pontotoc, then the right turn into Vance. "This side will do," Eben said.

When the cab stopped across the street from the green bungalow he gave the driver a fifty-cent piece, held ready in his hand, and got out on the traffic side, slamming the door behind him without waiting for his change. He crossed the street at a run. Fortunately the gate was open, and he did not slow for the steps. On the porch he did stop, but only to snatch the screen door ajar, and there they were in the living room, Martha and Mamma Cindy and Sister Baby.

"Oh, Eben!" Martha cried, coming toward him.

"Where's Teddy?" he asked, and stopped. To his surprise, he sounded gruff, if not downright angry.

"We dont know," she wailed, and she stopped too, just short of where Eben stood waiting in the doorway.

For a moment he felt relief. His guess, first off, had been that the boy, struck or run over by a car or truck on his way home from school, had been hauled away in an ambulance, dead or dying, and Martha's garbled report over the phone had been the result either of her hysterical grief or else of some misguided notion of breaking the news gently until he could get there to hear the worst of it in person. It didnt make much sense, but neither then did anything else he allowed himself to imagine, back at the office or on the way here in the cab. Now, though, other possibilities began to occur to him, all devilish, whether they made sense or not; a sudden bolt of thunderless blue-sky lightning, for example, or even spontaneous combustion, which left no vestige of the victim, and the victim was his son.

Dear God, Dear God, he thought, and asked, still in a tone that held more of sternness than concern: "What do you mean? What do you *mean* you dont know?"

"We dont know," she said again, and held out an unfolded piece of paper. "Look at here."

It was a single sheet, torn roughly from a cheap, ruled tablet, and the writing was in pencil, legible but crude in a meticulous kind of way, just this side of illiterate or maybe on the far side of retarded. He skimmed it fast, the first time through — *got your boy. say anything the cops. your last of him. will hear from us* — then carefully the second time, word by word: *We got your boy. If you say anything to any one, expecially the cops local or other wise, you will have seen your last of him. We mean this. So stand fast, you will hear from us in the next day or so. Wait till then.*

He started to read the message still a third time, perhaps as a way of delaying the moment in which he would have to stop and consider what it meant, when suddenly there was a piercing howl, mounting so swiftly up the scale that it seemed not so much to stop, though it did stop, as to pass beyond the range of hearing. It came from Sister Baby and was broken off by sobs.

All this time since she last saw her brother back on Linden, she had been big-eyed with wonder, but up to now she had not cried. Some people had taken Teddy — white people, and she knew next to nothing of white people except to see them on the street — perhaps as an extension of the punishment he had received from old Miss Pitkin for letting Juny Partridge talk to him in class. Despite her fears and growing confusion — including the fear that she would forget and tell what he had told her not to tell, lest their father refuse to take them to the fair — she viewed the event mainly as one in a series, almost a game, and she was waiting for those that would follow, now that the grown-ups were in charge and presumably would know just what to do. After all, Teddy had gone with those people willingly enough, riding in style, and had even left his books for her to carry, along with the note the lady gave her, saying, "Make sure your mamma gets this," and she had.

Her grandmother's reaction, then her mother's, though extreme, seemed to her no worse than you might expect of women in distress, which was plainly what they were. It was when she saw her father read the note twice over, the expression that came on his face while he did so, that she knew a true disaster was at hand, a threat to all of them, including herself. Her reaction was to howl, then break off in tears — for him and for Teddy as well, now that she saw in her father's face, instead of the anger he had displayed when he first arrived from the office in response to her mother's frantic and outrageous summons, the grief brought on by the trouble she now perceived had come their way.

"*Hush* that!" Martha cried with a start, unnerved by the sudden, full-voiced wail, though in fact it had stopped before she spoke.

Eben and Mamma Cindy moved at once to comfort the child: as did Martha herself, once she had time to realize what she had said. "Dont cry. Hush now. Hush," she told her, in a tone that gave the word a quite different meaning. Eben had bent and caught his daughter in his arms, her face against his collar. He patted her back to reassure her, and took out a clean white handkerchief to catch her tears and dry them when they stopped, which they presently did.

"*I* dont know what to make of it, any more than she do," Mamma Cindy said, shaking her head while standing by to help. "Mainly, I dont believe it. Chillun. Stealing chillun. Lord to God. What is this world coming to, these days?"

Eben's first thought, even as he scanned the note the first time, had been to call the police: not in defiance of the warning not to do so, but rather in acceptance of a suggestion to be snatched at, if only because it was the only one around. Before calling them, however, he had to know what he would tell them, and that meant having to discover, as best he could from those on the scene — Martha, Mamma Cindy, and above all Sister Baby — just what had happened. Strangely enough, his daughter's sudden yelping wail, so disruptive in its immediate effect, and the ministrations required to ease the pain she was so obviously feeling — the sound, he realized even before it ended, was like one he once had heard a small dog make when it was run over in the street — served to settle them all down, even Sister Baby herself, at least to a degree that made it possible for him to question them about the events of the past half-hour or so. The result was a rather full conception of what had occurred, on Linden and since, though not without certain gaps only time could fill, if ever anything or anyone was going to fill them between now and the hour of his son's return, if he returned.

Once the car had disappeared around the red mass of the schoolhouse, with Teddy somewhere inside it out of sight, Sister Baby took up his books and set out for home by their accustomed route. She was troubled, but more than troubled she was excited by the doubly prideful notion that she not only had a secret to keep, lest their father refuse to take them to the fair, but also had a note to carry and deliver to her mother, after the long walk home all by herself. Opposite Saint Patrick's she turned left, off Linden onto Fourth, and walked the two blocks south to Vance, much admired for her solitary valiance, she could tell, by watchers in the houses on the way. At Vance she crossed to the other side of the street, and there, a little more than midway down the block where Tio lived, was Mamma Cindy waiting on her porch as usual.

"I was getting worried," she called across the banisters when Sister Baby came within hearing distance. "Where is Teddy?"

"I'm caring his books for him."

"I see you are. Where is he?"

"He left. With some people."

"People? What people?"

"White people," Sister Baby said as she reached the stoop.

That was when the excitement began, slow at first, then fast. "You come up here. Tell me," Mamma Cindy said when Sister Baby had climbed the steps with the two sets of books, hers in the satchel, Teddy's under one arm, "what white people?"

"A lady, and two men. In a car. The lady said for me to get on home, and soon as I got there to give Mamma this."

She removed the folded paper from her shirtwaist pocket and held it out. Mamma Cindy unfolded and looked at it cautiously from all angles, turning it this way and that.

"Dolly!·Dolly!" she called in the direction of the door behind her.

Lame Dolly appeared promptly in the doorway, peering through the screen. She clutched a broom with both thin hands, her pale gray headrag fitted so tightly to her skull that it resembled polished bone. "Lucindy?" she replied.

"Come out here a minute," Mamma Cindy told her, and when she hobbled out, bringing the broom with her, handed her the note. "What do it say? See can you puzzle it out for me."

Dolly took and studied it, much as the other had done, before giving it back undeciphered. "I just reads printing writing," she said with a slow shake of her small round head, "not this here longhand kind."

"All right," Mamma Cindy said. She studied the paper again for a while, once more from several angles including upside-down, and Sister Baby realized for the first time that her grandmother couldnt read. At last, after turning and turning the note in her hands, she reached a decision. "Wait here," she told Dolly — making even less sense than Eben would make, some ten minutes later, when he gave Martha the same instructions over the phone; for Dolly never left home at all, aside from perhaps a half-dozen times, all told, since her uncle brought her here from Moscow on his wedding day, close to forty years ago. Mamma Cindy and Sister Baby set out, and Dolly stood looking after them, clutching her broom, as they walked up Vance together.

All the grandmother knew, for now, was that some "people" — white people — had taken Teddy somewhere, willingly or unwillingly, in a car. Worried though she was, she took it as a good sign that Sister Baby, who had seen him leave with the three people — a lady and two men — did not seem to be upset by his departure, which she surely would have been if the manner of his going had been forceful, let alone violent. And having reasoned this far in the attempt to relieve her fret, Mamma Cindy went still further. Perhaps it had something to do with the school, she thought; some kind of official business, maybe involving a reward, a medal or special certificate, she decided, for she had a high opinion of her grandson as a scholar, based mainly on having watched him read the Sunday funny papers unassisted. Maybe the lady was a teacher from one of the white schools, chief judge of the contest he had won, and the men were two of Mr Crump's politicians on the school board. It occurred to her then that the hand-written note, which she kept a careful grip on while they walked, probably explained all this to Martha and included instructions on where to join them for the ceremony, whatever it was and wherever it was being held. In any case, she told herself, she would know as soon as they reached her daughter's house and found out what was written on the paper.

"Mamma Cindy," Sister Baby said as they crossed Hernando.

"What, child?"

"The lady said for *me* to care the note."

"Well — all right," Mamma Cindy said, and gave it to her to hold for the rest of the way.

Then they were there, turning in at the gate of the green bungalow, and within a couple of minutes — scarcely time to adjust her thinking for the shock — all her wishful reconstruction and extension of the facts at her disposal, the suppositional edifice she had built to house and hide her fret, collapsed around her ears.

"Where is Teddy? What happened to Teddy?" Martha asked, almost shouted, after one look at their faces and before they had a chance to speak a word. Her own face took on a stricken look, and all of Mamma Cindy's fears came crowding back at the sight.

"White lady took him, *she* say," her mother told her, indicating Sister Baby.

"And two men, in a car," Sister Baby declared, and added, out of sudden recollection: "One had a musstache."

"Took him? Took him?" Martha cried.

"Took him," Sister Baby said, nodding gravely. "And told me to give you this, soon as I got home."

She held out the refolded note. Martha snatched it from her, unfolded it hastily, and read it much as Eben would do in turn, first fast, then more deliberately, though still not really slow; she had always been a quicker reader than her husband. The stricken look intensified, then faded into shock when she completed the second reading. She just stood there.

"What do it say?" Mamma Cindy asked.

"That Sister Baby's right. They took him." She seemed altogether calm, both hands at her sides, the note held loosely in one. "They got him and they say we've seen our last of him unless we do exactly what they say. Theyll let us know. It's a kidnap."

"Lord to God," Mamma Cindy said. She shook her head at that awful word and a doleful expression came on her pale aristocratic face with its high-bridged nose and amber eyes. "The world gone crazy, white and colored. White and colored, they done lost they mind."

"Eben! Eben!" Martha suddenly cried.

As abruptly as it had descended on her, half a minute back, her calm was gone. She ran to the phone, but was so unstrung that she had to dial the office number twice. "Eben. Get me Eben," she told Lucy Provine, and once he came to the phone all she could do was blurt out her troubles incoherently, in a way that made little sense even to herself. "Come on home!" she shouted into the mouthpiece, and felt no incongruity at all when he told her to wait there until he came. She was glad to have someone tell her what to do, especially when it was something she could manage.

This steadied her somewhat, and while she waited, as instructed, she tried once more to question her daughter. "What did they look like?"

"White people," Sister Baby said.

"And one had a mustache?"

"Yessum. And the lady had light-colored hair."

"I see; yes. But what did they look like? Old or young? Tall or short? What kind of clothes?"

"White people," Sister Baby said.

Martha stopped trying, on the theory that it would be better not to confuse the child, disturb her recollection of what she had seen outside the school on Linden, before Eben got there to conduct the questioning properly. Besides, she reminded herself, he had always been closer to their daughter than she was; just as she had always been closer to their son. She nearly burst into tears at the thought, but then she heard Eben's running footsteps on the porch. When he snatched the screen door open, she moved to meet him, only to be checked by the sternness of his face and voice as he stopped in the doorway. "Where's Teddy?" he demanded, almost as if he believed she had the boy hidden somewhere about the house, and "What do you mean? What do you *mean* you dont know?"

The note changed that, even more for him than it had for her. Whereas her immediate reaction had been an intensification of the alarm she brought to the reading in the first place, his was rather a softening of manner, a descent into all-but-ineffable sadness, as if he was already grieving for the loss the note informed him he might suffer. Moreover, their secondary reactions also differed. She had gone into shock almost immediately afterwards, an icy immobility that gave an impression of absolute calm, however false, but he no sooner finished the second reading — or so it seemed to Martha, watching as he read — than his expression began changing from one of sorrow to one of studied practicality, of preparation for coming to grips with the problem thus presented, even before Sister Baby let out the animal howl that claimed the attention of all three of them, Martha, Eben himself, and Mamma Cindy.

And it was Eben who helped their daughter most. He not only got her quieted; he even succeeded in calming her down enough to answer questions he formulated after finding out from her mother and grandmother all that she had told them up to now.

"You say one had a mustache. Good. What color was it?"

"Black."

"Good. And the lady had light-colored hair. What color?"

"Yellow."

"Good. Anything else? Who else saw them?"

Her mouth shook. Up to now she had answered bravely and decisively — however wrongly in each case — nodding in response to her father's nods, each time he said "Good." Now, though, she seemed about to start crying again, but nothing like as hard as she had done while watching him read the note. "What is it, Baby?" Eben asked.

"Oh, Daddy," she said, "I promised, promised Teddy I wouldnt tell." She began to weep in earnest, speaking between sobs. "He got kept in, for talking with Juny Partridge. He didnt talk; *Juny* did. And told me, told me not to tell. Will you still care us to the fair?"

"Yes, Baby, yes. Now quit your crying. I'll care you to the fair; course I will. And Teddy too; course I will — to lots of fairs." He patted her shoulder. "Was anybody else around to see him when he left?"

"Just me," she said. "The others all had gone. Even Juny."

Across the room, Jesus smiled calmly upward from his chromo on the wall above the telephone. Eben sighed. From all he had learned, questioning Sister Baby and Martha and Mamma Cindy, he could see that he would have very little to give the police to go on when he called them. He wondered, wondered. Then the phone rang.

He was there, alongside the curtained doorway to the dining room, and took up the instrument before the second ring stopped ringing. Behind him, Martha, Sister Baby, and Mamma Cindy watched and listened. "Hello," he said. Somehow he knew what it would be, and he was right.

"Eben Kinship?"

"Speaking."

"Listen, Eben. We got your boy, and got him good. Whether you ever see him again, alive, is up to you — you and the cops, like it said in the note. You get the note?"

"Yes."

"O.K. Cops; that means local or F.B.I. If you try and get in touch with them, no matter how much on the sly you think it is, the boy is done for. Done for," the voice repeated, and paused.

"What is it? What *is* it?" Martha cried at her husband's elbow. She had crossed the room and stood beside him, leaning forward toward the phone. "Is it them? Where's Teddy? Have they got him? Ask them have they got him."

Eben wagged his free hand at her, signaling for quiet as the voice resumed, nasal, flat, and altogether deadly, yet not without a touch of mockery, which increased the deadliness by denying any element of pity in the nature of whatever lurked behind it. Redneck, Dixiecrat, he thought, remembering them of old, back in his Mississippi boyhood, sitting on the galleries of country stores or come to town on Saturdays to stand around the streets. All his life he had made it a point never to look at one of them directly, especially in the eyes.

"Remember," the dead-flat nasal voice went on. "We are watching you round the clock, on Beale and there on Vance. Every move you make, we'll know it soon as you do. And remember, too, youve got another child; the little girl. One false move, Teddy's done for and we'll take her in his place. Keep that in mind."

"Let me talk to them," Martha interrupted, overriding what came next.

"Goddammit, woman, *hush!*" Eben shouted.

"What?" the phone voice said.

"Not you," Eben hurriedly replied, glaring across the mouthpiece at Martha, who had hushed.

"O.K." the voice told him. "We'll be in touch, by phone and mail. Youll hear from us again real soon. Stay by your phone and watch the mailbox. And remember, no cops, local or otherwise; we've got watchers down at headquarters. The thing to keep in mind right now is to do as we say do, nigger, if you want your boy back. Understand?"

"Yes. How is he?"

"He's fine. Just fine."

"Tell me — "

"He's fine, just fine. Dont worry. All we're going to want in the end is money, and youve got that. Or can get it. We'll take good care of him, however long it takes."

The line went dead. Whoever it was behind the voice had eased the receiver down with the faintest of clicks. All there was now was wire-hum. "Hello, hello!" Eben cried, although he knew it was no use.

He jiggled the phone impatiently until he remembered it had a dial, then dialed O in whirring haste. "May I help you?" a new, machine-like voice inquired; a woman, though just barely.

"Can you trace a call?"

"Sir?"

"Can you trace a call I just had?"

"What is the nature of your problem, sir?"

"A call; I had a call. Can you trace it?"

"I am sorry, sir," the voice declared, as if repeating the words by rote or reading them off a card. "The equipment we now have will not allow us to trace a call."

"Give me the supervisor."

"Certainly, sir. But what is the nature of your problem?"

"A call; I had a call."

"What was its nature?"

Exasperated, he hung on for a moment, hearing the instrument give him back the sound of his frantic breathing, and during that brief span he perceived two things in rapid sequence, almost at once: first, that the call could not be traced, even if the telephone people could be persuaded to try, which seemed unlikely: and second, that he was even then attempting to do the very thing the other voice, and the note itself, had warned him not to do — the one thing, that is, that would result in Teddy's being "done for. Done for." Those were the other voice's words, the altogether deadly redneck one.

"Thank you," he said, and hung the phone up.

He stood there, looking down at it, and the grieved expression on his face was like the one he had worn, a short time back, while reading the note that also began with the words, "We got your boy." If this new grief was sharper, that was because it was less general, more particular in its source. Just as he knew he would make no further attempt to trace the call, so too he now abandoned his notion of calling the police. "We are watching you round the clock," the voice had said, and he foresaw the consequences. He would call the station, give them what few facts he had, and within minutes a squad car would arrive, siren wailing, and somewhere up or down the block a lookout would pick up the phone, dial a number, and pass the word, "O.K. He's queered it, called the cops," and Teddy would be done for. Not only done for, Eben realized, but replaced by Sister Baby, whose turn would then come round, and the thing would start all over; "We got your little girl."

Whatever else he did, he knew for certain that calling the police would not be one of them. He was left in fact with nothing whatever to do — and he could see, already, that this was likely to prove the most difficult of all the things he would have to do or not-do: nothing.

"Eben. *Eben.*"

It was Martha, still beside him. Mamma Cindy was there too, by now, though Sister Baby was still on the couch across the room, where Tio watched from his oval on the wall. "Tell me, tell me," Martha begged. So he told her.

"They got him, all right, like they said in the note. They say he's fine and all they want is money. They'll call or write and let us know. They said not to worry."

"It's the times, is what it is," Mamma Cindy muttered, arms folded across her waist; "the Adam bomb and all them Russians killing people, roasting them alive in ovens."

Martha stood stock-still. When Eben had told her to hush, a couple of minutes ago, she obeyed him in part because she was not at all sure she wanted the answers she all but knew she would get to those brief, terrible questions she had been interrupting him to ask: "Is it them? Where's Teddy? Have they got him?" But now that she had them — the one big answer, anyhow, which left no room for doubt or comfort — she stood quite still for a moment before she started keening. Presently, though, she stopped that, too, frantic but comparatively quiet.

"Daddy," she cried. "Call Daddy. Call Tio. *He'll* know what to do."

Teddy by then was asleep on his cot in the attic, though the process of getting him there — in contrast, that is, to the hitchless ease of the snatch itself, an hour ago on Linden — had been hectic for the most part, laced with danger, and sometimes ludicrous as well. First there was the matter of the clown white.

Podjo had watched with growing apprehension Reeny's application of the flat-white greasy substance to the face, ears, and throat of her glassy-eyed charge in the back seat; but this was mild compared to the alarm he felt when he saw the finished product. Union Station, between Third and Second, had just slid by on their left. A block-wide granite and limestone pile, with twin red-capped towers flanking the high-roofed central mass with its six tall columns, the building had two entrances, broad, terraced flights of steps leading up from the ground level, a straight one on the left for colored, a curved one on the right for whites, longer but more gradual and therefore less steep to climb. In its high-rolling prime, back in the twenties when he was a boy, better than three dozen passenger trains a day pulled in and out of its cavernous sheds, hissing and panting, breathing steam and sweating oil. Now, though, the place was in sad decline, with scarcely half that many arrivals and departures in a week. Forty-five years in operation as the gateway from the Mid-South to the world, it had one limping decade left, and for three of those last ten years it would sit there trainless, empty as an abandoned barn — or, better, the desanctified cathedral it resembled — outdone by the airplane, just as in its day it had outdone the glittering river packets, the sidewheel floating palaces of an older time; after which the wreckers would move in with their cranes and two-ton headache balls for their share of the ten million dollars the government would spend to establish a new postal installation on the site. Union Station, knocked down and hauled away for landfill, would be abolished so completely that not one of its hundred thousand hand-cut stones would remain to signify that the massive structure they once formed had ever been there, let alone testify to the bustle of life it once contained. Podjo watched it slide past, beyond Rufus bent over the steering wheel in profile, and felt a certain sadness, not only for the building itself, which had begun to look dingy from soot and disuse, but also for himself, since he and it were close to the same age. Then he looked into the rear seat again, and what he saw made him forget his other troubles, including his lost youth.

Reeny's careful application of the clown white, avoiding the rims of Teddy's eyes and mouth for fear of irritating the delicate membranes there, had produced a startling result — startling not only to those closest at hand, Podjo realized, but also to anyone who happened to glance into the back seat of the Ford in passing; some random cop, for example, walking a downtown beat or cruising in a squad car. "Jesus Christ," he said in a tone approaching awe. For the boy had the look of a death's head, of a dwarf made up hurriedly by amateurs to play the role of Death in a morality play or pageant. His drug-glazed eyes glittered like agates lodged in fuliginous sockets and his red-black mouth described an outsized lopsided grin, set off by a surrounding expanse that was at once as white as chalk and shiny as new porcelain or wet paint. On second thought, now that he could study the sight without the distraction of the original shock he had suffered, Podjo could see that what Teddy in fact resembled was a blurred photo negative of a diminutive minstrel end man.

"Jesus Christ," he said again, and added sidelong to Rufus, in anger and consternation, "You and your goddam Canada Lee!"

Rufus risked a rearward look, and had much the same reaction. "He dont look too white," he admitted as he returned his attention to the traffic up ahead.

"Yair. He looks *too* white," Podjo said, and asked Reeny: "Cant you rub it in better or something? Sort of tone him down, or up?"

"I'll try," she replied, and took a compact from the pocket of her skirt. It contained loose powder and a puff, which she began using to pat the powder liberally onto Teddy's highly stylized black-and-white African mask. "All it needs is a little flesh tone," she explained as she worked.

But this was not only no better, it was worse. The puff soon became a greasy wad, and all the supposed repair supplied was a smeared, off-color, mottled appearance, even more unreal — if possible — than before.

Rufus turned for a second look, and once more was dismayed. "Holy Mother. We got us a freak on our hands."

"Well," Reeny said defensively, "he's sup*pose* to have been sick."

"Sick, yair, but Jesus," Rufus cried, "what with? Leprosy? Bubonic plague?"

They were approaching the Main Street crossing now, the most critical point in their drive back to the bluff. It was here that they were likely to be observed and stopped if some policeman, or some overzealous citizen, saw anything he considered suspicious or out-of-the-way; which Teddy certainly was in his present state.

"Here," Podjo told Reeny, reaching back and unfolding the quilt they had decided to bring along at the last minute. "Wrap him in this. Bundle him up real good. We'll smuggle him home all right, so long as that stuff you gave him dont wear off before we get there."

She wrapped him securely, with the result that he rode the rest of the way disguised more or less as a bundle, hooded and swathed in folds of the quilt as if in a sort of burnoose. They crossed Main with little danger of detection, passed under the brownstone Central Station viaduct just beyond, then crossed Front, another crucial intersection, to enter a bustling region of warehouses, trucks and trailers parked for loading, and many spur tracks, each of which gave the Ford and its occupants a hearty shaking — including Teddy, whose teeth Reeny could hear rattling under the hood of his improvised burnoose at such times. Here the streets were mostly named for states, and beyond Tennessee they made a left turn off Calhoun, south on Kentucky down a long block cobbled with bricks that made the tires give off a constant rumbling sound like distant thunder.

Perhaps the rumbling woke Teddy, or perhaps it shifted something in his dreams. In any case: "I'm thirsty. Thirsty," the others heard him say, his voice sepulchral under the layers of quilt.

"Is he coming to?" Podjo asked, alarmed.

Reeny folded the hood back gingerly and looked. He seemed no different, eyes still glazed and glassy, as unfocussed as before. "I dont think so," she told Podjo, replacing the hood to cover the mottled face.

"We'll fix you up, kid," Rufus said over his shoulder, "soon as we get where we're headed. Home sweet home."

"Let *me* talk to him," Reeny protested. "You scare him."

"Yair," Podjo agreed, still angry about the clown white. "You just drive. Let her do the talking."

"Dont worry," Reeny told Teddy, who had lapsed into his former hypnotic state, if in fact he had ever been out; "I'll look after you. It wont be long till we are home."

And it wasnt. A right turn, off Kentucky onto Georgia, and a two-block ride due west, across Kansas, brought them back to Riverside. They had come full circle, or almost full; Carolina was one block south and Arkansas the same distance west of the Chinaman's, where they turned right again. Rufus drove those two blocks carefully, hand-signaling the turns, and grooved to an easy stop in the driveway at 705, alongside the mulberry screen on the left side of the house. "Well, we made it," he announced, and added, conductor-style, as he cut the ignition, "All out. Watch your step."

"You go pull the steps down," Podjo told him. "I'll bring the kid in, then come back and change the plates before you leave to make the call."

Rufus went inside. Podjo got out and opened the rear door of the car, and when Reeny emerged he leaned across the width of the back seat, took up the elongated bundle in both arms, and sidled out, careful to see that the quilt did not fall open while he followed her into the house. Rufus had the steps down, as instructed, and Podjo, moving past Reeny with his burden while she held the screen door ajar, went directly up them to the attic, where he laid Teddy carefully on the farther of the two cots.

Reeny was close behind him, Rufus behind her. She unfolded the quilt with swift unwrapping motions, left and right, and the three of them stood looking down at the boy, who lay flat on his back, clutching the empty cream-soda bottle with both hands, his feet crossed at the ankles like those on the tombstone effigy of an old crusader, back from Jerusalem. He might have been sleeping except that his eyes were open, directed upward from deep in their sooty, clown-white-circled sockets, but still unfocussed and glazed over, just as they had been a while ago, back on Kentucky, when Reeny opened the hood for a look at him after he suddenly declared that he was thirsty.

Now he did it again, speaking abruptly, without preamble, out of the mask that somewhat resembled a child's drawing of a raccoon. "Thirsty," he said. "I'm thirsty."

"I'll be damned," Rufus marveled, standing over him, gazing down. "Look how he does it. Is he asleep or not?"

"Goofed up. Zonked," Podjo said, watching too.

"Looks like fun," Rufus said. "I might try it myself, sometime, if there's enough of the stuff to go round."

"Go bring up a glass of water," Reeny told him.

"Right," he said. He turned and started down the steps.

"I'll change those plates," Podjo said, following. "It wont take long," he told Rufus when they reached the bottom.

"Right. Whenever youre ready I'll go make the call," Rufus said, and went back toward the kitchen for the water. Before he got there, however, he turned and called through the ladder-like hallway steps to Podjo, who had stopped in the bedroom: "Goddammit, Podj, we sure brought it off, didnt we? Didnt we?"

"So far," Podjo said, more to himself than to Rufus.

He was on his knees, groping under the foot of the bed for the Mississippi plates that had been on the Ford until he removed them around midday. When he found them he went out and switched them again, lest someone unseen had spotted and jotted down the number during the pick-up or the drive back to the bluff, and returned to the attic in time to watch Teddy finish his second glass of water.

"Some kid. He'll make a great little drinker one of these days," Rufus was saying when Podjo reappeared. "O.K. I'm off to put the screws to them," he said, and went past him, down the steps for the third time in the past five minutes.

From outside, through the louvers in the gable toward the street, Podjo heard the car start and the slewing of gravel as it backed out of the driveway, then roared off. Hutton-Hutton, he thought, irked by the unnecessary racket.

Reeny had the boy sitting half-up on the narrow cot, one arm around his shoulders to support him as he drank the last of the water. His eyes, though still not in focus, turned this way and that when she took the glass down. When he saw Podjo — if in fact he saw him; she could not be sure — he seemed to flinch, as if with fear. Mustache, she thought. It's the mustache scares him.

She eased him back on the pillow, but his eyes continued to roll a bit in their dark sockets, looking up at the rafters, which ran crossways, and the slanted raw-pine ceiling, high in the brown gloom. "Where is this?" he asked, quite distinctly, to her surprise.

"Home. It's home, for now," she told him, but he appeared not to hear her. His lids came slowly down, extinguishing the glitter in his eyes for the first time, so far as she knew, since she administered the Noctec to him, more than half an hour ago.

They stood there, she and Podjo, looking down at Teddy sleeping behind the outlandish mask she had given him in the car on the way here.

"We've got to get some things I didnt think of," she said presently, as if musing to herself. "Milk, for one, and some different kinds of cereal. You know — kinds that kids like. Maybe ones with prizes in the box. And some picture books. Comics, things like that."

"Why not?" Podjo said.

They stood there a while longer, watching, until Podjo spoke again. "Well, he's sleeping good now; really sleeping. He'll probably keep it up the rest of the day, according to the folder. You want to come down for a break?" He turned toward the trap-door-looking rectangle of pearly, real-world light that seemed to have made its way up the steps from the floor below. Reeny stood there for another long moment, looking doubtful, then turned too, and they descended.

When Rufus got back they were in the kitchen, Podjo nursing a bottle of Jax and Reeny sipping from a cup of soluble coffee so diluted with Pet that it was the lightest of tans, not quite lukewarm. His mission, which had taken him to the nearest public telephone over on Crump, had returned to full flower the euphoria he displayed on Wellington and Calhoun, driving south and west from Linden, before it was diminished, just short of the Main Street crossing, by one quick rearward look at what had resulted from his brainstorm about clown white. He had only been gone around ten minutes — three to get there, three in the phone booth, three to get back — but that short span had been enough to send his spirits soaring.

"Boy, did I put it to him," he exulted as he came through the kitchen door. "*Kin*ship! Hey, I had him pissing all over himself. Youd have thought he had a whole klavern of Little Rock klansmen paying him a visit right there in his living room, pointy hoods and all. I could hear his wife in the background, going on about 'Teddy. Oh, where's Teddy?' till he had to shut her up so he could hear a word I said. I think he must have popped her one or something. Anyhow she hushed. 'Whether you see your boy again, alive, is up to you,' I told him." Rufus imitated the voice he had used, nasal and deadly, with an edge of mockery in it. "I laid it out real strong, right down the line, about how we'd grab the little girl next, if anything went gronky about this one, and how we were watching him round the clock. 'All we want is *money*, and youve got it or can get it.' That was how I brought old Wiggins into the act. He started trying to ask questions, like his wife before he shut her up, but I just told him the boy was all right, so far, and we'd be in touch. Then I hung up on him still trying to get a word in edgeways. Yair. It went just the way we planned; I had that klansman voice down pat. Pat as pat — if not patter," he concluded with a grin.

"Good then," Podjo told him. "Have yourself a nice cold beer."

Reeny caught the slur in this, the recurrent note of disapproval; Cool down, cool down, he seemed to be saying. But when she glanced from the older to the younger man she saw that the latter had taken no apparent notice of it, being altogether too involved in his elation. He's really enjoying this, she thought; enjoying it too much to let anything interfere. Her inclination, despite her own disapproval of the pleasure he took in the pain he had inflicted, was to speak sharply to Podjo in defense of Rufus, who after all had carried out his assignment and evidently had accomplished it in style. She was even about to do so, hackles up, when there was a jarring thump from overhead.

All three froze. Reeny was the first to move, and was also first to make it to the hallway steps and up them to the attic. Podjo was close behind her; Rufus brought up the rear. There on the floor, between the two cots, Teddy crouched where he had fallen, his mottled clown-white mask scrunched up for crying though neither the tears nor the wails had yet begun.

"Jesus," Rufus said with relief when he cleared the top of the steps; "I thought he'd tried for a breakout."

Reeny was with the boy by then. "It's all right, it's all right," she murmured as she bent to comfort him.

But it was not all right; not for Teddy anyhow. He had had some kind of nightmare and had fallen in his sleep. Emerging to find three white strangers bearing down on him, he thought he was still in the terrifying dream.

"Mamma! Mamma!" he cried, and tears burst from his eyes to run down his painted cheeks toward the still-dark corners of his mouth.

"It's all right — all right," Reeny told him again as she picked him up and held him. "I'll be your mamma; I'm here, I'm here. Dont cry. You just had a dream. I'm here. Dont cry."

She continued to comfort him, sitting sideways on the near cot with Teddy on her lap. Presently he quieted and she even persuaded him to lie back down. He seemed better, though not in looks, for the mask had been further distorted by the channels his tears had worn in the splotched powder, on their way from his eyes to the extended corners of his mouth.

"I know what," she said, brightening at the prospect. "We'll get that gunk off. Youll feel better once we do." Podjo had gone back downstairs but Rufus was still there. "Bring me that box of Kleenex by the bed," she told him, "and a washrag and some soap and a pan of hot water."

He brought the Kleenex first and she got to work at once. It took most of the box, but by the time Rufus came back up with the soap and water she had made a respectable beginning. Gentle scrubbing removed the last of the clown white, even from behind the boy's ears, and the soothing effect of the warm damp cloth, moving softly over his face and throat, restored his former drowsiness to such an extent that he was of little help to her in shucking off his shoes and socks and then his pants and shirt. He lay there in his drawers and sleeveless undershirt, both of which looked dazzling white against the darkness of his skin, and his eyes were no more than threads of a similar white under his lowered lids. She turned the covers down on his cot and shifted him to it, pulling them up to his chin when she got him settled. After she emptied what remained of the soapy water into the drain box under the water heater, she gathered up the scattered tissues and put them in the pan with the soap and washrag, then sat down on the adjoining cot to watch Teddy while he slept. A skinned rabbit, she thought. She smiled, but then corrected herself: Whoever saw a rabbit that was still black after you skinned him?

Toward sundown, Rufus came back up the steps. "Let's go eat," he said, whispering when he saw that Reeny had placed a finger over her lips.

"You and Podjo go," she told him. "I'll stay here."

"No. We talked it over. He wants to stay. He said so."

"I'll stay here and scrap something up. For you too, if you like."

"Goddammit, Reen, come on!" he hissed furiously. "You know you got to *eat*. Come on. The kid's sleeping sound now anyhow. He wont wake."

"He did before."

"Goddammit, Reen — "

Rufus was close to shouting now and she saw it was no use. Besides, Teddy showed no sign of stirring under the covers drawn to his chin. "All right," she said.

She took up the tissue-filled pan, turned on the hanging light bulb, for which she had improvised a conical shade by tying a piece of cardboard round the socket, and followed Rufus down the steps. In the kitchen, when she left the pan, Podjo was pouring bourbon over ice cubes in a glass.

"Sure," he said, "I'll listen for him. Quit your fretting; he's my meal ticket too. Just see you bring me that jumbo brown."

He meant a large-sized barbecue sandwich made from the crisper outside meat; for they were going to K's, over on Crump, and that was the special, jumbo browns. On the way there, Rufus recovered his high spirits, patting the steering wheel in approximate time with Connie Francis singing "Black Orchid" on the radio. The sun had gone down beyond the river, and up ahead, when they turned east, the new moon had risen somewhere out beyond the suburbs. Thin as a sickle, it seemed to gather unto itself what little light remained of the long day.

Inside the restaurant, glare from the overhead fixtures glistened on formica-topped tables. Rufus chose one toward the rear, removed from the rush-hour bustle up front, and began to study the menu, which bore on its cover a large black K.

"The proprietor's a character from Kafka," he told Reeny.

"Where is that?"

"It's not a where, it's a him; Kafka's a writer, German or Czech or something, from back before the war."

He seemed amused by this exchange, and hummed a few bars of "Black Orchid" until the waitress arrived to take their order. Middle-aged and harried, she had brass-colored hair and purple nails. Rufus looked up at her brightly, showing his teeth. "Congratulate us, miss," he said. "We just adopted ourselves a little boy. A dark one, cute as a button. My wife is just crazy about him. So am I. He's sleeping now though, and we stole away for some light refreshment. What do you recommend?"

Reeny was frightened to hear him talk that way, frightened to think what Podjo might do if he was there to hear him; except of course, she told herself, Rufus wouldnt have said it at all if Podjo had been there. He gave the order — two barbeque plates, with cole slaw and french fries — and also requested a jumbo brown "to go." He grinned. "It's for the boy," he explained. "He gets hungry up there all alone."

"And a bacon-and-tomato sandwich," Reeny broke in. "Also to go. And a carton of milk."

When the waitress had left, she said earnestly in a low voice: "You ought not do that, Rufus. You scare me with that talk about what we're up to, hints and such. Podjo'd go right through the roof."

"What the hell." He scowled, ignoring the reference to Podjo. "What fun is anything if you dont have fun *doing* it?"

"I dont know, but I think we ought to get this done first — what we came up here to do. Then have fun later, back home or wherever, after it's over."

"Later," he scoffed. "Horse piss. Sometimes later never comes."

On their way back, the moon rode high and bright behind them, then off to the right, a glistening sickle above and beyond the glow of the city. Reeny sat with the bagged sandwiches warm in her lap, the milk carton cold in one hand. When Rufus clicked on the radio Johnny Mathis was just ending "It's Not for Me to Say." Then Connie Francis came on again, this time singing "Eighteen." Rufus clicked her off in midnote. "Eighteen, hell," he said scornfully. "What she needs is a good banging."

He was in a strange mood, at once positive and unstrung. Parked beside the driveway mulberry screen, he said as he reached out to cut the ignition, "Let's get in the back seat."

"I have to get these in," Reeny said. She had one hand on the door latch, about to press down, and the other on the sandwiches. "While theyre warm," she explained.

"Come on, Reen," he told her. "Take your pants off. Cock yourself up on the seat there. It wont take long. The sandwiches wont get cold. I really want you."

She hesitated, hand on the latch but still not pressing down. For a moment she considered climbing back there — partly for Rufus's sake, the strangely urgent, assertive mood he was in, and partly for her own; she wanted it, too. But then she put the thought aside. "No, Rufe, we really have to get them in. You know what barbeque's like when it's cold."

"O.K." He said it casually, though there was nothing casual under the surface of the way he said it. "I just took a notion and I thought you might have taken one, too."

"I did — I do. But I think we ought to get these in, first."

"O.K." he said again, lightly, with a shrug of disinterest and dismissal. He got out at the same time she did, and even moved ahead of her up the steps in time to hold the screen door ajar for her to enter with her warm-cold burden of sandwiches and milk.

For all his politeness, she could see that he was miffed. She could see too, despite the feigned indifference, that he was even more needful than he had let her know when he stopped the car in the driveway. He would soon renew his suit, resume his plea, his pitch; she knew that, too. And sure enough, after Podjo started in on his jumbo brown, washing it down with a thinner bourbon-and-water, and she climbed the steps to the attic with Teddy's sandwich and milk, waiting for him to stir before she waked him all the way to eat his supper, Rufus came up and sat beside her on the spare cot where she would spend tonight, along with all the other nights the boy was here.

"Reen," he said, speaking low to keep from disturbing the sleeper on the other cot, just over a yard away, "I dont like you being up here and me down there. I want you where *I* am, where I can reach out when the time comes, day or night."

Then she saw what it was. Rufus's reaction to the new arrangement, now that Teddy was here, resembled that of a young husband to the introduction of a child into the household. He was jealous, petulant at the inattention, not to mention resentful of having been put to running errands, up and down the steps, for such things as Kleenex and soap, washrags and hot and cold water. She almost smiled, even as she felt a rush of affection for him in his new role as suitor and neophyte husband. He hadnt stopped talking, for fear she would interrupt him.

"Day or night — whenever I get the urge. In fact," he declared, remembering to keep his voice down, "Ive got it now, the urge, something awful. This thing today has got me all wrought-up. I want you now, tonight; I really do, Reen, real bad. Cant Podjo take the night shift? He sleeps alone anyhow."

"Teddy's scared of him. Because of the mustache, I think. He'd wake in the night and there Podjo would be, with that mustache cross his face."

"Maybe we can persuade him to shave it off."

"Rufus, you know better than that," she said, and again she had trouble keeping from smiling. "You told me yourself, it's part of his poker game. He uses it to hide behind when the cards go round."

"Yair," he admitted reluctantly.

He let that notion go, along with logic, and hurried ahead on a different tack. "But couldnt you sort of take the duty turnsabout? Podjo tonight and you tomorrow maybe? I really want it, Reen, I really do. Want it and need it, Reen; I mean really." She noted the shift from *you* to *it*, and almost laughed aloud, partly from pleasure at being carried back to her girlhood, when so many of her suitors acted much the way Rufus was acting tonight, alternately importunate and gruff, and sometimes both at once. He hadnt stopped talking all this time. "I want it now," he told her, "or anyhow tonight. This thing's got me all wrought-up or something, Reen. I'm half coming already, I'm so wrought-up. That's a fact." He paused at last.

"I want it, too," she said earnestly, looking directly into his pale blue eyes, arched over by the breaking wave of yellow hair, which had come unsprung. "You know I do. When didnt I, ever? But we made the arrangement this way from the start, back in Bristol, and we'd better stick to it. We'll have chances, off and on, out back or somewhere, maybe right here in the house from time to time. And anyhow, all this wont last more than a week at the most."

"A week? Sweet Jesus!" Rufus fairly shouted, slapping his knees in his distress. "What do you think I'm made of?"

Teddy sat bolt upright on his cot, translated from sleep to sudden wakefulness by the force of Rufus's protest. He did not seem alarmed, however, and his eyes, though still a little vague in focus, were no longer glazed. "I want to go home," he said, shifting his attention from the cardboard-shaded light to the two people seated facing him on the cot beside his own.

"You *are* home. For now," Reeny told him. "And look. I brought you your supper, a nice sandwich and some milk. Are you hungry?"

"I want to go home," he said.

"You *are* home," she said again, "until you get back to your old one. Your mamma and daddy want us to look after you till the time is up and they send for you. Maybe tomorrow or the next day; sometime soon. We're right here with you, and we'll be here all the time. You want your supper?"

"I have to go to the bathroom."

"Of course you do. Here," she said, and took from under his cot an empty two-pound coffee can she had brought up from the kitchen to use as a slopjar, complete with a snap-on plastic lid. "This is for when you need to teetee. Can you manage?"

He looked puzzled, and she saw what the trouble was. "Isnt that what you call it? To make water?"

"Peepee," he said.

"Oh." This gave her pause. "Well, I guess that's just as good. Anyhow that's what the can is for, in case you need it. I'll take you downstairs to the toilet for the other. Just let me know."

She snapped the lid off the can to pass it to him, saying to Rufus as she did so: "This will take a while, along with giving him supper and getting him tucked back in and back to sleep. You go on down and work on your letter or talk with Joe. I'll come down, soon as I can, and we'll go out back or something. I want to, much as you do, Brother. It wont be long."

Brother: she remembered to call me Brother, he thought as he came down the steps, and I forgot not to call her Reen. But that's all right; the kid was asleep all through it. I wont do it any more.

"Reeny's tending the kid," he told Podjo — Joe — who was on his couch in the living room, nursing a third Old Crow and watching Robin Hood. "I'm going to wind up the letter to put in the mail tomorrow."

Podjo replied with a wave of his glass and Rufus went back to the kitchen and sat on a tall stool at the counter to escape the television racket while he worked. He had already done several drafts of the letter, which included additional warnings about the necessity for secrecy, as well as a listing of the particulars of the ransom money pending notification as to the time and place of the payoff. All that remained was to put it in final form for mailing, and even under the strain of having to wait for Reeny to finish her attic ministrations before she could come down and join him, as she had promised, he worked hard and well; or so at least he told himself, with considerable pride in certain effects he managed to bring off.

He wound it up, both pages, and even addressed the envelope — *Eben Kinship, 279 Vance Avenue, City* — before he heard anything from Reeny. His watch was pushing nine-thirty by now. God damn, God damn, what's *keeping* her? he wondered, beginning to fantasize on what would happen once they reached what she had called "out back."

In point of fact, she had just finished giving Teddy his night-time dose of Noctec ("I dont like it," he said, looking down at the spoon brim full of the pink, bitterish liquid; "I dont." "Youll like it better as time goes on," Reeny told him. "It's what will keep you healthy. So here now. Bottoms up") and was sitting beside him waiting for it to take effect: as, indeed, it had already begun to do. Within a few minutes he seemed to be sleeping soundly under his patchwork quilt.

She waited a short time longer, then came down. From the foot of the steps, through the kitchen doorway, she saw Rufus pacing up and down like something caged. "I'll be right back," she told him from the hall, and went up front where the television was booming. It was some kind of cowboy picture, the dusty street of a frontier town, and a shoot-out was in progress.

"Going out back!" she shouted at Podjo on his velvet couch.

"What?" He cupped his ear in her direction, not taking his eyes off the flickering violence on the screen.

"Out back! We're going out back to look at the river and the bridge lights! Listen for Teddy; we wont be long!"

Podjo gave a brief salute with the dregs of his drink, much like the one he had given an hour ago, when Robin Hood was on and the glass was full. She turned rearward, but stopped by the bathroom on her way to the kitchen.

"Dammit, Reeny, dammit," she heard Rufus say about two minutes later, as he rapped at the latched door.

"Coming," she told him. But while she was hanging her pants on the towel rack above the tub and pulling her skirt down from where she had hitched it round her waist, the rapping continued, steady as drumming, light but insistent. "I'm coming, coming. Hold your horses," she called through the tattoo of knuckles against the plywood panel.

"Jesus, Reeny, I'm fit to be tied," Rufus said when she emerged at last. He took her by the wrist, there in the narrow, step-filled hallway, and led her through the kitchen, across the porch, down the stoop, and across the slippery backyard grass out toward the bluff, stumbling a bit in his haste, with Reeny in tow, and causing her to stumble too.

Just to the south, about on the property line of the adjoining house, the drop-off was gentler for a short distance below the lip of the ninety-foot bluff, leading down to a brush-choked gully or ravine. He had spotted the place some days ago, and now he led her in that direction, over the rim, and settled her there, snug on her back with her head uphill. While the bridge lights swooped westward over the river, red and green and amber, rocketlike in their rush toward Arkansas, he crouched over and then on her, undoing her blouse to mouth her breasts, and made little mewling sounds as he tugged and tugged at the nipples with his lips and teeth. "Oo, hurry, hurry," Reeny murmured, excited by his excitement, and Rufus slid downhill a bit, flung her skirt up around her waist, and put his face between her thighs. By then the mewling had changed to a whimper and now it became a whinny, high up the scale. Almost at once she began to repeat what she had said while he knocked at the bathroom door a couple of minutes ago, except that it was a good deal intenser now and proceeded not from exasperation but rather from delight. "I'm coming. Coming!" she cried. So was Rufus, and presently did again, along with Reeny, who followed through with still a third paroxysm — "Wait! Oo, wait," she told him, quieter now but somehow even more fervent than before — while he was coasting. He had indeed been wrought-up, and so had she, as it turned out, by the events of this long last day of summer.

They remained a while in that grassy notch, gazing out at the bridge lights and up at the high thin gilded paring of new moon. Reeny's bones felt limber to her and her breasts lay nearly flat. "Holy Mother," Rufus said at last, face-down alongside her, one arm thrown across her moonlit belly just below her upturned skirt. His tone was that of a man emerged from a rigorous ordeal, still a little winded but delivered, fully dressed and in his right mind again. Presently they rose, smoothed their clothes and hair when they regained the lip of the bluff, then walked back across the yard and into the house.

Podjo was on his couch, though he clearly had not stayed there all the time they were gone, for a new, darker-brown drink was in his glass and the television volume had been lowered. The shoot-out was over, the bodies cleared away, and the ten oclock news was on. "Watch this," he said when Rufus and Reeny entered. Faubus was on the screen, still at Sea Island, wearing an I-told-you-so expression but frowning to mask his satisfaction. "The trouble in Little Rock vindicates my good judgment," he declared.

"Looks kind of prissy, dont he?" Reeny said.

"Take it easy. He's on our side," Rufus told her.

All three watched — Podjo intently, Rufus intermittently, and Reeny with a yawn from time to time — as reruns began of this morning's violence, much of which they had seen before they set out for Leath School in the early afternoon; angry faces, flailing arms, the wrecking of the barricades, sudden flurries of group activity which the camera could not follow, such as the pummeling of newsmen of both races. Then the nine intruders were withdrawn and the crowd's howls turned to hoots of celebration, a celebration still in progress over there, less frantic, perhaps less joyous, but on a larger scale; larger, the announcer said, because carloads of new arrivers had been added to the mass and more were expected all through the night, attracted from miles and miles around by the news of what had happened today and seemed likely to happen tomorrow if the integrationists — "mixers," they were called — tried again what they had tried this morning.

So much was fairly clear. Yet it was hard to tell from the announcer's voice and manner whether he was apprehensive or hopeful, whether he feared or welcomed the continuance he foretold. Podjo's view, while not altogether coherent because of all the whiskey he had drunk, was that what the fellow was issuing was not so much a warning, an alert, as it was an invitation, an appeal for various yahoos roundabout to come and get in on the fun.

# 4

# *Voices*

I slept upstairs on the cot alongside Teddy's. Rufus didnt mind; not any longer *that* night anyhow. And though I'm a poor sleeper most nights when it comes to dropping off, it wasnt that way this night by a long shot. That business out under the lip of the bluff had turned my bones all limber — something like what someone told me once about a way around insomnia. You imagine youre a rag doll stuffed with sawdust; Raggedy Ann. You imagine the tips of your fingers and toes are slowly leaking sawdust, and you lie there, leaking, leaking, getting flatter and flatter, more and more relaxed, until finally, by the time youre close to level with the mattress, youre asleep. That was how it was with me that first night in the attic, only faster, even on that drum-tight canvas cot. Earlier, below, my eyes were drooping shut before the man on the news finished telling how things had popped across the way in Little Rock. I went up and bedded down and slept right through, and Teddy too; we both did, all night long, he from his Noctec and me from my trip out to the bluff and back, when Rufus drained my bones.

Next morning when I woke he was still sleeping under his patchwork quilt, so I went down to fix myself some coffee and him a bowl of cornflakes to wake up to. Rufus was square in the middle of the double bed, out from under the covers in his drawers but still asleep, hair tousled, mouth ajar, arms and legs bent like a swastika at the knees and elbows, all in the same direction. Up front, Podjo had the television going, and I could hear the man running on about Little Rock and Central High. Today it was mainly a celebration; the Negro children werent there.

I put water on to boil, and while it did I filled a cereal bowl with cornflakes, sprinkled them good with sugar and doused them with Pet, then mixed the coffee, sugar-and-creamed it too, and went back up. Teddy was stirring a little by then, so I poured the spoonful of Noctec, gave him a nudge, and got it down him just as he sat up. I doubt he even tasted it, woozy as he was, because by the time he really woke I already had him going on the cornflakes, spooning them down him like feeding a gape-mouthed bird.

"How you feeling, roommate?"

"Mm," he said, mouth full of cornflakes.

He was hungry; thirsty, too. I let him have my coffee, which I guess was a special treat for him, the way it was for me when I was his age, weakened down with milk and lots of sugar. By the time he finished he was drowsy again from the Noctec. I tucked him in and came back down the steps to fix myself another cup of coffee.

"Come on up here, Reen!" Rufus called from the living room. "Something I want you to hear before I go."

He was up and dressed, hair combed and everything; a fast riser. What he wanted was to read us — Podjo and me; Rufus had turned the TV volume down to silence — the letter he wrote the night before, while waiting for me to come down from the attic. He cleared his throat, like a preacher or politician, and started reading as soon as I walked in with the cup of coffee steaming in my hand. First came the particulars of the payoff, so many bills of such-and-such value, unmarked and not in sequence; how they would fit in a shoebox and how the Kinships, once they had the money ready, were to stand by for the phone call that would tell them when to deliver it, and where. He read that first page sort of crisp-like, radio style, biting the words, but when he reached the second page he began to breathe them like an actor, or anyhow his notion of an actor.

"Get this now. 'A word about the cops, Memphis or FBI, in case they find out from you or anyone else what's up, whether by accident or on purpose. They dont give a damn about your boy. They want us. They dont care for a split minute what happens to some little nigger, if losing *him* can get them *us* — a feather in their cap. Bear that in mind. Remember, you have as much if not more to fear from them as we do.' That's putting it to them, aint it?"

"Tough stuff," Podjo said. He seemed to want to get back to his program, some kind of game show with a bell and the contestants running around the screen in silence, like an old-time movie.

"Right," Rufus said. He waited for me to take my first sip of the cooling coffee, then went on. "But listen what comes next, the windup. 'One more thing. We dont want to kill the child, so as not to have a murder rap added to the charge in case of a slip-up. But we will most certainly kill him if it's a case of skedaddling without a payoff. Put yourself in our position. Why should we leave a witness, even an eight-year-old one, if you have not lived up to your end of the deal? Whereas if you pay us we owe you his life.' End. No signature."

For a good few seconds he stood there waiting for us to clap or something. I sipped my coffee.

"Well," Podjo said. He paused, thinking, then went on. "That ought to do it — if it dont overdo it."

"No, no," Rufus told him. "You dont get the drift. I tried for a balance; something that would scare and reassure them, both at once. What it says is, if they do right theyll get their boy back. If not, they wont. Theyll see that. Dont you?"

I didnt know about Podjo but it seemed to me if I was Teddy's mother I'd go running out in the street, hair on end, and yell for help from anyone around, cops or whatnot. Podjo by then was off the couch and crossing to the television. "O.K."

he said. "Go on and mail it. We'll figure some way to ease the shock before it gets there."

The sound came up and the bell rang and the people jumped and cheered for a won game. Rufus scowled. He'd been expecting praise, and instead what he got was criticised. Not by me though; I hadnt said a word. "All right," he said, and left.

By the time he got back from the post office I had rinsed out some things in the bathroom sink, including Teddy's one pair of socks, and gotten up the week's wash for the laundry, which I should have done the day before — a Monday, but not *that* Monday; Jesus, no. Up front, the TV was droning on, and sometimes the radio in the bedroom; Podjo switched from one to the other, chasing down news of the Little Rock hooraw still going on across the river. I tried not to listen, and mostly succeded, though some of it came through. When Rufus got back I left him on lookout while I rode over to Crump to leave and pick up the laundry, this week's and last, and on the way back stopped at the Chinaman's, up on the corner, to load up on cereal and canned goods — mostly soup — eggs and milk, and half a dozen funny-books to help Teddy pass what time he wasnt sleeping, if in fact such a time ever came. So far it hadnt, but I figured it wasnt reasonable to expect he'd keep on snoozing round the clock, Noctec or no Noctec.

Sure enough, he wasnt sleeping when I got back a little before noon. Rufus was up there with him, talking, talking, telling him some kind of story he made up, more for his own entertainment than for Teddy's; I could tell. He just got lonesome and Podjo was all wrapped up in the news.

I sent him downstairs and had him draw the bathroom shade and close both hallway doors, so Teddy couldnt look out and see where he was when I took him down for his bath. He liked it, the warm deep water, what time he wasnt shy, and soaped up all by himself until I rinsed and rubbed him dry and gave him one of Rufus's clean tee shirts to wear for a nightgown while his drawers and undershirt dried from the washing I gave them while he bathed. Poor little thing, with his tiny blue-black pecker — circumcised, too; I didnt know they circumcised them. The wooly skullcap he wore for hair was all but waterproof, and the whites of his eyes were the whitest white I ever saw, partly I guess because of the dark around them, but mainly I think because I never looked that close at one of them before.

I took him back up to the attic and tucked him in. He was good as good, and I said so when I came downstairs after he got drowsy and fell asleep.

"He's a brave little boy," I told Rufus, who was eating a candy-bar lunch on the back porch, washing it down with a glass of Teddy's milk. He sort of grinned a halfway smile to show he doubted it was true. "Well, he is," I said. "He takes all this real well. All that talk I heard all my life about niggers being cowards, no good in the clutch and all, is a bunch of blah. Maybe it's true, once we get them broken in to suit us, but it's not true where Teddy's concerned, beforehand. He's a brave little boy."

"Just what did you expect him to do?" Rufus said.

It made me mad, to have him say that; grinning, too. It took away the credit. "I dont know," I said, "but I know what *youd* do, Rufus Hutton. Bawl your head off."

I didnt all-the-way mean it, even though I knew it was true, but it made me mad to have him grin and talk like that, when I knew better from all I'd seen ever since we picked the little thing up on Linden the day before, like a sack of flour or something, and whisked him off.

"You sure are getting protective, Reen baby," Rufus said, still grinning, munching on his Baby Ruth and sipping Teddy's milk. "Maternal, too."

I let it go; just went in the kitchen and fixed and ate a peanut-butter sandwich while warming up a can of beef-with-vegetable soup for Teddy, then climbed back up to the attic to cool off. I cant stand spats.

Cool off was a manner of speaking; it was getting hot up there. I'd heard the radio say between bulletins that the ther-

mometer was up into the eighties. So while Teddy ate his soup
I got the fan going, swooshing and swooshing from side to side,
side to side, and when he finished I gave him his second Noctec,
tucked him in with just the top sheet for cover, and lay down
on the other cot to wait for him to fall asleep. Sure enough he
soon drifted off, but I still didnt go downstairs. It was nice up
there in the brown gloom, with the fan breeze coming and
going sideways, left to right, right to left, and the radio down
below was no more than a murmur except when the Little
Rock announcer got excited over something he saw happening
round the schoolyard, a fist fight or a shoving match or something.

The radio went on about it all day long, between Top Forty
songs and ads. On the TV it was sandwiched between game
shows and soap operas, but not so it would interfere with the
commercials, which mainly had to do with underarms and
bowels, hair and headaches, bad breath and congestion, and
every now and then a fire sale or a warehouse clearance. Sometimes it seemed they were doing things over there in Arkansas
— the rioters, I mean — just so they could sell things over
here in Tennessee. Even the President up in Rhode Island
seemed to be in on it somehow, squeezed as he was between
pitches for remedies, bargains, and soap. To keep from looking,
which was hard, I'd stopped going into the living room at all.
Hearing, though, was something else, even up in the attic. We
ought to have flaps for our ears, to keep the sound out, the
way we have lids for our eyes to keep out light.

Maybe it was that brown gloom, Teddy asleep in his knee-
length tee shirt under the sheet, the stillness except for the
radio down below, like voices in an adjoining motel room when
you cant quite make out the words. Anyhow, something got
me to thinking; all the way back.

My father — Billy Jimson, before everyone started calling
him Brother Jimson — was originally a roaming ginner, a
rounder in his early days, including a spell at Parchman for his
share in a roadhouse shoot-out. That was where he later claimed

he got the Call, though he didnt act on it till he met my mother
at a revival on Lake Jordan, south of Bristol. I think what he
was was crazy for women after she died; it was his way of
grieving, paying respect. He had always been religious between
sprees, giving testimony at services and all that, but now he
took to the pulpit, when he could find one, and to women after
hours. He'd preach to them, a big rough-shod man with clumsy
rough-shod ways, and then he'd ride them down. It all tied
in — lust and the Lord. I used to watch him up there, straddle-
legged, flailing his arms around, and watch the women, too.
They knew what was going on, but they didnt mind sharing
him any more than they minded sharing rain and sunlight. Lust
and the Lord — he saw it that way, gave over to it, and he was
right; the Lord won out. By the time I started school, still down
on Lake Jordan, the Lord had drawn him to Him. He was
Brother Jimson now, a full-fledged preacher, with or without
a church of his own, except at the height of the ginning season,
when he made enough to live on, preaching free, for the rest
of the farming year.

Sin — the need for sin — had led him to salvation. Yet he
couldnt abide it when my turn came round, no matter what it
might be leading to, including salvation. I had to be my mother,
born of her dying, and God had designed it that way from the
start.

So he thought; or so I think he thought, and here is why.
I found out later — a good while later, just on the verge of my
teens, from the back of the Bible — my name wasnt Reeny, or
at least it wasnt spelled or pronounced that way. It's French;
Renée, with a little upslanted kicker over the ee before the last
one; Ren*nay*, they call it. And it wasnt until still later, one day
in the dictionary, that I found out what it meant. Not that a
name has to *mean* anything, just that this one does. It means
reborn; born again, as they say in church. But I dont think it
was religious in that sense. I think he meant me to be my
mother, brought back, born again out of her dying womb.
Naming me that, if I'm right — and I may not be; he never

said so — was part of his grieving, like all those women he ran after till he stopped, and another part of it came later, up in my teens, sprouting breasts and widening out in the hips, when I turned out to be nothing like her, either in looks or anything else. That grieved him, too, and his reaction took the form of being strict on me, long after the time for it was past, in hopes he could make me like her after all.

He gave up, though, when he saw it wouldnt work. I was a good deal more like *him*, he saw at last; especially when, like him when he was my age, I took off.

The way I did it was I married Len Perdew, home from boot camp in the spring of '42. We'd been sweethearts all through school till he joined the Marines, right after Pearl Harbor, and I went back with him to live in a trailer at Camp Lejeune till he shipped out, two months later. It was fun, except for a pump-up gasoline stove I kept thinking was going to explode; I think maybe that's what turned me against cooking all the balance of my life. Len was a corporal by the time they left for the Pacific, and all that time we'd spent together was like a glowy mist, lit from within, until early September, just before my twentieth birthday — I had stayed in North Carolina, waiting tables in an all-night restaurant — when I got the telegram saying he was dead, killed in action on Guadalcanal.

It wasnt a canal. They just called it that. It was a jungle and I started having jungle dreams, with Japs for monkeys in funny-looking shoes, swinging knives and talking monkey talk. What scared me most, though, was I began forgetting what he looked like. Len Perdew, corporal, USMC, killed in action, Guadalcanal; faceless, as if theyd cut or shot his face off with their knives or guns. They buried him out there, what was left of him, and I came home to Mississippi.

Then I met Hippo Morgan, some kind of salesman passing through Bristol the following April; sort of on the rebound I suppose. I didnt know why they called him that — he wasnt even fat — until later, on the marriage license, I saw his name was Hippolite, the word for marshmallow goo. Morgan wasnt his last name, either; it was something unpronounceable from up above St Louis, maybe Polish. He was the downright best-looking man I ever saw, always combing back his coal-black hair and smoothing down his eyebrows, coal-black too. Youd never guess he was 4-F, the way he was set up, but he was; something about his kidneys or spleen, one of those inward things. Outside he was something else, except in one regard. He was like those Greek or Italian statues you see pictures of in books, with great huge muscles and a teeny tiny penis. And, oo, he was mean; I mean *mean*. He used to curse me all the time we were making love, if you could call it that. "Come on, bitch. Git it up there, git it up there, damn your eyes."

I liked him a lot at first, till I learned he really meant it. He started beating on me, out for blood, and spending my money. By the time I knew it, he had been through Len's insurance and was scrabbling round for more, without much luck. We were in Dallas by then and he left me, Oldsmobile convertible and all, probably for some other woman though I never really knew. I was twenty-two, almost twenty-three, and broke, and he didnt even say he was leaving. He just left.

Art Kinsella showed up then from down in Waco. He was Irish but looked Jewish, with a Spanish-sounding name. I had met him before, out nights with Hippo in clubs and such, and he generally had a good-looking girl along. We got to talking.

"What are you going to do?"

I said I didnt know; "go home I guess."

"Dont do that."

So we started going together. He paid the rent and bought me things and got me the divorce. I took Len's name back to blot out Hippo; a sort of way of telling him I was sorry, out there in his grave in the Pacific. Then Art and I got married.

He was short and fat, roly-poly, close to forty, in horn-rim glasses, yoked shirts, high-heel boots, and whipcord trousers; a one-time Hudson dealer with a used-car business on the side. Those were the high-rolling years right after the war. Money was fluttering down all over Texas and he couldnt do enough for me while it lasted, including fancy restaurants. Vichyssoise turned out to be potato soup, and cold at that.

Most of it, though, I liked, and I liked Art, mainly because he had a kind of *happiness* about him that was good to be around, even when things were coming all apart. "Everything's going to be all right," he used to tell me; "the radio said so."

Two years, three, coming up on four; then things turned downward. Deals got harder and harder to swing, especially sizeable ones, and he began asking me to help him on a few.

"This fellow's been watching you, Reeny."

"I know."

"He likes you, Reen."

"I know. It's all right. I like him too."

That was the first, a Waco lumber dealer close to sixty. Others followed, to swing deals, promote relationships, and sometimes just to get living-money; grocery bills, rent, vacation expenses, things like that. It wasnt near as bad as it sounds to some people. In the first place, I only had six or eight months of it really full-time, so to speak, and in the second there were only about thirty or forty of them, all told, and never more than one a night except once when there were two at the same time, oil men in from the field and out on a rip. Lots of them were just nothing, or close to nothing. You hardly knew they had been there, once it was over and they were gone or you were. Others, though — no more than a few, say half a dozen, including the ex-show-girl wife of a Fort Worth banker — were something else. They could really let you know what it was all about, and did. I learned a lot from them I never could have gotten any other way. As a profession it's got its points, provided you dont stay in it so long you stop learning and start enduring.

Art was a big help through all of it, thick and thin; it turned out he'd been in this line before. Then in '52 he died of a heart attack, the one truly good-hearted man I ever knew. Those five-plus years with him, after the one with Hippo Morgan, were the best consecutive five that came my way.

Best of all, though, roly-poly Art with his horn-rim glasses and cowboy clothes, his hard-times cheerfulness round the clock, helped to wipe out Len Perdew for what he wasnt. I saw that now for what it was, a boy-girl thing overblown in my mind because he wound up dead. If he'd come back from the Pacific we'd likely have turned into any two people. What made him special was dying before he was twenty-two, with our whole life before us. That way, I could turn it into anything I wanted, depending on what I wanted at any given time. It not only wasnt true, it was nothing fit to live by, asking everything that came along to measure up to something that never could have existed in the first place. One thing I found out about life is it will undo you if it gets half a chance, and mostly it doesnt need that much if you get in the habit of looking at it as something it isnt; such as staying forever twenty and living in a trailer with a pump-up stove on money from the Marines.

So this time too I took Len's name back, but more for the sound of it — Perdew — than for sentimental reasons. I knew well enough I was on my own. I was crowding thirty and it hadnt been much of a life up to now; just three men I tied onto, or who tied onto me. Two of them let me down by dying, the first and third, and the other I'd rather not mention, he was so mean. But what else was there? I couldnt type or go into nursing or clerk at the five-and-dime. All there was for me was men, and I kept trying.

I didnt do too well just then. First in Dallas, then back in Bristol, I spent a good part of two years each on men — businessmen, and middle-aged at that — who claimed they were waiting for divorces, though neither was. I got nothing from the Texan, not even train-fare home, and all I got from the Mississippian was a second-hand Ford, my worldly goods. I decided I'd better take it day by day, not get tied up, and trust to fortune. Around that time, Grace Kelly got to be a princess without putting anything down, or very little. But she had folks and money to take her wherever she wanted to go, and where was I going to find myself a prince?

At Bull Eye's, that's where; Rufus. He was there with some

poor little done-up thing in a too-tight sweater, lanky hair and a ballerina skirt. I saw he wanted what I wanted; it passed between us, across the space between tables, and I egged my date into going home alone, then left with Rufus and the girl till he dropped her off and we went out to the Shady Rest. That began it — no more than a notion I took, a pastime thing, like patting your foot while waiting for something to happen. So I thought, but he surprised me. Partly it was his *need*; he trembled with it, and partly it was his youth; he was the first really young one I'd been with since Len at Camp Lejeune, when I was as young as Len and didnt even know what I was getting, let alone giving. He told me he was thirty, but only to make me feel better about us; I didnt believe him and I didnt care, even when it occurred to me that by the time he really was thirty I'd be pushing forty.

*Forty*. That came as a shock, but I didnt care. I liked waiting for him to come off shift at Gypsum and all that. Getting it three-four times a day from the same person, day after day and night after night; that draws you, makes its claim. Then, lo, he came up with the Kinship thing in Memphis, and I was hooked. Not only getting my bones drained, liking it better all the time, but also a chance at something real — the money, of course, which would bring us lots of things, once we had it, and above all the notion of crime. I'd been on the rim of it from time to time, with Hippo and Art, but now I'd be crossing the rim, into the center. It's more exciting than you might think, and being scared is part of it; a lift.

So we came up, the three of us, and it went fine at first. The bluff, the river, the bridges, the house to ourselves; I always did like Memphis, except on Sunday when everything closes down. Then Rufus started getting edgy, more-so as the time drew nigh, and made me edgy, too — including bed; he couldnt get outside himself, it seemed. Then the snatch went down, and after that first flurry of excitement, Teddy in his clown-white mask and Podjo nudging at Rufus, tearing him down while propping him up, he began sort of unraveling at the seams. I watched it happen. Even out under the lip of the bluff that night, it wasnt so much *me* he was after as it was himself, something inside him that wanted out but couldnt make it. He turned resentful. He turned sarcastic. "What did you *expect* him to do?" he said next day, and though I got angry I saw well enough what was looming; I'd been down that road before, too many times.

Oh-oh, I told myself. Here's another one going sour on me. It's coming round again. He wouldnt know what to do with love if someone gave it to him. All he knows is he cant live without it.

I guess it was that snug brown gloom, the fan turning, turning — breeze then no-breeze, breeze then no-breeze, over and over — Teddy asleep on the other cot, the radio droning, droning down below. Anyhow I drifted off, and by the time Rufus woke me, climbing the attic steps, I could tell by the light coming golden through the louvers that the sun was going down.

"Hey, Sis," he said when his head came through the opening, about on a level with my own. "You want to go see the Lone Ranger?"

Lone Ranger? It didnt make sense. "What Lone Ranger?"

"The fair," he said. "Let's catch it tonight. Come on."

Then I was awake, or almost. Lone Ranger; the Mid-South Fair. "Not tonight. Ive got — "

"Yes. Tonight," he said. "Joe's got a fight he wants to listen to on the radio; Sugar Ray. He'll watch out for the kid. We wont be late."

I saw I couldnt any more argue with him tonight than I could the night before, when he had a different bee in his bonnet, a different kind of jimjams. So I gave over. "All right. I'll have to fix him some supper first, though" — meaning Teddy.

"Sure. O.K. Do it. Then we'll take off."

So I did; chicken noodle soup and crackers, a glass of milk, and the other half of the can for Podjo, down below. While

Teddy ate I put the new funny-books on the floor between the cots, within reach. "In case you want them theyre right there," I told him. "I wont be long. Anything you want, ask Joe. I wont be long."

"Yessum," he said, already groggy from the warm soup in his stomach, and we took off, Rufus and I, leaving Podjo hunched by the radio in the bedroom where he could listen for Teddy at the same time he heard Sugar Ray Robinson and Carmine Basilio slam away at each other at Yankee Stadium in New York.

We didnt stay long; I was worried about Teddy. After two rides, the ferris wheel and the pippin, a walk through the cow barn, two pronto pups, and some time in the shooting gallery — he was good at it; won a stuffed bear two feet tall — I persuaded him not to wait for the Lone Ranger rodeo. We headed back for the bluff, Rufus talking all the way, happy about how well he'd shot and rattling on about the Marine Corps, where he learned it. I didnt mention Len or Camp Lejeune; I never had, to him.

I was remembering Miss America night, more than two weeks ago, and Podjo, the way he was. Rufus, poor Rufus, he was flopping around like a fish that night. I landed him easy; brought him in just right, like on a reel. "Sweet Jesus," he said — as if to me. I'll say one thing; it's great to be appreciated. But the fact was he almost always said something religious at such times; "Sweet Jesus," "Holy Mother," and once all four Gospels in a row; "Matthew, Mark, Luke, and *John*." Then generally he slept, the way he did that night while all those Miss Americas paraded their twats around the stage in Atlantic City. I went out and put the bee on Podjo, more or less for lack of something else to do, and sure enough he didnt know whether to look front or rear, at me or Miss America parading, and I just let him hang there, biding my time. My girl won. Then next evening, a Sunday out on the bluff with the moon coming up full and bullbats flying, I watched him while I told about coming out of a cake, all that foolishness, and saw the way his mustache darkened in the moonlight while I talked. He wasnt listening much, but he was watching and thinking; I could tell. I kept biding my time. I'd know it when it came, if it came, and so would he.

We got back around nine-thirty and found him angry about the fight. Sugar Ray had it won, he said, then lost by a split decision because of heat prostration near the end. I went up, gave Teddy his nighttime Noctec, put the stuffed bear by his cot for him to see when he woke up next morning, then came back down in time for the ten oclock news on television.

Mostly it had to do with Little Rock, the two-day hooraw over there. Eisenhower was sending in paratroopers; that was the big news. Then it went back to scenes from yesterday that showed the mob surging this way and that, tearing down sawhorse barricades around the schoolyard, milling and shouting, waving fists and cussing the niggers, and moved on to today — Tuesday — when all they did was sort of stroll around, feeling good about keeping the school from getting mixed. Then Eisenhower came on, sounding righteous about what he would or wouldnt put up with, and there were films of soldiers coming out of planes and loading onto trucks bound for Central High School, wearing jump-boots and steel helmets, all with the Screaming Eagle patch of the 101st Airborne tacked to the left shoulder of their battle jackets. They looked like they meant business; all-round tough.

"Paratroopers," Rufus said. "What does that change?"

"Nothing — for us," Podjo told him. "We've gotten all we want out of it by now. Whatever those troopers do tomorrow wont change what was done yesterday and today, before they got there. We stand pat and keep up the scare. One thing, though," he said. He turned to me. "I been thinking. Instead of sending still another note to the Kinships, we'll just stick to the one Rufus mailed this morning. But I want you to call them tomorrow, before the postman gets there. Talk to the wife; Martha's her name, and brace her for the shock, so she wont do anything crazy when she reads it, out of fear or some kind of hysterics. Tell her youre looking after the boy, taking good care of him, and he's in fine shape, looking forward to coming home. She'll like to hear that, especially from a woman, the woman who's looking after him. Tell her again that if she and her husband *do* right — do as theyre told about the money, that is, and keep out of touch with the cops — theyll get him back in good shape, good as new. Can you do that?"

I didnt much like it, the notion of talking with her after taking her boy the way I did, and Rufus liked it even less, hearing that his final note was canceled after all the planning he invested in it. Still, Podjo had the say-so in such matters; that was what Rufus brought him in on the job for, in the first place; it didnt make sense not to do what he said, right as he had been from start to present. So I said I would do it, or anyhow try.

"I'll try it," I said. "I'll do it if I can."

"You can do it," Podjo said.

"Sure you can," Rufus said. "I'll rehearse you."

One main trouble I had was he would call me in the night. I dont mean he would *call* me: I mean I would *hear* him call me. Mamma! Mamma! And I would come awake, jerked up out of sleep there in the dawn or moonlight. Mamma! Mamma! — real as real, but whether near or far I couldnt tell. "Here, here I am," I'd call back, and it would be Eben trying to comfort me. "Youre dreaming. You had a dream. Lay back down." And I'd say, "He needs me. I heard him need me." And he'd say, "Youre dreaming, Martha, dreaming. Lay back down." And I'd wake up all the way at last and it was true: I'd been dreaming. That didnt mean he wasnt calling me, wherever he was. It just meant I dreamed it, whether he was calling me or not, and I'd start

crying. Eben would tell me not to — "Dont cry. Dont" — but
I kept on, crying for myself as much as I was for Teddy, sick
with worry from my imagination, the things it kept telling me
he was, including hurt and needing help, or dead beyond all
help including mine. I saw him both ways, and one was about
as bad as the other because I couldnt reach him either way. I
couldnt any more help him, hurt, than I could help him dead.

That might not make much sense, but sense had next to
nothing to do with what I was feeling there in the dark, awake
or sleeping. Wait till someday they take *your* child. Youll see.

Reason — sense — is no help at all in easing a burden on your
heart. I know, because another thing I did was tell myself I'd
lost him: he was gone, and gone for good. That way, if it
turned out not to be true, I'd be all the happier when I got him
back, and if it turned out to be true that he was gone, and gone
for good, I'd already have the worst of my grief behind me.
So I thought, before I tried it. Then I tried, and it was too
sharp for me to bear. I couldnt even try it beyond the first
half minute: I shied back from it, fast as I could get it out of
my mind. But what was I going to do if it turned out to be
true in the end?

I asked myself that, and I didnt know. All I could do was
keep hoping and waiting. In other words, nothing. And that
was the hardest, that and the thought of what it was for. It
wasnt as if he was off to war or something, the way it sometimes is with sons and mothers. In the first place, he wasnt much
over one-third old enough to be a soldier, and anyhow they
have people looking out for them in war — officers and the
government and all, including doctors — while all Teddy had,
if he had anything, was the very ones who grabbed him. And
what kind of people could it be would do a thing like that?
Terrible people. Terrible, terrible people. I couldnt imagine
them in my dreams. They stayed faceless even in my night-
mares.

Eben let that govern his reaction. First off, soon as he knew
from the note that Teddy was taken, he'd been for getting in

touch with the police. Then the phone-call came and scared him out of it: that is, till he realized we were left with nothing to do but wait, and he veered back again. "How can you deal with people like that?" he said. "How can you trust them to do what they say, even after they get around to saying it?"

He went on about it to Daddy when Daddy got there a few minutes later, straight from the office as soon as Miss Lucy told him I had called. On second thought — or was it third? — Eben was for going to the police, because that was what the note and then the voice on the phone kept harping on as the one thing he mustnt do. "If it's what they are most afraid of," he told Daddy, "maybe it's what we most ought to use against them."

Daddy read through the note again, then looked back at Eben, level-eyed, and set him straight.

"I dont think so," he said, and told him why. "It's been a longtime rule of mine to stay clear of the law whenever and wherever the two colors are involved. You got to remember, the law is first of all the white man's law. He wrote it, he enforces it, and he sits in judgment on it. Ever once in a while he lets us borry it to use against each other in a pinch, but then he always takes it back for his own use and purpose. It's his, not ourn, and nothing but trouble can come of not facing up to the fact that that's the way it is."

"It ought not be."

"Ought-not's one thing. Be's another. What we want here is to get little Theo back."

"Teddy," Eben said.

"Well — whatever," Daddy said.

"You think *I* dont want him back?"

"I think what you want and what you get might turn out to be two different things, once you start messing with the law. The only thing we know about those people, so far, is theyre white."

Eben quieted down at that. He'd only acted ugly out of stubbornness, out of knowing he was in the wrong and not being willing to admit it, especially there in his own house, or anyhow the house he was paying rent on, even if it was to Daddy and with money that had been Daddy's in the first place. I sympathized with his distress, if not his judgment, which fairly made my blood run cold until I saw he didnt mean it. Having to choose between doing nothing and pretending to think about getting in touch with the police, he chose the police, but only by pretense. He knew he wouldnt, couldnt, even while he said it, and knowing he couldnt made him so distressed he even bristled up to Daddy — something I'd never seen or heard him do before, either here or at the office.

I breathed easier once it was past, and Mamma and Daddy went on home to wait and hear from us that we had heard from the people who had Teddy. "All we want is money," Eben said the phone voice said, and now it was up to us to wait and find out when, either by mail or over the phone again, the phone voice said.

Fixing supper, such as it was, helped calm me down at least a little. Eben missed his news: forgot it, brooding. But when I came back from putting Sister Baby to bed ("How long before Teddy will be home?" she asked me, lying beside the empty other half of the mattress after she said her prayers. I told her, "Soon. You go to sleep now. Soon") he had the television going, most likely to keep from looking at the picture of the children on the wall, alongside the one of him and me at the time of our wedding, the little round one of Mamma, and the big one of Daddy staring out from under his hat brim, large as life.

After a while, after some kind of western thing with cowboys shooting at each other down a dusty street, the news he missed earlier came on. First it was Governor Faubus, off on some island, saying he'd been right, and then it went over to Little Rock, the crowd yelling round the schoolyard, smashing things, and the nine young coloreds in their Sunday clothes, going in and coming out. I almost couldnt believe what I was seeing: couldnt understand, that is, how their mothers could put them through all that, knowing what would happen, what the whites were bound to do in turn. I felt about it, now that

I saw it there on the screen, something like the way we felt in the old days when a lynching came along. We tended to blame the one who got himself cut and burnt for doing what he'd done, not the whites, who after all were doing exactly what they said theyd do if he crossed the line. We held it against him, even while he hung there burnt and cut on, for proving to the whites that theyd been right all along in saying we were animals: not just the low-life killer or raper who got what he had known he'd get, but the rest of us as well — animals out of Africa. Faubus was a bad, sly man. Anyone could see that, right there in flickering black and white. But he sure had called the turn, and now the crowd in Little Rock had proved it with the help of all those mothers who sent their children to be cussed and spit at over there in Arkansas, just as Faubus had foretold.

"That's downright awful," I said: to myself, I thought, till I heard Eben answer.

"There's worse things, worse by far," he said.

I heard something in his voice, a catch, and when I turned sideways, away from the screen, I saw he was looking up at Teddy on the wall, eyes shining with tears that brimmed and brimmed, then overflowed to come rolling down his cheeks. Seeing him cry I cried too, not just to myself, the way he had been doing with me beside him unaware, but full-voiced, wailing. I let go. And it wasnt only for Teddy, I know now, or even Eben. It was also for those poor children across the river, abused and spit at because they tried to cross a line the crowd had drawn between them and the education their government had told them they could have. Things move in on your feelings before your mind knows they are there.

He got me quieted, some, and then we went on back. For the first time since Teddy was born, eight years and nearly a month before, we were about to sleep in a house that didnt have him in it. I went to check on Sister Baby, asleep next to Teddy's empty half of the mattress, then returned, and I was already in bed, head on the pillow, before I realized I'd undressed and put on my nightclothes without even using the closet door for a screen. All that time, for all I knew, Eben had been lying there looking at me around the bulge of his feet under the covers. But I was too tired, too done-in from all the worry and the weeping, to feel much more than a twinge of shame. I thought of Teddy, the empty other half of the bed back there where Sister Baby was sleeping, until he blurred into those children I saw a while ago from over across the river, the whites yelling their faces out of shape, shaking their fists at the children going in and coming out. I saw again the tears glisten in Eben's eyes from the flickering light off the television screen, glistening, glistening, till they broke and came trickling down his face. Eben, Eben, I said, or thought I said. I was asleep, my mind gone blank.

So I thought, till: *Mamma! Mamma!* — real as real. I sat bolt upright, waking Eben too, if he had been asleep. "He needs me," I said. "I heard him need me."

Eben told me I'd been dreaming, and I had. "Lay back down," he said, and I did, and he put his arms around me, hugging my back, close up. "Dont cry. Dont," he said, and after a while I stopped.

I quieted down, and when I did I felt him hard against my backside, through my gown. I wanted it too, and so we did.

That was Monday, and I woke next morning, for another first time in all those eight-plus years, to a house without Teddy in it. Eben was in the kitchen making coffee, risen I dont know how long before. I fixed his breakfast, then got Sister Baby up and washed and dressed and fed and off to school. He would walk her there, returning by way of the office to have it open in time for Miss Lucy, then come on home, and I would go for her at letting-out time. That way, he would only be gone when the phone was least likely to ring. We told her, if anyone asked, to say her brother was down with a cold. So they left and I had the house to myself — like any weekday morning, except it wasnt. I sat in the living room to wait, though for what I couldnt say.

At times like that, with everything still and empty-feeling all around you, you see things you never saw before: the way sunlight falls on a rug, say, and shows you colors you didnt know were in it until then. So it is with people, sometimes, in the lives they lead. What you have been makes you what you are, and in times of strain you see things in the pattern you never saw before.

Most everything I was, and am, came from getting my daddy's looks and not my mamma's. If I'd been born willowy like her, high-nosed and light of skin, instead of squat and froggy, dark like him, I wouldnt have had to spend so much time rising above my appearance. I could even have laughed, the way some girls did, at things they taught us in St Louis at Miss Endicott's Finishing School for Young Ladies of Color. Myrtle Endicott was long since dead, a gold-frame portrait on the parlor wall. Priscilla Carter was head mistress now: Miss Priss we called her. According to the catalog she taught English, but what she really taught was Deportment — capital D. "When seated, dont cross your legs except at the ankles, never at the knees. It's suggestive. Dont lick your lips. That's suggestive. And dont wear red. Red's suggestive." She showed us how to sit down in a chair without looking back to make sure it was there, how to get up out of one without touching the arms, how to come down stairs with a book on your head, and how to walk with your feet put one in front of the other, not overlapping, to keep from swishing. Swishing was maybe the most suggestive of all, next to going without a girdle or brassiere.

Others could afford to laugh, especially the pretty ones, half white and sometimes more. I even laughed sometimes myself at the fun they made of Priss Carter behind her back. But they didnt need what she was teaching as much as I did, with my bullfrog look and my dark skin. I took it to heart, both years I was there, and brought what I learned back to Memphis to help me take my place in the life Daddy had aimed at for me even before he sent me up to St Louis to get what they called finished.

So I came home, past twenty now, and the war was on, with lots of events canceled for the duration, the Miss Sepia contest, the Christmas parade on Beale, even the Cotton Carnival. I was learning things, local things they didnt know to teach us at Miss Endicott's, such as what to wear with what down here, when and when not, and war-time clothes, broad in the shoulders, short in the skirt, waiting without knowing it for the New Look and the men — boys, we called them — to get back home from being shot at. Twice a year, spring and fall, Daddy would take me with him on the train to Chicago, where he went on business, and buy me clothes. Mamma didnt go. He did the choosing, mainly by the price tag, the higher the better, so long as they were sturdy, made to last, the same as he did with his own. I seemed younger than my years, even to myself, mostly I guess because so little happened all that time. I learned words, too, which to use and which not; Neegro, Nigra, even Niggero, but never "nigger" except in contempt or sometimes affection, the way Jews say kike or Italians say dago. "Keep away from niggers," Daddy often said. I learned to take my place and bide my time, though for what I didnt know, any more than we knew about the New Look till it got there.

Then the war was over, first in Europe, then Japan: I was twenty-three, young for my age, and the men came home not boys at all. Almost before I knew it, with barely time to get used to there being parties, movie dates and such, I was engaged to Lydel Partridge and mixed up with Snooker Martin, both at once.

I hadnt known him very well — Lydel I mean — except by sight before the war, when he was so much the older, already in his twenties by the time I reached eighteen. He'd been at Camp Polk the past two years, home on furlough from time to time to see the girl he was engaged to marry. Lilly Matlock was her name, the last Miss Sepia before they closed the contest down for the duration. She eloped with a one-legged sergeant from Kansas she met at the veterans hospital out on Getwell (Shotwell it had been called till then, but Shotwell was too grisly, so they changed its name to Getwell) on the eve of VJ Day. Daddy more or less arranged the match with Mr Partridge, who was looking round for someone to help Lydel recover from Lilly Matlock before he took over from him in the undertaking business. I had the veto, though, just as I always had with my clothes up in Chicago, once Daddy chose them. Anyhow I liked Lydel and always had, what little I'd known him. Then too I knew that sooner or later I'd have to marry *some*one, and it already wasnt all that soon. I told myself it might as well be Lydel Partridge. The wedding was set for June at the Beale Street Baptist.

That was in early 1946, and it was in April, two months later, that I took up with Snooker Martin on the sly. Going to visit Daddy at the office I'd see him standing outside one of those places along Beale. He'd sort of grin at me, just short of tipping his hat — rakish — as if to say he knew something I didnt know but someday would. "Hidy, miss," he began to say, and though I knew better than to speak to him, there on the street, I watched him out of the corner of my eye. He was tall and slim, about my age, dark-complected, with bulgy eyes, a chin that sort of went away, and clothes only a little short of zoot, including a watch chain that looped about knee-length down one trouser leg. "You look out. He's *dangerous*," Lydel's sister Edwina said one day on Beale.

I already knew that, just from looking at him sideways, and something else as well, which was that he was exactly what Daddy meant when he told me, "Keep away from niggers." Once at the Malco he sat right behind me and pushed at the back of the seat with his knees. I didnt look round, even to tell him to stop, till we got up to leave, Lydel and I, and as we did, moving past him, he nodded. To my surprise I nodded back, and his hand crept out in the aisle and brushed my leg and then crept back, too quick to follow.

Things moved faster after that. Next day I was walking to meet Daddy, and when Snooker spoke ("Hidy" — pause — "miss") I looked away and he came up beside me from behind.

"You ever take a walk after supper? Alone?"

"No."

"Well, could you?"

"I might could," I said, still looking straight ahead.

He leaned toward me, right there in broad open daylight on Hernando opposite Clayborn Temple, and I didnt know what to make of it. Here I was, twenty-four years old, and I didnt know what to make of it, the life I lived had been so sheltered. Nothing Miss Priss ever told us prepared me for what I was feeling, much less for what I was about to do, except I knew she wouldnt approve. And that night after supper, when Lydel called to say he was involved in a special embalming job, I told Mamma I was going to the picture show with Edwina. I set out across Vance, and hadnt reached the middle of the next block — right opposite where I later lived, at 279 — when a car pulled up at the curb just ahead, with Snooker at the wheel. I wasnt surprised. He reached over and opened the door and I got in.

We rode around some, barely speaking, till he turned south, then west, and parked in a vacant lot on the bluff overlooking the river and its bridges just downstream, lights twinkling in color like the ones on Christmas trees, red and green and yellow. His name wasnt Snooker, he told me, it was Richard: Snooker was a game he played in pool halls. While he talked, what little he did, I watched him sideways by the light of a streetlight not far off, the glittery look on the whites of his eyes and the way his chin left no bottom to his face. Call him Richard, he said, and I said I would. I was waiting, waiting, feet braced so hard against the floorboard that my legs were aching at the knees.

Finally he turned and put one arm across my shoulders, the other around my waist, and leaned over from under the steering wheel, sort of lifting me up, and kissed me. I braced harder, knees all tight, and he began moving his tongue in my mouth. No one had ever done that before: especially not Lydel, with those quick little goodnight pecks he handed out. Then Snooker

— Richard, he said call him — folded the hem of my skirt up a ways and began to stroke the tops of my thighs, above the stockings, till I was so scared and excited, both at once, I felt like bucking off the seat. *Do, do,* I thought, and all of a sudden, as if on some signal I didnt hear, he stopped and folded the skirt back down and took his mouth away from mine. Dont, dont, I thought, and he took his other arm from around me.

"Come on," he said. "We got to get you home before they miss you and start hunting."

That was the first time. Two nights later he parked in the same place — Arkansas Street it was called, a colored district at the end of Carolina — and once more stopped as if on signal. He had my blouse open down the front and my bra unhooked in back, stroking and fondling my breasts while he kissed me, and this time I said it out loud, "Do. Do," not rightly knowing what I meant, just what I wanted. But all he did was keep fondling, fondling, till the unheard signal came.

"Time," he said, and started and turned the car around while I re-hooked my bra and buttoned my blouse back up.

Then there came a gap, over the weekend. I didnt see him for five days, on the street or anywhere, and I thought I'd lose my mind with worry: first about him, Snooker-Richard, and then about myself, all I was feeling. I still didnt know what to make of it, any more than I had at the start, but I was beginning to get an inkling. Either this was the way it was done — like in the movies, where he wont take her till the time comes, even if they are snowbound in some cabin — or else he figured if I got what I thought I wanted, maybe I wouldnt want it any more. Then too, I began to get on the edge of the notion that it wasnt me he was courting, it was Daddy, and I was only someone in between: between him and Daddy, that is, or Daddy's money, which came to the same thing in Snooker's eyes.

I thought that, or anyhow on the edge of that, and still it didnt matter. Five days was just too long, including one night at a party, one for supper at our house, another at the Partridges', above the funeral parlor, and then the weekend, when there was no chance anyhow. I almost hated Lydel, I wanted Snooker — Richard — so. He loves me, I told myself. I know he does. If he didnt love me I wouldnt feel this way. Even in church, right there in the pew with Mamma and Daddy beside me and the preacher in the pulpit holding forth about damnation, I'd think *Fucking. Fucking*, a word I'd never said out loud. Then it was Monday and I still didnt see him on the street, and I made it out of the house that night and he didnt come.

It's the end of the world, I told myself. He's been shot or cut or something. He cant reach me.

Tuesday I made it out again, right after supper, and there he was. He'd been gone: to *Detroit*, he said later, on a deal. "Get in, babes," he said now, and steered directly for the river, that same blufftop lot with the streetlight down the way. He held and kissed me, sliding part-way over from under the steering wheel, and then instead of touching and fondling me, the way he did both times before, he had me touch *him*. And more than touch, as it turned out. When he took my hand and put it on him, down there, I found he'd opened the front of his trousers.

"There. Hold that," he said. I did and then he said, "Look down now at what youre holding." I did and I could see it by the reflection from the streetlight, lying there along his thigh. Forever after, when I looked back on what I saw that night, it put me in mind of a long dusty blacksnake just run out from under a stump. "Bend down," he said, and I did. "That's yours," he said. "Now taste it." I did and it began creeping, alive inside and lengthening itself along his thigh. "Wait now. That's enough for now," he said. "The best comes later, after you two get thoroughly acquainted." He took it away from me and slid it back inside his trousers, out of sight. "That's yours," he said again, "full-time yours, when the time comes. We got to study-up first how to handle your daddy, though."

He should have known better. For when it came to *handling*, as he called it, things turned out the other way around. Daddy never had much to do with the riffraff there on Beale, but this was the exception to the rule. When he heard next day from someone who saw me get in Snooker's car the night before — a favor: people were always ready to do him favors, in hope of receiving a favor in return — Daddy got in touch with Emile Spicer, and before the sun went down that evening Snooker was on his way. I didnt see him again for years, and not even then to speak to. Emile Spicer gave the job to three men he knew — part-time gamblers, full-time thugs or "rousters," as they call them — to serve him his walking papers. Two of them were long-time friends of his, but that didnt weigh much, there on Beale, alongside a request from Emile Spicer. They all three wore straight-edge razors hung on a string around their necks and under their clothes, so that all they had to do was reach inside their shirts, snap the string, and there were the razors, open in their hands. When the three called Snooker out of a pool hall and gave him the news, he didnt even go back to finish his game. They would have cut him where it counts, and he knew it. "Here, Rooster," he told one of them, handing him the cue he'd brought outside. "Rack that back up for me in there." He was gone by sundown, as I said before.

I didnt know. Nobody told me: least of all Daddy, who engineered it. Snooker was just *gone*. It's Detroit again, I said to myself. He'll come back. Youll see. Then when he didnt I told myself, He'll send for you. Youll see. And when he didnt do that either, when I knew for certain he was truly gone, I reacted first with a feeling of heartbreak, then of shame — a shame that went deeper than the sorrow it drove out. I could see then what lurked inside me, locked in my blood till something beckoned and it came raging out like some wild animal, all teeth and claws and snarling, when someone swings the zoo cage door ajar. I remembered all I felt with Snooker those three times: how it had been me begging *him*, wanting and ashamed at the same time, but with the wanting so much stronger than the shame that when he said, "Bend down. Taste it," I not only bent and tasted, I all but cried when it went away like a snake ducking back in its hole. "Do. Do," I said, out loud, and it was him who wouldnt, who said no. I couldnt control what I thought or did, even when I was *fix*ing to be with him, let alone *with* him. Fucking. Fucking, I said to myself, right there in church. All my raising went by the board: Miss Endicott's, Mamma, Daddy, everything I'd been told and taught since my Sunday School days at Beale Street Baptist. In my shame I decided what I felt went back to Africa, jungle doings, and we really were animals, wild animals, the way some people said of those who did the things that got them lynched — wild animals deserving of being cut and blow-torched, not only for what we did, but for what we were, deep down in the blood brought here from Africa two hundred years ago.

Pretty soon the word got round, what Martha Wiggins had done on the sly and how Snooker Martin lit a shuck when the rousters told him his time was up in Memphis. Edwina Partridge knew, for one: which meant Lydel did too, and somehow that made it easier to give him back his ring and tell him the wedding, still two months off, was off. He might have borne what I did to him, but not me: I couldnt. Besides, Lilly Matlock had braced him for the shock by giving him a still greater one the year before, when he lost a wife that had not only been Miss Sepia, in her time, but also looked a good deal like Lena Horne except for her hair and nose and skin a few shades darker. In any case, he was married before the end of the year, this time without one of those risky long-drawn-out engagements, and soon had children coming regular as clockwork, including a set of twins, cute as a pair of buttons, and a boy just Teddy's age. All I had, right after the breakup, was the shame I felt, plus the relief of knowing I wasnt going to marry an undertaker and live with his folks above the funeral parlor.

A year and a half later, after I passed twenty-five, here came Eben, up from Mississippi and working for Daddy. We met at Sunday dinner soon after he went to work on Beale, and I knew from his being asked to the house, along with his light-skinned look and careful manners, that Daddy was signaling his approval and inquiring after mine. I still had the veto, now as ever, and I watched and waited. One thing I saw was that he was frightened, and that was in his favor from the start. Maybe he had heard of Snooker, though Daddy never so much as dropped his name in my direction, and the way I gave up on Lydel Partridge with the wedding less than two months off. Or maybe it was just marriage itself that scared him, the wife being the boss's daughter, and only child, with all that money swirling round her head. What would people think of him? Above all, what would he think of himself?

Whatever it was, he was skittish as a jump-shy horse — and I took that as a good sign, different from both Lydel and Snooker, who were so different from each other except in the sense of putting me in the middle, something to be stepped across to get at Daddy. It worried me some that he was handsome, but it seemed not to bother him overmuch or make him demanding, the way Ive seen it do some others. Christmas came and went, and I told myself, as I had done before, that I was biding time I didnt have to spare. After all, I told myself, you have to marry *some*one, and it might as well be Eben Kinship, up from Mississippi. Moreover he was getting more and more skittish, every day that passed. The wedding came in February of 1948, a bare two weeks before I was twenty-six, and I heard later he came within an inch of bolting — of jumping out of the car, they say — less than a block from where I was waiting at Beale Street Baptist in my satin wedding dress.

So there we were, married. Married up, as they say: him at the office, plugging along, and me at home, plugging too, and between times we were both there, making what's called a marriage: married up. In bed, eight hours a night, and the other eight leading up to or away from it, I took care to see that what Snooker Martin had shown was in me, caged in my blood, did not come raging out. And it didnt: I didnt let it. What made it easier than I'd thought was, now that I had what I wondered and even bucked about, I found it was less than I had supposed or anyhow wanted it to be. It didnt rage unless you let it, and I didnt let it.

I kept a tight rein on myself, and on Eben too. He plugged along, got himself raises and promotions timed to Teddy's arrival and then Sister Baby's, named first for Daddy, then for Mamma, and the only change was them, the children, there to be looked after, cared for, loved. It was a long straight road to be traveled, more or less like the one I foresaw with Lydel Partridge, and everything on it was tied directly to Daddy, just up the street. He had chosen my husbands, including the one I didnt marry, just as he'd chosen my clothes and school. Nothing we had didnt come from him, and we both knew it. Job, house, promotions, expectations, all tied in to Daddy and what he wanted, what he thought. In bed it was that way, too, in its way, and it led me to think a terrible thing, no less clear for being terrible: Eben has the prick but Daddy pumps it.

Just at that point — and remember, that point had lasted almost a full ten years by now — they took Teddy: snatched him off the street on Linden and told me in a note, "We got your boy." I came close to dying, that day and the next, and on television, over across the way in Arkansas, the white mob yelled and milled around while the children came and went in their Sunday clothes, dressed up as if for church, and I thought how right Mamma was in what she said when she first learned that Teddy had been taken. "The world gone crazy, white and colored. White and colored, they done lost they mind." Now, Tuesday night, it changed direction and turned somehow even crazier over there. Paratroopers were coming off airplanes, decked out in helmets and automatic rifles, dressed for war right here in the USA, each with a screaming eagle on his shoulder. "White and colored," Mamma said. "White and colored, they done lost they mind."

All day Tuesday we hadnt heard a word. Eben sat by the telephone all that day, once he got back from walking Sister Baby to school and opening up the office, and all that day it didnt ring except Daddy and wrong numbers. We went to bed right after the news, worried sick, and did it again. Twice. I told myself it was some kind of nervous affliction.

Then next morning — Wednesday now — when Eben left with Sister Baby I went in the bathroom to wash my hair, more to be *doing* something than anything else. What's more I was trying to deal with a shame I felt. When they left and I stood watching them walk together on Vance, Eben and Sister Baby, I couldnt help wishing they had taken her instead of Teddy: not because I loved him most or because he was my child and she was Eben's, but because she was little and a girl and they wouldnt be as likely to hurt her, or she to hurt herself as much as he was, being a boy and more reckless. All the same, no matter what I told myself was the reason behind my wishing, I no sooner thought it than I was ashamed, deep-down ashamed. So I went back and washed my hair. At times like that, it's what women do: wash their hair.

Before I finished drying it to rub in the straightening cream, the phone rang — hard once, breaking the stillness, then hard again while I was on the way with the towel round my head. I picked up the phone on the third ring, a little out of breath. "Hello?"

"Martha? This is Thelma Pitkin."

"Yes?"

"It's about Teddy," she said, and my heart sank.

"Yes?"

"How is he?"

"What?" And then I knew: Miss Pitkin. Thelma Pitkin meant nothing to me, though I knew *Miss* Pitkin as well as I ever knew anyone in my life. She taught me in the same grade she taught Teddy in, the third, but I'd forgotten her first name was Thelma, if in fact I ever knew it. "He's better," I told her, "but we still thought we'd keep him home till he gets over his sniffles."

"Why, yes. Do. I just wanted to call — I'm down in the office — and see how he is. I'm glad he's better. Tell him I said to hurry back. We miss him, I and all his little classmates."

"Thank you, Miss Pitkin. I'll tell him. Thank you."

"Goodbye. My regards to your father."

"Yessum, I will. Goodbye."

I felt weak all over, first from thinking it was them, without Eben there to talk or take the message, and then from disappointment that it wasnt, that all there was about to be was another day of silence, of not-knowing.

But I no sooner hung up the phone than it rang again. Old Miss Pitkin. How could she call back again so fast? "Hello," I said, put-out at still another interruption.

"Is this Martha? Martha Kinship?"

"Speaking."

"Teddy's mother?"

My heart gave a tilt and I couldnt answer. I knew what it was, right off, mainly because the voice was white and had a coldness in it: a coldness that went to the marrow of my bones. "Then listen, Martha," the cold white voice said; "listen carefully."

"All right," she said in a sort of sinking tone, and I bore down on her, just the way Rufus rehearsed me back on the bluff.

"Youll get a letter in this morning's mail," I told her. "Do as it says do, to the dot, and your boy will be home soon afterwards, safe and sound. If you dont" — I remembered to pause — "he wont and youll never see him again. Dont let it scare you. Just do as it says. You understand?"

"Yessum," she said.

She was frightened; deathly frightened. I could hear her breathing, almost as if she was there in the phone booth with me, before what came next. "How is he? Is he safe?"

"He's fine," I told her. "Just fine. I'm looking after him myself. I wouldnt let anything hurt him."

"Is he eating?"

"He eats fine. Soup and crackers, milk, cornflakes; all those things."

"Does he say his prayers?"

"His what?"

"His prayers. Do you hear them?"

"Oh — prayers," I said. And me a preacher's daughter. "Yes, I do. Or anyhow I will. Dont worry. I'm looking after him myself, all round the clock. I like him. He likes me, too. Goodbye."

"Wait — "

I could almost feel her clutch the telephone, off there two miles away at the other end of the wire on Vance, trying to hold onto the connection. But Podjo said keep it short, so it couldnt be traced, and so did Rufus when he rehearsed me.

"No. Goodbye," I said. "I've got to go."

"Wait!"

"Goodbye. He's fine," I said, and hung the phone up.

Driving back from over on Crump, back to Arkansas Street and the bluff, I felt strange from having talked with her after all we'd done and were doing to her. She seemed a lot realer, now that I had talked with her, and somehow I seemed *less* real; that is, I had an even harder time believing we'd done what we had done — what we were doing. But we had; we were. Today made three weeks we'd been up here, and the end of September was only five days off.

Podjo and Rufus were sitting there reading the morning paper, and Podjo's part had a thick black three-decker headline all across the top of the front page. 1000 BATTLE-EQUIPPED ARMY PARATROOPERS/ ENTER LITTLE ROCK TO ENFORCE INTE-GRATION;/ 'MY INESCAPABLE DUTY,' EISENHOWER CLAIMS.

"How'd it go?" Rufus asked when I came in.

"It went all right. She was scared but I think I made her feel some better. Anyhow I braced her for what's coming in the mail."

"Good. Hey, Podj," he said, still talking across his section of the paper. "Theyre getting films at the Malco today of the

Sugar Ray fight last night; flying them down for a showing at five-thirty, it says here. How about that. Basilio creamed him, didnt he?"

"Nah," Podjo said. "Robinson was just so worn down by the heat he couldnt hold his hands up. Split decision."

I went in the kitchen for coffee, and when I got back Rufus was off on something else. He wasnt much for reading the papers, but when he did he liked to talk about what he was reading while he read it. "Faulkner's sixty today," he told Podjo.

"Who's that?"

"A writer, from over at Oxford. William Faulkner. I used to see him sometime walking round the square." Then I remembered; *Sanctuary*. I read it once, part of it anyhow, back in my school days when people were saying how dirty it was. I didnt think it was all that dirty — or all that understandable either, far as that goes. "He'd speak to you or he wouldnt," Rufus was saying, "depending on how he felt that day. Count No-Count."

He had more to say about him, how he'd gotten to know him there in Oxford, talks they had, but I went up to check on Teddy, who was sleeping with the button-eyed bear's head on the pillow beside his own. When I showed it to him first thing that morning, after his Noctec and cornflakes, he pretended not to care. "I'm too big for dolls," he said.

"It's not a doll," I told him. "It's a bear. A teddy bear, they call them. Brother won it for you last night in a shooting match."

"I'm too big for dolls," he said, and wouldnt take it.

Now though, only about an hour later, he had it up on the cot and under the covers with him, head on the pillow. Teddy, he named it, and from then on he was seldom without it within reach. It was as if he kidnapped it, just as he himself had been kidnapped — whether he knew it or not — and was mounting guard to see that it didnt get away. It slept beside him, head on the same pillow; Teddy One, himself, and Teddy Two, with button eyes; one close to black, the other fuzzy brown. I stayed up there a while, watching him sleep — watching them both sleep, you might say — then came down.

Rufus was in the kitchen pouring himself a glass of milk. "He likes the bear," I said, and he nodded, putting the carton back in the icebox. On the way down the attic steps, just now, I remembered the way Teddy's mother begged, "Wait. Wait!" when I had to hang up on her, and now it was coming home to me. I almost wished I hadnt made the call and heard her voice.

"Those poor damn people," I told Rufus.

"What poor damn people?" he said, glass in hand.

"Over there on Vance, the Kinships. You should have heard her asking me to wait. I couldnt wait; I hung up on her. And nothing I told her really helps. How could it? 'He's fine, just fine.' What good is that? How could she believe a thing I say, one way or the other? I'm the one that snatched him. And she's most likely got that letter in the morning mail by now. She must be going crazy with worry, this very minute. And the daddy too. They must both be going crazy."

He sipped his milk, watching me over the rim of the glass until he took it down. "What the hell, Reen," he said. He sipped again and took it down. "Any fretting they do is up to them, not us. It's for extra; something they do to fill up the time while they wait to get their boy back, like we told them from the start. Hell, it's not only for extra, it's for nothing. You know as well as I do, the boy's in no danger and never was. What the hell." He sipped and lowered, sipped and lowered, then gave a little positive nod that made the wave of hair across the top of his head break forward, then bob back, as much in place as if he hadnt nodded. "And you too, Reen. Your fretting is for extra, something you use to fill up your spare time. Let it go. The kid's in no danger; never was. You know it better than they do. What the hell."

I watched him set the glass in the sink and run the back of his hand across his mouth. All this time I'd watched him, saying nothing, thinking *Jesus, Rufus, Jesus.* Winning the bear last night for Teddy, and thinking to give it to him for company when we got back home, had made me feel kindly toward him, warmed the warm spot in my heart. But when he turned back from the sink with a sort of halfway smile, after all he'd just now said, my anger ran all the way over like a pot on a too-high fire. He was making me madder and madder with that kind of talk — and I think he knew it, too.

"You ought to be ashamed of yourself," I told him. I hate spats, but I was so angry I couldnt help myself; I just let go. "You say it's up to them whether they worry or not. It's not. You think worry is some kind of switch or tap you can turn off when it suits you? Well, it's not. Theyre worried about their little boy, whether he's alive or not, or hurt or not. How can they not worry? Durn you, Rufus, you think the whole wide world is made like you. It's not. It's made like me — like me and those poor damn people in that house on Vance, fretting over that little nigger up in the attic without even knowing he's there or where he is, or *if* he is; alive or not, hurt or not, crying or lying quiet, too scared to breathe. Durn you, Rufus Hutton. Durn you."

He smiled again, only this time it wasnt halfway. He was wrong and he knew it; how could he not? So he smiled to cover it up and get around me — make me see he didnt mean it, even if he did. Besides, I could tell he was amused, by the way he showed his teeth.

"You want to send him back?" he said; "send him back tonight and forget about the money, our half of the sixty thousand, now that it's right within our reach?"

"Oh, for Christ sake. For Christ sake, Rufus," I told him, "I'm in this too, to stay, as much as you are. I might as well be talking to a post."

I left him standing there, grinning at me around his teeth, and went up to be with Teddy. In the living room, Podjo was still fine-tooth-combing the *Commercial*, the way he did every morning of his life, but I didnt want to be with him any more than I did with Rufus. Different as he was, he was still a man. Men. I told myself I'd rather be with Teddy and his bear, up in the attic. At least they didnt go around hurting people and pretending it was up to them whether they felt hurt or not.

Between the cots, when I lay down on the near one, the funny books were beginning to look thumbed-through. I wondered if Rufus had been up there reading them, using Teddy to keep him company while I was gone and Podjo wouldnt talk or listen to him. I took up one of them, *Doctor Doom*, and was browsing through it — something about a space flight, a Buck Rogers kind of thing; "The whole cabin is charged with electricity!" the mad scientist was yelling, rimmed with fire — when I felt someone watching me in the stillness. I glanced up from *Doctor Doom* and it was Teddy lying there with his eyes open, head turned sideways on the pillow, looking at me or not; I couldnt tell, groggy as he still must have been from the Noctec only a couple of hours before. I didnt say anything till he spoke. Then he did, solemn as a papoose.

"Are you my mamma now?" he said.

"N-no," I told him, with something like a catch in my throat, "I'm just taking care of you for her till your daddy sends us word to bring you home. I talked to her this morning, though. She was glad to hear you are doing so well, and she said for me to make sure you say your prayers at night."

He thought about that a while, still solemn, head resting sideways on the pillow, eyes unblinking, one above the other, round as ohs. "I will if you remind me," he said. Then he said, "Is Sister Baby staying somewhere strange, like me, till Daddy sends?"

"She might be," I told him, knowing he meant the little sister I gave the note to, two days ago on Linden; or was it three? "I dont know for sure, though. I'm just looking after *you*."

"Mm," he said, and his eyes went slowly shut, two curtains closing sideways, one above the other. He was back asleep, if in fact he'd been awake.

It was a long day; sultry, too. I turned the fan on. Around noon, when he began stirring, I went down, closed the hallway door, drew the bathroom shade, and ran the tub, then came back up and brought him down. "Bears dont bathe," I told him, but he brought it with him anyhow to watch from a grandstand seat on the toilet tank. While he bathed I rinsed out the tee shirt he'd been wearing, got him a clean one out of Rufus's drawer, the one with the pistol, and put it on him soon as I rubbed him dry. Back upstairs, I left him and the bear reading the funny books while I heated our soup in the kitchen. Up front, Podjo and Rufus were watching the midday news; paratroopers with bayonets on their rifles, bulging the Little Rockers backward from the barricades, down sidewalks and across the yards of houses near the school.

"You-all want some soup?" I asked them.

"No thanks," Podjo said. "I'll eat downtown when I go see the fight."

"Me either," Rufus said, watching the soldiers move against the civilians, bulging them back. "I'll round up something later."

"You want to catch it with me?" Podjo asked him. He meant the fight film at the Malco, Sugar Ray and Whoever, sent by air from New York City.

"I'll just stick around here," Rufus said, eyes still on the screen, where a chunky-looking sergeant was telling his squad, "Keep those baynets high. Right at the thoat."

I went back, spooned out the two bowls of soup, and ate upstairs with Teddy. When we finished — chicken noodle again; he liked that best — I gave him his second Noctec, and when he drifted off on his cot, once more sharing his pillow with the bear, I began a nap on mine. The slap of the screen door woke me, and as I lay there, not quite knowing where I was, I heard the car start in the driveway, then pull off. Almost at once I heard Rufus tipping up the steps.

"Reen?" he said, forgetting to use Sis or Sister, and his head floated up through the opening like a toy balloon reeled out from below on a string. The rest of him followed, and he stood there looking down at me on my cot. "Podjo's gone," he said. "We got the whole house to ourselves. Let's dont fuss."

Here he was, at it again; bound to have it; mostly, I think, because he thought I'd say no. "Let's dont fuss," he said, knowing that was the best way around me, knowing I'd rather do anything than fuss — especially what I saw he had in mind. The trouble was he didnt want to wait any more now than he had two nights ago, with another bad case of the jimjams, when he dragged me out to the lip of the bluff and back; Podjo was no sooner clear of the driveway than here he came tipping up the steps, saying "Let's dont fuss."

He stood over me, looking down, and when I saw the sunlight coming almost level through the louvers I knew I hadnt just begun my nap; I'd had it, two full hours if not more. "Come on, Reeny," he was saying. "It's nice up here with the fan and all. Let's test-hop that canvas cot."

Teddy's eyes came open while he spoke, then closed again, the way they did a while ago when he asked me if I was his mamma. I shook my head and pointed, meaning Teddy was half awake, but Rufus sat beside me, bending over.

"What the hell," he said. "He's sound asleep. And what if he does wake up a little? Let him watch."

I didnt get as mad at that as you might think. For one thing, I knew he didnt mean it, at least not altogether, except as a way of letting me know how much he wanted what he came up there to get. And for another, I wanted it too; not up there, of course, but *some*where. Just because youre mad at someone doesnt mean youve turned to stone where theyre concerned; especially Rufus, with all those tricks he knew. So I persuaded him to go back down while I made certain Teddy was fast asleep again. Then I'd come join him, I said. "I wont be long."

By the time I got downstairs a few minutes later he was already naked, sitting cross-legged on the bed. Over beyond the river, I saw through the back door when I came down the hallway steps, the bottom rim of the sun had touched the landline so that its light glowed rosy yellow through the bedroom shades. I got my shoes and skirt off, my blouse undone and one arm out of its sleeve, but he was after me before I reached my pants; shoved me back and peeled them off, the way youd skin a rabbit. He was flustered — wrought-up, as he said, and fairly trembling.

As usual, it was catching. In no time, still with one arm in its sleeve, I was looking down past my stomach at his yellow hair with its breaking wave, forehead and eyebrows neat and pale in the rosy yellow light, and just the top half of each eye, first open, glaring at me through the fringe of hair at the bottom of my stomach, then hooded, both of them squinched close-shut the way theyd be if he was picking up on something heavy. Above them, all this time, the hair-wave broke and bobbed, breaking forward, bobbing back, in rhythm with the effort he was making to get outside himself, and the moans and slurps and growls were like the sound of some animal feeding — some wild animal. I quit looking; put my head back, the way you do at times like that, staring first at then toward the ceiling, and if I could have heard it I would have known that I was moaning too.

I did hear something, though, or thought I did. "Whut yaw doon," I heard a voice say.

It couldnt be Rufus, God knows. But who? No matter, I thought, and put it out of my mind. Anyhow I tried, until a sort of follow-up translation got through to me: What you-all doing?

I rolled my head, looking sideways, and there, less than six feet away, stood Teddy in his knee-length tee shirt, clutching his button-eyed bear. He had come downstairs and stood in the doorway to the hall; how long I didnt know, but long enough to wonder and ask, What you-all doing? I yelled, "Rufus! Rufus!" and squirmed to get free.

But he had a death grip on me, hands hooked over the tops of my hips and thighs from underneath, and the harder I tried to shake him loose the tighter he hung on — thinking I was yelling and writhing because I was all the way into what he was just on the rim of, closing fast — till I managed at last to get one foot on his shoulder, alongside his neck, and push down hard enough to break his hold. He was grabbing, walking forward on his elbows, when he happened to see Teddy.

"Jesus Christ!" he shouted, whether at me or Teddy or Jesus himself I couldnt tell. Not that it mattered. Left hanging like that, just on the rim, he was fit to be tied.

Scrabbling round, I managed to get my other arm in its sleeve and found my skirt to slip back on, though not my pants, which most likely were tangled up somewhere in the bedclothes. "Be back," I told Rufus, collapsed face-down on the mattress as if he'd fallen off the ceiling, and caught Teddy by the arm to take him upstairs.

"What were you-all doing?" he still wanted to know.

"Wrestling," I said, and kept him moving up the steps.

"Who won?" he asked when we reached the top.

"Nobody. It was a draw," I said. God knows it was — like Sugar Ray and his split decision, so worn down he couldnt hold his hands up. "Now climb right back in bed and go to sleep."

That was easier said than done, despite if not because of my impatience to get back down to where Rufus was lying all in a heap as if he'd fallen out of the sky. Teddy got in bed with his bear, all right, but his eyes stayed open, full of what theyd seen. It was half an hour, maybe more, before they closed for good, and I took another few minutes to make sure. When I came downstairs at last, intending to take up the match where we left off, the sun was all the way gone in a glory of red over Arkansas and dusk-dark was settling down outside the bedroom windows. By way of precaution I folded up the bottom section of the attic steps, so Teddy couldnt get down them without making some kind of racket.

Rufus was a pale dim shape, still naked on the bed, sitting with his neck and shoulders propped against the headboard and holding something that glinted in his hands. It was a bottle, I saw then, a half-empty fifth of Old Crow he had brought up from the kitchen. That was a surprise, because Rufus almost never drank and had no stomach for it when he did. Still, I could see how he figured he needed some kind of medicine or something, locked up as he was, half in and half out of himself, with a bad case of jimjams in the first place, even before the half-in half-out interruption. Who could blame him? — least of all me, who was in more or less the same condition.

"That was a near thing," I said, by way of a beginning, as I sat down facing him across the width of the double bed.

"Yair."

"He could have walked right out of here, by the back door or the front, for all we knew."

"Yair."

He shifted his weight and the bottle glinted in his hands. I could tell he was angry and I didnt blame him, except for what came next. "But not, by God," he said, "if we'd done what I'm beginning to think we should have done at the start, when we first grabbed him."

"What's that?" I asked, and held my breath for the answer.

"You know damn well what's that," he said. "The Green-lease way. Knock him off; put him down for good, under a flower bed or something. He wont run off then, or talk afterward. After the payoff."

"You dont mean that."

"I mean that," he said, and he tilted the bottle for a swallow, making a strong smell of bourbon in the room.

Here we were, back again at what we fussed about before, whether he meant it or not. I still didnt think he did; not all the way. He was just mad, I told myself, from the strain the interruption had put on him where he could take it least, and his bitterness came out. Besides, he was drinking — something he couldnt do.

All the same I didnt let it pass. "You ought to be ashamed of yourself," I told him.

"Goddammit," he said, "I'm getting tired of you putting me down every chance you get. You and Podjo." He didnt say it all that loud or angry-sounding, and certainly not in a way that warned me of what was coming next. "Bitch! You old bitch, I ought to rip your fucking head off."

Bitch was all right; I could take that. *Old* I couldnt. It showed that he was trying to hurt my feelings. What's more, it was mostly him with the fucking head, not me.

"You ought to be ashamed of yourself," I said again.

"Yair?"

He leaned forward, bottle in one hand, and gave me a shove in the chest. At that, before I stopped and thought, I slapped him hard as I could across the face. I hadnt slapped anybody in years, not since a Texas fellow cured me of it by slapping back. Almost at once I wished I hadnt, but it was too late then. He came at me; banged me one, up on the side of the head, open-handed yet hard enough to make it ring. I tried to scramble off the bed, but he got hold of my arm and snatched me back, face-up on the mattress, and got astride me, first on his knees, then sitting on my stomach. What made it so strange, above all else, was I'd come back down to get on with what we'd been interrupted in, both for his sake and my own, and here he was trying to maul me — rip my head off, as he said. Anyhow he had one arm up, fist clenched, fixing to bring it down, when all of a sudden the room was full of glare.

We looked, and there stood Podjo in the doorway where he'd flipped the light switch. "What the hell is this?" he said.

Then Rufus did the strangest thing of all. Sitting astride me, naked on my stomach, one arm lifted to bring it down and smash me, he looked at Podjo standing in the doorway to the living room, and "How was the fight?" he asked in an almost normal voice, as if he really wanted to know, as if I wasnt underneath him on the bed.

"Lots better than this one," Podjo said, and just stood there.

Rufus got off me — dismounted, you might say — and I heard the bottle gurgle as the last of the bourbon ran out on the sheets. He must have drunk more of it than I knew, for then a sort of surprised but thoughtful look came on his face, as if he'd just remembered something calamitous out of the past, and he got up from where he was sitting on the side of the bed and made a stumbling run for the bathroom.

He barely made it. Podjo and I could hear him being sick in there, and when I went to see about him he was on his knees in front of the toilet, the way it would be if he was praying to it, chin hooked over the front curve of the seat. He never could drink, but mostly — unlike this time, when first his distress and then his anger were just too much for him to bear — he had sense enough not to try.

I wet one end of a towel to wipe his face and make him feel a little better, then helped him up and half-carried half-guided him back to the bed and got him in it, covers pulled up to his chin. His eyes were partway open and the overhead light made them glitter icy blue. He lay there, stretched out like a corpse, the covers making a long sag from his toes to his throat, as if being drunk and sick had caved him in.

"You all right?" Podjo asked, still in the doorway.

"Yes. Just click that light out of his eyes."

He did, then turned away, and Rufus lay there, still as still, in a reek of vomit and spilled whiskey. "Goddam woman. Goddam woman," he muttered, about as sick as he was drunk, and finally turned on his side and went to sleep. Up front, the TV came on, and there beside me Rufus began to snore, a rasping sound.

Half-lying there alongside him, shoulders propped against the headboard, I tried to make allowances. He'd never been like that before; never hit me, never tried to, even once. But he did scare me now — on that account and the other, the things he'd been saying about Teddy, what-all he'd do. I hadnt believed he meant them, at least not all the way, till now. Now, though, I was beginning to see he might; might mean them, and might do them, too, if it came down to a choice. On the other hand there was still that warm spot, the gratitude I felt for all he'd brought me to, in bed and on the seats of cars, in a phone booth once against the wall while I was talking to another fellow on the phone, and once even in a crowded roadhouse when he crawled up under the table and I nearly cracked both kneecaps in my excitement when I came. You dont forget such things, such moments, all the balance of your life, wherever it takes you.

In those days I couldnt keep my hands off him afterwards — next morning when we woke, then at breakfast, or waiting at the Gypsum gate when he came off shift. Affection matters, getting and giving, even if it amounts to no more than a squeeze or a pat, a kiss on the cheek or just a look across a coffee cup. Lately though, up here I mean, it hadnt been that way at all. Between times I didnt touch him; didnt want to, because I could see he would have flinched back if I tried. I'd always known he was at his worst under pressure, strain or fright of any kind; like that time in the warehouse robbery when he wet his pants. But that didnt matter. What mattered was what was between us, and what was between us now had changed, even such times as out on the lip of the bluff, the night of the day we grabbed Teddy. None of it, such as it was, was really for me, no matter how much I wanted or enjoyed it. It was all for him, a kind of wrestling, a struggle to get outside himself by catching his excitement from mine; *feeding* on me, as I said before. And tonight was worst of all. He'd left me hanging.

Well, I knew a cure for that — right there at hand. I got up, took my skirt and blouse off, put on my robe, and went up front.

Podjo was watching the television; Father Knows Best, I think. He sat on the couch, sort of musing on the screen, and his mustache lay like a bar across the middle of his face.

"Thank you for that in there," I told him. "You got here just in time."

"He probably wouldnt have done you much harm anyhow, considering the shape he's in."

"I guess not. Mind if I sit down?"

"No. Here." He moved over and I sat down, pretending to watch the foolishness being picked up by the rabbit-ear antenna on top of the flickering box. "You rather see something else?" he asked. "Vic Damone's on 3."

"This will be fine," I said.

"How about a drink?"

"I'm fine," I said, and was.

We watched and I felt him looking at me, although I didnt check; Ive been told my profile's my best feature. This wasnt at all like Miss America night, going on three weeks ago, when he was so torn between front and rear.

Finally he said, "I think youve got a bruise there, up beside your eye. You may have yourself a mouse by morning." I turned and he looked closer. "Yair. There's a little swelling here."

He put his hand out, not quite touching where Rufus had bopped me. I watched as he looked, as he bent closer, and let my mouth fall a bit ajar, as if in surprise, when he kept moving closer still and kissed me.

There had been something almost shy about him up till then, unlike the Podjo I expected, but all that ended now. Over his head, while he opened the top of my robe and kissed my breasts, his mouth all trembly under the mustache, I saw Robert Young for a moment on the television screen; a prim little man, not at all like the one in my arms. He drew back — Podjo I mean — and began undoing his trousers while I opened my robe all the way. Then we came back together and he began turning me lengthways on the couch, already forcing my legs apart with his own.

"Wait. Wait," I told him. "I'm not ready. It'll be better if we wait."

"I'm ready enough for both of us," he said.

And he was; God knows he was. Poor couch, poor robe, poor me. He barely managed to make it in before he was half done. And no wonder; all that time he'd been up here alone, with Rufus and me having at it, day in, day out; no wonder. Yet he enjoyed it, I could tell. Brief as it was — he'd gone in a rush from shy to ravenous to tender — it freed him up. He lay there, softening, while I held him, so different from the Podjo I'd expected, and there beyond him was Robert Young, still flickering on the screen as if nothing whatever had happened out here in television land. And the fact was, very little had.

"Hey, I'm sorry," I said in a whisper, my mouth beside his ear.

"Yair? Well — " His mustache tickled my throat when he spoke, and I felt him tense up a bit in my arms. Here came the old Podjo back again. "Look," he said. "I'll worry about me. You worry about you."

"Worry?" I said. I tilted my head enough to look him in the face. "I'm not worried. You just answered something Ive been wondering from the start. You been wanting me all along, havent you? I know that now, from this. Unless, that is, you do this all the time."

I said it to kid him, put him more at ease, and it did.

"Wellp." He got up backward, tucking my legs back down to make me comfortable, then went over and clicked the television off. Again in his drawers, but not his pants, he stood there in his shirt and shoes and socks. "I'm for a drink. You want one?"

"Just a small one. Lots of water."

He went back to the kitchen and I lay there on the soft gold down-stuffed velvet, just clear of the wet place, and behind me, through the wall, heard Rufus snoring and Podjo knocking ice cubes from a tray. I was still left hanging, bad as before, but what I mainly felt was affection. All that indifference, all those weeks, and now this — with more to come. He returned with the drinks, one dark brown, the other pale amber. I took that as a good sign. Most men wont make you a weak drink; they think it's unmanly or something. He gave me mine and took a swallow of his own, then sat down on the couch and took off his shoes and socks. "Here, let me help you off with that," he said, meaning the robe. I was glad to get rid of it because of a wet splotch on it too, between the seat and the hem. Then he took off the rest of his own things, drawers and shirt, and we settled down.

This time was more like it. Though it still was a long way from the best I'd had — God knows I'd had better — it did indeed solve my problem, practically all the way. What's more, there was something about him, now as before, so different from what I had expected. And I could tell it would get better, later on. Lots better; I could tell.

Afterwards we lay there. He was smoking and my head was on his shoulder, my own shoulder in the crook of the arm he wasnt using for the cigarette. Behind us, Rufus snored and snored. "You dont know how much Ive hated this damn couch," Podjo told me. "Until now."

"I like it," I said.

"Strange, though, how it's comfortable for two but not for one."

"Mm," I said, all but drifting off to sleep in spite of my long nap that afternoon.

In another little while, drowsing or not, I felt him shift, then get up. "Ten oclock news," he said, and clicked the set on.

It had already started, and there again was that chunky sergeant with his squad. "Keep those baynets high. Right at the thoat," he said, the same as before, and they bulged the crowd backward, down sidewalks, across yards. Then the scene changed to Cape Canaveral, an Atlas launching earlier that day, and a great long ninety-foot silver rocket sat upright in its scaffold on the pad, fuming at the nose. Three, two, one, zero — "Lift-off!" someone shouted. It flamed and trembled, hovered, and began rising, up and up, roaring, soaring. "Go, baby, go," the announcer told it. But it didnt; not for long. At five thousand feet out over the ocean, that great long beautiful silver thing turned on its side, began to wobble, and exploded in a sudden ball of flame, pieces of it tumbling back to earth, burning too. Aborted, the announcer called what they had done to it, and told how they had had to blow it up.

I got to laughing; I couldnt help it. Podjo scowled, thinking

I was laughing at the Air Force or something. "What's so funny?" he said. So I told him.

"That rocket thing, Atlas, going off like that. It reminded me of you, first time around."

He smiled, but not entirely, then got up and clicked the news off and we lay back down again. Behind us, Rufus kept on snoring in his sleep, a rasping sound, but so steady in its pitch that after you heard it a while you didnt hear it any more.

# 5

# *What Went Down*

Thursday was a slow day for all concerned, except Theo G. Wiggins, who at least had the experience of drawing sixty thousand dollars from the bank; three banks, in fact, to keep from arousing suspicion. "A cash transaction," he explained, and took the money in tens and twenties, as instructed — two thousand of each. Now he and his son-in-law sat at his daughter's dining-room table, transcribing the serial numbers of the bills for possible future use, once the "transaction" had been completed and he had his grandson back.

Actually, though no doubt he would have thought of it on his own without being prompted, the notion of taking down the numbers had come from the letter delivered Wednesday morning in the wake of the phone call advising Martha that it was on the way. Eben returned soon afterward, before the letter got there. She still had the towel around her head, worn turban-like to keep her hair from dripping, and she greeted him with mixed emotions of relief and heightened apprehension. "At least they got a woman looking after him," she said, "no matter what's in the letter. But she told me not to be scared, so it must be scary."

It was indeed: especially the second of the two hand-written pages, the one Eben read first in search of some kind of signature. There was none — not even the skull-and-crossbones or block-lettered KKK he half expected — but the words, which he had begun to read before the postman cleared the gate, fairly leaped at him off the page. *We dont want to kill the child so as not to have a murder rap added to the charge in case of a slip up. But we will most certainly kill him if its a case of skedaddeling without a pay off. Put yourself in our position. Why should we leave a witness even a 8 yr old one, if you have not lived up to your end of the deal? Where as if you pay we owe you his life.* The words above these, concerning the police, were nearly as bad, and in some ways were even more disturbing, considering the danger of accidental disclosure. *They dont give a dam about your boy, they want us. They dont care for a split minute what happens to some little nigger if losing him can get them us, a feather in their cap. Bear that in mind. Remember you have as much if not more to fear from them as we do.*

Back inside, he read the first page, which consisted mainly of instructions on getting ready for the payoff: *$20,000 in tens, $40,000 in twenties, $60,000 total, used and not in sequence. Do not mark bills with ink or chemicals or take numbers — we will know when we examine before releasing boy and deal is off. Pack tight in shoe box tied with cord to keep from spilling. Take your time, a couple of days to get up money — no hurry, Ted. in good hands. You will hear from us Fri or Sat by mail or phone, where and when to deliver package, not until, and boy will be returned soon afterward safe and sound, unless you try to cross us up with tricks or cops, in which case he is goner and we move on to little sister. Do no use radio for tracking or interception, as we are on all frequenceys and have lookouts at Hq in case you try. Remember, do as told here and Ted. will be home in 24 hrs. If not — never, and we move on. You have been warned. Stand by.*

Eben passed the sheet to Martha, and while she went through it, badly confused, reread the second, which was every bit as frightening as before. *Why should we leave a witness even a 8 yr old one, if you have not lived up to your end of the deal? Where as if you pay we owe you his life.*

Martha's confusion matched his own. In both cases, no matter which order they read them in, the fright they got from the second page interfered with their comprehension of the first. Eben perceived from the start that the information was there, all right, but the jangle of interwoven threats prevented him from reducing the instructions to some followable pattern.

"What does it mean?" Martha asked, after a second reading.

"I dont know yet," Eben told her. "Give me some time to take it in and I'll explain it to you."

He read the first sheet through for the third time before he felt able to try, and even so it was only after he began to explain the words that he began to feel he understood them. "It's sixty thousand, half the bills in tens, half in twenties. Theyll give us two days to get it up, then tell me where to bring it, and Teddy will be back with us next day. Put it in a shoebox tied with cord, they say, and then stand by. How in God's name am I going to get sixty thousand dollars in a shoebox?"

"I dont know," she said; "just do. If that's what they say do, do what they say. Daddy will know."

"Yes. I'll go see him when he comes home at noon."

A more pertinent question might have been, How am I going to get sixty thousand dollars? period. Of course he already knew the answer to that; from Tio. But still it bothered him that a man in such distress as this, required to scrape up money for his son's deliverance, should be obliged to go outside himself to get it — especially from his wife's father, even though the father in question was also the child's grandfather and the child in question was his only grandson. Besides, Eben was to remind himself repeatedly in the course of the next few days, it was Tio's money that provoked the crime in the first place, so it was only proper that Tio's money should provide the solution to that abbreviated question.

He told himself that, at any rate, and soon after noon set out up Vance for his father-in-law's house in the next block.

Tio was in the dining room as expected, just finishing the midday dinner he came home to every day, to be followed by

a short upstairs nap before he went back to the office for
another half-day's work — or sometimes a full one, if something substantial was in progress. Lucinda sat at the table with
him, as always, although she seldom did more than pick at her
plate until Dolly brought in the dessert. Today it was peach
cobbler, a large helping for him, a smaller one for her. "You
want some pie, son?" she asked Eben.

"No thank you, Mamma Cindy," he said, tempted; Dolly
made perhaps the best peach cobbler in the world. He turned
to Tio and held out the two-page letter, taking a chair at his
end of the table. "This came this morning. It's from them.
Instructions."

Imperturbable, his napkin suspended in folds from the corner
tucked at his throat to shield the high boiled collar and snub
tie, the pearly shirt-front and expanse of chain-looped vest, Tio
received the letter, placed it beside his empty plate, and after
taking the last swallow from his glass of buttermilk, removed
from an inner pocket of his coat a snap-lidded case with his
steel-rim spectacles inside. He took them out, unfolded them,
and set them astride the broad flat bridge of his nose, hooking
the flexible shanks over his ears with a ducking motion of his
head. Then he unfolded the letter, as deliberately as he had
done the glasses, and began to read. He did not seem affected
by either page, much less confused, though he did take the
trouble to read them twice.

"Yes. We can do that," he said at last, refolding the two
sheets and handing them back. He took off his spectacles, returned them to their case, and snapped it shut with a pop not
unlike the discharge of a small-caliber revolver. "They give us
two days at the least. All right. I'll get the money up tomorrow
and we'll be ready when they call, next day or the next. That
will give us plenty of time to take down the numbers."

"They say not to do that."

"Yes, I saw. That was what give me the notion. How will
they know? We'll do it and use the numbers to track them
down with, once Theo's home."

*Teddy*, Eben thought in reflex, but refrained from making the correction. Let him call him what he wants, from here on in, he thought, so long as he comes up with what theyre asking.

"Maybe that way we'll get the money back," Tio had gone on to say. "What's left of it by then. Right now though," he said, rising and removing the napkin from under his chin, "I'm going up and catch my nap."

"Change yo mind about the pie," Lucinda urged Eben when her husband had gone. "You looking kind of peak-ed nowadays."

"Yessum, thank you," he said, and lame Dolly brought him a helping of cobbler nearly as large as Tio's own, along with a glass of ice-cold buttermilk.

Back home there was nothing to do but wait, and so he did, he and Martha, that night till bedtime and all day Thursday, which seemed to them the longest of their lives. Over across the river, according to the *Commercial*, the Central High situation had settled down to a simmer, though the headline was still a full eight columns wide and black as yesterday. INTEGRATION BEGINS IN LITTLE ROCK SCHOOL/ ENFORCED BY THREAT OF FEDERAL BAYONETS;/ WHITE STUDENT ATTENDANCE OFF ONE-THIRD. *Citizens Stand Tight-Lipped as Grim Soldiers Ring Area*, the subhead read. *Crowd Chased Away; Phony Bomb Scare*. "Lord God, the trouble, the trouble," Eben said as he sank into his Morris chair to read the paper after walking Sister Baby to school and doubling back on Beale to open the office for Lucy Provine.

All day, or nearly all day, the phone didnt ring. Then in the afternoon, soon after Martha left to walk Sister Baby home, it did.

"All right," Tio said when Eben answered. "I got it up and I'll come round after supper. Six-thirty."

"Yes sir," Eben said.

At six-thirty, sharp, while Martha and Sister Baby were putting away the supper things, Eben heard the gate creak. By the time he got the front door open, Tio was up the steps, crossing the porch. He carried in one hand a small black leather grip about the size and shape of a traveling hutch for a lap dog. "Evening," he said as he came in, and inclined his head toward the curtained doorway to the dining room. "How about in there? Go draw the shades."

They went in, and while Eben attended to the shades Tio stood beside the table, still with the grip in his hand and still wearing his brown derby — the one he had been married in, just under forty years ago in Moscow.

"Evening, Lucinda," he said when Sister Baby and Martha came out of the kitchen. He bent for the girl to hug his neck and kiss his cheek. "You dont mind us using your study room for business this one night, do you, honey?"

"No sir," Sister Baby told him.

"Thank you," he said. He straightened up, his face solemn again in the oval shadow of the derby, and spoke to Martha. "Daughter, get us a shoebox. A good stout one, and some string."

By the time Martha got Sister Baby started on her lessons, back in her and Teddy's bedroom, and returned to the dining room with the shoebox — a quite new one, labeled *I. Miller*, from which she removed an unworn pair of low-heel pumps — the two men were at work on opposite sides of the table, transcribing the serial numbers of the bills. "Just the twenties," Tio had told Eben, taking packets of money from the grip. "Nobody looks much at tens any more, even to see if they are homemade. But a twenty, that's something else. For a while at least." Accordingly, he set the tens aside and divided the twenties into two piles of a thousand bills each, one for him and one for his son-in-law. "All right, let's get started," he said, and took an outsized silver-mounted fountain pen — another relic of early days, even older than the derby — from still another of the several inner pockets of his coat.

Their hands and heads in the pool of light that poured from the lamp suspended above the table, they worked steadily at jotting down the ten-digit figures, Eben rather feverishly, with a good deal of lost motion, Tio so methodically that he appeared to be in no hurry at all, though in fact his pile diminished considerably faster than Eben's in the course of the first hour. It's because he's used to it, Eben thought; used to counting stacks of money all these years; used to watching Andrew Jackson stare past his right shoulder a thousand times a night.

So he told himself, by way of excuse, but there was more to it than that. For one thing, he was still recovering from the double shock he had suffered when Tio unloaded the grip. The first shock was at seeing that much currency tumped out before him, stacks and stacks of it, green as green, and the other was at the sudden realization that it would perhaps fit in a shoebox after all. Once he adjusted to this, he began to transcribe a good bit faster, though he still had four twenty-five-bill packets in front of him at nine-thirty, when Tio's were all gone. Without comment, Tio reached across the table and took two of them, adding those fifty numbers to his list. They finished together, and while Eben packed the bills in the shoebox — they did fit, and not all that snugly — Tio wrote on the lid in his flowing copperplate script:

> *Eben Kinship, Assoc. V.P.*
> *Wiggins Development Corp.*
> *185 Beale Ave., Memphis*

"In case you misplace it or something," he explained as he screwed the cap back on his big-barreled fountain pen and stowed it away inside his coat.

Here again, as so often on other occasions, it was hard to tell whether he was making a joke or offering an admonition. Probably neither; he just said it, Eben decided, putting the lid on the box and tying it round and round with string, which he then knotted tightly, across and lengthwise. His guess, when he took it up from the table — sixty *thousand* dollars — was that it weighed about fifteen pounds, a figure hardly commensurate with all it represented in the way of hopes and fears, his and most men's, here and elsewhere down the long slopes of the world.

Tio had his derby on, the empty grip in his hand. It was crowding ten oclock by now, his invariable bedtime. "Well, goodnight, Daughter," he told Martha, who was waiting in the living room when he came through the curtained doorway.

"Goodnight, Daddy," she said.

"And thanks, thanks again," Eben said as he opened the front door, made awkward by the burden of the shoebox.

"Well, yes. Yes," Tio said, and went out and down the steps.

They waited till he cleared the gate, then closed the door and started back. Eben however made it no farther across the room than the couch, where he sat with the string-tied box across his thighs, gripping it tightly with both hands, as if someone might appear at any moment and try to snatch it from him. Martha hesitated, looking at him from where she waited beside the clouded crystal ball of the dead television screen, then returned and sat beside him. He looked worried, and he was.

Earlier in the dining room, during a pause the two men took to rest their eyes, Tio remarked that he had considered calling in Emile Spicer to get up a private force to ferret out the kidnappers and deliver Teddy by moving in on them, but had decided against it as being too risky on several counts, not the least of which was that Spicer's rousters might not be trustworthy with that much cash involved. Hearing this, Eben was discouraged by the thought that not even Emile Spicer, with all the resources of the Memphis underworld at his command, could help them now. And if he could not help them, dealing as he presumably would be with his own kind, of whatever color, then who could? The answer seemed to be that no one could; no one except the kidnappers themselves, the very ones who had pointed out, in their letter that morning, the folly of leaving a witness behind to identify and testify against them; *even a 8 yr old one*, they had said. With his son's life in forfeit he was dependent on their good will and good faith, neither of which, in the light of all they had done up to now, he had any reason to believe they practiced or possessed.

Now that he had the money, the actual cash tied up in a shoebox in his lap, he perceived that it was Teddy's one sure link with survival — not in the way he had formerly supposed, but in reverse. So long as he had it, and they did not, his son was presumably safe. Once it was gone, once they had it, that assurance was removed. And in his weariness and distress, both much greater now on the living-room couch than they had been an hour ago at the dining-room table, where he at least was kept busy transcribing number after ten-digit number from his half of those two thousand twenty-dollar bills, he made the grievous mistake of passing his fears along to his wife, together with the possible solution of withholding the ransom until he secured some better assurance of Teddy's survival.

"It's the only thing that can really stop them," he declared, clutching the money in his lap. "Holding it back would hold *them* back. You see? What could they do?"

"*Do?*" Martha looked at him, level-eyed, and he began to suspect that she had not heard him right. Frown lines, first of disbelief and then of outrage, began to appear around her mouth, which flattened as he watched. For a long moment she did not answer. Then she did. "You must have lost your mind," she said.

"No, no, you dont understand. I mean as a way of saving him."

She did not even shake her head at this. She merely repeated what she had said before, in the same level tone of voice. "You must have lost your mind."

"I was just thinking," he told her, perceiving at last the error of his ways, but too late to disown or contradict the words.

"You a cold-hearted, close-fisted man, Eben Kinship. Ever was."

He understood what she meant by that, and even wondered how much of it was true. Now that he had the money in hand — sixty *thousand* dollars — maybe he was finding it harder than he knew to turn it loose. Maybe his fear, or rather his attempt to allay that fear, was designed to mask that reluctance, even from himself. The thought of this made him so angry that his resentment matched her own.

"Dont talk to me that way, woman," he told her sternly, turning on her there beside him on the couch.

She rose, eyes blazing in her face. "I'll talk to you any way I want, you start saying things like let them kill my boy!"

"I didnt say that and you know it."

He rose too, fuming at the unfairness of the charge, the swift and easy logic she employed to reverse the meaning of his words. Half a head taller, but bent a little forward so that they were face to face, he delivered himself of a judgment, a historical assessment of her attitude and manner: "My daddy wouldnt a put up for a minute with my mamma talking to him that way."

"You dont know what yo daddy would or wouldnt a put up with," she told him, adopting and mocking the patios he fell back on whenever he was emotionally aroused, as he was now. "Besides, you aint yo daddy," she went on. "And I sho as hell aint yo mamma."

Now that it had come down to this — Eben with no ground left to stand on, Martha with a bit more edge than she had really meant to grab, and both of them holding tightly to their anger lest it slip away and either of them be left without the advantage of moral indignation — he struck her, open-handed and high on the head to spare her jaw and eyes. There was a good deal more noise than damage from the blow. Caught off balance as she was, however, she tripped backward onto the couch and into a proper sitting position, not even sprawled, much like the one she had occupied before she rose. She was not hurt, and in fact was no more than a trifle surprised; for while it was true that he had never before slapped her, it was also true that he had never been so provoked till now.

It seemed to him, looking down at her, that her face softened, though her voice still held a measure of indignation. "What good did *that* do?" she inquired.

"No good a-tall — for you, I reckon," he told her. "A little for me though. Anyhow it helps to clear the air. Next time I'll close my fist, and now you know it."

"I dont know nothing of the kind," she said, still talking Mississippi. Then she stopped, about as abruptly as she had begun, and delivered a judgment of her own. "All I know is you cant deal with a big problem, so you prop yourself up by pretending to deal with a little one. Me. And you cant deal with that either."

"Hush now. Hush," he said, and sat beside her on the couch.

This had gotten too close to the bone and they both knew it; especially Eben. He remembered his mother and father in the old days, the shouts and cries, the broken crockery downstairs in the cafe. "Aint they having *at* it!" his sister Julia used to marvel. Upstairs too, sometimes, there were sudden pistol-like explosions in the adjoining room — slaps — followed by sobs and accusations involving money or another man or woman, then still more slaps, almost as rapid-fire as applause, and occasionally the police would arrive and break it up. "You damn Kinships get to bed now. Stop this foolishness," they would say, and mostly that would be the end of it; unless, that is, the thing flared up again, in which case the police returned and took his father off to jail and sent him back next morning with the marks of nightsticks grooved along his scalp. Those nights, those mornings, had been among the things that made Eben gun-shy about marriage, that had urged the near leap from the car on his wedding day, en route to Beale Street Baptist. They had been part of his life, and Julia's too, until both of them left home, he for the army and she in various directions. "Aint they having *at* it!" she used to marvel, head cocked sideways on her pillow to catch the words those two downstairs were screaming at each other in the night.

He reached out and laid his hand on Martha's shoulder, and though she gave one quick shrug, a sort of reflex, she let it stay there. Moreover he could detect, behind the pout she wore, a certain pride or anyhow satisfaction at having provoked him into striking her. "I'm sorry," he said.

"I'm — I'm sorry too," she told him.

"We're just all wrought-up about Teddy."

"I know. I know we are."

Then he looked down and saw the shoebox on the floor where he had dropped it. He stared at it for a moment, then realized with a shock that he had forgotten its existence. How could I do that? he asked himself, and bent forward and picked it up.

"Let's get to bed," he said. "It's late."

It wasnt really all that late; just past ten; but the words, "Let's get to bed," had acquired a new significance in the course of the past three nights, and tonight was no exception to the change. By the time Martha returned from checking on Sister Baby, who had been asleep more than an hour by now, Eben had stowed the shoebox under the bed, gotten his clothes off and his nightshirt on, and lain down with the covers pulled up to his chin, braced for the nightly floor show, the modified strip-tease his wife would perform behind the partial screen of the half-open closet door. The gown went on, the underclothes rustling beneath it, and then the nightcap, but more from habit than from need, since there was no grease to rub off on the pillow. Interrupted in her shampoo yesterday morning by the two phone calls, she had never gotten around to applying the straightening lotion, and instead wore a scarf wrapped around her head to hide her unslicked hair while she moved about the house and went to walk her daughter home from school. All the same, whether from habit or from modesty carried forward by some form of secondary inertia, she put the nightcap on, and the wooly socks as well, before she came from behind the door and got in bed alongside Eben.

"All right?" he said, one hand on the lamp.

"All right," she said, and he clicked the switch.

Everything was as before, up to that point, and then it changed. It changed even more tonight than it had done on any of the three preceding nights since the change began. Perhaps the urgency, so evident on both their parts, grew out of the fight they had just patched up between them. In any case the connection was sudden, almost without preamble. She even hitched up her nightgown herself, while he threw the bed-clothes back, and in no time at all they were joined in a strain of mutual need. "Do it! Oh, do it!" she cried, churning her hips and raising both feet in their fuzzy socks to pound the backs of his thighs with her heels.

Eben was somewhat taken aback, like a man who has watched what he thought was a spring breeze develop abruptly into a windstorm. It occurred to him, as if between two ticks of the bedside clock, that she might be trying desperately to have another child, a son to replace the one that had been taken, but he soon abandoned all such speculation to concentrate in-stead on the enjoyment of this gift that had come his way with Teddy's loss.

He woke once in the night from a dream of money, stacks and stacks of it, green as green, and remembered what lay on the floor beneath his head — the string-tied box, one of whose corners was slightly crumpled from the fall it took when, for-getting there was any such thing as money in the world, he rose from the couch to smack his wife — then drifted off and did not wake again till close to getting-up time. Martha slept facing him, near the middle of the mattress, one hand under her cheek, profoundly relaxed. He studied her in the pearly early-morning light filtered through the screen of the bedroom window.

Somehow, overnight, she had lost her lace-trimmed cap, so that her hair, ungreased and unrestrained, bushed out all round her head, sooty black against the whiteness of her pillow. His first reaction to this unfamiliar neglect had been regret; he had never thought she would let herself go like that, even under the strain of the past four days, ignoring the "beauty hints" whose application filled so large a part of her life. But now he recalled how soft her hair had felt last night, the whispery dryness fragrant of itself, and it seemed to him, watching her sleeping there beside him, so much closer than before, that much else was softer about her, too. The curved lift of brow, the peaceful mouth with its tender disappearing corners, the rounded chin, all seemed softer and somehow fuller — and so, though he had never seen them uncovered except fleetingly, by accident, in all the nearly ten years of his marriage; so did her breasts, rising and falling under her high-buttoned gown with the slow rhythm of her breath. As he watched, her eyelids trembled and her eyes came suddenly open. They were fuller, too, he thought, unless it was just the magnification that came with being at such close range for what seemed the first time in his life. Or perhaps it was even simpler than that. Perhaps he was falling in love. "I like your hair that way. It's soft," said.

Before she could wake enough to react to this, however, the alarm clock rang and she was up and off, head re-scarfed, to get Sister Baby roused and breakfast started.

*Fri or Sat by mail or phone*, Wednesday's letter had said, and this was Friday. But there was nothing, no word either by mail or phone, all day or all night either. There was rain again, a finer kind, with a touch of fall in the way it dripped and smoked, and across the way in Arkansas the jump-booted soldiers kept their vigil, though the morning headline had contracted to six columns. FAUBUS LASHES FEDERAL GOVERNMENT/ FOR 'POLICE STATE' INTEGRATION ACTION;/ TROOPS EXTEND LINES AROUND SCHOOL. On television, the news cameramen fell back on shots of girls in ballerina skirts and eyelet blouses giggling at the helmeted paratroopers, teen-aged too, for the most part, as they passed in both directions through their ranks. None of it meant anything to Eben, who spent the day with his ear cocked for the phone, and much of the night as well. Several times he woke in the heavy silence of the bedroom, thinking he heard it ring, but it always turned out that the ringing was in his dreams.

Next morning was that way, too, until around ten-thirty the phone gave a sudden peal. He answered and the voice said, "Eben Kinship?" — the voice he had heard on Monday, five days back.

"Speaking."

"You got the package?"

"Package. Yes."

"O.K. Now get this. Handy Park: high noon today. Come alone. Be by the phone, the double phone booth there, and bring the package. Got it?"

"Yes, but — "

"That's it. Noon: Handy Park. Be by the phone." Click.

Eben was left hanging, looking down at the dead instrument in his hand. "Was it them? Was it them?" Martha asked, close beside him.

"It was them," he said. "I'm due to meet them at noon."

"Can I go too?"

"No. They said come alone."

"Where?"

"Never mind," he told her. But then, seeing her face, he relented. "Handy Park. By the phone booth there, at noon."

"What about Teddy?"

"They didnt say."

"But how *is* he?"

"They didnt say. They hung up on me before I could ask."

"Oh Jesus, Eben. Jesus."

"I know. I know," he said. He put his arm across her shoulders. "I know. I know," he said.

He left within the hour, to make sure he would not be late, and though he walked the familiar route at a slower pace than usual, cradling the shoebox first under one arm then the other — Vance to Hernando, half a block, then three blocks up Hernando to Beale and the southeast corner of Handy Park — he arrived with nearly a quarter-hour to spare. Four of the park's half-dozen benches were occupied, all by Negroes, singly or in couples, some of them spending part of their midday break here in the open, others just loafing, having no job to take a break from.

One of the latter, a shabby man in rumpled clothes, was on the bench adjoining the double phone booth. When Eben sat down, the man turned and studied him.

"Got you some shoes," he remarked, nodding approval.

"What?"

"Shoes." He pointed. "You got you some shoes I see."

"Yes."

For a moment Eben had thought this might be the contact he expected, but now that he looked he saw it could not be. He looked away.

"Say." The man edged closer, and Eben, looking back, saw that the jaundiced whites of his eyes were threaded with red; red on yellow. What was more, he was old — past seventy at least. "You want to hep a old fellow git sump'n teat?"

"What?"

"To *eat*," the man said. "I'm hongry and broke. I played in my time with Handy, here and all through the Delta in my day, till my hands went bad with arthuritis and a woman done me in. Now I'm down on my luck and I'm hongry."

Thirsty you mean, Eben thought, drawing back from the stale reek of whiskey coming at him. He extended one leg, reached deep in his side pocket, and brought out a quarter. "Here," he said, conscious of the sixty thousand dollars in his lap, and dropped the coin onto the pale yellow palm of the crippled hand that had moved toward him while he probed his pocket.

The man got up, tall and cave-chested, specter thin, and shuffled in his broken shoes toward a beer place on the other side of Beale. I guess he dont need to say thank-you, Eben thought. He just lets his condition say it for him, whether he played with Handy back in the olden days or not.

Handy. Alone on the bench beside the double booth, the ransom-laden shoebox in his lap, he thought of Handy, whom he had never seen. Blind now and crowding eighty-five, the Professor, as they called him, had left for New York nearly forty years ago, even before Mr Crump closed down the sporting life in response to having Prudential Life declare Memphis the murder capital of the nation. From time to time he would return, as for the dedication of this park in the early Thirties, but not any more. He would die in the spring — March 28, just six months from today — and two years later, after a fund drive, friends would set up a statue of him, here in the park that bore his name, a little larger than life and dressed in a double-breasted suit of bronze, head uplifted, holding a trumpet with both hands and looking out over the ruin of Beale, which urban renewal soon would reduce to a rubbled waste. By then, the electric guitar having begun its amplified abolition of the music he knew and wrote, he would be about as outdated as the leather-winged pterodactyl and would have gone to join other forgotten heroes in the Memphis pantheon: Ed Crump, dead almost three years now and buried out in Elmwood, whose own statue, wearing its overcoat in even the hottest weather, had been unveiled this spring in Overton Park, and Machine Gun Kelly: Casey Jones, who began his last run out of the old South Street Station, and Bedford Forrest: Davy Crockett, who flung a blufftop farewell whiskey bust on his way to the Alamo, and Andrew Jackson — none of them born here, yet all of them Memphis-connected, like Eben himself and his father-in-law, Theo G. Wiggins, the door of whose office was in plain view beyond the Beale-Third intersection close at hand.

But that was mostly in the future and the past, a past that was peopled with ghosts from the far beyond. All there was now for Eben, left alone on the bench after the departure of the man who might or might not have played with Handy in his day, was the shabby little quarter-acre park, with its starved patches of withered grass and its few scrubby trees, and one of the phones ringing insistently in the adjoining booth.

For a time he did not connect the ringing with himself, having considered the phone booth, like the park itself, nothing more than a convenient landmark — a landmark within a landmark, so to speak — readily identifiable as a place to meet with those who had his son and turn over to them the money he hoped would secure his son's release. On about the fourth ring, however, it came home to him that he was expected to answer. He got up and did, and the voice was the one from before. "Eben?" it said, as if familiarity through repetition — this was, after all, the third time they talked — had put them at last on a first-name basis, at least in one direction.

They could see him from their high window, Rufus with his naked eye, the hotel telephone in hand, Podjo with the help of opera glasses. "Yes," he said, and Podjo saw him nod as he spoke, almost as if Rufus was there in the phone booth with him, face to face, in a more or less casual encounter.

"Right. You got it with you, the package?"

"I do," he said, nodding again into the mouthpiece.

While they talked — Rufus and Eben — Podjo continued to sweep the park with his glasses, studying the half-dozen people seated on benches and others walking along the two-block stretch of Beale, visible from west of Third to east of Hernando, or standing in doorways, one of which was old Theo G's own, whose goldleaf medallion he could not quite read, despite the four-power magnification, at a distance of more than six hundred feet. Now as before, there was nothing suspicious anywhere in sight.

"O.K." he told Rufus, touching his shoulder to get his attention. "All clear. Tell him goodbye till tomorrow."

He was pleased at how well the thing had gone since they left the bluff that morning for a dry run designed to assure success when the real thing went down. Just as they had rehearsed the snatch itself in the course of the week leading up to the Monday the boy was taken, so now they set out on Saturday to rehearse the Sunday payoff. Podjo explained that the two most dangerous times for them were the two pickups, first of the boy, then of the ransom, and of these the latter was by far the worse, since it was then that the payer, alerted beforehand as to time and place, was likely to try for a swoop.

"That's where most of these jobs go wrong, at the pickup," he told Rufus, and outlined a procedure he had devised, after a good deal of study on the ground and in his mind, to make reasonably certain there would be no tricks when payoff time came round. The thing to do was get Kinship out in the open, where he could be observed under circumstances similar to those that would obtain next day. That way, if he called on the law or some private source for help, they would find it out and know to avoid the trap that had been laid. Podjo wondered and reconnoitered, but not for long; Handy Park was the answer, there at hand, along with the Hotel Tennessee, whose south windows overlooked it. "If he's called in help, we'll spot it and let him know we know. You see?"

Rufus saw, all right, and found in what he saw still further confirmation of his good judgment for having brought Podjo in on the operation from the start. They left the house around nine-thirty, Podjo with his still-packed suitcase, and their first stop was at a pawnshop across Beale from the Wiggins office. Podjo chose a low-power opera glass, inlaid with badly chipped mother-of-pearl, in preference to some other superior models because of the price, four dollars, and the fact that their cash was running low by now. No matter how rich they might be tomorrow, today they were down to about forty of the original five hundred dollars they had scraped together for a stake. From the pawnshop they walked up to Handy Park, where he took down the numbers of both phones in the double booth, then came back and set out again in the car, turning left on Third. Two blocks beyond the park and a half a block short of Union Avenue, directly across from the more prestigious Peabody, was the Hotel Tennessee. There, by luck, they parked in a space just beyond the glass-doored entrance, and Podjo got out with his bag and went in, followed by Rufus.

"A single," he told the desk clerk. "High up, with a southern exposure. I'll pay in advance."

"Four fifty," the clerk said, and taking the money, along with the signed registration card — *Joseph Joplin* it read, in a back-slanted hand, *Pine Ridge, Ark* — passed him the key to Room 823. "Top floor south, Mr Joplin. You want a bellboy?"

"No thanks," Podjo said, hefting the suitcase, and told Rufus, "Come on up while I get settled."

Aboard the elevator Rufus shook his head. "I dont like it," he said, and nodded morosely in the direction of the key in Podjo's hand. "Room number. It adds up to thirteen."

Podjo shrugged at this, and presently — "Eighth flow," the operator announced, his bald scalp glistening like polished mahogany as he slid the elevator door ajar — led the way to the left, down the hall to Room 823 at its end. Inside, he dropped his suitcase by the bed, crossed to the window on the right, and leaning forward with both hands on the jambs, face near the glass, peered out and down. There below him, in oblique panorama, its northern border less than two hundred yards away, plainly visible beyond the rim of the flat-roofed three-story parking garage just south of the hotel, was Handy Park with its few stunted trees, already all but leafless, its half-dozen benches, only one of them occupied at this hour, and its double phone booth near the Third-Beale intersection. He took the toylike glasses from his pocket, lifted and focused them, and began to sweep the park and the two-block stretch of Beale on its far side.

"O.K." he said as he took them down. "Give him a call at home."

Rufus did. "Eben Kinship?" he said. "You got the package? . . . O.K. Now get this," he told him, and set up the appointment. "That's it," he ended. "Noon: Handy Park. Be by the phone," and hung up on him.

"How'd he sound?" Podjo asked.

"Scared. Scared and anxious."

"That's just the way we want him, start to finish."

It was ten-thirty by then. With an hour and a half to wait for Eben to show up, down below, Podjo stretched out on the bed, the pillow folded double for a headrest, and lit a Chesterfield. Uncharacteristically silent, even broody, Rufus sat by the telephone and the window, looking out at the all-but-empty park and the slack midmorning traffic on Beale and Third.

"You know," Podjo said at last, blowing smoke toward the watermarked ceiling, "I used to come up to Memphis on basketball trips before the war, those years we made the finals. We stayed here at the Tennessee because it was cheaper than across the street at the Peabody, but we hung out in the lobby there, what time we werent practicing or playing and could get away from the coach. We would see planters and businessmen from down around home, out with brass-haired women and other businessmen's wives. Far as we could tell, they might as well have been up here with their own, so far as looks went, except I guess cutting down on the notion of misbehaving would have cut down on the fun. Anyhow we slept four to a room, two of us in each twin bed. That was to save money too. It wasnt so bad; basketball players werent as tall in those day, not nearly. We liked the high-up rooms the best — ones like this — because at night, when the traffic died down some, car horns used to sound like fox hunters three fields off, and you could leave the shower running all night long, so youd sleep to the sound of rain like on a tin roof back down home. Memphis for us was the city. Whatever one you saw in later life, youd see it in terms of Memphis, whatever its size. Even New York. I saw it once from a troopship railing, back from overseas. It looked brand new, all straight up and down, sort of glittering in the sunlight, and I thought, 'Jesus. Jesus,' I thought. 'It's ten times bigger than Memphis.' Later I found that was just about right; five million to half a million. But to me it wasnt the city. Memphis was. Like on a hill."

He fell silent, nursing the stub of his cigarette till he ground it out on the ledge of the window by the bed. For another full minute he lay there, uncomfortable in the knowledge that his volubility, his long-windedness, was as incongruous as Rufus's mute brooding. Maybe we swapped parts, he thought, remembering Reeny and the way she tucked herself up under him on the couch the other night.

"Wellp," he said as he swung his legs off the bed to rise, "I'm going down for a paper. Want to go?"

"I'll wait here and keep a lookout," Rufus told him.

"Right. Be back shortly."

In the lobby he picked up a *Commercial*, which he scanned while having a cup of coffee in the Tennessean, as the coffee shop was called, before returning to the room. By then it was past eleven oclock and Rufus was still in the chair by the telephone and the window, looking out at the park and the traffic.

"Whynt you go down and get you some coffee?" Podjo asked with an up-from-under look.

"I'm fine right here."

"Anything shaking?"

"Naa. It's just like any other Saturday down there; tuning up for sundown, when the neon lights go on."

On the bed again, Podjo began a careful reading of the paper, page by page, picking up the continuations as they came along. Little Rock was still the lead, but the headline had dwindled to three columns. Faubus Urged to Issue/ Special Session Call/ In Integration Crisis. The Mid-South Fair would close tonight, and daylight saving time would go off in the small hours of the morning. He read on, finding most of it dull, until Rufus at last broke the silence.

"There he is! And by God he's got the shoebox under his arm."

Podjo reached the window in time to see Eben take a seat on the bench adjoining the phone booth, next to a man who was already there. When the man spoke to him, pointing at the same time to the shoebox in his lap, Rufus asked in alarm, "Is that some kind of undercover contact?"

But Podjo, with the glasses, could see better. "Nah. It's just a bum." And sure enough, they saw Eben reach deep in his pocket for a coin that sent the man shuffling toward the other side of Beale. Podjo continued to sweep the park, stopping for a careful examination of the people on four of the six benches, and then the buildings across the way, including the upper windows of those that had them. As before, there was nothing suspicious anywhere in sight.

"Let's take him now," Rufus said, all of a sudden.

"Hey, old son," Podjo replied, still with the glasses to his eyes. "Dont get jumpy in the homestretch."

"Jumpy, hell," Rufus sputtered. "He's right down there with the goddam sixty thousand in his lap! You can see yourself the coast is clear. Let's *take* him."

"You take it easy, that's what you do," Podjo told him, and removed from his shirt pocket the slip of paper on which he had written the two numbers when they stopped by the phone booth two hours before. "Now go on; put the call through. Either number."

For a time, while Eben sat there on the bench, Podjo thought the phone must be out of order. "Is it ringing?" he asked. "Try the other number." Before Rufus could answer, however, Eben rose and stepped into the booth.

"Eben?" Rufus said, and Podjo, adjusting the focus of the glasses till the view was icy clear, saw Eben nod at the instrument in his hand, then nod again when Rufus asked if he had the package they both could see him holding against his chest. "O.K. You came up clean as a whistle," Rufus told him. "Youre well on the way to getting your boy back. . . . Hold it."

Cupping the mouthpiece with his palm, he turned and spoke to Podjo, who continued to watch Eben. "I say again, let's get it now. I'll hold him on the line till you get down there, then tell him to walk off and leave it in the booth. People leave all kinds of things in phone booths. Then you can pick it up and we'll head for the bluff and split it, home free. What do you say?"

"Stick to the plan, stick to the plan," Podjo told him, still with the glasses raised, watching Eben cling to the silent phone, two football fields away.

"O.K." Rufus said regretfully. He sighed and uncupped his hand. "Eben? Yair. Listen. This was a dry run, a test. . . . No, we're not trying to devil you. What the hell. We just want to make sure youre not up to anything spooky, like bringing in the cops or some private muscle. That could have cost you your boy, for keeps. But you did fine. We trust you. Now go on home and wait for one more call tomorrow, during church. Thatll be it, the real thing, and you will have your boy back, soon as we check the money."

Bending so that his ear was near the receiver, Podjo heard Eben squeak and gibber like Punch in the Punch-and-Judy show, trying to get a word in edgewise before Rufus hung up on him.

"But how's Teddy? How *is* he?"

"He couldnt be better. He's fine."

"How can I know that?" Podjo heard Eben protest.

"What's the matter? Dont you trust us?" Rufus said. He smiled down into the mouthpiece, apparently recovered from his daylong doldrums. "We trust you. Why dont you trust us? Teddy's fine; youll see. He'll be with you in jigtime, once you pay us and we get the money counted. Right? Now go on home and wait for the call. Tomorrow, during church."

The hotel phone went down, and across the distance Podjo saw Eben wilt, the shoebox clutched to his chest with one hand while the other still held the dead instrument to his ear. Wait! Wait! he could almost hear him shout. Presently he came out of the booth, but he only made it as far as the bench, where he sat for a couple of minutes, as if to catch his breath or re-cover his balance, then rose and made his way across the park toward Beale, once more with the shoebox under his arm.

"I still say we ought to take him," Rufus said, watching too. "Hellfire, Podjo — sixty *thousand* goddam dollars! The way he's poking we can catch up with him before he's halfway home; pick our spot, then pull up at the curb alongside him, grab the box, and be long gone before he knows what hit him. What do you say? Because who the hell knows what might happen between now and tomorrow, to him *or* us?"

Podjo kept his anger under control, though only by the

hardest, so great was his resentment of this scatterbrained proposal to convert his carefully laid-out operation, with all its built-in safety factors, into a daylight mugging on the public street. "Stick to the plan, old son," was all he replied, now as before. He turned and took up his suitcase, tossing the room key on the bed. "Let's get out of here," he said.

Downstairs, he got in the car on the passenger side, hoisted the suitcase onto the back seat, and when Rufus settled under the steering wheel told him, "Let's go by the drop site one last time before tomorrow."

"Check," Rufus said brightly, his spirit still up despite the triple rejection of his plan for immediate action, and eased out into the Saturday midday traffic.

He turned left on Union, left on Second, then drove four blocks south to Pontotoc, where he turned left again, drove another two blocks east, and pulled over to the curb just short of Hernando. They were now only a little farther south of Handy Park than they had been north of it in the hotel room a few minutes ago, and were even nearer the Kinship house on Vance, one block south and a half a block west. Ahead and to their left, on the northeast corner of the Hernando-Pontotoc intersection, a broad sixty-foot stone tower soared out of sight beyond the upper rim of the windshield, and to the right of the Gothic doorway in its base a weathered metal sign read, CLAYBORN TEMPLE. A.M.E. CHURCH.

Podjo had wondered about this before, and now he asked. "What does that mean? A.M.E."

"African Methodist Episcopal," Rufus told him, ready as always with an answer, along with the trimmings. "What it really means is Methodist. There's three kinds: northern Methodists, southern Methodists, nigger Methodists — like this. African, they call it."

"Whatever they call it, that's one hell of a church."

"Yair. It used to be white, until about ten years ago. Second Presbyterian, like it says in stone over the other door, there on the left beyond those three big stained-glass windows. I looked it up once. When it was built, back before the turn of the century, it was the largest church building in the whole country south of the Ohio. This was a high-class white neighborhood in those days, before the colored ooched them out. The Presbyterians built themselves a new one in '47 or so, well out east where most of them lived by then, and sold this one to the nigger Methodists."

"All the better," Podjo said. "That means theyll make more racket singing and shouting when theyre packed in there tomorrow during the pickup."

"Right."

"O.K. Ease on forward, alongside the store there."

This was on the southeast corner, directly ahead and to the right of where Rufus had parked. Dwarfed by the dark stone mass of the church that loomed beside it, the two-story concrete structure, with rooms for rent above the downstairs shop — or sundry, as it called itself in crude but ornate lettering on the showcase window: *O.K. Sundry, Welcome All* — was built flush with the sidewalk, front and flank, so that the intersection was blind on the right when approached from the south, as Eben would be instructed to approach it when he walked here from his house on Vance tomorrow. Some fifteen yards east of the blind corner, beside the rear entrance to the shop, a near-full trash barrel awaited the weekly rounds of the sanitation department. It was here that the drop and pickup would be made, reasonably secure from observation either from back on Hernando or from the church, sideways across Pontotoc, with its opaque windows of stained glass. That was why Podjo, after a careful reconnaissance of the region within easy walking distance of the Kinship house, had chosen this as the place and Sunday as the day, both of which he believed would greatly reduce the likelihood of interference by some accidental witness.

He explained his choice of Sunday. "The sporting half of the people will still be in bed, sleeping off Saturday night," he told Rufus, "and the other half will be in church, here or in the

dozen-or-so others roundabout. That leaves Kinship and us —
him to drop the shoebox in the barrel, us to lift it out as soon
as he's rounded the corner, headed back the way he came.
Got it?"

"Got it," Rufus said, easing past the rear of the O.K. Sundry
and on toward Fourth, a block away.

"One more thing," Podjo told him. "And I really want you
to get this straight for minding down the line, whatever happens. I'll make the pickup, back at the barrel, then walk up here
and get in the car. You watch me through the rear window,
casual-like, and if something goes wrong, for whatever reason — I mean if you see them grab me, the cops or whoever —
you get the hell out. Go back to the bluff and lay low for a
couple of hours to catch your breath. Then get in touch with
Kinship or old Wiggins and maneuver for my release. Me for
the boy, the boy for me; with or without the ransom, but pref-
erably with it. You understand?"

"Right," Rufus said with a positive nod. "You can count on
me, Podj, and you know it. Till hell freezes over. And you can
count on me then on the ice."

"Hm," Podjo said, watching the traffic up ahead as Rufus
made the right turn onto Fourth, headed for Crump and the
river.

Driving south, Rufus began losing the euphoria he had shown
while talking on the hotel telephone. By the time he turned
west on Crump he had reverted to the brooding petulance of
that morning, before the phone call perked him up. Podjo,
though he normally had small use for any kind of music,
switched on the radio to see if that would help, and by luck it
was Ella Fitzgerald. Ella was Rufus's favorite singer, all the way
back to his boyhood when she played a one-night stand with
Chick Webb at the Bristol Casino. He was nine at the time, that
last spring before the war broke out in Europe, and his mother
and her date, a traveling salesman, let him sit out in the parking
lot and listen. "Undecided" was one of the songs she sang, the
same as now on the car radio. He remembered seeing her

through an open window of the club he was too young to enter. She was playing a slot machine during a break, and Webb was beside her, hunchbacked, in a white tuxedo. "She was just nineteen or so," he would recall, "all-over brown, in a red dress, still with some of her baby fat on her. I'll never forget how she looked. Or him either, high up on that motor-cycle seat he used for drumming." Two months later he read in the paper that Webb had died of an operation in Baltimore, and he was not long in inventing a conversation they had that night, out on the club steps in the moonlight, in which Chick told him he knew his time was nigh.

Listening now to "Undecided," he brightened a bit. "She really swings it, dont she?" he declared when the number ended.

He was smiling again, but not for long. He went back to frowning when the announcer played another bygone record, this one featuring Bing Crosby, whom he despised almost as much as he liked Ella. "Bubba boo, bubba boo," he muttered scornfully, and reached out and clicked him off. "Goddam crooners. We had us a great country here until they came along, Russ Columbo and the rest. Horse-hockey, all of them, right from the start. I looked for Johnnie Ray to save us, till he fell by the wayside. Now I pin my hopes on Elvis, if he dont up and get curdled the way Ray did."

They were on Riverside by then, within sight of the China-man's on the corner at Carolina. Rufus made the turn, went past the nipple company without comment, then turned left again on Arkansas and pulled into the mulberry-screened drive-way. While he sat looking down at the steering wheel, brood-ing dejectedly on the hands that gripped its rim, Podjo got out with his suitcase and went up the steps, into the house.

Reeny was in the living room watching a quiz show while she filed her nails. "How did it go?" she asked, rising to meet him.

"Went good," he told her. "We cased the action in Handy Park and set up the drop for tomorrow, like we planned. One more day after that, for getting squared away, and we'll be gone."

She stood facing him, smiling until Rufus came in, and then she turned away. What had been a slight mauve-violet bruise alongside her right eye had faded by now to a trace of yellowish green, barely discernible in this light unless you knew it was there and searched it out. Tonight would be the third night since Rufus swung the roundhouse left that did the damage, such as it was, and she had spoken to him as little as possible since then, day or night. She sat back down on the couch and returned to filing her nails, more or less as if Rufus had not entered.

"Well, Reen, we're all set," he said, standing just inside the doorway and looking a little sheepish despite his cheerfulness, which seemed forced. "Tomorrow's the payoff and we're home free. A cinch."

"Podjo told me," she replied, not looking up.

"Who's for a beer?" Podjo asked, and headed for the kitchen without waiting for an answer.

He was staying out of it, ostensibly at least. Partly this was because of his native caution, which had kept him single all these years, uncommitted to anyone or anything that might draw on the resources or disturb the concentration he was determined to devote to his vocation, his calling as a gambler. Much as he was drawn to what he had experienced on that velvet couch three nights ago, while Rufus lay snoring in the adjoining room, he reminded himself that he had felt about as drawn before, on similar occasions, and yet had managed to hold out until the attraction passed or anyhow paled enough to let him off the hook. It's just tail, he told himself — though not as successfully, so far this time, as in previous encounters which had threatened his unencumbered state. He kept remembering sensations, the way Reeny had tucked herself up under him, the way his heart knocked at his ribs, and above all the way there had been no following letdown, even after that first nick-of-time connection, which in fact had not been quite in the nick after all. What he wanted was more; not only then but later as well, when he found that desire was no less compelling because its edge had been dulled. An ache could hurt as much as a pain, he found, when the ache was this persistent.

I'll just sweat it out, he told himself, incurably optimistic even in what, after three days of abstinence, he had come to see would surely be defeat. What he wanted, maybe most in all the world, was a little touch of Reeny in the night.

On the other hand, putting first things first, he was concerned about Rufus's reaction to the swap, once he discovered that it had been made or was pending, and what effect that reaction would have on the current operation, the caper whose end was practically in sight. Early on, before she went up to the attic after their night together on the couch, he had warned Reeny not to do or say anything that would encourage whatever suspicions Rufus might entertain in their direction.

"He'll go right out of his skull," he said, "and God knows what might come of that, in all kinds of ways. It's not like we are dealing with any part of a whole man. He's dangerous, the way a coward's dangerous because you never can tell what he will do; not so much to you or me — we can take care of ourselves, or *I* can — but to the job. He might blow it sky high, just out of having no other way to let off steam, no other way to show he wont put up with being ripped loose from what means the most to him in all the world."

"But he'll come at me; I knew he will. He'll be trying to make it up with me tomorrow, soon as he gets over the hangover he's got coming. What will I do?"

"That's up to you," Podjo told her. "If he comes at you, he comes at you. Give him what he wants, or dont, this one last go-round. It's up to you; I'm not about to tell some woman how to hold a man off. But I am telling you not to let him know about us until we've got that sixty thousand collected and divided. You and I will have lots of time together, once we get this Kinship thing behind us, but until then we've got to lay low, and I mean *low*. You understand?"

"Yes," she said. "But I dont like it. He'll come at me, I just know."

She was right; he did come at her the following evening, up in the attic, just after she got Teddy dosed and bedded down for the night. "Let's dont fuss," he said, much as he had said before.

He stood beside the cot where she was sitting, the bruise still purple beside her eye. His face was pale from his daylong hangover and the continuing effects of last night's untimely interruption, which had left him dangling all this while. "I need it; really need it, Reen," he told her, also as before.

"No. You might hit me."

"Hit you? I wouldnt hit you, Reeny. You know that."

"I do?"

"Sure you do."

"Then what's this?" she said, indicating but not quite touching the bruise beside her eye.

"That was an accident and you know it; I was drunk. Besides, after what that little bastard put me through, busting in on us like that" — he did not bother to indicate Teddy, asleep with his bear on the adjoining cot — "it's a wonder I didnt hit everything in sight, including the woodwork and the ceiling. Come on; you know I wont do it any more, even by accident. I'm not like that, and you know it. Come on, Reen," he begged, growing more frantic as he spoke; "I'm asking please. We'll go out back on the bluff, like the other night. You do me or I'll do you, whichever. Or the other, if that's what you want. I'm asking, Reeny, asking; asking *please*. Youve got to jack me off or something — I cant do it by myself."

"No."

"Come on. *Please*."

"No!"

Almost a yelp, the word came out a good deal louder than she had intended, but the result was all she could have wanted it to be. Rufus stood there for a long moment, gazing down at her, and his look of intensity faded, as she watched, to one of sorrow. "Jesus, Reen," he said, and turned and went down the attic steps, recovering with his descent at least a measure of the dignity he had abandoned in the desperation of his plea. She felt a pang of sympathy for him, out of their old time; a pang so sharp that she might have called him back if Podjo had not been downstairs. Just then, however, Teddy stirred, half wakened by her sudden shout, and she turned her attention to getting him reassured and settled.

She did not go downstairs that night, except briefly once to use the bathroom, and Rufus did not come back up, despite her fears and expectations. Next day, moreover — Friday — he avoided her in much the same way she had been avoiding him since their set-to Wednesday night. There was a fine rain falling, on past sundown, with a first touch of autumn in the air. He kept his distance, and Podjo continued his role as a non-interfering third party on the fringe of a lovers' quarrel. They watched television that night, all three of them, and turned in early, going their separate ways to bed. Saturday morning, after the two men left on their expedition to the hotel overlooking Handy Park, Reeny gave Teddy his bath and took him back upstairs, then came back down and washed her hair.

When the men returned, early that afternoon, Rufus had changed again. Although his cheerfulness was forced, Reeny perceived at a glance, not only that he had abandoned his feigned indifference to her, but also that he had reverted — or anyhow would revert at the first private opportunity — to his old approach, combining outraged importunity and wheedling indignation.

Podjo must have seen it too, and yet when the six oclock news signed off he announced that he was driving over to Jim's Kitchen at Crump and Third, for three take-out orders of barbecued ribs. "I wont be long," he said as he went out. "Half an hour at the most."

He had no sooner left than Rufus got up and cut the television off, then came back and sat beside Reeny on the couch.

"Reen," he said. He paused. No longer pale, he was red-faced from the congestion of his emotions, rather as if he'd been holding his breath the whole time he'd been dangling. "I asked you before, I ask you now." He paused again. "I —" Again he paused, and this time, instead of trying to go on, he undid the waistband of his trousers and unzipped his fly. "Just hold it, Reen, that's all I ask. Just hold it."

She looked at him, down, then up, then down again, and her expression softened. "Goodness, Rufus," she said. "I'm sorry."

"Just take hold is all I ask," he told her. She took hold. "Oh," he said. "Oh, Reeny, you —" He semed to be weeping, eyes close shut, and the old attraction his urgency held for her returned. She crouched and took him in her mouth. "Oo," he moaned, and it was over almost as soon as it began.

She stayed with him a while, then lifted her face and looked up, amused. Not only the old attraction, but even a measure of the old affection had come back. "Goodness, Rufus, you were about as bad off as Podjo," she exclaimed.

Just as she had not considered her words before she spoke, so did he not consider them afterwards, at least for a moment or two. He had his head back, as if asleep, and presently he raised it. "What?" he said.

"Nothing," she told him, recovering from her slip. "Just that Podjo's been up here alone all this time and must be bad off. What did you think I meant?"

"I dont know," he said, and put his head back, once again as if asleep with Reeny crouched between his knees.

Afterwards, alone in bed, he continued his three-day assessment of the situation. He did so, however, only to discover that while his nerves were undoubtedly calmer as a result of Reeny's abrupt, compassionate ministration, he was also a good deal more worried in his mind. It was as if her easing of his surface frenzy, out on the couch a couple of hours ago, had produced an effect not unlike the removal of static to clarify a radio transmission. The words got through, and in this case the message was one of great distress. Mayday! Mayday! it seemed to be wailing, for all around him were indications that he was about to crash.

Reeny's postfellatio slip had not been one of these, at least at the time she made it; he accepted her explanation readily enough, partly because of his lassitude, but mainly because he wanted to accept it. The real trouble — that is, the worst of those crash indications — came about twenty minutes later, after Podjo returned from Jim's Kitchen with the ribs. They ate them there in the living room, wiping the grease from their faces with paper napkins from a stack he brought back with him, and Rufus believed he saw the two exchange glances while gnawing on the bones. 'I took care of it,' Reeny seemed to say with her eyes, and Podjo acknowledged the look with one of his own. 'Good. Good work,' it seemed to say.

Rufus could not be sure. Neither look was repeated, so far as he could see, though he studied the two of them carefully in the flickering light of the television screen — Jimmy Durante, Two for the Money, and Gunsmoke — before he and Reeny retired, upstairs and down, in anticipation of tomorrow's windup of the operation he had conceived two months ago in Bristol.

Lying there in the half-empty double bed, he reviewed his behavior over the past two days, in reaction to Reeny's rejection of his advances Thursday night, and perceived that at best it had been erratic. All day Friday, through Friday night, he had pretended an indifference matching her own, on the theory that this was the quickest way to bring her round. He believed she would not go long without what he was sure she wanted; especially if he feigned a reluctance to give it. Childlike, she would soon be in pursuit of whatever was denied her. So he thought, through Friday night. But then next morning, while he and Podjo were on the way to Handy Park, it occurred to him with a sudden shock that it might not be in his direction she would turn — it might well be in Podjo's, there at hand. This frightened him so, in his jangled, dangled state, that all he could think of for the next few hours was how to get her out of there, away from Podjo and temptation, before it happened.

Three times in rapid sequence, looking down from the high window of the hotel, he proposed that they shorten the operation by moving in on Kinship, then and there, and thus reduce the time remaining before they would go their separate ways, he and Reeny in one direction, Podjo in another. All three times, Podjo refused to modify his plan; so Rufus proceeded to modify his own. He decided to abandon pretended indifference as a tactic for bringing Reeny to her senses, and move instead in his old wheedling forthright fashion, a combined appeal to her pity and her lust.

What was more, it worked, or anyhow it seemed to; Podjo was scarcely out of the door that evening, gone for ribs, before she was on her knees, between his own. It was only after he emerged from his swoon of pleasure that he perceived that this had not really been like all those many times before, up here or back in Bristol. Something was missing, and it occurred to him now that what had been missing was Reeny. She had not done what she had done because it was what she wanted for herself, or even just out of compassion for his torment. She had done it, rather, for some other reason; some reason which, though he could not define it, he suspected was not a good one, so far as he was involved in the outcome. "You were about as bad off as Podjo," she told him, obviously without thinking, and though he accepted her explanation at the time she gave it, looking up at him from down between his knees, he soon began to have his doubts, especially after he saw her and Podjo exchange what he believed were conspiratorial glances, sidelong, brief, and all but undetectible in the flickering glow from the TV screen where Durante — "Good night, Mrs Calabash. Wherever you are" — moved from pool to pool of limelight, leering under the brim of his fedora while making his exit.

Whatever had or hadnt happened between her and Podjo so far, Rufus was determined to get her away from here as soon as possible. He wasnt too sure what was going on, but he had an unmistakable notion that *something* was. He knew Reeny well enough to guess at all her possible reactions to the current situation, and though he could not be sure, where Podjo was concerned, he knew him well enough too, by now, to feel certain he wouldnt pass up anything he decided he really wanted; including Reeny.

After Martha and Sister Baby left for Beale Street Baptist with Tio and Mamma Cindy, who called by the house for them around ten-thirty, Eben sat near the phone in the living room, the shoebox in his lap, awaiting the call he had been told would come this morning during church. From time to time he looked at the framed chromo on the wall above his head, but it seemed to him that Jesus, who was also looking upward, was too occupied with his own concerns to be troubled much about what might be happening down below. No doubt his problems were white ones, Eben thought, since he himself — like his Father before him, invisible somewhere in the direction he was gazing, beyond the gilt upper limit of the frame — was a white man.

*Ugly*, he told himself in quick reaction to the rage that had been with him since the day before, when he hung up the phone in Handy Park. It's a good thing I didnt go with them to church, he added, else I'd be dodging bolts of lightning there in Tio's pew before the service even got started.

As if in answer, though whether by way of forgiveness or reproach he could not tell, bells began tolling all over that part of town, first one, then another, then suddenly more than a dozen all together, near and far, summoning worshipers churchward in the bright September weather of this next-to-last day of the month. Sextons tugged at ropes and the people moved toward them, young and old in their best clothes, hymnals in hand, each in response to the bronze or iron tone that drew him along that same path every Sunday. For ten minutes this continued, full-voiced and peremptory, yet pleading, before the bells began to fall away, withdrawing one by one from the chorus, far more gradually than they had joined it in response to that first peal. The last of them was still clanging, slow and solemn, high in the belfry of its soaring dark stone tower — Clayborn Temple, a block and a half away — when the phone rang.

"Yes," he all but shouted, snatching the instrument up before its completed that initial ring, and waited for the voice he knew.

"Eben," it said — no question this time. "Listen. You know Clayborn Temple, where Pontotoc crosses Hernando?"

"Yes."

"Just this side of it, on the near side of Pontotoc, that same corner, is the O.K. Sundry. You know that? The O.K. Sundry, on the corner?"

"Yes."

"All right. You make the turn at the corner there, to the right, on down alongside the sundry, sideways across from Clayborn Temple, and youll see a trash can near the back door, in a gateway about twenty steps off Hernando, where the high board fence begins. Put the shoebox in the trash can there, then turn around and go back the way you came — back to Hernando and down it to Vance and then on home, and dont look back. Put the money there and dont look back, anywhere along the line from start to finish. If you look back," the voice went on, "we wont touch it and you wont see your boy again, I mean *ever*, unless it's when he comes floating up from where we sink him. You got that?"

"I wont look back," Eben said, frightened. "The money's here. I'll put it right where you say, in the trash. I wont look back."

"All right. Now one more thing. You got ten minutes; I mean from right this minute. Look at your watch."

"I'm looking."

"All right. Five after eleven, right? You get there by eleven-fifteen or just dont bother to come at all. You understand?"

"I do. I'll be there. But how about Teddy?"

"What about him?"

"I mean how is he. How is he?"

"He's fine is how he is; he's fine. Youre wasting time, yours and ours. If what you want is your boy, you better get going. O.K. Sundry; back door trash can, there on Pontotoc. You got it?"

"Yes."

"All right, get going. Ten minutes. Put the box in the can and get the hell out, the way you came. And remember, dont look back."

"All right," he said in turn, and even nodded, but the phone was dead in his hand before he spoke.

So he set out, as he had done the day before, again with the shoebox under his arm, within half an hour of the same time and even by the same route, half a block up Vance to Hernando, where a left turn would leave him only a one-block walk to the O.K. Sundry instead of the previous three to Handy Park. Another difference was his frame of mind. Hope was still what it mainly held, but part of that hope had been displaced by the rage that came over him when yesterday's excursion turned out to be nothing more than a test devised by his tormentors.

A dry run, the telephone voice had termed it then, and instructed him to go back and wait for one more call tomorrow — meaning today. "We're not trying to devil you. What the hell," the voice had said. But it seemed to Eben, there in the public booth, that that was exactly what they were trying to do, and with considerable success. Nervous exhaustion underlay his rage; so much so, indeed, that when he emerged from the booth he had to sit for a while on the bench and collect himself before he felt able to set out for home.

"Theyre deviling me, that's what theyre doing; deviling me," he told Martha as he came up the steps, the shoebox still under his arm, heavy as any millstone, after his long walk, or anyhow long-seeming walk, back from Handy Park through the bustling Saturday streets.

His rage was twofold, in the sense that it extended in two

directions. First it was directed toward those who had taken his boy on Monday, just across the way on Linden, and second it was directed toward society, the very life he led. The first of these two rages was nearly a week old, and the second, he now was beginning to see, had been with him as far back as he could remember, in Tennessee and Mississippi and overseas as well, though he had not become aware of it, at least to the point of protest, until the pressure of the first was brought to bear and he began to buckle; that is, until he stood in the booth in Handy Park, the dead phone to his ear, and told himself, in words the voice itself had used just now, that he was being deviled. From the outset he had wanted to bring in the law to help him get his son back, but it had taken little persuasion, on the part of his wife, his father-in-law, and the kidnappers themselves, to convince him that this would be a mistake. *They dont give a dam about your boy,* the letter read, and it was true, along with the expansion of the warning: *They dont care for a split minute what happens to some little nigger if losing him can get them us, a feather in their cap.*

That was the root cause of this latest phase of his rage, that and the feeling of helplessness it brought. He was part of a system which asked certain things of him — things he gave, if not gladly then anyhow willingly; taxes, for one, and close to four years in the army for another — yet which turned out to be unavailable when he got around to needing something in return; in this case, assistance in the recovery of his son. There was no refusal, not even the occasion for refusal, since, knowing as he did that almost nothing worse could happen than for him to be granted that assistance, he did not ask it. Thus when he returned from his Handy Park excursion, still with the shoebox under his arm, and protested to Martha that he was being "deviled," it was not only the kidnappers who were the object of his wrath.

She too was distressed by the delay, but on practical grounds. "Suppose wherever he is catches on *fire,*" she cried, opening whole new areas of concern.

Tio, however, took the news calmly enough when he arrived from the office in response to a call from Eben.

"Well," he said, after he had been told of the Handy Park experience, "I can see how they would do that; look it over to make sho they not getting waylaid." He sat on the couch, still wearing his hat to cover his baldness, hands resting on his thighs, looking up at his oval-framed photograph, which looked down at him in turn — a mirror image, even to the dead-level angle of the derby, except that the image was not reversed. "It's just a day, one more day," he continued; "no longer for us, most likely, than it is for them. I expect they want the money about as bad as we want Theo."

"Yes, the money," Eben said, with an edge to his voice.

"And a good deal of it, too," Tio replied with a nod.

Eben watched him sit there, solid and stolid as an idol, a somewhat leaned-down ebony Buddha, and anger was like the rising taste of copper, far back at the base of his tongue.

"A good deal," he found himself saying, gripped by a resurgence of the rage he had brought home from the park an hour ago; "no more, though, than you gave Mr Crump and others like him, down the years."

"Yes," Tio said mildly, "but I got something for it, then."

"Dont you call Teddy something?" Eben cried.

"Eben," Martha broke in, or tried to.

"Besides," he went on, "what did you get?"

"I got left alone," Tio told him, unperturbed. "That, and business thrown my way; more of it than you might think, just from looking at the books. What was colored was mostly mine and we both knew it, Mr Crump and me, though we never even spoke to say good-morning on the street."

"You got the leavings from Mr Crump's table, is what you got."

"Eben," Martha said again.

"Leavings," Tio said, as mildly as before. "It's those leavings that will get your boy out of kidnap."

"Yes, and got him there in the first place," Eben said.

"Now hush this," Martha said.

There was a pause, a heavy silence in which Eben, having relieved at least a measure of his wrath by attacking one of the figureheads of the forces that aroused it — a convenient one, moreover, there at hand — had trouble believing he had said the things he said.

Tio was the first to move or speak. "Well," he declared, once more exchanging glances with his portrait on the wall, "I guess we all of us tend to get a little outdone with each other when trouble comes along. Ive seen it often enough, myself, in business. Speaking of which," he added as he rose, "I reckon I better get on back to the office. Daughter. Eben."

"Yes, sir," Eben said, and saw him to the door.

Walking now on Hernando toward the O.K. Sundry, more than twenty hours later, he remembered Martha's reaction to the scene. "What got into you?" she asked when he turned from seeing Tio out, and he had been pleased to see that she wasnt mad at him, just puzzled. All he could say was, "This, all this," with an at-large gesture; "the things we have to live with, all around us, and Teddy will have to live with, too, when he gets back and gets a few years older. It's not only when trouble comes; trouble just makes you see it for what it is. It's all the time." And to his surprise, as they stood there looking at each other across the room, she seemed to understand him better than he understood himself. "Yes, I know," she said, nodding slowly as she spoke. "I know."

Up ahead, at the end of the block remaining after he made the turn off Vance, the stone tower of Clayborn Temple stood dark-brown against the bright blue Sunday morning sky. When he first arrived from Bristol, after the war and Tougaloo, a twenty-foot steeple had crowned the tower, visible throughout the city as its limits then were drawn, and presently, after the white Presbyterians sold the church and moved out east to be with their own kind, the steeple was condemned and taken down. He remembered it now, slender and sharp as an uplifted lance, and regretted its loss, though even without it the tower reared higher and higher, or anyhow seemed to, as he approached its base.

Just short of the end of the block, he shifted his grip on the shoebox to look at his watch. Twelve-eleven, it said — an hour fast because he had neglected to reset it the night before, when daylight saving time went off. In any case he was a safe four minutes ahead of schedule when he passed the shop window with its flowery lettering, *O.K. Sundry, Welcome All*, and rounded the blind corner onto Pontotoc.

It was then that he began hearing the singing from behind the stained-glass windows across the street; a soaring chorus that rode on pipe-organ billows of glory and lifted the banal words of the hymn beyond their earth-bound meaning.

> *All hail the pow'r of Jesus name!*
> *Let angels prostrate fall;*
> *Bring forth the royal diadem,*
> *And crown him Lord of all.*

Swept over by the waves of sound, which crashed against the windowless north wall of the stuccoed concrete building on his right, Eben made his way down the narrow sidewalk, clutching the shoebox in both hands, and there ahead, half out of the open gate in the high board fence that began where the wall ended, was the trash can he had been told he would find some twenty steps from the corner.

That was about the distance, all right, but the can turned out to be a barrel, close to five feet tall and filled to overflowing with empty cans and bottles, wadded cartons of all kinds, and what appeared to be several armloads of excelsior. He stopped beside it, hefting the shoebox as if testing its weight while he wondered how to find room amid all that trash. At last he solved the problem by making a nest in one of the clusters of excelsior, pressing down firmly so that the bottom edge of the box was wedged against the rim of the barrel to keep it from sliding off. When he turned loose it rose a bit, though not enough to clear the rim. For a moment he stood looking down at the string-tied box, reading his name and business title and address written in Tio's copperplate script across one end of the lid stamped *I. Miller*. Then he turned, mindful of the admonition not to look back, and walked rapidly toward Hernando, retracing his steps as directed.

The music now was on his right, the organ pealing, and the congregation had reached the hymn's refrain.

> *Bring forth the royal diadem,*
> *And crown him Lord of all.*

*Ah-ah-men*, they sang in a lower tone as he rounded the corner and passed out of earshot. *O.K. Sundry, Welcome All*, the shop window hailed him again as he went by.

Fifty yards down the street, he stopped. He stopped quite suddenly and stood there, still not looking back. Then he did; not only looked back, but turned abruptly and began walking in the direction he had come from, back to the blind corner and around it, toward the barrel twenty steps away. In part the cause was another resurgence of the rage he brought home from yesterday's fruitless round-trip excursion to Handy Park, but there was more to it than that. There was also fear — fear and the apprehension of grief as a consequence of the thing he feared. He had just been struck by the knee-buckling thought that in obeying the instructions for depositing the shoebox in the barrel, then turning and walking off, he had given not only the money but also his boy away. "It's the only thing that can really stop them," he had told Martha three nights ago, meaning a delay in payment of the ransom or possibly a refusal to pay it at all. "Holding it back would hold *them* back. You see?" All she had seen was the risk in the other direction, the risk of a quick fulfillment of their threat, and he had abandoned the notion in the wake of the quarrel and reconciliation that followed; he put it out of his mind as no more than a symptom of his desperation, his fear that his son would be killed as soon as the kidnappers had what they wanted. Yet it returned with such force, fifty yards down Hernando, that it stopped him in his tracks, then spun him about and sent him walking back to the corner and around it, almost at a run.

Across Pontotoc, the singing had stopped; the preacher or one of his deacons was speaking or praying. "Gret God A-mighty!" Eben heard the deep voice roar from the pulpit, beyond the stained-glass windows.

Then he reached the barrel, halted by still another shock, and stood looking down once more into the overflow of trash. The box was not there. He could see its nest, the print of its shape where it had rested, but not the box itself, either in the place he had made for it or on the sidewalk at his feet. That quickly — two, maybe three minutes at the most since he nestled it there in the cluster of excelsior — it was gone.

# 6

# *Voices*

We made off fast, for once without Podjo telling me to hold it down; that is, till I made the right turn onto Fourth, tires squealing against the quiet of the Sunday morning streets. Then he did. "Hold it down now. Hold it down," he said, sitting there beside me with the shoebox jiggling on his knees.

I slowed, but only by the hardest; I wanted to get where we were going, back to the bluff, so I could find out what sixty thousand dollars looked and felt and smelt like, all in a lump and half of it mine. Hot damn, hot damn, I kept thinking. We brought it off. We really brought it off.

"Lift up the lid and let's see what we got," I told him, but he just sat there with it jiggling on his knees, tied up with string.

"Easy now, old son," he said. "There'll be just as much in it when we get there if we wait."

Partly my excitement was plain greed, the high-breathing thrill of having all that cash money within reach, but partly too it came from having the pickup go so well, the way we planned. That's how it is when something goes well; you get excited. Easing along Pontotoc beforehand, before I put the call through from a phone booth around the corner on Fourth, I got worried because the trash can had been filled to overflowing since we checked it yesterday. I didnt want the least least thing to be off balance. "Quit your fretting," Podjo said. "Just pull over and park, short of the intersection, and walk on up and put the call in." So I did. It was five after eleven then, and when I got back he told me, "O.K. Keep a lookout through the rear window and do what I said do if it blows."

He got out and walked back to where the board fence ended and stood behind it, watching, and within a couple of minutes — maybe three — here came Kinship, box in hand. After hesitating a moment, looking down, he laid the box on the bulge of trash, and by the time he turned the corner, headed back, Podjo had it and was coming toward me, walking fast. "O.K. Let's go," he said as he got in, and I took off.

It went that well, that easy; not a soul in sight, white or colored, and I was so set-up I forgot my troubles, tooling down Fourth past Vance and Butler, Griffin and the others, and finally took a right on Crump, headed west for the bluff and Reeny, though I wasnt sure yet whether it was for me or Podjo she was waiting. All I knew was I'd soon find out.

I found out all right; not all that soon, but sooner than I wanted, considering the way it went. It wasnt me, but I didnt know that yet, for sure. That came later, a little farther down the line.

When we reached the house, around eleven-thirty, she was waiting at the door, looking out through the screen, which she pushed ajar and held open as Podjo came up the steps, box in hand and me behind him, on his heels. He went on through the living room to the bedroom, and lo, for once, Reeny had made up the bed — out of nervousness, I guess; a lack of anything else to do while she waited for us to get back or not.

"How'd it go?" she asked, following close.

"Went good," Podjo told her over his shoulder. "But let's see."

He stopped beside the newmade bed, jerking at the string on the box to break it. Then it broke and he took the lid off and there they were, packed in snug but showing their color round the edges. Greenbacks, greenbacks, acres and acres of them; enough to paper all the walls.

"Oh Lord," Reeny said, watching. "Lordy Lord."

"Holy Mother," I said, looking too, like into a well or down a mine shaft, with something bright at the bottom, way way down. "Holy Mother, Mother, Mother."

Podjo tilted the shoebox and began tumping the money out sideways, using one hand for a scoop. It fell on the tight-stretched sheet and mattress with little bounces, packets and packets, each with a rubber band around the middle; twenty-five-bill packets for the twenties, fifty-bill packets for the tens. Spread out, though, they somehow didnt seem to amount to as much as they had when they were snugged together, and that was a surprise; I had expected them to stretch out like an accordion, much wider than they did. I guess that's just another way of saying there's never enough money to satisfy the hopes of those who've got it. Not that it still didnt look like a lot. It did, and was.

"Well, let's get to counting," Podjo said, once the box was empty.

While Reeny watched, saying Lordy Lord to herself every now and again, he and I separated the packets of tens and twenties into equal piles, then split each pile in two, half for him and half for me. We counted a few of the packets to make certain we hadnt been short-changed, and we hadnt. There were two thousand tens and two thousand twenties, a thousand of each apiece, just as we planned from the start — sixty thousand dollars; half for him, half for me, and all of it pure gravy.

That was what you might call the bookkeeping aspect of the matter, the cash return on our investment of time and risk and know-how. But for me it was only the second half of a whole whose first half was Reeny, and neither half would amount to much without the other — in the long run, I mean, and the long run was the only run that counted.

So Podjo used to say from time to time. His main concern was gambling; he was headed for Las Vegas with his gains. Mine was fucking, in one form or another, and for me that meant Reeny, wherever we went. I had an investment in that direction too; not only my time and know-how and now the risk, the risk I mean of losing her, but something else as well. We'd had close to five hundred comings since that night at Bull Eye's and the Shady Rest; enough, in all, for me to fill a gallon jug brim full. I thought of that too as an investment, and Reeny was the container for the thing contained, a sort of trophy, an outsized demijohn of jism. filled to overflowing with the viscid, pearly essence of myself, my very seed. The problem was how to keep her, keep the trophy from passing to someone else, by abolishing the risk I'd been fool enough to run the other night. One clew was greed; I'd seen it on her face, just as she no doubt had seen it on mine when the lid came off that shoebox. "Oh Lord. Lordy Lord," she said while I was saying, "Mother, Mother, Mother." I could dangle the money under her nose; that might do it, when it came down to the crunch. Podjo damned well wasnt about to give her any of his — or spend it on her, either, or even on himself except for gambling — and I counted on her taking that into account where he was concerned.

Now he was off on one of his lectures. Pete and Repeat, they should have named him, because he had given it before, like so many others this past month. The fact is, I was getting fed up with them; up to here.

"My guess is they took down the serial numbers off the bills. Maybe not the tens," he said, "but anyhow the twenties, and it's likely theyll report them to the cops as soon as they get their boy back tomorrow. So only spend the twenties when youre on the move, or are about to be, and cant be traced. That's important."

Reeny was all ears, drinking it in, the way she'd been these past few days whenever Podjo was around and holding forth; whereas, with me, she was about as distant as she'd been through that same time — except briefly the night before, when she was down between my knees, munching on the top third of an erection behind that curtain of hair that always fell across her face when she bent forward. Now youd think it never happended. She didnt look ready to give me the time of day, and what was more, as it turned out, she wasnt.

The notion was, we'd spend tonight and part of tomorrow squaring the house away, getting packed and all, and then in the afternoon we'd take the kid somewhere, not too far, and let him out to find his way home, the way we'd promised in the arrangement for the payoff. Up to that point there was no hurry, since the Kinships were bound to keep on keeping quiet until they got their son back, and we still had that day left on the lease, which ran through the end of September. Then we'd come back here for our bags and a final look-round before we went our separate ways, Reeny and I in one direction, Podjo in another. So we'd said, until the falling out. Now of course it was up in the air, what we'd do or what we wouldnt at that stage; I mean the parting, now that things had changed between us.

Anyhow, we were sitting there on the bed, the three of us, Reeny down at the foot, Podjo and I on opposite sides at the head, each with his pile of money stacked beside him. I was somewhat off balance from watching the way she looked at him and took in all he said, and in consequence I told myself the showdown might as well come now as later. A mistake; I should have waited; but I was provoked. Still, except for a little trembling of the hands, which might have come from counting all that money, I managed to hold onto myself well enough not to give the impression of being overeager or concerned. I sidled into it, asking him more or less casually, off-hand, "You heading out for Vegas, then, tomorrow?"

"Part way anyhow," he said.

"How do you plan to travel?"

"Train. Plane. One or the other." He shrugged, as if to say it didnt matter, just so he got where he was going in the end. It seemed to me he was pretending as much as I was. Maybe he wasnt, but it seemed to me he was. He put on his poker face, stroking his mustache with one hand, the other resting idle on the mattress by his money, and then seemed to make up his mind. "Probably the train first, over to Little Rock, say, or Texarkana, then the rest of the way by air — to throw them off the track in case the wind's up."

It was pretty convincing. I dont mean it *convinced* me; I just mean I couldnt tell. "Right," I said, and turned to Reeny, down at the foot of the bed. "We ought to be getting squared away ourselves," I told her. "Like maybe packing some of our stuff in the trunk of the car today, so we wont have so much to do tomorrow."

While I watched, she kept her eyes down, looking at something on the sheet, a stain or something, and I could feel what was coming. Then it came.

"I'm not going with you," she said.

Her eyes were down; I waited till she raised them. "What do you mean youre not going with me?"

"I'm just not."

"Who are you going with, then?" I asked, not looking in Podjo's direction, though I could almost feel him signaling from his side of the headboard.

"What difference does that make? Nobody."

"Hm." I had more or less expected that, but I still didnt know whether it came from anger or conviction. If it was anger it would pass, maybe even by tonight, like the night before. Whatever it was, I decided to counteract it, then and there, by playing my ace. "Then I guess you dont expect a share of this," I told her, patting the stack of money under my hand.

That gave her pause all right. But then, having paused, she answered. "Not unless you think I earned it. *I* think I did."

"Well, I dont. You didnt go with me down to the wire, or dont plan to, and that's what matters." I turned my head at last. "How about you, Podjo? You think she earned it?"

"It's your money," he said.

"But what do you think?"

"I think she earned it; whatever you agreed on."

"Then give her a share of yours," I told him.

That stopped him. But then he surprised me. "I tell you what I'll do," he said. "I'll match whatever you give her."

"Yair?" I wasnt falling for that. Once they got together — if my suspicions were right and that was what they were planning — he'd get his back, along with mine. "Well, dont sweat it, old son," I said. "All youd be matching is flat-out nothing."

Reeny sat there looking outdone, as if she'd been run over by a steamboat.

"What you need's a union," Podjo told her.

"Dont we all?" I said, and gathered up my money.

I went back to the kitchen and rooted around till I found a stout paper sack to put the bills in. While I ate a candy bar, along with a glass of the kid's milk to wash it down, I concentrated on finding a place to hide the cash, between now and taking-off time, in case Reeny got light-fingered in her resentment and chose that way of solving the problem I hoped would bring her round. Whatever else I was going to do, or not do, giving her up wasnt one of them; especially to Podjo, who'd been offered her back at the start, and turned her down. And in that connection, the last thing I wanted just now was to have her taking off with her pockets stuffed full of what she might consider was her fair share of those two thousand tens and twenties.

She was up in the attic by then, checking on Teddy, and Podjo was out in the living room rereading the Sunday *Commercial*. So I returned to the bedroom, walking soft; got my pistol out of the underwear drawer of the chifforobe, put it in with the money, and rolled the top of the sack down tight to make it compact. Looking and thinking, I decided the bedside closet, jammed to the hinges with the cotton man's spare and off-season clothes, was the best hiding place. I put the sack on the high shelf, well back in the far corner behind a clutter of stuff, to conceal it in case either of them got to rooting around, then went out into the living room where Podjo was sitting behind the curtain of his paper. The Little Rock headline was still on the right, but it had been shrinking day by day ever since the paratroopers got there. SPECIAL SESSION CALL/ MAY COME VERY SOON,/ GOVERNOR FAUBUS SAYS.

I said, "He's bad-off if that's all he's got to offer."

"What?" Podjo looked at me over the rim of the paper; just his eyes.

"Faubus," I said. "He seems to be running out of devices."

Podjo folded that corner of the paper back and looked at the headline upside down. "Yair. Well, he dont need any more devices than he's used already. There's not much doubt, by now, which way that governor's race is going to go, come November. He's gotten all he wants from both the government and the rioters. Like us. We've gotten all we want from them, too."

He was friendly; as friendly as he ever was, that is. Youd have thought we hadnt had our three-way hassle back there a while ago. What it came to was he didnt want any trouble; anyhow not at this stage of the game. Neither did I — at this stage of the game.

And neither did Reeny, as it turned out when she came down from the attic around sunset and found us watching television. She was a long way from friendly, but she wasnt much different from the way she'd been all through these past few days, aside from that one little quick-snacking incident last night on the couch where Podjo was sitting now, watching Douglas Edwards and the News.

When it was over he got up and clicked it off. "Well," he said as he straightened up from the darkened tube with its little fading moon of light, "I think we earned ourselves a treat today. Who's for a sack of burgers from K's? There's still a couple of bottles of Jax left over to wash them down with."

"I'm for that," I said, trying to be friendly too.

"O.K. Your turn to fetch; I went last light."

I might have known it, I told myself, and turned to Reeny. "You want to come along?"

"I'll wait here," she said. "Teddy's restless."

I might have known that too, I told myself.

It didnt take much over twenty minutes going and coming, including one run stop-light and a squabble with the counter-man to get the cook to hurry. But what the hell; twenty minutes was long enough for almost anything. Sure enough, when I got back with the sacked burgers warm in my hands, Reeny was in the bathroom and Podjo was sitting there in the living room with the TV off, not even reading the paper. That wasnt like him. And something else I detected on my way through the bedroom to the kitchen, after plates. It was my opinion theyd been screwing; I could smell it — the friction — or anyhow I told myself I could. Passing the closed bathroom door I heard the toilet sigh from being flushed, and right then I began to feel the whole three-cornered thing change gears, from rivalry to revenge.

When I came back with the plates she was there, and while Podjo went for a couple of beers from the icebox I studied her out of the tail of my eye. She didnt look rumpled, much, but what did that prove except she'd squared herself away?

We were sitting there afterward, waiting for time for the Sunday Night Movie, when she began thumbing through one section of the paper. "Hey, look at there!" she hollered all of a sudden, holding up a picture of a young woman wearing what looked like a croaker sack, tight at the bottom and the top, where her legs and head stuck out, and bulgy in between. A middle-aged man in a Homburg was looking round at her, startled bug-eyed — and no wonder. The dress, if that was what it was, made her look as if someone had puffed up her midriff with a pump. Beneath was a sort of explanation. *Paris, France. Givenchy and other Paris designers staggered men's imaginations (and milady's walk) when they came out recently with the "sack dress," also called the "bag,"* and so on and so forth, the way they talk.

Bag was right; but Reeny liked it. "Hey now," she said. "There's something a girl could really move *around* in. A surprise package, too, when she takes it off."

"Yair," Podjo said, bent forward and sideways in her direction to study the picture. "Sort of like coming out of a cake."

Reeny laughed, loud and on a rising note. I didnt get it till I remembered she told about that cake business one day out back, soon after we got here. Even Podjo was grinning, but I didnt see all that much to laugh about, even the dress, let alone the cake.

I was so put-out I had to walk out onto the back porch for a while to settle down. The bridge lights skittered across the river, out and out, reflected green and red and yellow on the water shimmering down below with the glittery light of a bright first-quarter moon. I remembered that night just over the lip of the bluff, a week ago tomorrow, and the thought of it was like a razor moving across and across my heart. "We could have had us a life here. A good life," I told myself, aloud. It wasnt true, but I enjoyed saying it anyhow, out there alone on the porch.

Inside, the movie had started by then — one of those Joan Crawford things. I hardly noticed; *Mildred Pierce*, perhaps. A couple more times, and not necessarily during commercials, I had to get up and walk out back because of the way the television flickered homelike on their faces. Then at last it was over and we turned in.

"Good night."

"Night."

"Good night."

And I lay there alone in the dark on that double bed, past midnight and into the last day of September. A man fools himself as long as he can, until finally he knows he's got to stop; if he can. In this case, all in one short tail-end of one day, the evidence had mounted up so high it was bound to topple. First off, her refusal to ride with me over to K's was a clear passing-up of a chance to reclaim her share of my share of the ransom. She was saying she didnt want any part of it, if any part of me went with it. Greed hadnt worked, and I came back from K's to the notion that someone had thrown a quick screw into someone in the brief time I'd been gone. Then there was that business of drinking one of the bottles of Jax. Always before, knowing I didnt drink the stuff, she didnt either. Yet now all of a sudden she did; with him. Then came the newspaper picture of the girl in that sack thing, and they joked about it, laughing and happy, with me not even onto what cake they were talking about until I stopped and thought. He knew her better than I did, now, because I didnt know her at all. All I knew was how she *was*; how she used to be, I mean, back in the olden days almost a week ago, when it was me she was with, all round the clock, and the jokes we made were our jokes. And then, when I returned from cooling off out back, they sat there like any two homebodies, television flickering like firelight on their faces: God bless our happy home. It was too much. I had to get up and walk out back again, then return and grit my teeth some more till that goddam Crawford thing went off and we said good night and went our separate ways, upstairs and down. For all I knew, she was carrying on up there with Teddy, even now, on one of those drum-tight canvas cots. I even got to imagining I could hear it squeaking overhead.

"The thing you ought to do, and you know it," I told myself, "is get yourself another girl." And the answer came back:

"Trouble is, she wouldnt like it as much as Reeny does. Or did."

"Yes, and that means you wouldnt either, dont it?" No need to answer that. "Still, you cant tell. You found *her*, didnt you?"

"Well, yes I did," I told myself — my other self, there inside me. "But who's going to have that kind of luck twice in a single year, or even a single lifetime?"

Various elements of a plan were swirling round me in the dark. Some I'd use, others not. One thing I had to do was get myself some wheels, some kind of car away up the scale from that ramshackle Ford theyd be after me in, maybe before I was out of sight. What the hell; I could afford most anything I wanted now, without even denting my roll. Maybe one of those new Edsels, I thought, in spite of the split front bumper and a radiator that looks like a toilet seat. Yes, and a cover story of some kind, to allow for being gone a while; say a girl out east I was going to pick up in a cab I'd call when the time came.

All those various elements swirled around me, and I decided to let them swirl right through a good night's sleep, so theyd come together when I woke, like a jigsaw puzzle interlocked by magic overnight.

Sleep; a good night's sleep, I told myself, only to find I was so tense it wouldnt come. I tried masturbation, but found that, raunched as I was, I could just barely get it up, and then when I got it up a bit, thinking of Reeny out under the bluff or on the couch, I couldnt get it off. Nothing new about that; she'd had that effect on me, those few times she wasnt handy, ever since the night we met at Bull Eye's. She had my balls in her pocket, whether she wanted them or not.

Sure enough, though, when I finally got to sleep and then woke up hearing Reeny come down the attic steps to fix break-fast for the kid, all that swirl of notions had worked itself out in my head. I knew what I was going to do, and how, including what I was going to tell her and Podjo in the meantime by way of a cover. They kept busy and so did I, all that Monday morn-ing, sorting out things to pack and things to throw away. One of the latter was the two spare sets of license plates, after Podjo went out and put the Missouri ones on the Ford. An-other was what little was left of the Noctec, once Reeny had given the kid his final wake-up dose, which we figured would have about worn off by the time of his release that afternoon. We didnt go so far as to sweep out the place or anything so strenuous as that, but we did sort of square things away — strip the bed and take out the collection of empty cans and bottles, paper napkins, candy wrappers, stuff like that — for the cotton man to come home to without blowing up com-pletely at what he found waiting for him to settle back into after the Ole Miss law student and his hot-looking wife got through with it, along with their child who would have gone blind except for the operation and a place for his mamma and daddy to lay their heads through a time of strain. Lies work wonders, properly used; such as this time, which got us the house on the bluff with an attic to store the kid in, safe from prying eyes. The only rule is dont lie to yourself, except some-times when it helps.

Late in the morning, crowding eleven, Reeny drove over to Crump for last week's laundry and Podjo walked south along the lip of the bluff toward the bridges, where a path led down a more gradual slope, to throw the spare plates and the leftover Noctec into the river. "Listen out for the boy while I'm gone," he said, careful as always in all he did, or *I* did.

I said I would, and soon as he left I went in the bedroom and took five thousand dollars in twenties out of my rolled-up grocery sack in the closet; ten packets of twenty-five bills each, a bulky wad. To keep them from bulging overmuch I distributed them among the various pockets of the coat and trousers of my good blue suit on its hanger in the chifforobe, then rerolled the sack, pistol and all, and put it back in its top-shelf hiding place, minus those two hundred and fifty twenties. "Only spend them when youre on the move or are about to be," Podjo had said the day before. And that's what I was about to be *on*, all right, the move.

By the time they got back, almost together — she from one direction, he the other, front and rear — I was in the tub with the bathroom door ajar so I'd see the kid if he woke and tried for a getaway, the way he did five days ago when he damned near stripped my gears and brought on so much of the trouble that followed, right up to now.

"Hey!" I called out to them, head lathered, eyes tight shut against the soap. "Something's come up! I'll be out in a minute to tell you!"

I took my time drying and combing my hair, got into my drawers and tee shirt, and sauntered out to sit on the side of the bed, putting on my socks and shoes. "It's a notion I had," I told them, out of sight in the living room. "Wait a minute. I'll be right out." I was in no hurry; let them wait and wonder. I got my trousers on, a clean white button-down shirt, tie untied, and then went out to join them, buckling my belt a notch tighter to take up the slack from the five-or-so pounds I'd lost those past few days going out of my mind with worry. She loves me. Loves me not.

"I got to thinking, remembering old times," I said, "and it seemed to me I ought not be moping round about something as replaceable as a woman. Even you, babe. You know what they say about streetcars; wait till the next one comes along. Only I decided to do more than wait."

They were sitting there, Reeny in a chair, Podjo on his couch, holding the morning paper she'd brought back from her laundry trip. They were waiting and wondering, just as I intended, and I was still in no hurry. "Well, look at that," I said. "They took the bayonets off." That was because of the headline. FAUBUS FOE DEPLORES/ HIS MOTIVE IN CRISIS;/ BAYONETS DISAPPEAR. "Looks like the Little Rock hooraw has wound itself down at about the same time ours did, over here on this side of the river. Yours and mine I mean," I told her.

"Anyhow," I said — back to Podjo now — "I got to thinking about streetcars and I remembered this little creature I used to knock around with, some, up here on weekends. Christ; how I could ever have forgot her I dont know. Except I didnt, as it turns out; I just misplaced her for a while. She lives out east toward Germantown, one of those slick society twats just out of college, about twenty-two or -three, with gold hair down her back all the way to the tuck of her ass, dressed to the nines all hours of the day or night, and a pair of knockers the size of the moon coming over the mountain. Loves it, too. We had us some good times up here last winter, till I got sidetracked this spring out at a joint near home called Bull Eye's." I didnt so much as glance in Reeny's direction. "You know Bull Eye's?"

"I been by there," Podjo said.

"Yair. Well, that's all over now. Off with the old, on with the new. I put in a call for this little cutie a while ago, for old time's sake and new time's sake as well, and I could hear her all but jumping up and down, off at the far end of the line. Celia's her name; Celia Dawnbrook. She's got her own car and everything — like Reeny here, only more so — and we thought we'd take a ride down to New Orleans, by way of the Teche, and eat ourselves some crawfish étouffée. Where we go from there is anybody's guess till the money runs low, and then I reckon we'll fall back on hers. Or maybe I'll think up a new job to pull, the way I thought up this one."

I paused to let that sink in, and then went on. "I'm due at her house in an hour or so, out near Germantown. So most likely I wont be here when you leave to drop the kid off. Around three, isnt it?"

"Right," Podjo said, cold-eyed, with a nod.

"But I'll be here by the time you get back, most likely, to pick up my gear and say goodbye. I figure you dont need me any more, anyhow, and I'll be here when you get back. Or if I'm not, if I'm late and youve already left, that's o.k. too, I reckon. What the hell; the world's not all that big our paths wont cross. I'll see you later, somewhere down the road; say in Vegas in a couple of weeks, if you last out that long at the tables."

He didnt say anything to that, and neither did Reeny, who hadnt said anything all along. "Well," I said as I turned to go back to the bedroom after my coat, "keep your toes clean."

What?

"Nose; I mean nose. Keep your nose clean." I laughed it off, or tried to, hating to lose my dignity after a speech like that; like an actor stumbling when he exits. It's not easy being a clown when it's not in your nature. "I cant seem to get my tang untongled. It must be this new girl Ive got lined up."

I went back to the bedroom and put in a call for a cab — the first time I'd used that paper-stuffed phone since we got there, close to a month ago — then tied my tie and put my coat on, patting the pockets flat so the money didnt bulge much more than would make up for the weight I'd lost since Reeny turned against me. Out in the living room, she and Podjo were keeping mum as mum, no doubt wondering how much or little to believe of what I'd told them. No matter, I thought; let them wonder. Just so they dont know for sure.

The cab still hadnt come, so I went back to the kitchen and ate another Baby Ruth, washing it down with a last half-glass of the kid's milk, which was my way of charging him rent on all those tee shirts he'd been wearing. I was standing again in the bedroom, suitcase packed and ready to be picked up when I returned in style from where I was headed, and was giving a final touch to the knot of my tie — "Boo, you good-looking devil," I told my reflection in the chifforobe mirror — when I heard the cab horn give a couple of blasts out front.

"So long; see you shortly," I said as I passed through the room where Reeny and Podjo still hadnt moved from their separate places, chair and couch. I scarcely glanced in either direction, no more than a one-handed wave as I walked between them, then went out and got in the cab pulled up at the curb. "Cormac's, out Union," I told the driver, and he took off.

That was the dealer, and while we rode I got to thinking, getting it clearer in my mind what theyd been up to, Reeny and Podjo, those past few days behind my back. They were probably on that sheetless mattress by the time the cab cleared the nipple company up the block. "You lock the door; I'll go check on Teddy and be right back," I bet she said, as soon as she heard the tires growl on the gravel. My guess was she shucked her pants up there, or jumped out of them on her way down the steps. But what did I care? I told myself *I* didnt care. All I hoped was the kid would come wandering in on them, bear under arm, the way he did that day last week on me.

We were tooling along Riverside by then, the river glittering in the midday sunlight on our left, and I kept telling myself I might not get far, but no matter; no matter what stopped me in the end, Podjo or the law, I'd sure as hell get far enough down the road to show them they couldnt do what they had done to me, behind my back, and then come out scot-free.

I know he's smooth, a smooth old con, I told myself. He's even scary. But did he really think he was going to get my girl and half the money *too*?

About all I did, from the time I got back hopping mad from the Sunday drop by Clayborn Temple, was fume and fret. Now here it was crowding noon on Monday, already past the twenty-four-hour promise made in the letter, and still my boy wasnt home. "Oh damn them. God damn them," I said when the clock struck twelve.

"You get aholt of yourself," Tio told me.

"I know who I'd like to get a hold of," I said.

"And what good would that do Theo?" he asked.

"It would do *me* good. It would do *me* good," I said.

"You have to think of Theo," he told me: as if I'd thought of anything else this whole past week he'd been gone.

The fact was, I had: lots else — mainly, I see now, to keep from going slap out of my mind from knowing there was nothing I could do about Teddy but pay the money and wait, dependent all the while on the word of some people I had every reason to know I couldnt trust, any more than they could trust me if I got within arm's reach of them. In that sense, the rage that came over me, first in the booth in Handy Park and then next day when I left the shoebox in the barrel there on Pontotoc, helped make the worry bearable by deflecting at least part of it in another direction, against the very life I had been living all those years, in Mississippi and the army and now lately here in Tennessee. The trouble was that the System, as I called it in my mind, was as faceless as the kidnappers, and therefore offered no real target for my anger. But I soon found a cure for that by giving it a face, and the face I gave it was Tio's, there at hand. He represented the system, for me, because he had done such a good job of going along with it that he had made money enough to get his grandson kidnapped.

Always, whatever direction my thoughts took, they looped back to Teddy before they got far. I couldnt help that: I just kept trying.

All the same, I knew even then that a lot of what I was feeling, as a way of letting up on my fret in Teddy's direction, had been festering inside me a good deal longer than I suspected up to then. Even before, though, while I was holding it down out of sight by talking and even believing all that Tom talk, I knew that, deep down underneath — and maybe not all that deep — it was because I didnt want to face up to being a man. If youre not a man, youre not required to act like a man, and acting like a man is a hard task when it's something youve been taught is not allowed, under penalty of losing your chance to hold a job and make a living for your wife and children. So at first, in my search for deflection as a way of easing the pain I felt for Teddy, I chose taking it out on Tio, who had provided the job and the living in the first place. And the fact was, for all his stiffness and never being contradicted, even by anyone his own age or older, let alone younger and working for him in his office, he took it a lot better than I had any reason to expect: coming back today, for instance, along with Mamma Cindy, after all I'd said to him the day before, when I got back from putting the shoebox in the barrel there on Pontotoc behind the O.K. Sundry.

It wasnt till I turned in midstride on Hernando and hurried back around the corner where the Clayborn Temple choir had stopped singing about Jesus and his diadem, then stood looking down at where the box had nestled in the barrel, but wasnt now, that I began to shake with fear from the thought of what might have come of what I'd done. "If you look back," the telephone voice had told me less than ten minutes ago, "you wont see your boy again, I mean *ever*, unless it's when he comes floating up from where we sink him. You got that?" Yet here I was: I had not only looked back, I had turned back, hoping to get my hands on them for what they had done, and were doing, to Teddy and me. Crazy: but I couldnt help it. All I could do, once I came to my senses, was be glad theyd gotten the money and were gone, nowhere in sight and no sign left to show theyd even been there, except the empty print where the shoebox had nestled for maybe one full minute in the excelsior. I turned and started home again, and then the rage returned, along with the fear, the knowledge that I had given them the only thing that would hold them back from doing all they had threatened to do if I didnt give them what they asked, and give it in exactly the way they directed me to do.

Part of the rage was reaction to the fear that had come on me. I was angry because they had scared me, and even angrier because they had made me scare myself by acting so much like a man that I decided I must have been crazy. But partly, too, it was a reaction to knowing I had nothing left to turn to: no help, now the money was gone, from any direction outside myself. All I stood for, as part of, all I belonged to as a person, let alone a man — here it came again, by way of deflection: the System — was designed to look the other way when it was me that was doing the asking. Put-and-Take didnt work here. For me, the system was all put, with no take whatsoever except for wages from the job that was my reward for going along. "Let down your buckets where you are," old Booker T. advised, and I believed him, along with Tio, until I let my bucket down, the way he said, and found it had no bottom.

Back home, I was alone with my fuming until close to noon when the others returned from church, Martha and Sister Baby, Tio and Mamma Cindy. I was wrought-up something awful by then: so much so, indeed, that they had no more than walked in the door, the four of them together, than I fairly shouted at Martha, who was in the lead. Wild as it sounded, I had thought out the words beforehand, brooding over them there in the living room, alone with my fear and my shame. "I gave the bastards the only thing that the lack of would restrain them!"

"*You* gave?" Tio said, bridling.

He was offended at my use of such language in front of Sister

Baby, not to mention our two wives, but more than anything he was riled by my self-centeredness, the way I kept leaving him out when I complained of the hardships that had come upon us this past week. I was fairly launched by then, however, and I turned on him even harsher than I had on Martha.

"All right, *we*," I told him. "You. What difference? It'll all be Martha's anyhow, once you pass, wont it? And what's Martha's is mine. Mine too, I mean," I said on second thought.

I half expected him to reply, as I had heard him do before when someone mentioned passing, 'I'm not going anywhere.' But he didnt. He just stood there, barely inside the door, looking shocked and determined, broadfaced in the shadow of his derby, slighted as a guest in the very house he owned and collected rent on. He didnt look so much outraged, though, as he did hurt, and not so much hurt as he did disappointed — not so much with me as with life in general, which he seemed to feel had let him down.

"Lucindy," he said, and stepped aside to clear the doorway. "Let's get on home to dinner."

This would be the first Sunday meal we'd missed at his house since Sister Baby was born, more than six years back, and even then nearly two-year-old Teddy had been at the table to represent us in his highchair. She — Sister Baby — stood there among us now in her church clothes, blue silk dress with a bow in back, shiny pumps and light pink socks, new yarn on her pigtails, and looked from one to another of us, wondering. So did Martha, in a different way. I felt ashamed but couldnt say so lest my rage flare up again, and though I tried to put what I felt in a look, I found I couldnt do that either.

"Tio," I said, and had to stop. "We'll stay in touch."

"Well, yes," he said. He motioned Mamma Cindy past him.

"Goodbye, son," she said, and they went out.

"Mamma," Martha called after her as they started down the steps. "Tell Dolly hello for us, and say we're sorry. Goodbye, Daddy."

"Daughter," he said, and they went on out the gate.

When we turned from the door Sister Baby was still standing there round-eyed, wondering. She had heard what she had heard, and she had drawn conclusions. "Is Teddy coming home today?" she asked us.

"Today, tomorrow, next day," Martha told her: "we dont know yet. All we know is he'll be here when he gets here. Now you go back and change out of your good clothes while I fix us something to eat."

Sister Baby went on back to her and Teddy's room, and I followed Martha into the kitchen. She opened a can of chicken noodle soup, put it on the stove to simmer, and got out a box of crackers and some butter. By the time Sister Baby returned in her everyday clothes, the soup was steaming in its bowls. "I'll do better by us tonight," Martha said, looking down at what passed for Sunday dinner.

Strangely enough, I was hungry. I'd be hard put to say how many crackers I ate, each with half a pat of butter.

When we finished, Martha told Sister Baby to go back and take her nap. But she didnt want to. She wanted to stay and listen. "I'm too big for naps," she said, sounding for all the world like Teddy.

"I'll go back with you and get you started," Martha offered.

"I want Daddy to," she said.

So I did. Sitting there by the bed, looking down at her face on the pillow, I thought again how loving her was like loving myself, we looked so much alike. At last she began to drowse and I got up and tiptoed out. By that time, two of the twenty-four hours were up. Twenty-two to go, I told myself. How am I going to get through them?

Up front, Martha had finished in the kitchen and was just coming out through the dining room curtain. I sat with her on the couch. We spoke low, so Sister Baby wouldnt hear us in case she woke, and I still felt what I had felt before: ashamed of myself and defiant, both at once, where Tio was concerned.

"You ought not be so hard on him," she said.

"Hard on him? I'm not hard on him," I told her — knowing

I was. "It's just that lots of things have come home to me all of a sudden, things I been living with all my life without letting them rankle me till now. 'Niggers dont vote here. Theyre voted,' is a saying up at the Courthouse. Yes. And my God, the things that go on in the courts themselves. 'What are you charged with, nigger?' 'Looking a white man in the eyes.' 'Uppity, hey?' and the judge bangs the gavel on the benchtop, loud as the crack of doom. 'Six years' hard labor. Maybe that'll learn you.' Yes. Well, perhaps it's just this place that's getting to me: Mr Crump's town, and what-all he'll allow and wont allow. He's dead now, yes, but his soul goes marching. Yes indeed. I heard it said that if God was going to give the world an enema, Memphis is where He would insert the nozzle. And to this good day there's a saying, amongst entertainers on tour here, that the three worst weeks in the show-business year are Christmas, Easter, and Memphis."

"There's lots worse places and you ought to know it," she came back at me, "being up from Mississippi."

"Leave Mississippi out of this," I told her. "No man can help where he's born. It's where he moves to that counts, and I moved to Memphis." There we were, both of us defending our birthplaces, and both of us having a hard time doing it. "But that's not what I mean — not what I'm talking about, really," I went on. "I'm talking about Tio. Not Tio himself, but what he stands for, represents." I was having trouble expressing myself, the way you do when it's something you feel in your bones before youve got it worked out in your mind. But I kept trying. "What do you make of a system, a set-up, that will always turn its back on you when the going gets its roughest, that will hand you the brunt end of the stick every time the crunch comes down? What do you make of a man who'll do all he can to keep that set-up in operation, not only for himself but also for his children who come after him to pick up where he leaves off?"

She started to answer but I wasnt finished. I kept on. "He does that, all that. It's his way, going along, and he did it to me: I bought the package. But he's not going to do it to Teddy —

put him on that treadmill leading nowhere, I mean, with no pause for seeing where youre headed or even where youve been. He's not, and I'm here to tell you he's not. He's not."

"But he's right," she managed to say. "He *knows*."

"Of course he's right. I couldnt any more go to the law for help than I could to the devil. Of course he's right — and that's what's wrong. It ought not *be*. It ought not be for me, and it sure as hell ought not be for Teddy when he gets back."

"But what will you do," she said, "if that's the way it is?"

"I dont know," I told her. "I dont know yet. That's the trouble. But I will know, once Teddy gets back and I can start to think straight."

We sat there, the two of us. Martha didnt say anything and I was about talked out. "I'll go check on Sister Baby," she said at last, and when she left I swung my legs up on the couch. This was my naptime, too, but I didnt think I'd take it without the usual heavy Sunday dinner.

I was wrong. I was asleep before she got back. When I woke it was close to three oclock and I almost couldnt believe it. Four down and twenty to go. Twenty to go, I told myself. How am I going to get through them? And the answer came back: You just will. The same as you did these last four. Somehow. You just will.

And did: somehow. Theyd had time by now to check and count the money, and I imagined them taking the blindfold off and lifting him out of the closet or the coalbin, wherever they had been keeping him all this time, here in Memphis or elsewhere, getting ready to turn him loose and send him back, the way they promised, *in 24 hrs*. I told myself if he wasnt home by dark it wouldnt be until next morning, because surely they wouldnt turn him aloose at night, all by himself at eight years old. Or would they? I decided they would, or anyhow might, but I didnt tell Martha that: I told her they wouldnt, and I believe she believed me. Anyhow, we ate supper and then came sundown and then dark, streetlights gleaming down all the Sunday-evening streets, and still no Teddy.

"I'll call Daddy," she said.

"No: let me," I said. And did.

"Well, Eben, it's what we expected," he said. "He'll be home tomorrow. That's what they told us and that's what they'll do."

"Yes sir," I said. "Good night."

"Good night, son" — the first time he called me son, the way Mamma Cindy always did.

Once Baby Sister had finished her dab of homework and been put to bed, we settled down in the living room to wait, one ear cocked toward the telephone, the other toward the door, in case they called to tell us where to get him or he came scratching in the night. After a while I lit up the television and even stayed with it till some kind of Joan Crawford thing came on. Then I cut it off and told Martha, "It wont be tonight. Let's get to bed and rest up for tomorrow." So we did. I went to sleep hugging her back, and woke up later to find her hugging mine.

Over beyond her, looking round, I saw the bedside clock was past eleven. The twenty-four hours were halfway up: I'd somehow got through half of them.

Going back to sleep I thought then of the coalbin. I imagined them lifting him out, his clothes all grimed. No, no, I said, still half asleep, and came all the way awake from hearing a scratching — Teddy at the door. 'Let me *in*. Let me *in*.' Then it stopped and I knew I'd dreamed it. Before long it was straight-up midnight. "Today, tomorrow, next day," Martha had said. Now tomorrow was today and next-day was tomorrow, and soon as I drifted back onto the rim of sleep I heard it again: scratching, scratching — Teddy at the door. 'Let me *in*. Oh, let me *in*.' So I got up in my nightshirt, careful not to wake Martha, and went out in the living room and bedded down on the couch, so if it really was Teddy at the door I'd hear and know it. That way, I got back to sleep till morning, full daylight in the room there, and Martha standing over me saying wake up, wake up now, the coffee's perked.

I got dressed and we ate breakfast and I set out with Sister Baby for school. Doubling back on Beale, I unlocked the office, waited for Lucy Provine, and hurried home almost at a run expecting Teddy might well be there already: 'Hello, Daddy —'

He wasnt. No word, no sign, and my heart took a drop like into a pit, a coalbin, down and down. In my mind I was back where I was the day before, standing over that bulging, empty barrel, knowing they had me.

Around eleven Tio and Mamma Cindy got there, he from the office, she from up the street, meeting as if by signal at the gate. I wanted to make up for yesterday, that ugly scene between us, but it was closing fast by then on the time-span being up, and I was too distracted. Then it was all the way up, twenty-four hours, and the clock swung on to noon and I broke out against them, cursing whoever they were, wherever they were, for not keeping their word.

Tio tried to calm my anger and my fears. "You have to think of Theo," he told me.

"*Teddy*," I said, shifting my rage from them to Tio, and once more it seemed to work at least a little, for a while.

Then it was Martha's turn to come unraveled. "Oh Mamma, Mamma — I'm so scared!" she cried.

"There, child," Mamma Cindy told her, leaning forward and taking both of Martha's dark hands in her own two pale ones that hadnt so much as lifted a dust-rag since she left her old daddy's house in Moscow close to forty years ago. She patted and held them, the dark and the pale. "Do like I do. Put your trust in the Lord. He'll see you through every time. Or almost every time," she said, wanting to be honest about those few occasions when He had seemed to be looking the other way just then.

That helped too, some, though in a different way from Tio's. We sat there, the four of us, ears cocked, *minds* cocked, and at last it was time to go fetch Sister Baby home from school.

"I'll go," I said, not wanting to, but thinking Martha might not be able, from all the tension.

"No. You stay here," she said. "I want to."

She set out, still in her turban, and when she'd left, on out the gate and then up Vance, Tio cleared his throat to speak. What he intended, and I knew it as soon as he cleared his throat, was to explain some things I'd been tearing him down about, mostly in private to Martha but also to his face, to some degree. It was as if he read my mind, the way folks say he can do sometimes with people he's taken the trouble to get to know for business reasons.

"Eben," he said, and cleared his throat again. I saw what he intended was an accounting, and then he gave it. "You gotten so you get all worked up over things that dont bother me hardly a-tall and never have. I long since learnt to live with them and expect still worse with every go-round: especially where the law, the power, is concerned. All them other scrabblers, black and white, I dealt with as they come along. You can catch more flies with honey than with vinegar, by a long shot. What I did, right down the line, was pretend to be on their side so I could get them on mine, unbeknownst. You think I ever minded some man having a low opinion of me? No indeed. That give me the best of all advantages over him. He wouldnt even take the trouble to look at my position and think what I might do: especially a white man. Handkerchief Head, Uncle Tom — what do I care what he thinks I am, so long as I know I'm me?"

A long speech, for him, with a whole great mass of things behind it, including disappointment and hurt pride. He had worked hard all his life for his money, and he resented seeing so little respect being paid it now that the need for it was greatest. Running money down to him, the way I'd been doing this past week, was like running down God to a preacher. He took it hard. That should have been understandable, even to me, considering the odds he'd faced and overcome, but it angered me more than ever — I guess because of the state I was in by then, seeing the money more as the cause than the salvation.

All through this time, while he was speaking and after,

Mamma Cindy smoothed her skirt in her lap, watching her hands ripple over the cloth, smoothing, smoothing, and she kept doing it now, right up to Martha's return with Sister Baby. They were both puffing from their fast walk home, like mine from the office that morning for the same reason, hoping Teddy would be there waiting: 'Hello, Mamma — '

He wasnt, any more now than then, and I began to come unraveled at the thought. Here it was crowding three oclock, almost four hours past the promised span, and still there was no sign of him, no word from any direction.

"I did wrong to give them the money," I broke out. "I did wrong — and I knew it at the time I gave it."

"You did right," Tio told me.

"Why aint he home then? Why aint he home? The twenty-four hours is up, and more than up."

"He'll be home," Tio told me.

"I dont know that, and you dont either. All I know is I did wrong. I lost my leverage, flung it away. It's up to me to say whether I did right or I did wrong about my boy: mine and Martha's. And I did wrong."

"You did right," Tio said again. "Didnt he, Lucindy?"

For a minute she didnt answer, not being accustomed to having her opinion asked. But then she did. "It's they *child*," she told him.

"And my money," Tio couldnt keep from saying.

"Yes, yo money," she told him, "and they child. I weighed them one against the other, and the child come out ahead."

"Hey, Mamma Cindy!" Sister Baby shouted. Ten years later she would be a cheer-leader at Central High — another Central High School, here in Memphis — and this was her first cheer: "Hey, Mamma Cindy!"

Tio sat there looking poleaxed, but I was mainly watching Martha. She even managed to smile, at a time like that, and I told myself as I watched her, She's not Daddy's girl any longer. She is mine.

Half an hour from time to go, we got up to dress, and after a while, from there near the bottom of the steps where I sat putting on my shoes, I could hear Reeny up in the attic talking with the boy. She laid it out for him the way we decided was best, which was to tell him the bedrock truth and count on him behaving, rather than have to drop him off just any old place, trussed up like a turkey or drugged to the gills, for someone to find and carry home. "We took you and now we're taking you back," she told him.

"Took me?"

"Took you; yes. Kidnap they call it. And now we're fixing to take you back. Youre going home."

There was a pause while I tied my shoes. He was thinking it over, trying to take it in. Finally he answered, but with a question. "Can I keep Teddy?" That was the button-eyed bear Rufus won at the shooting gallery, the night they went to the Mid-South Fair. He had given it his name.

"Course you can," she told him. "He's yours. Of course you can."

She was getting him dressed in the clothes he wore when we snatched him, a week ago today, and she went on to explain the blindfold and the quilt. They would come later, when we left. "It's so you wont know where youve been, in case they try to trace us," she said, meaning the blindfold. "And the quilt is so the neighbors wont see us carry you out to the car, the way we did when we brought you here asleep. You see?"

"Yessum," he said.

I dont think he did see, but he trusted her. And he sure was what she called him earlier; a brave little boy. Just so.

Her notion, and I agreed, was that it would be better all round if we let him out where he would know his way home, instead of somewhere strange that would make him feel abandoned. So far, what with all the attention she had given him, he hadnt been frightened without someone there to comfort him, tell him things were all right, and she didnt want it to happen here at the end. We had already decided the night before, while Rufus was gone after burgers at K's, to stop the Noctec after the last-morning dose so he wouldnt go home groggy, and then this afternoon she got the notion we could let him out where we picked him up, somewhere along that empty stretch on Linden near the school.

"He'll know his way home from there all right," she said, "and that's where he'll go, straight home. He's a brave little boy."

"O.K. We'll do it," I told her after thinking it over and remembering how there hadnt been a soul in sight within half an hour of the two-thirty bell. "We'll leave here sometime after three, to make sure, and he can walk home just the way it would be, Monday to Monday, if this past week hadnt happened."

We were lying there on that sheetless mattress, an hour or so after Rufus took off in the cab to pick up his new girl out east. Celia, her name was; Celia Something. Drawbridge? I couldnt remember, but Reeny had already said it didnt matter. "He made her up," she told me, right after he left.

"No."

"He did. I dont know why, but he's lying. He hasnt got any girl; not that one anyhow. I know him too well. He's just saying that for some reason he's got in mind."

"Sure he does," I said. "You heard him."

"That's what I mean; I heard him. It's his way. I can tell by his face when he's lying. And his voice. It gets lower-down in his throat. He's more earnest; more truthful-seeming, if you see what I mean."

"Maybe." The fact was I didnt much care. Let him do or not-do whatever he wanted about some girl out east or not out east; I didnt care. My mind was on matters there at hand.

"But Celia dont sound to me like a name youd make up on the spur of the moment, if what you wanted was to have somebody believe you."

"You dont know Rufus," she said. She looked worried. "And who says it was spur of the moment?"

"Maybe not." I was on the couch; she was in a chair across the room. He had been gone maybe two-three minutes, and it was a long time since Wednesday, the night of the Atlas launch. "Anyhow he's gone now, wherever and whatever for. We got the whole house to ourselves."

"I'll go up and check on Teddy. I wont be long."

Even so, I found myself thinking of him while I waited in the bedroom they shared till she moved upstairs. In part I felt sheepish about the way I'd acted in his direction these past few days since the night of the Atlas fizzle — calling him Old Son, I mean, and talking my head off about high-school basketball trips and such, to put off his suspicions until we got the money in hand, my half and her share of his half. I knew him well enough to know he might explode under that kind of pressure, blow the whole job to hell-and-gone before we wound it up. Nothing is as dangerous as a coward when he's crossed and cornered; that is if he's got some angle he can work to get back at you, never mind what's likely to come down on his own head afterward; especially when he's as keyed-up as Rufus was all through that time. The calming-down job Reeny did on him two nights ago, while I was gone to Jim's for ribs, barely lasted out the evening. There's no top to that ladder for men like him, built around their privates, with a brain that ticks like a time bomb in the shape of a clenched-up cunt. If it was big enough, and you could smoke in there, theyd live in it. And the lies; my God, the lies. Instead of making a life for himself, he made one up.

As I sat there on the side of the bed, waiting barefoot in my drawers, I heard her at last tell the boy up in the attic, "If youre not sleepy, look at your funny-books a while. I wont be long." She was going to be longer than she knew, if I had any say-so in the matter.

Presently she came down, remembering to fold back the bottom set of steps, and joined me on the mattress. Christ it was good; even better than I remembered from four nights ago, out on the couch while Rufus snored. The way she tucked herself up under me for a better fit, I mean — a sort of trick she had, except it didnt come out a trick. It amounted instead to a kind of closeness, breast and belly, arms and thighs; a round-trip ticket to glory. Rufus was right about the covey of quail, and a little later I found out he was also right about other things he said, back at the start when we first got here, except he neednt have drawn the line this side of Paris. I know; Ive been there.

"Where are you from anyhow?" I asked her, a little later still. We were lying there and I was smoking. I really wanted to know, by way of a clew as to what had just come over me, there on that naked mattress with the midday sunlight filtered through the shades.

"Down on Lake Jordan; near Ithaca, the same as you. You knew that."

I remembered then she had told it before, one time or another, back before I started paying much attention, let alone asking questions. She'd also said her daddy was a preacher, I remembered, but it hadnt registered till now that I really wanted to know.

"What was your unmarried name?" I asked her.

"Jimson," she said, and then I knew.

"Youre Brother *Jim*son's daughter? Little tow-headed girl in the second or third, when I was in the eighth? Jesus. I remember you being pointed out in the schoolyard. And I sure as hell remember him. He was one preacher even my old man wouldnt tangle with — and my old man made a practice of tangling with most everyone he met. I'll be damned. Little Reeny Jimson. I'll be damned."

I couldnt get over it; having things come full circle like that, I mean. One year, long ago, youre a boy in the yard at Tarfeller School, grades one through eight, and somebody points out a skinny little third-grader across the way, playing jacks or hop-

scotch at noon recess — ribbed stockings, a cotton dress with
no more shape to it than the flour sack it was cut from, hightop shoes, lank hair no color at all even in sunlight — and tells
you, "That's that preacher's daughter. Jimson. The one they
say jumps all the women. Her name's Reeny." You notice her,
say, a couple more times in the schoolyard there in Ithaca, and
then the year is over and youre gone; you dont see or think of
her again, if in fact you ever saw her in the first place. Then
twenty some-odd years go by — twenty-six, to be exact; a
whole goddam generation — and you are lying there on a sheetless mattress with her, little Reeny Jimson that you last saw
when she was nine and you were fourteen. She's Reeny Perdew
now, and you both have packed a lifetime into the years that
came between, including a trio of marriages and a war, Texas
and Parchman, a stretch as a whore and a stretch as a jailbird,
all part of a wheel that came full circle.

Maybe it meant luck; she'd bring me luck, in addition to all
she'd brought me already, first on that velvet couch out front
and now on the bare ticking of a mattress she had shared with
someone else, poor loused-up Rufus, before I came along. If
that means luck, I told myself, I sure could use some. Luck's
one thing I never had till now.

"What are you thinking?" she asked me.

"I dont know; all kinds of things. Lake Jordan, my old man
and yours, and you the way you were back then, a little skinny
thing in the schoolyard there in Ithaca all those years ago."

She didnt remember me, though she had tried. "I wish I did,"
she said. "I bet you were as country-looking as I was."

"Could be. It was a long time back. Hoover days; just before
Roosevelt came along and saved us for the war."

"I dont remember. I wish I did — unless maybe I dont want
to." She had been smiling up to then, but now she stopped. Her
face went solemn. "They do pile up though, dont they?"

"What do?" I didnt understand.

"Years. The years," she said.

I bent over my side of the bed to put out my cigarette in the ashtray on the floor there, and while I did I checked under it for the shoebox I hid there last night while Rufus was gone for the burgers, sliding it back out of sight through the dust that collected this past month. It hadnt been moved, no dust disturbed except the one clean track it made when I slid it back against the baseboard.

When I straightened up she began talking about the boy, wanting to let him out where he'd know the way home and wouldnt feel lost and abandoned. I had planned to turn him loose somewhere on Mulberry, the old redlight district not too far from his house on Vance, but Linden sounded fine to me now that she mentioned it. When I said so — "O.K. We'll do it" — she smiled again, happy as she had been a while ago, before her face went solemn about the piled-up years.

We lay back down. I could be calmer about her now, not only because of the past hour but also from thinking of all the hours ahead — between now and the time it ended, the way all things end at last. Just so. And before long it was past two-thirty; time to get up and dress, finish packing and set out for Linden.

My notion was to get as much done as possible beforehand, including loading the Ford with the cots and such, to keep from wasting time when we doubled back to pick up our bags and begin that nearly two-thousand-mile drive to Vegas. I was sitting there on the side of the bed, putting my shoes on, while she told the boy about the blindfold and quilt he'd have to wear when we set out. "Yessum," I heard him say as I tied my laces, and then went up front to wait some more while she finished getting him dressed for leaving.

This morning's paper, brought back by Reeny from her laundry trip, was there on the couch where I read it after I returned from throwing the Noctec bottle and spare plates in the river. Under BAYONETS DISAPPEAR a subhead read, *President Ending Vacation; Will Confer With Governors.* Rufus was right in what he said before he left, that Little Rock was winding down at the same time as our caper over here. So it

was, and a good thing, too, all round. Old Ike; I guess he figured he could come out in the open, back on the job, now that
the smoke had cleared and Faubus had gotten all he wanted
from him, including re-election. The poor half-assed West
Point son of a bitch never knew how to deal with any chal-
lenge unless it was personal, and then all he knew to do was
send in troopers. LITTLE ROCK IS TOPS IN RED PAPERS, another
headline read, inside. What this country needs, I told myself,
is a President; Dick Nixon maybe, or anyhow someone who
knows which way the wind is blowing nowadays.

"Joe!" I heard Reeny call down from the attic.

For a minute I didnt know who that meant, until I remembered and went to the foot of the steps to see what she wanted.
What it was was the kid was ready and so was she; I could
come up and fold the cots for loading in the car so we could
go. I went up, and there was Teddy in his clothes and shoes,
looking just the way he did when we first took him, barely a
week ago today, another Monday, before Reeny put the clown
white on him. "Joe is going to take the things down, then come
back and take you too," she told him. This time he was too
frightened to say yessum. He just nodded and sort of swallowed
to clear his throat.

Folding those cots was no easy job; I'd forgotten how since
my recruit days right after Pearl Harbor, more than fifteen
years ago. All the time I was rassling with them, Teddy stood
there alongside Reeny, watching and looking uneasy, especially
when I got mad at one of them after folding it the wrong way.
I hadnt seen much of him this past week; her notion was I
scared him, so I kept mostly away from him for that reason.
I think I did scare him. How not? But she was right, too, when
she called him brave, no matter how frightened he was of me
or anything else. Bravery's nothing anyhow but fear turned
inside-out. I never put stock in that down-home claim that
niggers are no good in the clutch. It depends on what kind of
clutch you mean, what's offered and what's threatened — and
life never seemed to me to offer them much of anything except

threats that any sensible person would shy away from in the first place. Yes; just so. Anyhow I finally got the two cots folded and took them down, along with the fan. On second thought, I left them by the front door, to be picked up when we returned, and came back up to the attic where Reeny was about to put the blindfold on him.

"I'm going to tie this round your eyes," she told him, undoing a blue silk handkerchief scarf she had put around her neck when she dressed in the bedroom, "then wrap you in the quilt you came here in." She had that too, folded over one arm. "They are so you wont see or be seen — like I said before. Then Joe is going to carry you down the steps and out to the car, and we'll head for home. Dont be afraid; Joe *likes* you. It wont be for long, and I'll be right there with you all the time. He'll put you in the back seat and I'll get back there, too, right beside you all the way. You understand?" He nodded. "All right; hold steady." She put the scarf around his head and knotted it in back. "Too tight?"

"Noam," he said. His voice shook. He was blind now.

"All right; now the quilt." She draped him in it, head and all. "That feel snug?" He didnt answer. "All right. Now Joe is going to pick you up. All right?"

"Yessum," he said, muffled alone there in the dark.

I picked him up, wrapped like an undersized mummy, and now as before, a week ago, it surprised me how light he was, how little he weighed — mostly I guess because I never had any child of my own to get me accustomed to the notion that a life could weigh so little as fifty-sixty pounds, one scant arm-load, with all those years stretching out ahead of it. Anyhow, as I started down, taking the steps one at a time to keep from stumbling because of their steepness, I heard him call out something, faint and far, through the layers of batting. "Teddy, Teddy" — his own name. I didnt understand till I stopped and thought.

"What's he saying?" Reeny asked, behind us.

"He wants his bear."

"I got him right here, I'm right behind you," she told him over my shoulder, through the quilt. "I'll give him to you soon as we reach the car."

That seemed to calm him, some. At the bottom I waited while she folded the steps and let the trapdoor up, one-handed because of the stuffed bear in the other, then went around us to open the front door. I went out and down the stoop, then over to the driveway, waiting again while she locked the house and hurried past us to open the back door of the Ford. I put him on the seat there, more or less like a rolled-up rug bent in the middle, and when she got in beside him, sitting close for reassurance, went round to the driver's side, got under the wheel, started the engine, and backed out.

Soon as we turned onto Riverside, by the Chinaman's, she part-way opened the quilt and put the bear in with him. "There you go," she told him. "Didnt I promise?"

She talked to him that way during the ride up Riverside and later, mainly to let him know she was there with him and to help get him through this first stretch of going without the Noctec that kept him sleepy-calm all the rest of the time he'd been with us. I turned under the viaduct onto Beale, then right again on Front one block to Linden, where I took a left, back east toward the school only six short blocks away. The three-thirty traffic lull was on and not many people were out of their offices or homes. I drove carefully, taking my time, but not so slow that it would draw attention. Reeny kept talking, bent sideways now so her head was near Teddy's, under that rolled-up patchwork quilt.

"We'll meet again, some day," she was telling him. "Youll be grown and you wont know me; youll have forgotten, because of the medicine and all. I'll know you, though, and I might even come up and say hello."

He didnt answer, so far as I could hear, but she kept talking, talking. I couldnt tell whether she meant what she was saying or was just running on to make him feel less alone there in the dark, behind his blindfold and the quilt. I think she meant a good deal of it, all the same, because of the way she told me a little later about him asking once if she was his mamma. Anyhow, I had crossed Main, then Mulberry, Second and Third, Hernando and Fourth by now; Turley was next, with Church Park on the left and the three-story red brick mass of Leath School just beyond the intersection. We were there, and no one was in sight in either direction along that stretch of houseless street or the schoolyard up ahead.

I pulled over to the curb, within ten feet of where we grabbed him that other Monday, one week plus one hour ago today. Now as then, when I checked up and down the block again, there was no one in sight, riding or walking. "O.K." I said. "Unload him. Make it quick."

Reeny folded back the quilt and there he was, like a shucked nubbin, hugging his button-eyed bear and turning his head this way and that, as if he was trying to see through the blue silk blindfold.

"All right, Teddy," she said. "Hold still now while I get the scarf off." When she unknotted and removed it, he clamped his eyes tight shut against the sudden glare of sunlight. "It's the school; youre back at school now, headed home," she told him, stepping rearward out of the curbside door, hands on both of his wrists to guide and keep him from falling when he came out behind her, groping blind with his feet. For a moment they stood there together on the grass between the sidewalk and the curb, he with his eyes still closed against the glare, the bear dangling head-down by one leg, and Reeny looking at him. "Goodbye," she said, hand on his shoulder, the way it had been that other time just before she snatched him up.

She got back in the car, up front with me, slammed the door shut behind her, and called out to him through the open window as we pulled off, "Be a good boy now. You hear? And go on home —"

We were rolling by then; she had to lean part-way out of the window to keep him in sight while she said goodbye. I saw him in the rear-view mirror, standing alone there in the clothes we took him in, hugging the bear to his chest, upside down, while his eyes grew more accustomed to the light. He looked somehow orphaned — bereft, they call it — as if he'd lost still another family. When I made the turn onto Wellington, he slid sideways off the mirror while Reeny sat stiff-backed beside me, a shocked expression on her face. One minute he was there, the next he wasnt, with scarcely an eye-blink in between.

It was then, as we passed the rear of the school, that she came out with what I mentioned earlier. "He asked me once if I was his mamma now."

"You want to go back and snatch him up again?"

A joke; but she didnt take it quite that way entirely. "I almost wish we could," she said. "I miss him already."

"Maybe someday we'll get you another one," I told her. She just sat there. "Or a stuffed bear," I said, still trying to bring her round. But she just sat there stiff-backed, looking about as bereft as the boy had looked, back yonder between the sidewalk and the curb, hugging his bear upside-down and trying to get his eyes accustomed to the glare.

By now I had turned over to Fourth and eased on south to Crump, where I took a right, headed west for the river. Beyond Third was Earl's Hot Biscuits, on the left; I pulled in there. The notion was, we'd get a good substantial meal before leaving, and by driving hard — five to six, maybe seven hundred miles a day, taking turns at the wheel and only eating when we stopped for gas — make Vegas by Thursday afternoon, three days off, with plenty of time to settle in, take a look-round, and line up a game that night at whatever club I thought would suit me best. I was down to about eighteen of the original five hundred dollars, which was cutting it pretty close but was still enough to keep us from having to dip into the shoebox before we put Memphis comfortably behind us. We had steak and French fries, okra and head lettuce, a plate of biscuits and cups and cups of coffee, rounded off with ice cream; vanilla for me, peach for Reeny.

I watched her eat, and I'll say one thing. For someone who

cared as little for food on a day-to-day basis as she did — cornflakes doused with canned milk, for instance — she was no
slouch at packing it in when something substantial came her
way. From the first bite of steak to the last shred of lettuce, on
through the three-scoop bowl of ice cream, she swept the board
so clear that Earl wouldnt even have to rinse up after her.
An appetite like that could make for problems; not to mention
clothes and shoes, movies and makeup, double rooms at motels
and boarding houses. Two can live as cheap as one, they say,
means two men can live on what it takes one woman — and the
cost would come out of my stake. Always before, wherever I
went, whatever I was after, I traveled alone. And now as I
watched her across the table there, with her various plates
licked clean as any cat would lick them, I asked myself: Are
you truly ready, at this late stage, to take unto yourself a
millstone?

"Hey, that was *good*," she said just then, meaning the ice
cream. And the answer came back, clear as clear: Yes. Yes, I am.

Between the question and the answer, there inside my head,
had come a sudden recollection of her on the couch that Atlas
night. "You been wanting me all along," she said, back then,
and it was true; I'd been wanting her even before I knew it —
all along — and now that I had had her, Atlas night out on the
couch and this afternoon in the bedroom, I knew just what it
was I'd been wanting, and knowing made me want her even
more. Yes. Yes, I am, I told myself, shaking off the buck that
had come on me there at the last minute, the way they say it
generally does. That's why they have a best man at weddings,
to keep the groom from bolting when the buck comes on him;
so Ive heard.

Anyhow, millstone or not, I'd already figured she would
bring me luck, along with the kind of attention at home that
would make me calmer in a card game, more able to maintain
my concentration. I'd seen the way she was with the boy up in
the attic all that week, outgoing and concerned, and I took that
as a sign of how she was; good-hearted, I guess I mainly mean,

combined with friendliness and caring. She was even that way with Rufus, till he spoiled it. I remembered the night of the snatch, when they went out back together; "to see the lights," she said. He was in a conniption and she wasnt far behind him, warming up for another of their duets. What a waste.

"Well," I told her, getting up from the table, "I reckon we better get rolling. We got a lot of road to cover between now and Thursday when we hit the bright-lights."

I left a quarter for the waitress, paid at the desk — six-forty plus tax — and we went out and got back in the car. One more stop, next door for gas — it had gone over thirty cents that weekend, even the off-brand kind I buy — and we headed for the bluff. I was down to a five-dollar bill and some change by now; enough, I figured, to take us through our first stop near the Texas border.

Just past the foot of Main, as we went under the railroad viaduct, Reeny switched on the radio, and when we came out the other side it blared at us, first with music, then an interruption, a bulletin from the newsroom. Two men — male Caucasians, the announcer said; a fancy way of calling someone white — had just hit the main downtown branch of First National and got clean away, so far. The take was somewhere between five and six thousand dollars and the police were in pursuit, though it seemed they didnt quite know what they were in pursuit of; descriptions varied. Stay tuned for details, the radio said, and the music came back up.

"Sounds like they made it," Reeny said.

"Could be," I told her, "if theyve got sense enough to lay low for a while. Hitting banks is one hell of a way to make a living, though. Not the heist itself; that's easy enough, with a little luck. The tough part comes later — the getaway — if some dumb guard didnt blow one of them's brains out in the first place. Guns; Jesus."

Up ahead, the sun was about to touch the top of the bridges, preparing to set a full hour earlier because of daylight-saving going off. The result was like a sudden leap into fall; short days, cool nights, the gins going full blast throughout the Delta and all the roads and highways full of unlighted cotton wagons creaking homeward in the dusk, invisible till you were right up on them, sometimes with a mule's head through the windshield. I remembered my old man hauling logs that time of year, early fall, and the many near misses he had along the backroads, until the day a chain snapped and the whole red-oak load came rolling down on him. 1938; I was close to twenty-two and we were about to come out of the depression. He was the one who named me, back before I was out of skirts. My mother had me christened Joseph, a proper saint's name, but he wouldnt use it. "You could at least call him Joe," she said. But he wouldnt; Podner he called me, until she raised so much fuss about it, in and out of bed, that he struck a compromise by telescoping the two names into Podjo. She didnt like that any better, if as much, but he had compromised as far as he would go; I stayed Podjo, then and since. One thing I remember best about him, back when I was a boy, was the way he came home from his barber-shop bath every Saturday bringing the smell of Lucky Tiger with him, mixed with the smell of whiskey when he laughed. Only half of me is my father, and I'm half the man he was.

There beside me, as I turned off Crump onto Riverside, Reeny too was watching the sun groove down across the way in Arkansas. She was over missing the boy already, or anyhow she seemed to be, after a solid week of spending more time with him than she probably spent with any other person in any one week in her life. "Pretty," she said, with a nod at the sun out over the bridge-tops. I nodded too, regretting that we had burnt so much daylight before setting out, but satisfied all the same that we at least had spent it getting ready. As we turned north off Crump she turned her head to keep the reddening sun in sight past the back of my head. Cut off early though it was by the end of daylight-saving, this last day in September had been a long one, and now it was sloping toward a close, not only the day but the month as well.

I watched her sideways, rounding the curve, sunlight glow-ing rosy on her face, and watching her made me want her again, the way it had been ever since that first night together on the couch; a kind of hunger I knew I mustnt let her know I felt — her or any woman — from knowing she would be sure to use it against me when the time came. A man's got to watch himself all round the clock. Just so, I thought, staving off the notion that she might want a good deal more from me than I would be willing to give except in my spare time. But that's *her* problem, I told myself. Just so.

We had made the turn onto Carolina by then, alongside the Chinaman's, past the nipple company, and up ahead, just as I turned left again on Arkansas, I saw a car parked at the curb in front of the house; a brand-new white Thunderbird, so new it still had a cardboard dealer's license on it, along with double headlights, an air-scoop on the hood, fins on the rear fenders, and a grill like a big frowning mouth under the curve of the front bumper. And there on the concrete stoop of the house sat Rufus, the coat of his good blue suit folded across his thighs and a handkerchief spread on the top step to protect the seat of his trousers. He was back from out near Germantown and waiting. When he saw us he grinned and raised one arm and waved a greeting.

"See there," I told Reeny, nodding at the car as we went past it to turn into the driveway. "He did have that girl-friend after all. Celia. Didnt I tell you?"

# 7

# *Some You Lose*

"Locked me out, by golly," Rufus said, rising and smiling as Reeny and Podjo emerged from the Ford and approached the stoop where he had been sitting. He flung his jacket across one shoulder to free both hands for refolding the handkerchief he took up from the top step when he rose. "I thought at first you had skedaddled on me. Man, it gave me quite a turn, till I looked through the bedroom window and saw your bags still there alongside mine. So I decided to wait instead of jimmying my way in. Besides, I wouldnt want to take off without saying goodbye, after all we been through together this past month. You drop the kid all right?"

Podjo answered none of this. Instead, as he came up the steps behind Reeny, who went past Rufus with the key, he jerked his thumb toward the shiny white Thunderbird parked at the curb. "That's some set of wheels your girl-friend Celia's got there."

"Yair." Rufus looked fondly back at it while following his companions through the door. "But that's not Celia's car. That's Celia," he said as he stepped inside. "I named it myself, the way rich men do their yachts, when I bought it just now at Cormac's out on Union."

"You *what?*" Podjo stopped in his tracks.

"Bought it, like I said, just now at Cormac's out on Union. A pretty good deal, if I do say so myself. It was $3358 f.o.b. Detroit; $4503 with shipping and prep and the extras. I got them all — radio, air-conditioning, automatic shift, chrome spinners, deluxe upholstery; the works. At first I thought I'd try for a straight four thousand, but then I decided I'd rather watch the salesman's reaction to a man who wouldnt dicker. So instead I just got him to knock off the odd three dollars, along with the sales tax, and gave him the even forty-five hundred, cash on the barrelhead. He almost dropped his teeth."

"In twenties I reckon," Podjo said, tight-lipped, standing there looking level-eyed at Rufus, who was smiling.

"What else? Sure. But dont worry; I told him I won them at Hot Springs yesterday on the daily double. I even looked it up beforehand, to see which horses won. Tampax in the second, Gloriosky in the fifth. That poor damned salesman near dropped his teeth at the sight of all that long green coming at him, without even a trade-in on the deal. His hands shook so, he almost couldnt write the ticket."

"Jesus, Rufus — "

"What? You mean about the money? Man, we'll be long gone by the time they start trying to trace it, even if youre right about them taking down the numbers off the bills."

"And how far do you think youll get?"

"Pretty far," Rufus said, still smiling. "Far enough, anyhow. It depends on where I'm headed. Far enough."

Podjo stood there a moment longer, turned halfway round to look over his shoulder at the sly pride of that smile, that blue-eyed smirk of satisfaction under the trained wave of yellow hair, then walked on through the bedroom and the hallway — the attic steps were down; Reeny was making a last-minute check up there — into the kitchen, where he unlatched the back door and stepped out onto the porch.

In his present state of rage he did not trust himself to say anything more until he decided how best to deal with this new situation, which in fact he had predicted at the outset. "I got to watch this fellow, I got to watch him," he had told himself, by way of reinforcing the admonition that if there was

any way to screw things up Rufus would certainly find it, if for
no other reason than that he always had. Sure enough, he'd
found it here at the very end of the caper, and now Podjo was
faced with the consequences he had foreseen but not fore-
stalled.

My trouble was I got distracted, he thought, gazing out past
the lip of the bluff at the river and the three bridges webbed
against the red declining sun. He remembered Reeny on her
birthday, drying her hair out there in the yard — on the half
shell, Rufus had said after offering her to him — and another
sunset, the following day, when she talked through moonrise,
on and on, about powing out of cakes. Yes: distracted, he told
himself, and pulled his attention back to the problem at hand,
the car parked at the curb out front and the money used to
buy it.

Once the police caught up with Rufus in that glittering '58
Thunderbird, which would stand out in the heaviest traffic like
a Christmas-tree ornament in a nest of eggs, they would in
effect have caught up with all three of them. Whether he talked
or not — and clearly he would, especially in his present venge-
ful state — it would be no trick at all to trace him back to
Bristol, where there were plenty of witnesses to identify the
two who had been closest to him for the better part of a month
before they all three disappeared together, just under four
weeks back. The thing to do, as in the case of the pistol on the
day they arrived and unpacked, was persuade him to get rid of
the goddam car at once. Not sell it; just abandon it somewhere,
wiped clean of prints, and write off the loss, the forty-five
hundred in twenty-dollar bills. That wouldnt be easy, for several reasons, not the least of which was his obvious pride in the
purchase. For a moment, casting about for straws in his distress,
Podjo considered giving him five thousand from his own money
in exchange for the machine, thus allowing him to boast of a
five-hundred-dollar profit on the deal. He had no sooner
thought of this, however, than he rejected it out of hand, not
only because Rufus was likely to go right back to Cormac's

and buy another, more or less its twin, but also because he decided that would put too deep a dent in his Las Vegas stake. Then it occurred to him that Reeny perhaps could handle the persuasion best by working it out in bed with Rufus, here or down the road a piece in some motel. But that too was rejected, on grounds that the authorities might well be hot on their track before enough time had passed to get him thoroughly persuaded. A better notion might be to knock him in the head, which he certainly deserved, and ditch him where he would never be found: except of course they always *were* found, and then there would be a murder charge on top of all the rest.

At this point Podjo fetched a deep sigh, in acknowledgment of the difficulties involved in trying to outwit a crazy man. In any case, he decided, if none of these shaky alternatives worked out, the thing to do was get clear of him — get as far away as possible, and leave no trail for the police to follow when they took up the second phase of the chase, after collaring Rufus. Just so, he thought. He felt better now, or at any rate calmer for having thought it over, even though he had reached no firm decision, and went back inside.

Reeny was down from the attic by then, and when he saw the frightened expression on her face he realized she had gone up there not so much to check on things as to escape the blowup she saw looming when she heard Rufus say he'd bought the car with bills he had been warned would put the law on their track. Podjo saw, too, that she was relieved to find him speaking calmly when he returned.

"I'll load up the car and we'll take off," he told her. "As for you," he added, turning to Rufus, who had come into the bedroom and was standing by the chifforobe on the far side of the bed, still wearing that sly prideful smile, "I ought not have to say it, but now that youve gone and risked our necks, you know damned well our only chance for a clean getaway — yours, anyhow — is to get shed of that damn T-bird, somewhere out of the way, by nightfall. Come morning, if not sooner, the cops are going to be on you like white on rice."

"Mmn; I dont know," Rufus said. He seemed to ponder.

"There's a sentimental factor youre not taking into account. You know how a fellow is about the first car he buys. Sociologists all agree it's one of the great American experiences. He gets attached and fond of it, that first car; they tell me he never forgets it, down the years. I cant see my way to giving it up just yet. Not even for you, old son."

His smile had dimmed. Now Podjo watched it brighten, and as it did he turned and went into the living room, where he took up the folded cots and the fan. The screen door slapped behind him when he went out to put them in the trunk of the Ford parked in the driveway.

"Well, babe," Rufus said, alone with Reeny in the stillness, "it looks like this is it, the parting of the ways. You sure you dont want to change your mind again?"

"Rufus," she said, part reproachful, part pleading.

"Yair. Well, I thought you might; you been known to. You see, I'm not forgetting how much you liked what I was putting down, all those months we spent together. That time might come round again. Who knows? And when it does, just give me a sign; I'll be there. *He* wont know it, but I will be. You just send up some kind of signal and we'll get it on again, like in the old days. Beaver, beaver."

The screen door slapped and Podjo came back into the bedroom. He glanced at Reeny, still looking frightened there beside him, then at Rufus, by the chifforobe on the far side of the bed.

"I'll ask you again, for all our sake," he told him. "Will you or wont you get rid of that damn T-bird? Or are we going to spend what little time is left us running from the law? You can come with us, once you ditch it, and we'll drop you off wherever you want, unless maybe we can work something out between us, down the line. O.K.?"

"I cant see it," Rufus said, drawling the words. He smiled at Reeny before turning back to Podjo. "You go your way, I'll go mine; in our two cars. For one thing, how do I know what youve got in mind for me, down the road a piece? And for another, old Reeny tore her drawers with me some time ago."

"O.K." Podjo shrugged, then knelt abruptly beside the bed

and reached under it, up by the headboard. He emerged with the shoebox in both hands.

Rufus was startled by the sudden movement, but soon recovered his composure and his smile. "So that's where you kept it. Hm; I wish I'd known. Well" — he opened the bedside closet door, groped amid the clutter on the shelf, and brought down the bulging paper sack — "here's where I kept mine. We're a couple of sly dogs, aint we? Each of us scared what the other would do while his back was turned." He held the sack by its rolled-up top, still smiling. "As for me," he went on, "I got to thinking about my new girl Celia. Trouble was, there wasnt any Celia; never was. So I decided to keep this one." He gave Reeny an up-from-under look, peering at her through the pale fringe of his eyebrows, then back at Podjo. "That's first-class stuff, I'm here to testify, just as I did before you found out for yourself behind my back. Yair. But then I changed my mind again; I decided to let you keep her. I'd rather" — he had unrolled the mouth of the sack, and now he reached inside — "have the money. All of it." The pistol came out, cocked and locked, and as he leveled it at Podjo he released the safety. "Just lay that shoebox gently on the bed there, and back off."

Podjo looked at the .45, staring literally down its barrel, which at that range seemed almost large enough for him to crawl inside. His ace in the hole, Rufus had called the weapon once. And now it was. Luck, Podjo thought. Here Ive gone and done it again; snatched defeat from the jaws of victory, all because I got distracted.

"Now wait up, kid," he said, doing his best to keep his voice level. "You got a problem here that takes some thinking. The law or me. Think it over and put that thing away. Theyll catch up with you or *I* will. Your problem is which, and one's about as bad as the other, where youre concerned."

"You catch up with me, old son, youll be sorry," Rufus told him. "I'll feed you this nine-round clip so fast youll never know what hit you. Christ almighty. Did you think you were going to get my girl and half the money, too? No way: and now you know it. Yair. So put that box on the mattress there, and back off like I said."

Carefully, even gently, as instructed, Podjo placed the shoe-box on the bed, then backed away to stand alongside Reeny by the doorway to the hall. When this had been done, Rufus reached across the mattress, never lowering his eyes, and pulled the box toward him, the dead-black pistol steady and level in his other hand. "Well now," he said, broadening his smile. "That's more like it. Share the wealth. And just to show you there's no hard feelings on my part — "

By way of finishing the sentence, he took from the left side pocket of his trousers the unspent tenth of the ten packets of twenties he had taken from his sack that morning, before head-ing out for Cormac's, and with the same hand, still without looking down, removed the lid from the shoebox, deposited the packet of twenties in it, and withdrew two fat five-hundred-dollar packets of tens, which he flipped on the bed in Reeny's direction. They landed with two little bounces, then lay still.

"That's for you, babe," he told her; "one cool thousand, for favors received. Maybe the best I ever had, bar none. Any time you want to let me have some more, come see me. I ought not be too hard to find — for you, that is. Old Podjo there, he's another matter. Dont come looking, old son, lest you run into something you dont want."

And with that he left. Sack and shoebox bundled in his jacket under one arm, he also carried his suitcase on that side, leaving his right hand free for the pistol, which he stuck inside the waistband of his trousers as he came out of the door, down the steps, and across the shallow front yard to the Thunderbird parked at the curb, already headed north for a swift depar-ture. After hoisting the suitcase into the back, he put the sack and shoebox on the other side of the front seat and laid his jacket across them. For a moment he stood there, speculative and intent, looking back at the house, then turned and walked quickly over to the battered Ford. Crouching beside the right rear tire he unscrewed the valve cap, inverted it to unscrew and remove the stem, and stepped back to watch the tire go flat with a sudden protestive hiss. "Now stay there a while," he told the Ford, flinging the cap and stem into the early-fallen mulberry leaves on the far side of the driveway, and returned to his own car.

He got in and started it, gave the engine a couple of trial stabs with the accelerator — hutton-hutton, hutton-hutton — and pulled off, slewing gravel. Just before the right turn onto Carolina, he looked back at the house and saw Podjo in the doorway, holding the screen ajar for a better view. Raising his left hand palm-outward in a gesture of farewell, Rufus tapped the horn for two quick hoots, then made the turn and was gone.

Up at Riverside, waiting alongside the Chinaman's for the southbound glut of off-work traffic to slacken enough for him to join it, he clicked on the radio in time to catch the start of the six oclock news. "A concerted search is in progress at this hour for two men who held up the main downtown branch of the First National Bank just over an hour ago, near Madison and Second, and escaped with an estimated five to six thousand dollars in cash. The bold daylight bandits — "

"Pikers!" Rufus shouted at the dashboard speaker, patting some ten times that amount in the two bulges under his jacket there beside him on the seat, and gunned the engine for a leap into a brief gap in the right-lane stream of cars flowing past him with an almost constant roar. He made it because the driver straining to close the gap managed to hit his brakes in time to avoid a crash. "Hi, pal," Rufus said, lifting one hand for a wave when the man appeared on his rear-view mirror, red-faced with anger at having been outdared and outmaneuvered. "Dont be mad at me, ripsnorter," he told the reflection, which now was shaking a miniature fist at him. "Take it out on your wife when you get home."

At Crump, three blocks away, the parent stream divided. Some drivers, all of them white, turned east for their homes in the clustered suburbs; others continued south, mostly colored, where the old-time residential sections were rapidly going

downhill or commercial; while still others took a right onto the
bridge approach, an ethnic mix headed west for Arkansas.
Rufus was among these last, and in that direction, across the
river and somewhat off to the left, the lower sky was one huge
glory of crimson boiling up from the sunken sun, a quarter-
hour gone.

Just in time, when he saw that the car ahead had stopped, he
stopped too, within six inches of its rear bumper, with a sudden
forward pitch like a ship in rough seas diving into a wave. He
leaned sideways to pick up his jacket, which had slid from the
seat to the rubber-carpeted floorboard under the dash. Refolding it to replace it, he looked for a moment at the rolled-up
sack and the shoebox there beside him, the latter with Eben
Kinship's name and business title and address written across
one end of its lid in a flowing Spencerian hand.

"That's the stuff," he said as he covered them once more
with his jacket. "Just you sit there steady till I get a chance to
spend you. Spend some more of you, that is," he added, reminded by the new-car aroma all around him despite the windows open on both sides.

He was prepared to move on now, but when he looked he
found that the car ahead had not budged: nor the one ahead of
that, he saw through the two windshields. "Faubus," the radio
said, and he clicked it off. Intending to step out for a better
view of whatever was happening up the line, he remembered
the pistol stuck inside his waistband, its grip protruding black
against his shirt, and delayed long enough to remove it and
slide it under the seat. Then he got out. There were five cars
halted bumper-to-bumper ahead of his own, he saw, and a
sixth beyond a thirty-yard gap where a young policeman stood
holding the others back. Two more policemen stood beside the
car in the distance, one of them talking earnestly with the
driver, the other listening alongside him. Then Rufus saw the
driver get out and stand by the open door, watched by the second policeman while the first leaned inside, evidently conduct-
ing some kind of search or inspection.

Alarmed, Rufus walked up to the second car in line, whose owner he had just seen return from a talk with the young policeman in the gap. "What's the holdup?" he asked him.

"The holdup's the holdup," the man replied. He wore a vested suit, a Kiwanis button in the lapel, and seemed pleased to be involved. "That First National thing a while ago; it's some kind of roadblock and they're checking for the loot."

By the time Rufus got back to his Thunderbird four cars were lodged bumper-to-bumper behind it. He was wedged. Nevertheless he got inside, not only because the pistol and the money were there, twin symbols of security, but also because it seemed to him the one place he could be alone to think his way out of the difficulty which had just come on him out of nowhere. The law or me, Podjo had said, and now Rufus was faced with the prospect of them both. One was in his immediate front and the other no doubt would soon be coming up in his rear, depending on how long it took Podjo to get the spare tire on the Ford.

I should have flattened two of them, he told himself, combining regret and self-reproach.

Across the way, beyond the river, the crimson flare of September's final sunset boiled and burned, shot through by now with bands of dusky purple and old rose. Observing this, Rufus was having trouble addressing his mind to anything but spilt-milk thinking of the past. He could scarcely consider the present, let alone the future, perhaps because he already knew the choice that lay before him. There was obviously no way to escape rearward, wedged as he was, and the pending search would surely turn up the fifty-odd thousand in cash, even if he acknowledged defeat in advance by flinging it into the river along with the pistol. His choice, then, narrowed down to surrender or a try for a getaway forward by running the roadblock, between or over the two policemen and into the clear on the far side of the bridge, where he could veer off onto some side road and avoid his pursuers by ditching the Thunderbird in a patch of woods before taking off on foot with his suitcase and the money. Somehow, with or without the help of the pistol, he would buy or steal or commandeer another car nearby and speed off north or west or south, into what by then would be the night.

So he thought, or so at any rate he told himself: not out of any conviction that what he proposed would be successful, but rather out of an absolute rejection of the alternative. What made surrender unthinkable was the knowledge that Reeny and Podjo most likely would arrive in time to watch the fulfillment of the latter's prediction that once Rufus was on his own the law would scoop him up in short order. They would arrive in time to see him taken, hands raised beside his head until one of the policemen jerked them down for the fixing of the cuffs and shoved him stumbling into the back of the squad car. That was a scene he could not face, and there was still another factor in his make-up which encouraged his resolution to avoid it. Without any real formulation of the thought, but rather under the influence of pressures he had lived with all his life, he also saw this solution to his present dilemma as a chance to go out in a way he had always wanted but had also always lacked the nerve to try. Moreover, there was a long-odds chance that it would work, and success against such odds might well cure him of the ache for failure which had goaded him through most of his twenty-seven years, in all his various areas of endeavor.

"I'll give it a go; I'll *do* it," he told himself, too involved in his thoughts to realize that he spoke aloud for reassurance.

He groped for the pistol under the seat, then turned it so that the grip, though still out of sight, would be handy for grasping. Up ahead, on the far side of the gap, the Kiwanian's car was being searched while he stood by, smiling, happier than ever at being more intimately involved. TV fan, Rufus thought, remembering the way the man had called the bank-heist money 'loot.' The car ahead of that one, containing as it did a single Negro, had been waved on by the policemen, and so was the one that followed with two women in it, though the next was stopped and the three men inside ordered out. Rufus now was first in line at the gap.

"T-bird!" the young policeman cried, walking over for a nearer look. He had tiny milk-white teeth, blue eyes almost as pale as Rufus's own, and the beginnings of a blond mustache. "Brand new, aint it. '58?"

"Yair," Rufus said, keeping his face partly turned away to avoid a close description once he had broken through the road-block and was gone.

Even as he thought to take that precaution, and prided him-self on having thought to do so, he was refining his plan in the brief time remaining before the signal came that would launch it. His notion was to kill the engine by switching off the ignition on the take-off, then pretend to have trouble starting again until the three-man car ahead had cleared the bridge for his high-speed run. He was shaking now, and his left leg was the worst, having no familiar clutch to prop its foot on. Mind-ful of the money on the seat beside him and the pistol under-neath, which he intended to use if it was needed, he did what he could to get a grip on himself — especially his bladder; for he was determined, if he failed and they closed in on him as they had done before, this time at least he would not wet his pants.

The shaking continued, hard, but then a strange thing hap-pened. Braced like a racer for the take-off, he began hearing Sibelius, passages from symphonies he had long forgotten, or thought he had: first, the clarinet solo at the start of the E Minor, plaintive and forlorn, and then a sort of melding of the later ones, toward their climaxes: a rustling, eerie and crepitant, then a ponderous, frantic beating as of wings in preparation for flight. This did not stop the shaking but it somehow put him in tempo, or anyhow made the shaking seem to matter less than he had thought before he heard the music.

"O.K. You can move on now," the blue-eyed young police-man said, and motioned him forward to where the other two were waiting.

Teddy by then — half an hour past sundown — was in his pajamas in the living room, bathed and fed and ready for bed, despite his protest that he was neither hungry nor sleepy, and did not need a bath. "I been bathed enough, since I been gone, to last me all my life. And slept enough, too," he complained. To no avail:

"You are home now. Mind your mamma," Eben told him.

Although the initial shock of his reappearance had subsided, it would of course return from time to time. For days, one or another of them would be startled by the realization that he was truly back, safely with them there at home, an integral, on-hand member of the tight-knit family of four; six, including Tio and Mamma Cindy; seven, including lame Dolly from the other house just up Vance. These later shocks, though joyous too, were a long way short of that first one, which occurred at precisely four oclock in this same room, two hours and twenty minutes back. Sister Baby, wearied by all the talk — her grandparents were doing what they could to comfort her mother and father, whose distress increased with every passing minute, now that the waiting time was close to five hours past the promise in the letter — walked over to the front window, aimlessly and mainly for lack of anything else to do. As it happened, she had no more than drawn the curtain aside to look out at the street, where in fact there was little to see at that hour, than she saw her brother turn in at the gate and hurry toward her, up the walk.

"Here come Teddy," she said in a surprised but almost conversational tone, not loud at all.

All four grownups heard her and stopped talking at once. Still, they did not react for perhaps two full seconds, which was how long it took them to believe or even realize they had heard what they had heard. Eben was the first to move, with Martha close behind him. When he paused to snatch the door ajar she passed him, flinging the screen outward to fall on her knees in the doorway, arms extended. Midway across the porch by now, Teddy half-ran half-stumbled into them, bear and all, and began crying with his face against her throat.

"Teddy! My Teddy!" she shouted, and so did Eben, kneeling to hug him too, but from the rear so that he was sandwiched between them.

"I was, I was — " He choked and began again. "I was gone so *long*."

"Now, now," Eben told Martha. "Come on in the house."

"Look at you. Just look at you," Mamma Cindy declared, not only to her grandson but to them all. "You look like you never been gone a-tall, no more than up the street for something."

"Well, Theo," Tio said from back on the fringes.

Inside, Martha sat with Teddy on the couch and the other three stood in front of it looking down at him, all smiling unawares. Crying had used up what little breath he had left from his four-block walk, but now he stopped crying and glanced around, as if in search of something that was missing. Apparently it was Sister Baby, who had stayed by her window; for when she came over and stood beside the couch, speculative and solemn in contrast to the others, he smiled for the first time.

It was not so much her brother she was studying, however, as it was the stuffed bear he held cradled in his arms. "Whose is that?" she wanted to know.

"Yours," he told her. "It's what they call a teddy bear, and that's what I named him; Teddy. Brother won him in a shooting match and I brought him home to you."

He held the bear out to her, legs dangling, button-eyed face expressionless at the parting. She took it and sat with it in her lap on the pull-out of her father's Morris chair. "He's nice," she said.

"Who is Brother?" Martha asked.

"Sister's brother. They used to rassle." Teddy paused, remembering. "She looked after me while we waited for Daddy to call and tell me to come home. There was another one called Joe. Had a mustache."

"We'll talk about that later," Eben said. "Right now we're just glad to have you back where you belong."

"Indeed, indeed," Mamma Cindy declared.

"Yes in*deed*," Tio boomed out alongside her.

There followed an almost awkward pause. Glad as they were to have their boy home, none of them knew quite what to say now that Eben had ruled out talk of where he had been for the past week; not even Mamma Cindy, though as it turned out she was the one who broke the silence. "Bless Jesus, our Teddy sho is looking fine this day. Now aint he?"

"He is that," Tio agreed, smiling under his derby, and all of them nodded except Sister Baby, who, occupied with her new bear, had shifted from the pull-out to the roomy chair itself — a breach of manners strictly forbidden in anything like ordinary times. "Well, Lucindy," Tio said, perceiving at last that the trouble was Martha's and Eben's need to be alone with their son, "I reckon we better be getting on our way."

Mamma Cindy was somewhat taken aback, until she saw it too. "Why, yes. All right," she told her husband, and turned to Martha. "I'll tell Dolly. She didnt know he was gone, or anyhow missing, but she'll be glad to hear he's back, getting his cakes and things on the way from school and having his Sunday dinner after church." Leaning down, she cupped her hand over one of Teddy's cheeks and kissed him lightly on the other. "You come by home first chance you have. I'll get our Dolly to bake you up a lemon pie this very night so it will be cold in the box for you tomorrow. And you too, child," she said to Sister Baby, who still was giving all her attention to the bear. "You come too. Theyll be plenty to go round."

Tio meantime was telling Eben, "I'll get in touch with the law first thing in the morning, at the office, and give them the numbers off the bills. I'd do it tonight but the day shift down there's better at such things. So I been told. Besides, them folks aint likely to be such fools as to start in spending that money right off anyhow, whoever and wherever they are by now. We can tend to that tomorrow, from the office."

While Eben was seeing Tio and Mamma Cindy to the door, Martha stayed on the couch with Teddy, smiling at him as she had been doing ever since she got up off her knees from their meeting on the porch. For a moment however, with Eben gone, she put on a stern expression. "Sister Baby, shame on you," she told her daughter. "Shame on you for propping yourself up in your daddy's chair like that. Havent you got lessons to get started on or something?"

"Not yet awhile," Sister Baby said, getting out of the chair to sit with her bear at one end of the couch, much as Martha was doing with her brother at the other. Reminded of school, she turned and looked at Teddy, beyond her mother. "I brought your books home for you, the day you left."

"Do I have to get mine too?" he asked Martha, meaning his lessons.

"Not tonight," she told him. Then, remembering: "Miss Pitkin called, one day last week."

"Was she mad?"

"No, no. She was worried how you were — like all of us. Youll be staying home tomorrow, partly to go see Dr Beck for him to look you over, and then next day, if he says so, youll be back in school with your friends."

He shook his head at that. "I got a lot of catching-up to do."

"I know," she told him, and patted his shoulder. "Right now though, what you need is a good hot soaking bath, then get your nightclothes on and eat some supper."

"I'm not hungry, Mamma."

"Well; you will be. Anything special you want, on short notice?"

"Lemon pie."

She laughed. "Dolly's most likely started in on one already. Youll have that tomorrow, cold from Mamma Cindy's icebox.

Tonight youre having ham and greens and cornbread, along with the rest of us, for coming home."

"That sounds good," he admitted.

"And *is* good," Eben said, back at last from seeing Tio and Mamma Cindy to the gate, where he and Tio had stopped to talk.

"But right now what you get's a bath," Martha declared.

It was then that Teddy protested that he had bathed enough, this past week, to last him all his life: only to have his father tell him, "You are home now. Mind your mamma. And Sister Baby, you go do your lessons while your brother's in the tub. If youre both good, we might can watch some TV after supper."

He sat there in his Morris chair, hearing the water run for Teddy's bath and watching Sister Baby go past him with her books and bear, through the curtained doorway to the dining room. Half an hour ago he had been on the verge of hysterics, sick with cumulative worry; now he was on the rim of contentment, feeling let-down and even a little sleepy or in any case very tired. It's just people, the way they are, he marveled. Already it was as if the boy had never been gone at all, or at most had just come in from play, except his clothes were clean. Eben wondered at the ease with which all four of them had returned to the dailiness of daily living, once the tension was removed, and wondered too at Teddy's pretended indifference to being made the center of attention, along with Sister Baby's resentment at being supplanted in that role — a resentment so pronounced that she withdrew, in turn, into pretending to be more interested in her new bear, which he had brought her, than in her brother, back from his ordeal — as well as at his and Martha's undelayed assertion of the discipline they both knew did much to hold the family together, whether in times of ease or strain. "Shame on you," she had rebuked Sister Baby for propping herself up in her daddy's chair, and he had been as quick to admonish Teddy, "Mind your mamma," for bridling at instructions.

It's just people, the way they are, he told himself, contrasting the unrestrained joy of their first greeting, out on the porch, with all that had followed, here inside, for the past half hour. It's just life, the way it is, he thought. But all the same it's strange.

At supper, an hour later, in contrast to his earlier action in cutting off discussion of the matter, he decided to risk upsetting Teddy by asking, "What was it like, where you were with those people all last week?"

"I think it was some kind of tent," the boy replied, "but all-over wood. Like Noah's ark."

"Noah's *ark*?" Martha said.

"Yessum, like they taught us in Sunday school. No windows, and long ribs going cross and cross, high up under the roof."

Eben thought perhaps this meant that Teddy had been taken out into the country and kept in the loft of a barn. He let that go, however, and asked instead, "What were they like, those people? Did they take good care of you?"

"Sister did."

"And how about the others?"

"They did too. But mostly Sister. I didnt see much of them, except sometimes Brother."

"All three white?"

"White," Teddy said, and nodded.

"Would you know them again, to look at?"

"Sister I would. And Joe, because of the musstache."

"How about the other one? Brother."

"Him I might not," Teddy said, and then added, as if by sudden inspiration, "He had yellow hair."

"I saw the one with the musstache," Sister Baby put in. "And the lady, too, that day I carried the books home by myself. She was the one had the yellow hair, not the other."

Martha and Eben looked at Sister Baby, whose pigtails bristled with resentment at having been left out of the conversation up to now. Then Martha turned back to Teddy and asked, "What did you eat, all that time?"

"Soup. Mostly soup, and sometimes crackers."

"Not like this?"

"No *maam,*" he said fervently, lifting another forkful of greens and taking a mouth-sized bite of buttered cornbread.

After supper, while Martha and Sister Baby cleared the table, Eben and Teddy went out into the living room and sat on the couch, both of them too full of ham and greens to do anything more than watch the tail end of Douglas Edwards. When Martha and Sister Baby came out, in time for the start of Robin Hood, Eben got up and sat in his chair and they joined Teddy on the couch. Martha sat in the middle, a child on each side, and before they were ten minutes into the program, which had always been one of his favorites, Teddy began to get glassy-eyed and started nodding. Presently, when his chin touched his chest, Martha spoke to him by name.

His head jerked up and his eyes came open, shining as if wet with tears in the flicker from the television screen. "I'm not sleepy. I'm not sleepy a-tall," he said.

"You were, too, sleepy," Sister Baby reproached him, leaning out to gloat from Martha's other side. "You were so sleepy you were sound asleep. You didnt even see Maid Marian come on, or Friar Tuck tip that soldier in the creek."

"Hush now," Martha told her, and turned to Teddy. "You want me to take you back? Robin's about over anyhow."

"I want Daddy to," he said.

Eben did, leading him by one hand like a sleep-walker, with a stop by the bathroom on the way. There was a little trouble there, groggy as he was, but none in the bedroom, since he already had on his pajamas. Up front, Robin Hood went off. "I *am* a little sleepy," Teddy admitted when Eben turned the covers down and tucked him in. His eyes closed, then came open, heavy-lidded. "Sister?" he said.

"This is Daddy," Eben told him.

"Daddy," he said. "Where is Mamma?"

"She's getting Sister Baby in her nightclothes."

"Sister?" Teddy said.

"Sister *Baby,*" Eben told him.

She came in then in her hand-me-down pajamas, still with her bear, which she propped upright on a straightback chair on her side of the bed. "I named him Buster instead of Teddy," she said as Martha tucked her in alongside her sleeping brother. "You think that's a good name, Daddy?"

"I do," he said. "I used to have a crook-tail bulldog I named Buster, back in Bristol long ago."

"You told me — I remember."

"I did? I guess I did. Well, goodnight, honey." He leaned down and kissed her. "Sleep tight."

"Dont let the bedbugs bite," she recited, solemn-faced. "Goodnight, Mamma."

"Goodnight. Sleep tight."

"Dont let the bedbugs bite," she said again.

Eben and Martha stood in the doorway, looking back, Martha with her hand on the light switch. They remained there a while, looking back and down at their two children side by side in the double bed, one asleep, the other not, watched over by the button-eyed bear on the chair near Sister Baby. Studying Teddy, whose face, so much like his mother's, was dark in profile against the whiteness of the pillow, Eben wondered again at the recurrent notion that he might never have been gone at all. Then Martha tripped the switch and they went to their own room, got undressed, and went to bed.

They lay there in the faint moonlight, on their backs. Presently Eben groaned and said fretfully, "I ought to get some of this fat off."

"I'll help you," Martha told him.

"How?" He looked over at her.

"Youll find out," she said.

They laughed, both at once, and turned and put their arms around each other, and it's likely there were no two happier people in all of Memphis on this last night of that particular September. Still, Martha got up twice before dawn, once with Eben and another time alone, to look in on Teddy, asleep again in his own bed alongside Sister Baby.

Next morning — October now, with a hint of autumn in the air; soon there would be cold snaps, hogs screaming under the knife, and presently the long year-end swoon of Indian summer, redbud and dogwood like flames in the wind, sunsets as sudden as they were early, and the lingering fragrance of woodsmoke high in the nostrils — Eben walked his daughter one last time to school. Teddy would be going with her tomorrow, after staying home today to rest up and be checked by Dr Beck. That had been the decision. "You want to hire some kind of guard or something?" Tio had asked the night before, when they parted at the gate, and Eben had not even had to think before replying, "No. We cant live that way, Martha and me, and neither can they, the children. What kind of a life would that be? No." So it was decided. He would walk her today and Teddy would walk her tomorrow, on his own.

Yet he had no sooner unlocked and entered the office on Beale than he received what at first was a terrible shock. The phone rang, and when he answered, taking it up for the first time in eight days with no clutch of apprehension round his heart, a voice said, "Eben Kinship?"

Dear God, here it comes again. *They got Sister Baby*, he thought; for the voice was white, with an edge to it, like all those other times. Still he managed to say, as he had said before, "Speaking — "

"Kinship, this is Lieutenant Grackle down at headquarters. What do you know about a shoebox with your name on the lid?"

"Full of money?"

A pause. "Yes."

"I know all about it. It's mine, or my wife's father's."

"Theo G. Wiggins?"

"Yessir."

Another pause. "Is he in?"

"He will be, in about half an hour."

"Tell him to call me, will you? Lieutenant Grackle, down at headquarters. Soon as he gets in."

"I will; yessir. He was going to call down there this morning anyhow, lieutenant."

"All right." And hung up.

Lucy Provine came in then, spectacles glinting, and not long afterwards Tio, who was early. He called Lieutenant Grackle at once, talked with him briefly, then turned from the phone to Eben, there beside him.

"They got the money," he said, "and one of those people, what's left of him. Some kind of car wreck. I'm going down there with the withdrawal slips and the list of numbers we took down, and soon as I show the bills are mine theyll give them to me. It ought not take long."

Eben was amazed at how little Tio seemed surprised by this happy recovery of his money. But when he said so, Tio shook his head, solemn in the shadow of his derby. "I always knew we'd get it back; just not this soon," he said. "The question was, how much or little of it. Money dont just disappear. It's earmarked. All I could lose would be what little wasnt run down or what the law got on the sly, along the way. We'll know more about that when we get it back and count it."

He was right. As it turned out, he got nearly all his money back; all but a thousand dollars, which he considered so reasonable a fee that he did not risk insulting the authorities by asking them to investigate the loss. First, $54,500 was recovered from the wreck, then another $4,500 from Cormac Motors when the car was traced. All that was missing in the end was a couple of five-hundred-dollar packets of tens, which he figured some policeman must have pocketed, either on the scene or later, down at headquarters, while the bills were being held as possible evidence before the case was written off.

That took three days, till Friday, and by then Teddy had become something of a celebrity, especially at school, because of accounts in both papers. Boy Returns Safely/ From Mystery Snatch, one headline read above a story that ran nearly one full column, accompanied by a murky half-column cut of Teddy himself. "I dont think it's such of a much," Sister Baby said when they showed it to her.

By that time Eben had begun to follow through on his resolution to change things; first of all, himself — meaning his situation, financial and otherwise. At home on Wednesday evening,
two days after Teddy's return, when Tio and Mamma Cindy
came to call, Eben braced his father-in-law right there in the
living room, apparently not caring who was listening.

"What I want's a raise, by way of a start," he declared. "Say
to fifty dollars a week, with others to follow as we move
along. And now that I mention it, Martha wants that three-
bedroom house across from you at 318; the brick one sort of
like yours at 311, except one-story. I think you ought to give it
to her so we can be paying taxes instead of rent."

Martha and Mamma Cindy watched as he spoke, and when
he stopped turned both their heads in unison to Tio. They
seemed expectant; Eben saw that Martha was smiling, though
she barely let it show.

For his part, Tio shifted uncomfortably on the couch, glancing sidelong first at the chromo of Jesus, then at his own
picture on the opposite wall. He shook his head with a shudder
of distaste. "Just listen at you," he marveled. "When I was
your age it never even crossed my mind to expect somebody
would give me any kind of a house a-tall, let alone a three-
bedroom one like that."

"Your wife didnt have a rich daddy, the way mine does,"
Eben pointed out.

This was a telling blow; Tio closed his eyes for a moment to
absorb it, conscious that Martha and Mamma Cindy were
watching him closely, awaiting his reply. "We'll talk about it
tomorrow at the office," he said at last, looking doubtful if not
outdone, now that his son-in-law had brought up the women
as shock troops.

Even so, next day on Beale, after waiting all morning and
most of the afternoon for his employer to call him over, Eben
was the one who broached the matter. Tio was at his desk,
near quitting time. Instead of standing, which he later decided
might have been more comfortable, Eben sat in the chair across
from him, as he had seen many supplicants do in the course of

the past ten years, and spoke again of the raise and the new house.

"Well," Tio said. He paused and began again, in a different tone. "What do you want with all that now, before your time?"

"It *is* my time," Eben told him. Then he too stopped and started over. "It's to square myself away for what I got in mind. Once I get that done, or anyhow started, I can begin to square away what's around me; or start trying. Mostly it comes out of what happened last week to Teddy and the way we had to do to get him back. On our own, I mean."

"We did get him back."

"That's right, and we had to do it the way we did, things being the way they are in this town and in this country. Maybe all countries. You were right, and you still are. And that's what's wrong."

"You mean the law?"

"I mean the law and a whole lot else. I mean what's coming up for Teddy — and for Sister Baby, too. I mean letting my bucket down and bringing it up dry. I mean the system."

"You want to change it."

"I want to try."

"It's a system that's been good to me. I used it against itself, and beat it."

"Well, it aint been good to me, except through you. Maybe I can beat it, too; not in your way but in mine, once I get in a position to decide what that way is."

"Son," Tio said, and again he paused, looking down at his hands clenched loosely on the polished desktop. His starched cuffs had a glaze like mother-of-pearl. "Let me take another night to think out what youre getting at. I want what's best for all of us, all round."

"All I'm asking for's a raise."

"And a house."

"And a house," Eben agreed, and rose and turned away.

I should have held off till later, on the house, he told himself in bed that night after Martha was asleep. But next morning —

Friday — Tio was no sooner settled at his desk than he beckoned Eben over. "About that raise — "

"Mr Theo!" Lucy Provine called from her place up front. The phone had rung. "Lieutenant Grackle on the line."

Tio talked briefly, mostly listening, then hung up. "It's my money," he told Eben. "I can come and get it, they say, now that they closed the case out. They dont even know who the one they got was, let alone them otherns, to start tracing and chasing. Now about that raise," he went on, as if there had been no interruption. "You got it; fifty dollars. And the house too — in Martha's name. I should have give you what you asked without you asking, only sometimes it takes me a while to understand things. New things, anyhow." He sat back, peering across his folded hands at Eben. "I decided you were right about a lot you told me, yesterday and last week, under all that pressure. Right for you, I mean; not me. I did what I did, in my way and in my day, and I outdid them. It could be I gave you a kind of base to stand on, you and others like you still to come; to stand on and say, 'He done it his way in his day. Now the time is come for us to do it our way.' Even Theo; Teddy, as you call him. Outdoing them your way wont be easy, though. You wont have the edge I had, using their own system to beat them with. Or maybe you will. Maybe you will find a way to do that too. Anyhow, what you do youll have to do it your way, not in mine. Mine's gone by, or it's going; going fast. I know that now. But knowing's one thing. Doing is another. I wont change."

He was wrong. He changed. We all did. For that was the Friday — October 4; thirty days, to the day, after the Edsel was unveiled — that the Russians put the sputnik up from Kazakhstan, a polished steel basketball with spike antennas, beeping in A-flat around and around a world that would never be the same.

From the time Rufus pulled away from the curb in front of the house, slewing gravel, Podjo had been as busy, so he told himself, as a one-armed paper hanger. Shielded by a jamb of the living-room window, he saw him flatten the tire on the Ford, and then from the door, with the screen ajar, watched the Thunderbird make the turn onto Carolina, hooting twice in derision as it did so; whereupon he ran out into the yard and up to the corner, less than a hundred feet, in time to see it pause beside the Chinaman's before taking a sudden leap into the all-but-solid wall of traffic roaring south on Riverside. That meant Crump, three blocks away, which in turn meant Highway 61, back down through the Delta, or else the bridge across to Arkansas. "New Orleans, by way of the Teche," wasnt much to go on, nestled as it was in that pack of lies about the nonexistent Celia, but it was all he had until he found out something better somewhere down the line.

"We'll make what time we can, in behind him," he told Reeny when she came out to watch him unload the cots and fan from the trunk of the Ford to get at the spare tire and the jack and lug wrench, "but speed's not what counts the most. If I know Rufus, he'll burn out that new engine, with its light-weight break-in oil, in five or six hundred miles or so. What counts is for us to get on his tail, no matter how far back, and stay there till it happens, then close in on him before he gets the damned thing fixed or trades it in. Here," he said, handing her the wrench. "Try this on those lugs while I get the jack set up, and we'll be after him in no time."

In point of fact there was a good deal more to fret about than he let Reeny know, though doubtless she was aware of most of it already. The pistol, for example. It could be as much of a factor, when and if they caught up with Rufus, as it had been a while ago when he used it to separate them from their share of the money in the first place. The answer to that would be to come upon him unawares, best of all when he was asleep in some motel, and surprise him before he could bring the weapon into play; at a roadhouse, say, with his arms around some girl or perhaps in a more intimate embrace, such as Teddy had caught him in five days ago. In any case, whatever was done in this regard could be improvised when the opportunity loomed. Beyond that, however, there was a larger problem involving a bitter paradox. When Podjo first learned that Rufus had spent part of the traceable ransom on a car, and found too that he could not persuade him to get rid of it, his first thought had been to steer as far clear of him as possible, before the law descended not only on him but also on whoever was with or even near him at the time. Now the case was quite reversed. If Podjo was to recover his share of the money, he was obliged to stick as close to him as he could manage, only hoping that the police didnt overtake him first, and thus get both their shares, or — worst of all — at the same time, which would mean that all three of them would wind up behind bars. Confronted with this possibility, as he now was, he was somewhat in the position of a man obliged to locate and defuse a time bomb set to explode at an unknown moment.

"We'll catch him all right," Podjo said, crouched to set the jack in place; "if the cops dont get him first. Almost any garage or storefront loafer looking out on any highway will spot that flashy T-bird going past. All we have to do, wherever it might have turned off, is stop and ask. Hand me the wrench." He needed it to use as a handle for the jack, and that was just as well; Reeny, who was far from mechanical-minded, had not yet even managed to pry the hubcap off to get at the lugs. "O.K. Now go set the hand brake," Podjo told her.

That she could do, and did. Podjo meantime, despite the crankiness of the rusty jack, was working fast, getting the tire clear of the ground, the hubcap off and then the lugs, which were also badly rusted. To save trouble when the opportunity came to get a new valve stem and reinflate the tube, he hoisted the flat onto the floor of the rear seat, then began lugging the threadbare spare in place. "Put the cots and fan back in the trunk," he told Reeny over his shoulder, straining on the wrench to make sure the lugs were tight before snapping the hubcap back in place. "Then I'll go get the bags and we'll be off."

He was sweating, badly grimed with rust and grease. Inside the house, after flinging the jack and wrench into the trunk and slamming it shut, he took a minute to wash his hands and arms, and then — leaving the grime-streaked bathroom sink as still another cultural shock for the homecoming cotton man tomorrow — reentered the bedroom and picked up the two bags. In the living room he set one of them down, freeing that hand to toss the front door key onto the velvet couch, then took up the bag and went out, clicking the lock shut behind him. Reeny was waiting in the car. He put the bags on the rear seat before going around to get under the steering wheel. "We'll catch him all right," he said again as he backed out of the driveway.

Reeny, however, had doubts about what was to follow. "What will we do when we do?" she wanted to know. "He'll still have that pistol."

"Make him eat it," Podjo said, teeth gritted. "Make him by God eat it, bullets and all."

Turning onto Riverside, where the off-work traffic had already slackened considerably, he reckoned that he was not over twenty minutes behind Rufus. At the stoplight on Crump, however, he had an uninformed decision to make: whether to turn left and head for Highway 61, or right, onto the approach to the Memphis-Arkansas Bridge. He chose the bridge. That seemed to him the likeliest route, and if he was wrong he would find out on the other side, perhaps at the weigh station there, and double back. By now it was straight-down six thirty, and he soon found that he had chosen right — though he also found that it hadnt really mattered which way he turned, so far at least as getting what he was after was concerned.

Up ahead, where the girders began, a jam was building up as cars arrived to add to the number already stopped. Apparently there had been some kind of mishap out on the bridge itself, so that traffic was stalled in both westbound lanes, waiting for the trouble, whatever it was, to be resolved. As soon as he stopped on the fringe of the jam, which promptly extended itself behind him as more cars arrived, Podjo got out and searched the mass of vehicles up ahead for some sign of the white Thunderbird. Finding none he cursed his luck. Rufus — if this in fact was the route he chose — apparently had gotten across before the bridge was blocked, which meant that he was even now increasing his lead, at the rate of better than a mile a minute, while Podjo waited for the way to be cleared and the jam untangled.

"Take the wheel," he told Reeny. "I'll walk up there a ways and try to find what this is all about."

He found out soon enough. Picking and pushing his way through the press of cars and people in the rapidly gathering dusk, he heard a man who had just returned from a similar expedition tell some friends, "It's those bank robbers; one of them anyhow. He tried to make a run for it and crashed." This raised about as many questions as it answered, but as Podjo continued to work his way forward he was not long in finding the solution to them all. Two policemen were coming toward him through the crowd, one of them bearing two parcels in his arms. The first was a rolled-up brown paper sack, such as might have come from almost any grocery store, but there was no mistaking the second. It was the I. Miller shoebox, and Podjo could all but read Eben Kinship's name on it, even though the blue uniform sleeve covered that end of the lid.

"Five or six thousand, the dispatcher told us," he heard one policeman say when they went past him; a lieutenant, he saw now, just as he also saw that the other had Rufus's pistol in his hand. "Hell, this looks to me like at least ten times that much."

Podjo stopped. He knew well enough the number of bills in those two parcels, half of which he had considered his; till now. Then he moved on. For he could see, no more than a couple of hundred yards up the bridge from where he passed the two policemen, the new white Thunderbird now sadly battered about the snout and along one flank. The closer he got the worse it looked, and it looked worst of all from dead ahead, where the chrome-rimmed frown of its grill, beneath the once-gentle upward curve of the front bumper, had been transformed into a crumpled grin. From there, too, he could see Rufus wedged between the seat, which had come unbolted from the floor, and the shattered steering wheel, on whose shaft the lower part of his body had been impaled when he was hurled onto and across it by force of the sudden impact with one of the upright girders of the bridge. Looking at him through the crinkled windshield, especially in the flat yellow light from the overhead fluoride lamps, which glowed brightly now that the sun was nearly an hour down, was like seeing him through a frosted pane or inside a block of ice. What was left of his face was pressed earnestly against it, mouth agape as if for a scream, though in fact he was very quiet and very dead.

"Sombitch took off like a scalded dog," a blond young policeman was saying there beside him, telling it for perhaps the third time in the scant ten or twelve minutes since the crash. "First, though, he stalled when I waved him forward. I thought he was just having new-car trouble. It wasnt till later I realized he'd flooded the engine to delay things so the car ahead would leave him a clear track. Anyhow, just as I headed back to give him a hand, he got it started. For a minute he sat there, hutton-hutton — goosing it back to life I thought — until all of a sudden he had it floorboarded, coming at me. Jesus; I bare had time to jump aside and holler up to Mick and Henry, 'Look out! *Look out!*' He went between them, picking up speed as he went, and I saw Henry pull his gun. He leveled down to get off a shot, two-handed, taking his time the way they taught us, but by the time he fired — *baloom!* — that T-bird was already into evasive action, swerving, swerving this way and that, and

I saw the driver squinch down, most likely reaching under the seat for that pistol we found later. Henry's shot missed, I'm pretty sure, and so did Mick's when he finally got his piece out, because by then that Bird was all over the place. Then it began to straighten out, some. Whoever he was had it almost under control again, when all of a sudden it took a kind of sideways wrench, still picking up speed, and mounted the guard rail on the right, sliding along it till it hit that girder. Mother of God. From all the racket, youd have thought a locomotive jumped the track from over on the Frisco."

A rookie, he was greatly excited by his first line-of-duty connection with violent action. Moreover this excitement increased throughout his description of what followed. He ran up and joined the other two, Mick and Henry, and all three approached the wreck, some three hundred yards ahead, half-crouched with their pistols drawn. There was no need for that, they discovered when they got there. "He was about the deadest rooster this side of Korea," the young policeman later said of what they found inside. While Mick jogged back to the patrol car to put in a call for the rescue squad, which would arrive with crowbars and acetylene torches to be used in prying or cutting the Thunderbird's hard-jammed doors ajar, and a wrecker to tow the car away when the body had been unwedged and trundled into the ambulance, Henry and Otis — such was the young policeman's name — looked in from opposite sides, through the open windows. "That was when I saw the money," he went on. "The paper sack was on the floormat, still rolled up, but the lid flew off the shoebox when it landed. Jesus; I never saw so much money in my life. It was ankle-deep in tens and twenties under the dash there, all done up in packets with rubber bands." About this time, on the driver's side, Henry saw the Army .45 down between the dead man's feet, and leaned in and picked it up. Otis did the same with the bills, returning them to the shoebox before removing it and the rolled-up grocery sack, which turned out to be loaded too. "They must of hit that bank a lot harder than headquarters told us," he declared, standing there beside the crumpled Thunderbird with both arms full of money.

Returning, Mick was obliged to jog back to the patrol car again with this latest information for the dispatcher, while Henry crossed to the opposite side of the bridge to halt the eastbound traffic so that the ambulance and wrecker could reach the scene. That left Otis guarding the wreck and the money, until a lieutenant and another patrolman arrived to relieve him of the sack and shoebox; after which he stood telling and re-telling his story as latecomers arrived to hear and marvel at it, including Podjo.

He had heard enough. Indeed, he had heard a good deal more than enough by now. After one last took at Rufus, frozen there inside his block of ice, Podjo returned to the Ford, where Reeny had been waiting all this time. He got in on the passenger side and collapsed on the seat, eyes closed. "You drive the first shift," he told her. "I'm next to bushed."

"It was him. Wasnt it?" she asked.

"Yair," he said. "It was him all right. But youd have to have known him awful well to recognize him now."

Reeny remembered Rufus: not so much his shenanigans now, which had to do with crawling under nightclub tables and into phonebooths to embrace her, as certain things he had said from time to time, especially up here. "What fun is something if you dont have fun *doing* it?" he had remarked on the night of the day they took Teddy, and that was true. "Sometimes later never comes," he also told her, and that had turned out to be even truer, anyhow for him.

"Did he have the money with him?" she asked Podjo, who was sitting there beside her with his eyes shut.

"Down to the last simoleon," he said wearily, "except what he spent on that goddam car and the thousand he gave you. Us. That was it the two cops had when they came by here a while ago, in the sack and shoebox."

Then it came; the sudden thump, or crump, of a low-key explosion somewhere up ahead. Podjo opened his eyes in time to see, through the dusty windshield of the Ford, a mushrooming pillar of gray-black smoke, shot through with crimson whips of flame, rear up beyond the tops of the cars and trucks jamming the two right lanes of the approach, and almost at once he identified its source. The Thunderbird was burning out there on the bridge, with Rufus still inside it.

Later there was disagreement as to what had caused the explosion. Some said it was a dropped match or cigarette, others that it was more likely something electrical under the hood, a spark from the cracked battery. In any case there was no doubt that a fuel line, ruptured in the crash, had been leaking ever since, and when the dripping gas caught fire, whatever the cause, the flames spread rapidly to the tank, which then blew up. The wrecker had arrived by then, but its crew was standing by, waiting for the rescue squad, whose ambulance, delayed by a collision at Crump and Third, pulled up in time to be greeted by the explosion, and whose members were then held back, by the press of heat, from performing their task of removing from its cocoon of twisted metal the body, now on fire itself, inside the burning car.

Firemen were there in a pumper from the South Main Station within eight minutes. By then, however, all twenty gallons of gasoline had been consumed. Only the upholstery and tires were still burning, and the gum-booted firemen were quick to extinguish them with a hose from the booster tank on their nearby bright red truck. For a while longer they played the stream of water on the wreckage, but that was only to cool it enough for the rescue squad to get to work. In some ways, mainly mechanical, their task had been made easier by the fire. The force of the explosion, for example, had jarred the seat back onto the floorboard where it had been bolted before the crash, and the body too had been hoisted off the steering wheel and dropped in a sitting position on the seat. Watchers early on the scene, seeing him crisping and curling there inside the roar of the fire, said that the dead man resembled a grasshopper caught in the flame of a blowtorch. Hair afire, he lifted his arms a bit, they said, and rotated them slightly outward in a gesture of supplication, before he collapsed entirely, folding inward on himself. Anyhow, once the metal had cooled down enough for them to move in with their crowbars, the rescue people finally got what was left of him out of the car and into a canvas body sack, which in turn was placed inside a long brown narrow wicker basket, about the size and shape of a horse trough, for transfer to the ambulance. Before it left, siren wailing, the wrecker crew began working a low-slung dolly under the burnt-out shell of the Thunderbird for its removal, too.

This time Podjo had not left the Ford. The fury displayed within that suddenly upreared pillar of smoke and flame, combined with the crackling roar that followed, told him plainly enough what he would find if he took the trouble to push his way again through that crush of cars and people for a look at what was happening up ahead there on the bridge. He and Reeny watched the wrecker, ambulance, and fire truck arrive and then depart in reverse order, fire truck, ambulance, and wrecker. When the ambulance came past them on the return trip, siren wailing — more from exuberance, it seemed, than out of any need, for both eastbound lanes were clear — he nodded in its direction with approval, as if he could see through its curtained windows, inside the wicker basket and even the canvas sack.

"Well, that's one piece of luck that came our way if nothing else did," he told Reeny. "Theyll get no prints off our friend there, even off his toes. Yair: luck. If I'd thought of it while I was up there I'd have dropped the match myself."

He was silent for a moment after the ambulance pulled away, remembering Rufus's admiration for that gas-chamber exchange betwen Bonnie Brown Heady and Carl Austin Hall. Are you all right, honey? Yes, mamma. "Aint that great? Just great?" Rufus had exclaimed, and Podjo, contrasting their departure with Rufus's own, wondered if their words had occurred to him, there toward the end when he saw that girder coming at him. Most likely not, he decided, and turned to

Reeny, patting his trouser pockets, left and right, where he had put the two five-hundred-dollar packets of tens he snatched up from the mattress before running out to check on which way Rufus turned after taking off from the curb in front of the house. "Well, anyhow," he said, his spirits rising at the thought, "this thousand he left us is twice what we had when we came up here in the first place, four weeks back. And what's more there's one less of us to spend it."

Alas, they were not to have it long. Four nights later, in Las Vegas, Podjo lost what remained of the thousand dollars to a cowboy, or anyhow a man dressed like a cowboy, wearing a sand-colored hat and holding a straight flush. He would have lost it sooner, given his luck, except for a rear-end breakdown just beyond the Texas panhandle Tuesday night, thirty miles short of Tucumcari. Replacing the Ford's differential cost him close to eighty dollars and better than twelve hours of travel time, one about as regrettable as the other in his haste to fulfill his dream of clacking chips and slithering cards on the green felt of some table out in Nevada. They got under way again before midday Wednesday, taking turns at the wheel and stopping only for gas all the rest of the trip. Even so, they never made up that lost New Mexico time and still were twelve hours behind schedule when they pulled into Vegas at sunup Friday, October 4. Here again was that thirty-day span, Edsel to Sputnik; thirty days, to the day, since the three of them rode into Memphis out of the Delta, Podjo and Reeny and Rufus, who was buried this day in an unmarked grave back there, about the same time Theo G. Wiggins recovered his money from the police — all but the thousand, of which all that was left was about to be risked in Las Vegas.

Podjo slept all day, and Reeny most of it, in a dingy four-dollar motel room on the outskirts, both of them watching the highway twist and turn beyond the bug-spattered windshield, even in their sleep. Then at sundown they rose and went on a tour of the gambling places. The one he settled on called itself the Shamrock in green neon over the door. He studied it carefully, from the bar and the back wall, and after waiting and watching for a couple of hours, observing the style and habits of the players at what he considered the best table, took the next empty chair. It was straight poker, draw or stud, which he preferred. He bided his time, folding often when confronted, more or less holding his own while awaiting a hand he could go with. After about an hour it came; a full house, aces up. The game was draw. In the course of the betting, all the other players dropped out except the cowboy-looking man in the pale hat, who had been laying back until the final go-round, with something over three hundred dollars in the pot.

"How much you got in front of you there?" he asked, after Podjo bet two hundred.

"Just what you see. Six hundred," Podjo told him.

"O.K." he said. "I raise you that."

Podjo, who knew a bluffer when he saw one, called and laid down his full house, aces up. The cowboy smiled. "Seven, eight, nine, ten, jack," he said as he spread his cards. "Theyre straight as Hiawatha's arrow, and all hearts."

"Well; those things happen," Podjo said, and got up from the table.

Reeny was waiting at the bar, nursing a double Pepsi-Cola. "How'd it go?" she asked.

"It went," he told her, and on the way out spent a dime of their last two dollars on a local paper so they could study the Help Wanted columns — faro dealer? waitress? — before turning in for the night.

But that was later; four days later. This was still Monday, back on the Memphis-Arkansas Bridge, where Podjo and Reeny, now that the wrecker had come past them towing the gutted shell of the once-glittering Thunderbird on its low-slung dolly, sat waiting in the Ford for the jam to be untangled up ahead. Somehow, the sight of what remained of that elongated sports car, which had served as a funeral pyre, affected Reeny more than the passing of the ambulance, with its known burden, had done a few minutes earlier. "Poor Rufus," she exclaimed.

"Ah, hell," Podjo said, turning back from watching the red blinker on the wrecker disappear beyond the rearward fringes of the jam. "Poor Rufus nothing. He got what he's been running after, all these years."

"Not so many. And besides, whatever he was after, I dont think he wanted to burn like that, with no one even knowing his name."

"He was dead then; he didnt mind. But I'll say one thing for him. If what he wanted was to go out in blaze of glory, he sure managed it in style."

"That's true," Reeny admitted, though she seemed to derive small comfort from the notion.

They sat there silent for a time with their separate thoughts. Ahead and below, on the left and right, the fragile glow of September's final moon, newly risen over the city in their rear, lent a shimmer to the surface of the river, which also reflected the red and green and amber lights they had watched so often, along with Rufus in his time, from the back yard of the house on the bluff, no more than an air-line quarter mile across the way. They had been waiting considerably better than an hour by now, all told, and Podjo was well on the road to recovery from the worst of the depression that descended on him when he saw that police lieutenant walking toward him with that shoebox. His mind had moved ahead of him, proleptic; he was anticipating Las Vegas, which he counted on reaching by early Thursday evening, in time to get started on his project for expanding the thousand-dollar stake.

"You know," he suddenly told Reeny, leaning forward so that his dark mustache looked darker in the flat light from the overhead fluoride lamps, "I got a feeling I'm going to burn them down, those Vegas hotshots, even without that whopping roll I counted on to back me up. All I been needing anyhow is luck, a touch of luck, and I figure youre it. Yair. My only trouble so far's been that my luck has all been bad. But that's going to change now; I can tell."

Up ahead, engines were starting and cars were beginning to

roll. So did the Ford, not long afterward, but only a short distance. Reeny had to stop again when a snarl developed.

"What the hell," Podjo went on. "It's all grist for the mill, whichever way it goes. What the hell if it turns out the cards dont run in my direction this time either? We can find ourselves a couple of jobs and build up a new stake to try again. Sooner or later it's bound to change. How not? Meantime I can always deal blackjack or faro in some house until it does."

"What will *I* do?" Reeny asked.

"Do? Well, let's see," he said. He seemed to ponder. "How about something steady, say like powing out of cakes?"

She laughed at that, on a single rising note, pleased to find him emerged all the way from his gloom and savagery, but also startled by his unaccustomed volubility. Then the car ahead jerked into motion and she eased the clutch out, rolling forward.

"Right now though," Podjo continued as the Ford gathered headway, its tires slapping the metal expansion joints on the roadbed of the bridge, "we'll have to try cutting corners on expenses, to keep from dipping much into our thousand. For instance, those cots in the trunk back there. If we both get sleepy at the same time, and the weather holds, we can save money sleeping outdoors on them, somewhere alongside the road. One of them anyhow," he added.

Reeny laughed, again on a rising note, then looked over at Podjo, who was smiling under his broad mustache, and drove on into Arkansas and October.

## About the Author

Although he now makes his home in Memphis, Tennessee, SHELBY FOOTE comes from a long line of Mississippians. He was born in Greenville, Mississippi, and attended school there until he entered the University of North Carolina. During World War II he served in the European theater as a captain of field artillery. In addition to *September September*, he has written five other novels—*Tournament, Follow Me Down, Love in a Dry Season, Shiloh* and *Jordan County*. He was awarded three Guggenheim fellowships in the twenty-year course of writing his monumental three-volume history *The Civil War: A Narrative—I. Fort Sumter to Perryville; II. Fredericksburg to Meridian; III. Red River to Appomattox*.